Hollywood Kids

Hollywood Kids

Jackie Collins

G.K. Hall & Co. • Chivers Press
Thorndike, Maine USA   Bath, Avon, England

This Large Print edition is published by G.K. Hall & Co., USA
and by Chivers Press, England.

Published in 1995 in the U.S. by arrangement with Simon & Schuster, Inc.

Published in 1995 in the U.K. by arrangement with Macmillan London.

U.S.	Hardcover	0-7838-1211-6	(Core Collection Edition)
U.S.	Softcover	0-7838-1212-4	
U.K.	Hardcover	0-7451-7848-0	(Windsor Large Print)
U.K.	Softcover	0-7451-3678-8	(Paragon Large Print)

The text of this Large Print edition is unabridged.
Other aspects of the book may vary from the original edition.

Set in 16 pt. News Plantin.

Printed in the United States on permanent paper.

British Library Cataloguing in Publication Data available

Library of Congress Cataloging in Publication Data

Collins, Jackie.
    Hollywood kids : a novel / Jackie Collins.
      p.   cm.
    ISBN 0-7838-1211-6 (lg. print : hc)
    ISBN 0-7838-1212-4 (lg. print : sc)
    1. Motion picture industry — California — Los Angeles — Fiction.
2. Hollywood (Los Angeles, Calif.) — Fiction. 3. Youth — California —
Los Angeles — Fiction. 4. Police — New York (N.Y.) — Fiction.
5. Large type books. I. Title.
[PR6053.O425H58 1995]
823'.914—dc20   94-44322

For my best friend —
you know who you are.
Love and friendship always.

The Man emerged from prison on Tuesday morning, filled with a pent-up rage he'd been keeping in check for seven years.

He was thirty-six years old and looked it. Pale, with a thin face, narrow slate-gray eyes, and a prominent scar slashed across his right cheek — a souvenir of his incarceration. He was five feet eight inches tall, and although once slight, in jail he'd had time to work on his body, and now he had muscles of steel and remarkable upper-body strength.

In prison The Man had learned many things — the first being that defense was everything. If you couldn't defend yourself, who would do it for you?

No one. That's who.

Seven years was a long time to be caged away from the real world.

Seven years was long enough to drive any sane person crazy.

Unless, of course, you were crazy to begin with. And you never let on, because the motherfuckers did not deserve to know the truth.

The truth was his business. Only his. And

woe betide anyone who tried to get it from him.

Freedom was the unknown. It beckoned — tempting him to do things he'd only dreamed about during his years behind bars.

First came the women. Faceless whores put on this earth to do his bidding.

The Man used them mercilessly, paying them more money than they deserved to do the things they couldn't get enough of — because whether you paid them or not, all women were whores, his father had taught him that.

When his appetite was sated he took out his list and studied it intently.

The Man's list, written neatly on a single lined piece of paper, was the only positive thing in his life. Without the list he couldn't have gone on. He would have given up and hung himself, like his first cellmate.

His list had kept him strong. Given him a real purpose.

If those motherfuckers in Hollywood thought they'd seen the last of him, they were wrong.

Very, very wrong.

1

"What a movie!"

"Quite unusual."

"Jordan, my pal, you've got another smash."

The praise came fast and furious. Jordan Levitt and his wife of six months, Kim, reveled in it as they stood at the massive front door of their Bel Air estate, saying goodbye to their guests.

Dinner and a private screening at the Levitts' was a weekly event. Only tonight was more of an event than usual, because Jordan, a veteran producer, had just screened his latest production.

Kim squeezed her husband's arm and gazed up at him adoringly. She was softly pretty, with flowing light brown hair and winsome features. At twenty-two, she was younger than his only daughter. "They loved it," she whispered excitedly. "And so did I. Oh, Jordan, you're so clever."

Jordan smiled down at his new bride. He was a powerful-looking man — over six feet tall, with a shock of unruly gray hair, craggy features, and a deeply lined tanned face. Soon he would be sixty-two — like Clint Eastwood, age suited him. "You never know," he said modestly.

"*I* do," Kim replied, her eyes never leaving his. "It's a surefire hit."

He put his arm around Kim, walking her back into the house. "It doesn't matter what this group thinks," he said. "The public make their own decisions."

"Not only clever, but oh *sooo* wise," Kim murmured, tilting her head to gaze up at him. "I wish I had time to write down everything you said. You always make such perfect sense."

Jordan kept smiling. With a woman like Kim to feed his ego, he never stopped.

"Piece of crap."

"Boring!"

"I fell asleep."

"Jordan's really lost it on this one."

So went the conversation as the guests got into their respective cars, parked in the Levitts' driveway.

Sharleen Wynn Brooks was particularly vocal. A voluptuous red-headed movie star of thirty-five, she seemed to take great pleasure in pulling her ex-lover Jordan's movie to shreds frame by frame.

Her Oscar-winning director husband, Mac Brooks, laughed as he got behind the wheel of their yellow Rolls Corniche. At forty-three, Mac was handsome in a rumpled, been-around-the-block way. He had curly brown hair and a once broken nose that told tales of his past — way back when, he was an amateur boxer in Brooklyn. "Come on, baby — tell me what you *really* think," he urged, patting her knee affectionately. "Don't hold back."

Sharleen couldn't help giggling. "He needs you again, darling."

"Not me," Mac replied. "Jordan's a control freak; everything has to be his way or no way at all. After making *The Contract* with him, I decided never again."

"You won an Oscar for *The Contract*," Sharleen pointed out. "And met me for the first time."

"I vaguely remember. . . ."

She giggled again. "You're so *rude*."

"If I recall, you didn't give me a second glance — you were too busy with that muscle-bound jerk who trailed you to the set every day."

"My trainer," she said demurely.

"My ass!" he retorted.

"And three years later we worked together again and fell in love." She sighed happily. "Isn't it romantic?"

"Yeah, yeah, yeah."

As their car left the Levitts' driveway, she snuggled closer to her husband, taking his hand and moving it under her expensive Valentino skirt.

Going down the winding driveway, the Rolls nearly collided head-on with a speeding white Porsche driven by Jordanna, Jordan Levitt's twenty-four-year-old daughter.

Jordanna honked her horn as she screeched her car to a halt alongside the Rolls. Lowering her window, she leaned out. "Did I miss the movie?" she asked, tossing back her long dark hair.

"What do *you* think?" Mac responded, surreptitiously removing his hand from under his wife's skirt.

Jordanna pulled a face. "Is my old man pissed?"

"He'll live."

Jordanna grinned at Mac. He'd been her lover

11

when she was a teenager and he was thirty-six; now they were nothing more than good friends. "Glad to hear it," she said, adding a low-voiced "or maybe not."

Sharleen waved. She wasn't fond of Jordanna, and it showed. "Hello, dear," she said frostily.

The feeling was mutual. "Hiya, Shar," Jordanna responded, wondering what a cool guy like Mac saw in the overstuffed movie queen.

"Your father's really mad at you."

"I'm shaking, Shar."

Sharleen peered into the Porsche. "Who's your friend, dear?"

Trust Sharleen to notice the stud in the passenger seat. Jordanna had no idea what his name was — and quite frankly she didn't care. They were all the same in the dark. Midnight Cowboys. Her life.

"See ya!" She gunned the Porsche into action and disappeared up the driveway.

"That girl's trouble," Sharleen said, pursing newly plumped lips. "Jordan should do himself a favor and throw her out."

"Don't be bitchy," Mac said mildly. "She'll grow up."

"She's twenty-four, for God's sake. I had my own child when I was her age." Sharleen moved closer and ran her fingers lightly up his thigh.

Mac prepared himself — he knew what was coming, and it was the high point of his evening. Sharleen was into car sex, and who was he to argue? It kept the heat in a four-year-old marriage.

As soon as she touched him he was hard. Oh yeah, Sharleen did it for him every time. She was one talented female — and he didn't mean her acting.

He'd met her on the job, so to speak. Directing Sharleen had been an experience. Sleeping with her had soon led to marriage.

Monogamy was something new for Mac Brooks. Before Sharleen he'd bedded all his leading ladies, now his exceedingly sexy wife kept him too busy for affairs.

"I see Little Big Man is ready for immediate attention," Sharleen whispered, deftly unzipping his fly.

This was Mac's favorite part. Driving down the dark, narrow hills with a mammoth hard-on. Trying to concentrate. Hoping they didn't get stopped by the cops — or, even worse, a couple of would-be carjackers in ski masks. It all added to the excitement.

Sharleen bent her head, tantalizingly licking the tip of his penis, her lightning-fork tongue flicking this way and that. After he was suitably turned on, she sat back and began unbuttoning her silk shirt, revealing a lacy black bra.

One eye on the road. One eye on her. "Take it off, baby," he muttered, hard as the proverbial rock.

"Should I?" she teased.

"Do it," he said tensely, the pressure building.

"Well . . ."

"Do it!"

She slipped off her silk shirt and unclipped her lacy bra. Sharleen had the best breasts in Hollywood — untouched by plastic surgeon, they were full and firm, topped with juicy hard nipples.

"Oh, Jesus!" Mac groaned, swerving the car to the side of the road.

Sharleen enjoyed enslaving him. "Jesus has nothing to do with it," she murmured sweetly.

"Wasn't that Sharleen Wynn?" the stud asked, barely able to keep the awe out of his voice.

"Huh?" Jordanna said vaguely, screeching to an abrupt stop at the head of the driveway.

"Sharleen Wynn," he repeated, looking like a reject drummer from a grungy rock band, with his long greasy hair, scruffy clothes, and dime-store shades.

"I'm surprised you know who Sharleen Wynn is," Jordanna remarked, getting out of the car.

"Sure I know who she is," the stud said somewhat indignantly. "My dad had a copy of *Playboy* with her on the cover. Kept it by his bed for months."

"Lucky him."

"Nice tits."

"Never mind about hers, how about mine?" Jordanna said boldly, pressing up against him.

He took the hint and started to kiss her. Long, hard kisses with plenty of tongue action.

She decided this one had possibilities. "Come along," she said, pulling him onto the path leading to the guesthouse.

"Aren't we goin' inside?" he asked, sounding disappointed.

"My apartment's in back." She laughed, a brittle laugh. "It's more fun back there. Trust me."

"If you say so," he said, grabbing her ass.

"Then be a good little boy and follow me all the way to an incredible time."

"I'm right behind you."

I bet you are, she thought. *Pretty girl. Great wheels. Magnificent mansion. What's to lose?*

She'd picked him up at a music-industry party, attracted by his black jeans. There was something about skinny guys in tight jeans that really got her attention. It reminded her of visiting one of her father's sets when she was ten and meeting Teddy Costa, a hot young actor with the best butt in the business. The very thought of Teddy had taken her through puberty, until at the age of fifteen she'd casually dropped by his trailer during the making of another of Jordan's films and seduced him.

Teddy Costa had taken her virginity and never called. Who said life was fair?

Jordanna was five feet six inches tall. Not conventionally pretty, she had a beauty, strength, and wildness that most men found quite addictive. Her eyes were dark and penetrating, the curve of her finely arched eyebrows a challenge. Her nose was just a fraction too long for perfection, but her high cheekbones balanced her oval face, and her lips were naturally full and luscious. She had a sharply etched jawline and deeply suntanned skin. Her long raven hair hung casually tangled below her shoulders. Her body was athletic, slim, and sensuous. She looked more European than American, her looks inherited from her mother's side of the family. Her mother, the beautiful Lillianne, had been half French, half Brazilian. A lethal combination.

15

"You got a great ass," her stud for the night said.

Mister Romance. She hoped he knew what to do in bed. So many of them couldn't get it up anymore — show 'em a condom and they lost the urge.

It wasn't easy being a single girl in L.A. in the nineties. In fact, it wasn't easy being a single girl anywhere.

Men. They were either gay, into kinky sex, cheating on their wives, mamas' boys, jerks, drug users, cheats, pimps, or — the worst kind — actors.

Mention the name Jordan Levitt, and she could have any actor she wanted. Except that an actor was the last person she wanted. Egocentric jerks. Me — me — me. *My* life. *My* look. *My* career.

She flung open the door to her apartment, and the stud followed her into chaos. So she wasn't the tidiest person in the world. Big deal, she was hardly planning a two-page spread in *House Beautiful*.

The stud was primed and ready to go — he didn't care about her housekeeping skills. Grabbing her, he pressed himself up against her, kissed her twice, then his rough hands began exploring under her T-shirt.

The phone rang. Her machine picked up, and the sound of her recorded voice filled the air. "Yo — don't waste my time — if you got something to say, go for it now."

The machine bleeped. Her father's voice, "Hello, skinny bird. You missed my movie. They liked it. Where were you?"

I was out trying to get laid, Daddy. And don't call me skinny bird — you know I hate it, almost as much as I hate your latest wife. Christ! Is age making you senile? She's the worst one yet. A phony, sweet-talking, perfect little bitch on wheels.

"Hey — " The stud began, going for the zipper on her jeans.

She'd lost interest. "It's over," she said, slapping his hands away.

He didn't believe what he was hearing. "What's over?" he asked belligerently.

"Our incredible time," she said, anxious to get rid of him.

"Now wait a minute — " he began.

She flung open the door. "Out," she said firmly.

He blinked twice. "Ya *gotta* be shittin' me."

"I have a black belt in karate," she lied, flexing her muscles. "Wanna put it to the test?"

He wasn't taking any risks. "How'm I supposed to get home?" he whined.

"You'll find a way," she said, hustling him through the door.

God, how she hated whiners! Why couldn't anybody stand up to her? There was only one man who'd managed that feat, and he was dead.

Jamie, her darling brother. The only person who'd really understood her, because they'd shared so much. Being the offspring of celebrity parents was no joke, but at least they'd had each other, and that had meant everything — until Jamie had checked out without so much as a goodbye. He'd jumped from a skyscraper window in New York when he was twenty and she was just sixteen.

To this day she couldn't bring herself to think about his suicide.

Jamie wasn't the only one who'd met an early death. There was also her best friend, Fran, whose father was a major-league comedy star. Fran and she had grown up together, close as sisters. They'd loved each other dearly, in spite of the fact that they'd argued over everything — especially men. Fran used to hang out with three dumb Italian guys, whose favorite pastime was screwing her in turn. Two of them were bit-part actors, and the third was a would-be singer. Fran — who was usually too stoned to know any better — thought it was cool to service them one by one. The guys viewed her as a major slut, which infuriated Jordanna, because she saw Fran as losing it big time.

"What are *you* getting out of this?" she'd demand angrily.

"Love. Attention. Sensational sex."

"Give me a break."

"What's the matter, Jordanna — jealous?"

Yeah, sure, jealous of three dumb creeps jumping your bones every chance they get.

Fran took an overdose on her seventeenth birthday.

At first Jordanna couldn't believe it. She'd felt numb — as if nothing mattered anymore. And then reality had set in and she'd wanted revenge, so she'd "borrowed" her father's gun, tracked the three Italian guys to their favorite club, and come on to them — leading them to believe they'd found another dumb little rich girl to admire their over-inflated egos. Back at their apartment, she'd pulled

18

the gun, informed them of Fran's suicide, and messed with their minds, threatening to blow them away. By the time she'd finished intimidating them, they weren't so cool anymore — just three nervous jerks with limp dicks.

The trouble with men was that most of them had no balls. Except her father. Jordan Levitt had balls enough for an army.

Sometimes she thought about Jamie and Fran. Just as she sometimes thought about her mother, the exquisitely beautiful Lillianne, who'd been dragged off to a mental institution when Jordanna was six. A few weeks later the fragile and famous Lillianne had slit her wrists and died a lonely, messy death.

Daddy had mourned for a good three months before marrying the first of four other wives. Kim was number five. Why did he have to keep getting married? What was wrong with staying single for a while?

Jordanna sighed. The truth was, if he could do what he wanted, so could she. There was nothing and nobody to stop her.

She considered phoning him back, then decided against it. She knew exactly what he'd say. *Are you all right, skinny bird? Do you need money? When are we going to see you?*

Her answers were always the same. *Yes, Daddy. No, Daddy. Soon.*

He loved her. In his own way.

She clung to the knowledge that he did. Without it she had nothing.

Sharleen climaxed with a piercing shriek. Mac

19

was surprised the occupants of the house they were parked outside didn't come running out to see what was going on. Would they get a surprise if they did! A half-naked movie star and a world-renowned director. What the *Enquirer* wouldn't give for that picture!

Sharleen began wriggling into her clothes, while Mac resumed his position behind the steering wheel. Soon they were on their way home to Pacific Palisades, where they shared a large house with Sharleen's sixteen-year-old daughter and Mac's seventeen-year-old twin sons from a previous marriage.

As soon as they hit Sunset, Mac drove fast, constantly checking the rearview mirror, making sure they weren't being followed. Crime was on his mind a lot. Two months ago some tall, skinny cokehead had sprung out at him in an underground parking structure, shoved a gun in his stomach, and demanded his solid-gold Rolex. He'd slipped it off his wrist and handed it over without a word. Once the robber had fled, Mac regretted the fact that he hadn't put up a fight.

He would never admit it to Sharleen, but after the incident he'd felt less of a man. Whenever he related the tale to his friends he made light of it, but deep down he was sick that he hadn't fought back. Now he carried an unregistered gun, and screw anybody who tried to take him.

Back in his Brooklyn days he'd had real balls. Was it possible that twenty years in Hollywood had softened him up?

Sometimes he thought his entire life was a dream — from amateur boxer in Brooklyn to

Oscar-winning director in Hollywood. Quite a leap. With a little help from his friends.

He tried not to think about the old days — his past was buried, and he didn't want anyone digging it up. The one time he'd done someone from his past a favor, it had ended in disaster. After that no more favors. Mac was an expert at keeping a low profile as far as his early beginnings were concerned. The truth would blow everyone's mind.

Lately he'd had a strong urge to get rid of the yellow Rolls and buy a less conspicuous car. Unfortunately Sharleen wouldn't allow it; she was into image in a big way, and as far as she was concerned the Rolls said it all.

As they approached their house he noticed two police cars with blinking lights up ahead. "Goddamn it!" he muttered. Cops always made him uncomfortable — a hangover from his Brooklyn days.

"What?" Sharleen said.

"There's two police cars parked outside our house."

"Why?" Sharleen asked, reaching for her powder compact.

"If I knew, I'd tell you," he replied shortly.

She studied her perfectly made up face in the small compact mirror and began applying more lipstick. "I suggest you find out."

Beautiful and sexy as she was, sometimes Sharleen got on his nerves. "Sweetheart," he said, trying hard not to let his aggravation show, "that's *exactly* what I intend to do."

2

Michael Scorsinni arrived in L.A. on a Friday night, worn out, fucked up, and ready to make a fresh start. He'd had it with New York.

The airline had lost his one suitcase and didn't seem to care. Eventually he flashed his detective's badge, informing them they'd better damn well care or he'd arrest every one of them.

That put a rocket up their collective asses. They tracked his missing luggage to Chicago and assured him it would be delivered to his door the next day.

Fine. So he couldn't change his underwear for twenty-four hours. What did they care?

Michael Scorsinni was a tall man with dark olive skin inherited from his Sicilian ancestors, an athletic body, thick jet hair, penetrating black eyes, and a straight nose. He was handsome with a dangerous edge — an irresistible combination.

Women loved his looks, which made him forever suspicious. Did they chase after him because he was good-looking, or did they genuinely like him as a person?

He'd never figured out the answer to that one. Probably never would. As it was, he'd yet to come across a woman who really understood him.

He glanced around the airport. His friend and ex-partner, Quincy Robbins, was supposed to be meeting him, but there was no Quincy in sight, and Quincy was not easy to miss — big and black, he looked like a retired ballplayer who'd put on a pound or two. Michael found a pay phone and spoke to Amber, Quincy's wife, who informed him that her husband's car had broken down on the freeway and there was no way he'd make the airport.

"Don't worry, I'll take a cab," Michael said.

"Hurry up," Amber said.

Oh yeah, like he was dying to hang around the airport.

Outside he hailed a taxi, gave the Iranian driver the Robbinses' address, settled back, lit a cigarette, and tried to relax.

Who'd have thought Michael Scorsinni would ever move to L.A.? Certainly not him. Certainly not his ex-wife, Rita — boy, was she in for a shock.

Over the last six months circumstances had changed his life considerably. One moment he was living in New York, doing his job, missing his kid, but getting along okay. The next minute he got himself shot — *fucking shot* — in a drug bust gone wrong. And for several days his life hovered on the brink because the bullet had lodged dangerously close to his heart.

Not close enough. They'd managed to remove it, and he'd lived to tell the story. Rita hadn't even called.

As soon as he recovered he'd taken stock. He had a daughter he never got to spend time with because his ex had moved her to L.A., a series of interchangeable girlfriends, and a family in Brooklyn he rarely saw — which was fortunate, because when they did get together all they managed to do was yell at one another.

Michael Scorsinni was thirty-eight years old and just about ready for a new life, so he'd requested a year's leave of absence from the police department, figuring that would give him enough time to get his head together and decide whether he wanted to continue being a detective. Because of the shooting, they'd allowed him the time.

Quincy had been in L.A. almost three years. He'd started a private investigation business and was always bugging Michael to join him.

He'd resisted, sure that New York was the only place to live. But after the shooting he couldn't wait to make a move, and the good thing about L.A. was that he'd be near his four-year-old daughter, Bella, whom he hadn't seen since Rita had shifted them both to the Coast with barely a goodbye almost a year ago.

Rita was in for one big surprise, because Bella's daddy was coming back into the picture with a vengeance, whether she liked it or not.

Amber Robbins opened the door of her modest house with a baby under one arm, a toddler clinging to her skirt, and a big welcoming smile. She was a pretty black woman with dazzling teeth and a touch too much flesh distributed over her five feet four inches. Quincy had met her through a dating service, which he'd joined because of a bet. He swore it was the best seventy-five bucks he'd ever spent, even though his family were not thrilled on account of the fact that Amber was a former exotic dancer. Quincy had solved that minor problem by moving to California.

"I'm forty-seven years old," he'd told Michael at the time, "and my mama still treats me like I'm a kid!"

"Michael!" Amber's delight was almost as big as her smile, she had a warmth that was very appealing.

"Well, well — lookit little mama." He grinned, hugging her tight.

"I put on a pound or two," she admitted ruefully, enjoying the hug, then ushering him inside.

"It suits you," he said, handing her an F.A.O. Schwarz shopping bag.

"Hmm . . . you always were a damn fine liar," she said, opening the bag and pulling out a giant panda and a cuddly teddy bear. "For me?" she said, smiling widely.

"Aw, just somethin' for the kids."

She kissed him on the cheek. "You shouldn't have bothered, Mike, but thank you."

The baby began to cry, while the toddler tugged impatiently at Amber's skirt.

Michael stepped back and raised an eyebrow, "Two of 'em, Amber. You couldn't wait, huh?"

She blushed. "What can I tell you? My husband's an animal, and I love it!"

"Yeah, he's an animal, all right," Michael agreed. "Where *is* the asshole?"

She settled the baby in its crib, talking over her shoulder. "He called. They're towing his car."

"Bet he's thrilled," Michael said, making his

way through the cluttered living room, nearly tripping over a large furry toy lying in the middle
of the floor.

Amber headed for the kitchen, her two-year-old
trailing behind her. "You know our Quincy, Mister Impatient."

"Yeah, do I know Q!" he said, following her.

She placed the toddler in a high chair and turned
to survey him. "Anyway, Michael, you look fantastic. I was expecting — "

"A wreck — right?"

"What with the shooting and all . . . ," she
said, taking a jar of baby food from the fridge.

He paced around the kitchen. "I'm doing fine,"
he assured her. "In fact, now I'm here I'm doing
great."

"Good," she said, spooning applesauce into the
child's open mouth. " 'Cause we want you to feel
right at home."

"You know I will."

"I'm sorry we can only offer you the couch."

"I've had some of my best times on couches."

"I don't want to hear about your sex life," she
scolded, still smiling.

"Hey — right now it's nonexistent. I was hoping
you had a girlfriend who looks exactly like you."

"Sweet talker! But I love every word of it!"

"I only speak the truth."

"The good news is you can stay as long as you
want. You know Quincy loves you like a brother."

"Yeah." He nodded, scratching his stubbled
chin. "I feel the same way about him."

He thought about his friend for a moment.
Quincy was one of the good guys, a very special

person who'd taught him a lot. Back in New York they'd been partners for six years. Quincy had been like an older brother to him — a calming influence, because Michael had a wild streak and a temper he couldn't always control. It was better now that he wasn't drinking, and getting shot was enough to calm anyone. Still, it was nice having a surrogate brother who'd watched out for him — especially as his real brother, Sal, was a low-life scumbag and he couldn't care less if he never set eyes on him again. Sal was a liar, a cheat, and a con man, yet their mother, Virginia, still imagined the sun shone out of Sal's fat ass. Sal had always been her favorite when the two brothers were growing up. Michael was the one who got to take the brunt of her anger, because she couldn't vent it on his father on account of the fact that the weak sonofabitch ran every time there was trouble, and in the Scorsinni household there was always plenty.

When he was ten his father had taken off permanently — kind of a moonlight-flit thing — leaving them with no money and no forwarding address. Virginia was forced to take two jobs just so they could get by.

It took her two years to track her missing husband. By the time she did, the man who was to become Michael's stepfather — Eddie Kowlinski — had moved in and taken over.

Eddie was a tough bastard who drove a liquor truck for a living and beat up Virginia and her two boys for sport. He was a bear of a man, with hands like lethal weapons and a vicious temper. He was also a bad drunk.

Eddie had kicked the shit out of Michael until one night, when he was sixteen, he'd run away, lied about his age, and gotten a job as a bartender in New Jersey. He hadn't gone home for eighteen months, and by the time he did he was over six feet tall, strong and athletic.

Shortly after he returned, Eddie got horribly drunk one night and tried to take a strap to him.

Michael fought back, breaking his stepfather's nose. After that Eddie left him alone.

A few months later he'd made it into the Police Academy, which really burned Eddie — not to mention Sal — because they both considered all cops the lowest form of life. Too bad. It had given him a feeling of strength and purpose, and after graduating with the highest score possible, he'd moved rapidly through the ranks, eventually — much to Eddie and Sal's continuing disgust — becoming a highly respected detective.

The memories of Eddie were too disturbing; even today Michael had trouble thinking about him.

So why was he? The aggravation wasn't worth it. It was almost as bad as remembering his real father, Dean, who'd lived in Florida for over twenty years with a new wife and family.

Since Dean walked out on them, Michael had seen him twice — two uncomfortable short meetings arranged by him because he'd felt it important to attempt to get to know his real father. But it was not to be. Dean Scorsinni had made it abundantly clear he was not interested in the family he'd left behind. He'd treated his son like a stranger, and after the second meeting Michael decided never to try again.

Such was life. A father who didn't care. A mother who wasn't capable of doing so. And a stepfather who was a sadistic sonofabitch. He'd survived. Just about.

"How about a beer?" Amber suggested, wiping a dribble of applesauce off her son's chin.

"You got nonalcoholic?" he asked, wishing he could grab a can of ice-cold Miller's and demolish it in three great gulps.

"Oops, sorry. I forgot," she said quickly. "Quincy told me you're in that . . . uh . . . AA thing."

"The program," he said dryly. "Twelve steps to peace and serenity."

Amber didn't understand what he was talking about, nobody did who hadn't experienced it. The program had saved his life long before he got himself shot. It hadn't saved his marriage — nothing could have done that.

"Quincy will go to the store when he gets back," Amber said.

"No problem. I'll have a Seven-Up."

"Diet?"

"Nope. I'll live dangerously an' take it regular."

"Help yourself," she said, gesturing toward the fridge.

"You know what? Maybe I'll smoke a cigarette instead," he decided.

She pointed to the back door. "Take it outside, Mike. You don't mind, do you? Quincy and I gave it up."

He smiled. "So what vice *do* you two have?"

29

Amber smiled back. "Never you mind."

He wandered into their backyard, mentally checking out all the things he had to take care of. First on his agenda was renting an apartment, because he didn't plan on spending too many nights on the Robbinses' couch. He'd already decided it wasn't wise to contact Rita until he was settled. When he did reach her, she needed to know he was ready to spend time with Bella on a regular basis, and he didn't expect to have to deal with any of her shit.

Rita was a piece of work. He'd married her because she was pregnant — for once in his life he'd done the right thing.

Yeah. The right thing. Soon after she'd given birth, Rita turned into a nagging shrew, blaming him for everything, from the loss of her showgirl figure — wrong, she still had a sensational body — to her stalled career. *What* fucking career?

Rita had been a waitress when Sal introduced them, but like many pretty women she'd harbored aspirations to become a model or an actress. She was furious when she realized the baby tied her to the house. "I have no freedom," she'd often complain. "I can't be stifled like this."

He couldn't understand what she was bitching about; as far as he could see, she had plenty of freedom. Every weekend when he wasn't working he baby-sat, while she ran riot in the shopping malls with her flashy girlfriends, spending too much of his hard-earned money.

Rita was charge card crazy. When the monthly bills came in, it drove him nuts. "How many pairs of shoes can you wear?" he'd demand, completely exasperated.

"As many as I want," she'd reply, spoiling for a fight.

Rita was a feisty one, with her flaming red hair and temper to match. She was also an outrageous flirt and knew how to press every one of his buttons. It had worked in the early days, when he'd thought he was in love.

Four years of marriage, and she could have fucked the New York Yankees for all he cared.

When Rita left New York he'd been relieved — except that it meant he couldn't see Bella on weekends. At first he'd spoken to his little girl every Sunday, but after he was shot, communication broke down, and whenever he called, all he got was an answering machine.

He'd felt guilty, but what the hell — he knew he'd make it up to her. He hadn't deserted Bella like *his* father had deserted *him*. He and Bella were going to spend a lot of time together, and if Rita didn't like it, too bad, she'd simply have to accept it.

He loved his daughter, and he was determined to start being a good father. It was time.

3

Kennedy Chase was thirty-five years old and couldn't pay her rent. Well, technically she could; she had savings, a small portfolio of stocks and bonds, several well-invested treasury notes, and a modest house she owned in Connecticut. But dammit, her one golden rule was never to dip into her savings, and she stuck to that rule rigidly.

The rent problem meant she'd have to do something she tried to avoid — a celebrity interview.

Oh, God, no! She hated the thought of sitting down with egomaniacs who considered themselves real hot because God had given them good genes and a few lucky breaks.

The lack of cash flow was due to the fact that at the urging of an overly pushy agent she'd finally abandoned everything else to sit in her apartment for the last three months, working diligently on a novel about love, sex, and relationships in the nineties. She'd written three hundred pages and torn most of them up. Finally she'd decided fiction wasn't her genre — if she was going to write a book, it had to be based on plain hard facts, because only the truth would do.

Once she made that decision, she realized she needed to buy more time, and the only solution that came to mind was to accept the offer *Style Wars* magazine editor Mason Rich kept tempting her with. Mason wanted her to write six celebrity interviews, plus six pieces on any subject she cared to cover, and in return she would receive a healthy paycheck for the next year.

She'd thought about it for two weeks now. If she accepted Mason's offer she wouldn't have to worry about paying the bills for a while, and that would be a big relief.

Call him, her inner voice urged.

Tomorrow.

Not tomorrow. Today.

Taking a deep breath, she picked up the phone and connected with *Style Wars'* New York office.

"Mason?" she said quickly, before she changed her mind.

"K.C. My favorite scribe," Mason said, sounding pleased. He was a white, heterosexual married man of forty-eight, with a strong urge to lure her into bed. So far she'd managed to keep their relationship on a purely professional level, but it wasn't easy. Married men were always the most persistent.

Taking another deep breath, she said, "Okay, put me in front of the firing squad."

"What's that?"

"Mason, I'm all yours."

He chuckled. "K.C., I couldn't be happier. I'll arrange a first-class flight for you on American and book us the Oriental Suite at the St. Regis. We'll have a memorable weekend."

She sighed. "Very amusing, Mason. You know exactly what I mean."

"You're missing out," he said ruefully.

"Send me an advance before I'm evicted. And give me the name of my first victim so I have time to throw up before the big moment."

"Welcome aboard."

"I'll be saluting all the way to the bank."

Decision made. No going back now, she was working for *Style Wars*, the thinking Hollywood executive's guide to the real world — or what was imagined to be the real world. Every month the Hollywood community devoured its subscription copies of the fashionable magazine — *Hey, I read* Style Wars, *I'm a well-read person.*

Actually, it wasn't such a bad publication, compared to the women's glossies and the men's jerk-off trips, it was a virtual mine of information. In with the celebrity interviews, reviews, fashion statements, and avant-garde photographs, there was usually one big story worth reading — some major scandal involving the rich and infamous.

It was the idea of the big story that attracted her. When Mason first proposed the deal, he'd assured her she could get into anything she wanted, and that appealed to her. Investigative reporting was her forte — she'd covered everything from the Anita Hill Washington debacle to political screw-ups, the war in Iran, and several juicy Wall Street shenanigans.

Usually Kennedy liked to be where the action was — her motto was *Have pen, will travel*. But six months ago her father had gotten sick, and she'd decided to stay in one place until the inevitable happened. Her dad was eighty-five years old and putting up an admirable fight against lung cancer. Three years earlier her mother had passed away. The loss was devastating — although Kennedy had learned to deal with grief when she'd lost her husband to a terrorist's bomb after twelve years of togetherness.

Phil had been a wonderful, smart, sexy man. They'd met in college, fallen in love, traveled the world, and after six blissful years gotten married aboard a boat on a crocodile-infested river in Africa. They'd both craved adventure like junkies chasing the latest high — if there was something going on in the world, they had to be there. Phil had been a brilliant photographer, capturing stark, honest images. Kennedy had written the pieces to go with his startling work. They'd been a formidable team, much in demand by magazines and newspapers.

Phil had died in Ireland, covering the ongoing battle. She would have been with him except that she was three months pregnant, and since she'd had two miscarriages her doctor had advised her to stay home and take it easy for once. She'd lost the baby anyway.

After Phil's death her life had stopped for a while. She'd sat in their small house in Connecticut for almost a year, trying to get past the overwhelming grief that enveloped her. At times she'd considered suicide, but she'd known Phil would regard it as a cowardly way out. He'd fully expect her to achieve all the things they'd planned to do together, and she knew she couldn't let him down. So finally she'd drawn on every bit of strength she could muster and ventured out into the world again, only to find that traveling by herself did not hold the same fascination. It was difficult, dangerous, and lonely.

Eventually she'd decided to find a base somewhere — not the house in Connecticut, because it held too many memories, but Los Angeles, so she'd be near her parents. Shortly after she moved to L.A. her mother got sick and died. Now it was her father's turn.

She did not regret her call to Mason. In fact, she was almost excited about the commitment of working for the same magazine for a year. The celebrity interviews were a minor irritation she'd have to deal with. It was the thought of the big story that got her juices flowing.

Phil would have a million and one ideas if he were around. But he wasn't. Phil had checked out. Deserted her. Not his fault, but sometimes — late at night, when the reality crept up on her — she couldn't help blaming him.

Why did he have to go to Ireland?
Why did he have to leave?

She'd never met a man who could measure up to Phil. Her closest girlfriend, Rosa Alvarez, assured her there were plenty of good ones around, but she had yet to find one, even though she dated sporadically — hating every minute of forced conversation and the obligatory good-night pass. "I'm too old and too smart for this shit," she wearily informed Rosa, who had a bad habit of trying to fix her up.

Rosa, a Hispanic beauty of forty who held the prime position of coanchor on a local TV station, was a determined woman who refused to give up on her friend's romantic situation. "You're five years younger than me, Kennedy," Rosa lectured sternly. "I will not allow you to sit at home by yourself. There's someone out there for you, and I intend to find him."

"Oh, good," Kennedy replied dryly. "I can't wait for you to come up with Mister Wrong."

She knew men were attracted to her, they took one look at the package and wanted a chance. She was tall — five feet nine — and curvaceous, although she tried to play down her sensational body. She had shoulder-length honey-blond hair and startlingly direct green eyes. Hers was an intelligent beauty touched with class.

Since Phil's death she'd had one semiserious relationship. Somehow — against her better judgment — she'd gotten involved with one of Rosa's colleagues, a Kevin Costner look-alike weatherman, who was two years younger than she and not the fastest brain in the West.

The sex was okay, but after six months she began to suspect he wasn't faithful, and that was enough to make her move on.

Dumping him was not easy — they'd broken up three months ago, and he still called every few weeks, begging her to change her mind.

She knew she never would. Celibacy was infinitely preferable.

4

Bobby Rush jogged every day. He arose at five in the morning, donned shorts and a T-shirt, put on his well-worn Nikes, and set off come rain or shine. Not that there was much rain in sunny California, most of the time it was too hot. Since moving back to L.A. from New York, he'd had a hard time readjusting to the constant heat.

At thirty-two, Bobby was boyishly good-looking, with longish dirty-blond hair and river-blue eyes. He'd inherited his looks and his talent from Jerry Rush, his famous movie star father. Thank God he hadn't inherited his personality, because Jerry was a womanizer, a bully, and an alcoholic.

Now finally, after years of being regarded as nothing more than one of Jerry's sons, Bobby had a hit movie of his own. A goddamn hit! And all of a sudden he was being heralded as the star of the family, and Jerry was being referred to as Bobby Rush's father! It was an amazing triumph!

His two older stepbrothers, Len and Stan, were not pleased. It was bad enough being labeled Jerry Rush's sons, now they had to contend with being known as Bobby Rush's brothers. It rankled — especially as they'd both tried to make it as actors, with no success. Len and Stan were the sons of

Jerry's first wife, who, after the divorce, had married a heart surgeon and now lived quietly in Arizona.

Len was a drunk, Stan a cokehead. Jerry still supported them, even though they were both married, with children of their own.

Bobby had not spoken to his father for five years. They'd fought before he'd moved to New York and had no contact since. Now he was back, his movie was a hit, and Darla, his Swedish stepmother, had arranged a reunion dinner the following week.

Bobby's feet hit the running track at UCLA. He was renting a small house in the Hollywood Hills, but he'd soon found that jogging up there was a chore. His first day out, he'd bumped into Madonna and her bodyguards. Jogging was not supposed to be a social occasion, it was work — gut-strengthening, heart-pumping powerful work.

He'd been back in L.A. for several weeks, and what with attending endless meetings, setting up new production offices at Orpheus Studios, conferring with writers about the movie he was putting together, and settling into the house, he'd had no time to do anything else. He hadn't called anybody, not even his brothers.

Darla had tracked him down because Darla was the best busybody in town. She knew everybody and everything, and now that he had a hit movie she was more than anxious to arrange a reunion with good old Dad.

Jerry Rush. An icon. A legend. Up there with Burt and Kirk and Greg — all the great stars from the fifties and sixties. Jerry had been one of the biggest, an action-adventure star when action meant killing the bad guys and adventure meant kissing the leading ladies. Now Jerry rarely appeared in a movie unless it was a character role, even though he still looked pretty damn good, thanks to a talented plastic surgeon who'd worked his magic gradually over the years. But Jerry was nearing seventy, hardly a desirable age for screen heroes.

Bobby wondered what his father would have to say about his amazing success. Their relationship had always been difficult — the belittling treatment he'd received when growing up would have destroyed a lesser man. His brothers had never made the break, they were trapped forever in Jerry's giant overbearing shadow.

Bobby's earliest memories were grim.

His first swimming lesson: Jerry had tossed him into the deep end of the pool and calmly watched him struggle for his life.

His first day at school: Jerry had gone with him and strutted around, introducing himself to the teachers, signing autographs, making sure everyone knew whose son little Bobby was.

His first prom date: Jerry had kissed the girl full on the lips, and starry-eyed, she'd done nothing all night but talk about how wonderful his father was.

His first fiancée: Jerry had screwed her regularly for two months before Bobby walked in on them one day. Jerry just laughed. "She was a tramp," he said. "Lucky you found out in time."

After that Bobby knew life with father was a

war, and to win that war he had to become as wary and devious as with any enemy.

Jerry wanted him to attend college in California, but with the support of his long-suffering mother, he'd made an escape to New York, where he put in time at NYU for eighteen months before dropping out and trying for an acting career. His father did not approve and gave him no support. That was okay, he didn't want any. He got a nighttime job as a waiter and a daytime job on a TV soap. It was good training.

Two years later, when his mother died of cancer, he'd returned to L.A.

The day of the funeral, Jerry had taken him aside, begging him to stay. "I'm lonely," Jerry had said, displaying a never before seen vulnerability. "Your brothers are married, and this is a damn big house. Whyn't you move back in, Bobby? Keep an old man company."

Against his better judgment he'd done just that. Big mistake. Once he was safely back, Jerry had turned into a monster again — putting the make on every one of his girlfriends, treating him like he was still a kid in grade school.

It became painfully obvious that cutting off his son's balls was one of Jerry's favorite pastimes.

When Darla entered his father's life, Bobby exited. He stayed in L.A. and rented an apartment in Sherman Oaks. He landed a couple of small roles in features, then got a part on another soap and started dating a series of girls he never took home to Daddy.

After Jerry married Darla, she tried to make

one big happy family out of them. It didn't work.

Christmas of '89, Jerry and Bobby had their famous confrontation. There was a big party at the family mansion on Bedford Drive. Jerry liked to go all out, no expense spared, so the garden was tented, the swimming pool covered to make a dance floor, phony Santa Clauses abounded, along with fortune-tellers and a seven-piece band. Fifteen round tables were place-carded to accommodate the one hundred twenty guests. Darla organized every detail — while Jerry took all the credit.

Bobby entertained a grudging admiration for Darla. The steely Swede succeeded where many other women had failed — she almost kept Jerry under control. However, on this particular occasion nobody could have controlled Jerry. Too much straight bourbon, a new movie about to start shooting, and he strutted around more cocksure than ever.

Bobby made the mistake of taking his current girlfriend to the party, Linda, a petite blonde with the requisite California body and gorgeous big blue eyes. Naturally Jerry tried to hit on her as soon as they arrived. Linda handled it well, but later a drunken Jerry grabbed her when she exited the powder room, jamming his lips on hers and plunging his sweaty hand down the neckline of her dress. Linda, a true innocent from Minnesota, was totally distraught. She slapped Jerry's face and ran to tell Bobby.

Bobby rose to the occasion because Jerry's bad behavior had to stop somewhere.

When his father appeared he faced him and said

42

in a low, angry voice, "Linda deserves an apology."

"What?" Jerry stood before him, swaying slightly, liquid slopping over the edge of his glass.

Bobby had no intention of backing down. "Say you're sorry, you horny bastard."

Jerry began to laugh in a nasty fashion. "Sorry — to *her?* You gotta be kidding."

For once in his life, Bobby stood up to his father. "Do it," he said tightly.

There was a heavy silence as everyone pretended not to watch the tense confrontation.

"C'mon, son, can't y'see she's nothin' but a tramp," Jerry said, slurring his words. "You sure as hell know how to pick 'em, Bobby. Gotta stop lettin' your cock rule your fuckin' heart. Be like me — get some class in your life."

Something came over Bobby, an anger so dark and overwhelming he couldn't control it. He hit Jerry straight onto his dumb ass. Then he grabbed Linda and got the hell out.

The next week he took off for New York, where he threw himself into making his career happen.

He soon realized nobody was killing himself to give Jerry Rush's son a job, but he was determined to make it — so he got together with a couple of friends from college, and they started developing properties with an eye to getting them made as low-budget movies.

They were a hard-driving team, with an excellent commercial eye. His college roommate, Gary Mann, line produced and handled the financial side, while Tyrone Houston, former college football hero, did the actual producing. Bobby starred in and executive produced, overseeing every detail.

Fortunately it all came together and they enjoyed making it happen. Gary was Mister Charm with his easygoing manner, but underneath the warm personality lurked a calculator mind. Tyrone was Mister Handsome. Black and athletic-looking, he was an excellent producer, who really got off on making killer deals.

It was hard, grueling, seventeen-hour-a-day work, but it sure paid off. Thanks to all their efforts, they put together two movies on an almost nonexistent budget, and when those films made money they were able to interest real investors and came up with *Hard Tears*, an erotic love story about a cop and a call girl. It scored big, and suddenly Bobby Rush was a star with a major development deal at Orpheus — which he made sure included Gary and Tyrone. Now they had plenty of Orpheus's money to do exactly what they wanted. The trick was picking the right project. A score was a score, but Bobby knew only too well that his second big movie was crucial. Right now he had a couple in development, and any moment he was about to decide which one was ready to go.

"Hi, Bobby." A pretty girl in cutoffs and a clinging T-shirt waved at him as she jogged past.

Lately everyone greeted him, it seemed that overnight he'd become public property. Never mind all the time he'd put in on the soaps — one hit movie, that's all it took.

Automatically he waved back, even though he had no idea who she was. He began to jog a little faster. The thrill of no longer being regarded as Jerry Rush's son was indescribable. It would be impossible for anyone to understand who hadn't gone through it himself.

Growing up with a famous parent.

Handicapped for life.

Goddamn it, he'd taken that handicap and crushed it underfoot. Now he was a winner all the way.

The Man moved into a room in a big, almost empty house on Benedict Canyon. It belonged to his uncle, who lived back East and allowed various relatives and friends to occupy its rooms. In the forties it had been the home of a legendary blond movie star who'd killed her lover with a butcher's knife and, when the deed was done, committed suicide by hanging herself from the rafters in the huge, gloomy living room.

Eldessa, the black woman who looked after the house, had told him the story the day he moved in. The Man had listened impatiently to the senile old crone, and when she was finished he'd instructed her never to talk to him again, and that she was not — under any circumstances — to enter his room.

To make absolutely sure, he summoned a locksmith and had heavy-duty locks put on his door. Nobody was allowed to invade his privacy.

The Man settled in because it was convenient. His family didn't want him back in New York, they'd made that quite clear. But they couldn't cut him off completely — he was their blood, and so they were obliged to take care of him. He was given a room in the uncle's house and a paltry allowance.

Did they really imagine they were rid of him forever?

No way in hell.

But for now it suited him. He had things to take care of before he dealt with his family.

The Man had a list — a long list. And he knew exactly how he was going to dispose of everyone on it.

Retribution.

Revenge.

Kill the motherfuckers who had betrayed him. Every single one of them.

Soon he would begin. . . .

5

Homebase Central was the hottest club in L.A. Situated on the edge of Silverlake, it was co-owned by Melinda Woodson, a sour-faced sometime actress, and Arnie Isaak, a former child star turned coke dealer. The two of them were close friends of movie star Charlie Dollar, who'd put up the money to get the place started. Charlie had done it as an insurance policy so he could be assured of a fun place to hang out — plus his two friends were driving him nuts and he'd come to the conclusion it was about time he gave them something to do so they'd quit sitting around his house all day smoking grass, snorting coke, and guzzling his booze.

Charlie Dollar was hardly your average matinee idol. He was overweight with a comfortable gut, fifty-three years old and slightly balding. But when Charlie Dollar smiled, the world lit up and every female around got itchy pants — for Charlie possessed a particularly wild stoned charm that was irresistible to both men and women. It helped that every one of his movies was a guaranteed box office smash, thanks to his quirky presence and offbeat performances. Charlie had a way of taking on a role and bending the character until it fit him to perfection. Some said that Charlie Dollar was a genius; others claimed it was just old Charlie up there on the screen, jerking off over anyone who'd pay attention.

Nobody knew the real story about Charlie, although there were many rumors. Prison, a drug bust, a difficult tour of duty in Vietnam. He'd burst upon the scene as a burned-out thirty-five-year-old in an underground rock 'n' roll movie, playing the crazed manager of a heavy metal group. After that one brilliant, insane performance he'd never looked back.

Charlie Dollar was the hero of stoned America. He enjoyed fame but pretended indifference. Life was simpler that way. After all, a man had to look like he had *some* ethics.

Because of Charlie, Homebase Central had instantly taken off. It was *the* place to see and be seen. The hipper, younger side of the industry took their lives in their hands and drove down to Homebase Central on Friday and Saturday nights, knowing it was good for business — knowing they were either going to get a deal or get laid. Agents, actors, producers, managers — they all made the scene.

Of course, getting laid was hardly difficult. Beautiful girls were everywhere. Girls with spectacular bodies and not much else. Girls with hungry eyes and a talent for spotting the real players. Girls who would do anything for a shot at the big time.

And Charlie was always there, sitting at his usual table, surveying the scene like a contented tomcat.

Jordanna cruised into the club late Saturday night. She knew everyone, and everyone knew her. After all, she was a Hollywood kid, one of the chosen few. She had a famous father — alive. And a famous mother — deceased. She was Hollywood royalty.

Arnie Isaak, who liked to play the genial host, greeted her with a friendly "Hey, Levitt, lookin' good." Arnie was skinny, with a straggly beard. He lived under the impression that he was irresistible to women. Wrong.

To Jordanna's annoyance, Arnie was always trying to hit on her, in spite of the fact that she made it very clear she couldn't stand him. Staying out of his face seemed to be the only way to avoid his irritating come-ons.

"Hi, Arnie," she said, moving quickly past him to join a group of her peers — the other Hollywood kids, all assembled:

Cheryl Landers, a cynical redhead with seen-it-all eyes, long legs, and real attitude — which surprised no one, since her father, Ethan, owned a major studio, and her mother, Estelle — a secret drinker in the privacy of her Bel Air mansion — was the high priestess of L.A. society.

Sitting next to Cheryl, Grant Lennon, Jr., the dissolute son of Grant Lennon, a wildly attractive movie icon. Grant, who worked as a junior agent at International Artists Agents, considered himself the town cocksman, but Jordanna suspected that unlike his studly father, he couldn't get it up as often as he would have liked, which was why he kept trying so hard.

Then Marjory Sanderson, the dreamy-eyed

daughter of a billionaire television magnate. Marjory was painfully thin, with long, wispy fair hair and a plain, pinched face. She was a recovering anorexic, who spent most afternoons on her psychiatrist's couch.

And lastly Shep Worth, the only son of an aging sex symbol. Shep resembled a smaller version of his famous mother, Taureen Worth — the woman with a body that never quit and a long line of ex-husbands.

The group had grown up together, sharing the experience of too much too soon. A Porsche at sixteen. Handfuls of credit cards. European vacations. The best tables in the hottest restaurants. And endless lavish parties.

Jordanna flopped into a chair. "I need a drink," she said, grabbing a handful of tortilla chips and tossing them into her mouth.

"Tough day?" Cheryl asked.

"It's a bitch doing nothing," Jordanna deadpanned.

Cheryl laughed a humorless laugh. "Tell me about it," she said dryly, knowing exactly what Jordanna meant.

Cheryl had moved out of the family home at seventeen, the envy of her friends because her parents had presented her with a condo in Westwood, a new BMW, and limitless charge cards. They were almost as delighted to see her go as she was to depart the family mansion. Since that time she'd been trying to get her life together, without much success. There was nothing for her to excel at. Being Ethan and Estelle's daughter meant living up to impossible expectations, so

51

she just didn't bother.

Cheryl was attractive without being dazzling. Had she not been a Hollywood Princess, she would have been considered extremely attractive. In a town full of outstanding physical beauty she was a six. Anywhere else she'd be considered a ten.

Cheryl had found that being best friends with Jordanna had taken getting used to. They'd never really clicked until after Fran's suicide, then they'd bonded — united in their grief, because they'd both been close to Fran. At first Cheryl couldn't stand Jordanna; as far as she was concerned, the coltish bad girl with the wild reputation was an outrageous pain in the ass. But once she'd gotten to know her she'd realized that — like herself — Jordanna came from an affluent dysfunctional family and was merely trying to survive as best she could.

They'd started hanging out together, bringing in Shep, Grant, and Marjory as their cohorts. Soon they were known as the Hollywood Five. It suited them fine, as they all carried the same burden — parents who were too busy being rich, famous, and successful to find time for their kids.

"I suggest you try a margarita," Cheryl said, barely looking up. "Three of those little mothers, and you don't even know you're on this planet!"

"*You* try a margarita while *I* try the blonde in the tank top," Grant said, getting to his feet. He was tall and lanky, with a long face, thick arched eyebrows, and brown hair slicked back in a ponytail. He was handsome, but not as handsome as his famous father — a fact that irked him considerably.

Jordanna glanced over at his soon-to-be conquest. She loathed what she termed the Bimbette Army. They invaded Homebase Central on a regular basis, all tight spandex, big hair, and plumped-up lips — every one of them available and stupid. "How you guys can get it up for them is beyond me," she sighed. "Haven't you heard of having a conversation first?"

"C'mon, Jordanna, get real," Grant said, preparing for conquest. "I'd like to get an ear on *your* pillow talk."

"Screw you, Grant," she said mildly.

Shep joined in. He had sun-kissed blond hair and small, well-defined features. "Yes, Jordy," he said accusingly. "You do the same as Grant — pick a body for the night, and a couple of hours later it's goodbye, don't call me I'll call you."

"At least mine don't have plastic tits," Jordanna retorted tartly. "And they don't show everything in girlie magazines with one leg in the air, claiming they love animals and have this burning desire to save the world."

"Personally I've decided I'm into celibacy," Cheryl announced. "Either that or I might try the dyke route. This whole AIDS thing scares me enough to keep my pants *on!*"

"Can I watch?" Grant asked, leering.

"Get *out* of here," Cheryl said tartly. "You're a real sicko."

Grant touched her shoulder. "And you love it."

"In your dreams."

Grant moved rapidly toward Miss Tank Top, who lurked at the crowded bar with a group of similar-looking girlfriends.

"God, I hope he's not going to bring her over," Jordanna groaned.

"Ignore her, she'll never notice," Cheryl said, knocking back her fourth margarita. "She's the kind of girl who only pays attention to the guys."

"I can't stand these would-be starlets," Jordanna complained. "They honestly believe if they sleep with a guy who's even vaguely connected to the movie industry he'll give them a part. Everyone knows what part they'll get, and the only place it's connected to is his balls!"

"Vulgar!" Shep said.

"But true," Cheryl said.

"They're so dumb!" Jordanna said.

"Not everyone has your rocket scientist IQ," Shep interjected.

Jordanna turned on him. "Why are *you* so pissy tonight? Got your period?"

"What do you mean by *that?*" Shep demanded, his cheeks reddening. Shep was gay, but he still thought nobody knew. They *all* knew, but the closet door remained firmly shut.

"He's always pissy," Cheryl murmured, causing Shep to glare at her too.

Naturally Grant couldn't resist bringing the hard-bodied blonde to their table. She had that glazed look — as if she'd recently posed for a center spread, revealing her big breasts, all-American teeth, and ever so slightly protruding eyes to the world.

"Everyone — this is Sissy," Grant said, placing a possessive arm around her bare shoulders.

Sissy focused on Shep, who was even more handsome than Grant. "Hello," she said, in a high-

54

pitched Valley Girl voice. "And who exactly am I meeting?"

Oh, great, Jordanna thought. *This one wants their résumé on the table before she puts out.*

"Shep Worth," he said obligingly.

"And this is Jordanna, Cheryl, and Marjory," added Grant, always the polite host.

"We're a singing group," Jordanna offered.

"Really?" Sissy was impressed. "And where exactly do you sing?"

Shep burst out laughing.

"Did she say something funny?" Grant snapped.

"They all say something funny," Cheryl murmured.

Grant took Sissy's arm. "Let's dance."

She was disappointed. "Aren't we going to sit with your friends?"

"Later," he muttered, pulling her toward the small, crowded dance floor, where the soulful sounds of Whitney Houston filled the air.

Jordanna narrowed her eyes. "Do you think Grant uses a condom?"

"He'd be crazy not to," Cheryl replied. "He sleeps with at least two different girls a week."

Jordanna tapped her fingernails on the table. "Yeah, well, it's that whole macho thing," she said knowingly. "Whatever they tell you, men are *not* into condoms. They figure it slows down their action."

"I hope you're not telling me *you* let them get away with that crap," Cheryl said sternly.

"Do I look like an idiot?" Jordanna replied, brushing back her long dark hair. "I buy them by the gross and keep them in a cookie jar on

55

the coffee table. They soon get the hint, and if they don't they're out the door."

Oh yeah? Who was she kidding? Twice the previous month she'd indulged in unprotected sex because she'd been too out of her head to care. Every so often she found herself on a self-destruct course. Drinks, drugs, wild sex, anonymous partners. When she came to her senses she swore she'd never do it again. And yet something always happened that pushed her over the edge.

Wife number five was responsible for her last binge. Gotta get over caring so much about Daddy. He obviously didn't give a damn about her.

The truth was she knew she had to gain control of her emotions and stop feeling that way. If she didn't get it together, nobody was going to do it for her. Right now she was off drugs. No grass. No cocaine. No crazed nights. She was cleaning up her act, and it felt good.

"I had another death threat," Marjory said, speaking for the first time in an hour.

Jordanna leaned forward. "A *what?*"

"I've been getting these letters," Marjory confessed.

"What kind of letters?" Cheryl asked.

Marjory clammed up. "I don't want to talk about it."

"The hell you don't," Cheryl said, signaling the pretty waitress to bring her another drink.

Marjory's voice was low and even. "He says he's going to slit my throat."

"For God's sake!" exclaimed Jordanna. "Have you contacted the FBI?"

56

Marjory looked mournful. "I haven't told any-one."

"Not even your father?" Shep questioned.

"He's too busy," Marjory said.

They could all identify with that.

Jordanna crammed more tortilla chips into her mouth and asked Marjory how many letters she'd received.

Marjory didn't care to talk about it anymore. "I'm sure it's someone playing a joke," she said, closing the subject.

"Some sicko joke," commented Cheryl. "Give the letters to your old man — he should have his security check them out."

"Yes, I will," Marjory said. "If you think I should."

"*Of course* you should," Cheryl insisted.

"Make sure you do," Jordanna added sternly.

Arnie approached their table, gap-toothed leer on full alert. "Hiya, Levitt," he said.

Being referred to by her surname always irritated her. She gave him one of her direct *don't fuck with me* stares. "What do you want, Arnie?" she asked, willing him to leave her alone.

He was host of the hottest club in town, and most women were ready to rock 'n' roll any way he wanted. He got off on the fact that Jordanna wasn't all over him. "Charlie's throwing a party at his house after we close tonight. Wanna go?"

"With you?"

"Yes, with me."

"No offense, Arnie, but I've told you before — I'm not interested in dating you."

"This wouldn't be a date."

"Oh yeah? What would it be?"

He scowled. "What's your problem, Levitt?"

She stared him straight in the eyes. "I don't want to fuck you, Arnie. It's *your* problem, not *mine*."

"You're a real bitch, Levitt."

"No. Merely honest. Makes a refreshing change, doesn't it?"

He kept his leer firmly in place. "Lighten up. Who knows? You and I could be this generation's Natalie and R.J."

"You're full of shit," she said offhandedly.

"That's what I like about you, Levitt, your gentle reserve."

"Gee, thanks. It's nice to know I'm appreciated."

"Give it a rest, you two," Cheryl said, yawning. "You're beginning to sound like you're married."

Jordanna leaped to her feet. "That's it. I'm out of here," she said restlessly.

"Where are you going?" Arnie asked, disappointed.

"To check out the competition."

"We have no competition," he boasted.

"I'll let you know," she said crisply.

On her way to the door, she caught a wink from a stoned Charlie Dollar. He was old enough to be her father but still quite sexy. Idly she wondered what he was like in bed — reports varied.

Out in the parking lot, her Porsche was parked right up front. She was a good tipper — learned that from Daddy. "So you give out an extra thousand bucks a year, it's worth it." Words of wisdom from the great Jordan Levitt. And he *was* great — when he wanted to be. When he had time. When whoever the current wife was wasn't messing with his brain. Strike that. Make it cock. Fact of life. Jordan Levitt was ruled by the great erection.

Growing up in Hollywood. Watching Daddy get laid. What an education!

Jordanna had many fine memories, one of the most vivid being of the time she'd discovered her father in the family swimming pool — which happened to be drained at the time — servicing a voluptuous movie star, while their respective spouses circulated at a lavish party taking place inside the house. Jordanna had viewed the entire spectacle from her bedroom window. She'd never told anyone — except Jamie — that it was she who'd switched on the pool's floodlights, illuminating her father's bare ass and the movie star's huge quivering breasts. Wife number three had departed shortly after. Jordanna was satisfied. Mission accomplished.

She hit the road in her Porsche and dropped by a couple of supposedly happening clubs. Unfortunately Arnie was right — Homebase Central *was* the only place to hang. There was no action elsewhere.

By two A.M. she was home. Alone. Another scintillating night in the City of Angels.

One of these days she'd meet someone who could take away the dull throb of loneliness that stayed with her day and night. Someone who would understand and love her. One of these days.

Maybe . . .

6

Five days on Quincy and Amber's couch was five days too many. Michael had an aching back and a permanent headache on account of the fact that the baby never stopped crying and the toddler kept up a particularly aggravating whine from early morning on.

"How do you put up with this?" he said to Quincy as they drove slowly through the residential streets of Beverly Hills — Quincy was giving him the grand tour.

"It's called marriage — don'tcha remember?" Quincy said, chuckling.

Yeah, he remembered, all right. Rita complaining every time Bella woke her in the middle of the night. The smell of dirty diapers. Toys and baby clothes all over the floor. A fridge full of formula. Ah, memories . . .

"I gotta get my ass outta your backyard," he muttered, thinking to himself, *The sooner the better.* He'd already looked at several apartments. Unfortunately, the ones he liked were too expensive, and the rest were crap.

"Why?" Quincy asked. "Amber loves you — an' I kinda get off on havin' you around. It's like old times, only we're not out bustin' our cans

60

chasin' low-life scumbags."

"True," Michael said, staring through the window at huge wrought-iron gates, sweeping lawns, exotic plants, and manicured palm trees. "Hey, Q — this place is unreal. People really live like this?"

Quincy laughed. He was a big man, verging on being overweight, with soft brown eyes, bushy hair, and extra-large hands and feet. He had a habit of waving his hands in the air whenever he got excited. "You've seen it in the movies, now get used to the real thing," he said, gesturing expansively. "These dudes got plenty of money an' don't mind spendin' it."

"Who? Movie stars?"

"Naw . . . Some of 'em, maybe. But it's all those producers an' Hollywood execs who cream a bundle off every movie they're involved with. Those guys make sure they're swimmin' in big bucks. They call it creative accounting."

"What are you — a Hollywood expert?" Michael asked, laughing and scratching his chin.

Quincy nodded knowingly. "I'm doin' some work for a couple of those hotshot studio execs."

"Yeah? Anything interesting?"

"Not compared to our New York days. Hey — at least I ain't puttin' my life on the line tryin' to nail some friggin' deadbeat with a bad crack habit an' a shaky trigger finger. Out here it's cream puff time, an' I get paid primo. I'm tellin' you, Mike, come in with me — we'd clean up mucho bucks."

Unconvinced, Michael said, "Doesn't it get kinda boring? Y'know, the sun shining all the time,

61

people telling you to have a nice day, everyone smiling — "

"You're forgetting about the riots," Quincy interrupted. "An' the carjackings, earthquakes, mud slides, fires, drive-by shootings, an' floods. It's not all Sunset Boulevard and big mansions."

Reaching for a cigarette, Michael lit up and said, "This is nice, Q, but after a while, I'd miss the streets, y'know what I mean?"

"If you stay here you'll be near your kid."

"I called yesterday," he said, taking a deep drag. "Same old thing — all I get is that frigging answering machine."

"So drop by. Surprise 'em. You must be achin' to see little Bella."

"I am, but I gotta be sure Rita knows I'm here to stay. I need my own place, that way I can take my kid for weekends, get to know her again."

"Whyn't you bring her over to us? Amber would love it, she's turned into a regular earth mother."

"I'm tempted."

"Tell you what," Quincy said, making a quick decision. "If you promise not to tell Amber, on account of the fact that she's startin' to call me fat boy, I'll buy us a pizza, then we'll drop by an' surprise Rita. How's that?"

"You know something," Michael said, nodding slowly, "that's not such a bad idea."

"Bobby Rush," Mason said, his voice crackling over the phone from New York.

"Don't you mean *Jerry* Rush?" Kennedy replied, cradling the receiver under her chin as she

62

reached for a notepad and pen.

"Jerry's cold. Bobby's hot."

She hated asking, but she honestly didn't know. "Who *is* Bobby Rush?"

Mason grunted disapprovingly. "Sometimes you surprise me."

"I've never heard of him."

"For Christ's sake, K.C. — keep up with what's happening, or I'm likely to think I've made a serious mistake hiring you."

She drew a stick figure on the notepad and added little pointed horns. "Movie stars are not my priority, Mason. I presume that's what he is."

"He's Jerry's son done good. Starred in and produced *Hard Tears*, it just passed the hundred-million-dollar mark. He takes his clothes off on-screen — that should appeal to you — a touch of the double standard reversed. I suggest you see the movie. In the meantime we'll FedEx you some of his clippings and a bio."

"How exciting," she said dryly.

"I want a very provocative piece. This'll be the cover story. Make him out to be a male Sharon Stone."

"Why — does he flash his pussy?"

"Don't be crude."

"I was hoping for Clint Eastwood, Charlie Dollar, or Jack Nicholson."

"You like 'em old, huh?"

"I like 'em to have a brain."

"He does."

"What are you — his PR?"

"Goodbye," Mason said, hanging up.

She called Rosa at the network. "Who's Bobby Rush?"

"Nice ass," Rosa said. "Why?"

"I've never heard of him," she repeated.

"I wouldn't advertise. He's famous."

"I guess I'd better start watching *E.T.* and reading *People*."

"How about going to the movies occasionally?"

"So shoot me. I prefer watching PBS."

"Bobby Rush is *very* sexy. Rumor has it he fucks like a rabbit and doesn't come for an hour and a half."

"Sounds like your kind of man, Rosa."

"I'm perfectly happy with my basketball player, thank you. He might be young, but he has stamina and . . . uh . . . other attributes I'm too much of a lady to mention."

"Sure!"

Rosa giggled. "Okay, okay — he's hung like a bull and I think I'm in love."

"Again?"

They both laughed. Rosa's love life was legendary, she used men for sex the way men usually used women, and she always got away with it because she never let them into the secret.

"Why are you questioning me about Bobby Rush?" Rosa asked curiously.

Kennedy sighed. "Because Mason — in his wisdom — requires me to write a cover story on this person I've never heard of."

"Check out the movie pronto and get back to me. I got a feeling you'll like what you see."

"I'll let you know."

An hour later she was sitting in a darkened theater, watching Bobby Rush emote. He was certainly movie star material, with his regular
features, dirty-blond hair, and incredible blue
eyes. The body was good too, and he flashed regularly — kind of like a Richard Gere for the nineties. At one point in the movie there was a brief
full-frontal shot — fast but worthwhile.

Male bimbo? she jotted down with a question
mark. *Beautiful but dumb?* If he was, she could
rip him to shreds without any trouble at all.

Now why would I want to do that? she asked
herself.

*Because I have no intention of writing the usual
love-struck female journalist puff piece.*

She called Mason. "Send me everything you've
got on him *and* the father."

"This is not supposed to be a father-son piece,"
Mason warned. "His press people were adamant
about that." A pause. "But do what you want —
make it hot."

"I intend to."

The Sunset View apartments did not live up
to their glamorous name. There was no sunset,
because they faced the wrong way, and absolutely
no view. The small cluster of run-down apartments was located in a seedy side street off Hollywood Boulevard.

"Shit!" Michael muttered, as Quincy parked his
car outside. "Rita told me she and Bella were living
in a decent place. This is a crap hole."

"Maybe it's better on the inside," said Quincy,
always the optimist.

"Maybe not," Michael said grimly, eyeing a couple of derelicts huddled in a doorway, surrounded by overflowing shopping carts.

"Let's go take a look," Quincy suggested.

They got out of the car, dodging a drunken bum who staggered by, singing to himself.

"No kid of mine is living here," Michael said, running up the front steps. "This isn't what I'm paying alimony for."

"Calm down," said Quincy, right behind him. "You haven't seen Rita in a while; don't start with the screamin' — see what she has to say first."

"I don't give a shit what she has to say," Michael said angrily, and he meant it. Quincy could try and calm him all he wanted, but no way was his daughter staying in a dump like this.

He pressed the buzzer marked Rita Polone. Trust his lovely ex to use her maiden name. Scorsinni wasn't good enough for her, Rita wanted better. She'd come to Hollywood to find it, and look where she'd ended up.

There was no reply to his persistent buzzing, so he leaned on the bell next to hers.

After a few moments a head poked out of an upstairs window, and an elderly fat woman wearing too much makeup and a pink bow in her hair croaked an unfriendly, "If ya sellin', I ain't buyin'. If ya buyin', I bin outta the business five years, an' why that dumb-ass freebie piece a shit magazine keeps runnin' my address ain't my concern."

Michael took a couple of steps away from the building and looked up. "I'm trying to contact Rita Polone," he shouted.

"Who?" the woman yelled back, cupping her ear.

"Rita Polone. She lives in the apartment below you with her little girl."

"Oh, *her*." The woman snorted. "That red-headed slut. Don't know where she is, an' don't care." With that she disappeared, slamming her window shut.

"Nice neighbors," Quincy remarked cheerfully.

"Christ!" Michael said, getting more frustrated by the minute.

Quincy tried to calm him down. "Maybe we should come back when she's home," he suggested.

"Maybe we shouldn't," Michael retorted sharply. "Get the door open — let's take a look around."

Quincy pulled a face. "That's breakin' an' enterin', Mike. You know Rita's temper. I don't wanna be here when it hits."

Michael threw him a dirty look. "What happened to you in California, Q? You gone soft?"

"Hey, hey," Quincy replied, gesturing wildly. "Gotta keep within the confines of the law, or I could get my license revoked."

"Fuck the law and fuck your license. I want in."

"Shit!" Quincy groaned. "I almost forgot what a trip it was workin' with you."

"Let's go," Michael said impatiently, clicking his fingers.

"Shit!" Quincy repeated, before using his skills and a Sears credit card to skewer open Rita's front door.

The first thing that hit them was the smell —
a combination of stale air, moldy food, and damp.
"Jesus!" Michael said grimly, pushing his way in.
"What's that stink?"

Piled on the floor behind the door was a stack
of unopened brochures, letters, and flyers —
mostly junk mail, but as Michael bent to sift
through it, he was startled to find his last two
months' alimony checks, still in their envelopes.

"Sorry to say it," Quincy said, walking through
the musty hallway. "I got a strong suspicion they
don't live here anymore."

7

"I'm going into the hooker business," Cheryl announced over cappuccino and a Danish, carefully monitoring her friend's reaction.

Jordanna raised her blacker-than-black shades and stared disbelievingly at her friend. "Ex*cuse* me?"

They were sitting at an outside table at Chin Chin on Sunset Plaza, watching hordes of Euro-trash pass by.

"Not street hookers," Cheryl explained matter-of-factly. "High-class party girls who get paid a ton of money for doing things they usually do for free. Call girls, actually."

Jordanna frowned. She was used to Cheryl's crazy ideas, but this was ridiculous. "Have you totally lost your sense of reality?"

"I always thought I'd make a good business-woman," Cheryl said evenly. "And now's my opportunity. Donna Lacey's father has summoned her back to London, and she's asked me to take over her business while she's away."

"And what exactly *is* her business?"

"Where have *you* been hiding? You must have heard about Donna. She's that English director's daughter who supplies girls to several of the studios on a regular basis. Her clients include agents, studio execs, and quite a few movie stars."

Jordanna sipped her cappuccino and said without much interest, "I guess I've seen her at Homebase, picking out talent. I had no idea she was a friend of yours."

"We go to the same shrink, and we got to talking."

"I see."

Cheryl desperately wanted Jordanna to understand that this was a legitimate business venture she could get into without any help from Daddy. She needed to separate from her family — show the world she had her own identity. "The thing is she's got the high-class-hooker bit covered because important men trust her. Donna's connected — like me. That's why she's decided I'm the perfect person to take over for her."

"Lucky you."

Cheryl chose to ignore the sarcasm in Jordanna's voice. "You see, guys are all the same," she explained, warming to her subject. "They either have the original wife, who's not into sex anymore. Or the sleek little trophy number, who, after one year of marriage, conveniently forgets what a blow job *is!* Sex and marriage do not jell — hence Donna's thriving venture. These men are *into* paying for it."

"Why?" Jordanna asked, genuinely puzzled.

"For the same reason they buy the most expensive cars, houses, clothes. Money equals status. They don't want a fifty-buck-a-night hooker, they want the top-of-the-line latest model, hardly used — *very* costly."

"You've finally lost it, Cheryl," Jordanna said, shaking her head. "Why would *you* get involved?"

"For a piece of the action."

"Oh, like you're hard up for money. Your father owns a studio, for God's sake. You can have anything you want."

Cheryl turned on her, eyes flashing. "I want to do something on my own for once, without taking handouts from my family. Right now my only claim to fame is that I went on a date with Eric Menendez in high school. This is my opportunity."

Jordanna snorted derisively. "Big fucking opportunity. Running call girls."

"Don't knock it," Cheryl said defensively. "They pull in fifteen hundred a trick, and *I* get to pocket forty percent. Of course, I'll have to put aside ten for Donna, but that's okay — I'll still end up with plenty."

"You'll be a madam, Cheryl. You could get busted for pandering — isn't that what they call it?"

"You've been watching too many of your father's movies. They can't touch me, I'm Hollywood royalty."

"Oh, really?"

A good-looking blond guy cruised by in a low-slung convertible. He beeped his horn and waved at them. Automatically Jordanna waved back.

Cheryl sat up a little straighter. "Who's he?" she asked.

"Do I know? Do I care?"

"Come *on*, be a little cooperative, he could be a future client."

Jordanna stared at her in amazement. "You're really serious, aren't you?"

Cheryl nodded, her gold earrings glinting in the noonday sun. "You *bet* I am. It's certainly preferable to marking time. I mean, take a look at us — what are we *doing* with our lives?"

The unfortunate thing was that Cheryl had a point. Jordanna realized she'd partied her way through high school; continued to party through two years of college; lived for six months in Paris, where she'd learned the language and had a hot affair with a married French movie star twenty years her senior. Until finally she'd returned to L.A., moved into her father's guesthouse, and generally bummed around, taking for granted the generous monthly allowance she received. Cheryl was right — what were they doing?

It often crossed her mind that maybe she'd be a lot happier if she could find something interesting to occupy her time. But what? For several years she'd thought about becoming an actress. Everyone told her she had the looks, and it was possible she'd inherited some of her mother's talent. Tentatively she'd approached her father, who'd laughed in her face. "Forget it, skinny bird. You have no idea what a hard business this is — especially for actresses." He'd gone on to convince her that as Jordan and Lillianne Levitt's daughter she'd have too much to live up to — people would expect the moon and then some. Sadly she'd been forced to agree, even though she still secretly harbored the ambition to act.

She'd considered several other careers, but none had really grabbed her attention, so eventually —

like Cheryl — she'd fallen into the pattern of lunching with friends, shopping, hanging out, going to parties, doing drugs. It soon became an addictive lifestyle — although it never made her happy, and it certainly didn't make her father happy. The summer after Fran committed suicide, he'd gotten together with Ethan Landers, and the two men had decided their errant daughters needed something more than parties to occupy their vacation time, so they'd put them to work as set assistants on *The Contract*, a movie Jordan was producing for Ethan's studio. Both she and Cheryl had hated every minute of it, although Jordanna had managed to have an affair with the director, Mac Brooks, and that had been quite an experience.

Now she was well aware she was at a crossroads, but she sure as hell wasn't becoming a madam, like Cheryl, who was even now leaning over her cappuccino with a self-satisfied expression. "I've had a brilliant idea," Cheryl exclaimed excitedly.

"What?" Jordanna asked, suspicious of her friend's brilliant ideas.

"You!" Cheryl said, eyes gleaming. "You'd make a shitload of money."

"Doing what?"

"You could be one of my girls."

"I *love* your insane sense of humor. Any more brilliant ideas?"

"I mean it."

"Stop it, Cheryl, okay? I have no intention of becoming one of your girls. In fact, there's no way I'm getting involved in this stupid scam of yours."

"You'll be sorry," Cheryl taunted. "Donna handed over her little black book, and it's full of important names. Aren't you at least curious?"

"Nope."

"Her book's worth plenty, and *I've* got it," Cheryl said.

"How fortunate for you," Jordanna replied with absolutely no interest.

"I now know everything about the players in this town," Cheryl continued with relish. "What turns them on — and off. The type of girls they like, and the ones they've had. All their kinky turn-ons. It's kind of a thrill discovering what everyone's into."

"I'm sure it is," Jordanna said, wondering if Cheryl had totally lost her mind. "I always had a feeling voyeurism was your thing."

"Donna's filled me in good. She has plenty of girls working for her, and when she needs new ones she simply goes on a recruiting spree."

"Sounds like the army."

Cheryl was still on a roll. "She finds them on Rodeo Drive, Melrose, at health clubs, restaurants, parties. According to Donna, gorgeous girls are everywhere, and they're all tempted by the money. I mean, we're talking big bucks. She discovered one girl checking out the jewelry in Pepe, and the next day she had her on a private jet to Paris, with five thousand bucks in her purse for one simple day's work! Nobody's going to turn down an extra thousand or two. And these girls get to go on great trips, just like the one in Pepe — who incidentally ended up marrying an extraordinarily rich Arab."

Cheryl had done some wild things in her time, but this was way out there. "I'm delighted you've found your vocation," Jordanna said coolly. "But it's not something I would even consider getting into."

"You're chickenshit."

"How about *you?*" Jordanna challenged. "Are *you* planning on putting out for the right price?"

"*Please!*" Cheryl replied scornfully. "Madams don't have to."

"I didn't think so," Jordanna murmured, clicking her fingers for the bill and watching as the good-looking waiter hustled it over.

Another out-of-work actor. Her weakness.

Idly she wondered if she'd had him. Maybe in her drug days.

"You'd *love* being a hooker," Cheryl continued, still trying. "Think of the illicit thrill!"

Jordanna shook her head. "I've never seen you this hyped."

"Keep watching," Cheryl said happily. "I'm about to be bigger than my daddy!"

Sharleen and Mac were on the outs. They'd hardly spoken for almost a week now — ever since they'd arrived home from the screening at Jordan Levitt's and found the police on their doorstep.

Sharleen blamed Mac's two sons for the trouble. Mac was equally convinced that Sharleen's sixteen-year-old daughter was to blame. Whichever of their offspring was responsible did not make much difference — the fact was there'd been a drug bust in their house, and Sharleen was mortified. "I'll be all over the tabloids," she wailed.

"It won't be the first time," Mac replied, remembering when she'd been labeled the other woman in his very public divorce. At the time, he'd been married to Willa, the daughter of the famous director William Davidoss. Willa had been his ticket to the big time — he'd started out as third assistant on one of her father's movies in New York and ended up moving to California and marrying her. Two years later — with a little help from William — he'd directed his first movie.

When he and Willa separated, the tabloids had gone into a frenzy, because some bigmouth had alerted them about his affair with Sharleen. For months they'd lived with the lurid headlines, right up until he'd divorced Willa and married Sharleen. Thank God they hadn't delved into his background, although it would be pretty difficult to find out anything about him; he'd covered his tracks well.

Sharleen was not to be appeased. "That was then — this is now. I have a reputation to protect," she said primly.

When Sharleen said things like that, he wasn't quite sure what she meant. Sharleen was a movie star, for chrissake. Movie stars were *supposed* to have reputations!

"Calm down," he told her, between attempts to find out exactly what had taken place at his house. Kyle and Daniel, his sons, were close-mouthed. Suzy, Sharleen's daughter, was sulky. The three of them were silent on the subject of who had invited the drug dealer — a twenty-something rich kid — to their house.

"He's a friend of a friend," Kyle finally ad-

76

mitted. "We had no idea he was a dealer."

Sure. They'd had no idea. Until the rich kid was arrested by an undercover cop posing as a high school dropout, just after he'd sold a gram of cocaine to Suzy's best friend, an angelic-faced blonde.

"It's your fault," Sharleen informed Mac.

"Why is it always *my* fault?" he'd asked patiently.

"Because you never discipline those boys. You allow them to run wild."

"It was Suzy's friend making the buy," he'd pointed out.

"That's right, change the subject."

At Sharleen's insistence, he'd arranged for his sons to visit their mother for a few weeks. Some punishment. Lounging around Hawaii, surfing and getting tans.

His ex-wife had moved to the big island shortly after their divorce became final. Her father had made sure she used a killer lawyer, who'd scored her an enormous settlement, with hefty alimony payments unless she remarried. Plus child support until the boys finished college.

Like she needed the money, Willa had trust funds coming out her ass.

Big chance she'd ever remarry. He was screwed. The moment all financial matters were in place, she'd moved her girlfriend in, a plump redhead with smoky eyes and soft hands. The ex Mrs. Mac Brooks was a dyke, and there was nothing he could do about it except continue paying big bucks for the rest of his life.

He *was* able to get custody of his boys. This

77

didn't thrill Sharleen, who went to great lengths to inform anyone who'd listen that they were merely her stepsons.

Mac was not happy about the situation. Getting divorced was one thing. But getting divorced and then having his ex set up house with another woman was downright insulting. Especially when *he* was paying for their cozy setup. Somehow he imagined that Willa's sexual turnaround reflected on him — and not favorably. Hadn't he satisfied her? Wasn't he an incredible lover, as women had always told him?

"Baby, you're the best," Sharleen crooned on a regular basis. She was a very intelligent woman when she wanted to be.

So Kyle and Daniel were banished to Hawaii, and Suzy was forbidden to see her angelic-faced girlfriend ever again. Case settled. Mac could get back to concentrating on his next project.

He had a lunchtime meeting with Bobby Rush regarding a script Bobby had sent him. *Thriller Eyes* was an interesting piece of material — a psychosexual edge-of-the-seat drama about a hero and a villain. The twist was that the villain was a beautiful psychotic young woman — although the audience didn't find out until the end of the movie.

Mac liked the piece a lot, but he wasn't sure about working with Bobby Rush. If he was anything like his father, he'd be a monumental pain in the ass.

"Have you heard about Cheryl's latest venture?" Jordanna asked Shep as they sat on the patio

78

of his two-bedroom Hollywood Hills house — purchased for him by his mother in a generous mood.

"The call girl thing?" Shep said.

Jordanna raised her eyebrows. "Is she crazy or what?"

"We all know she's crazy," Shep stated matter-of-factly.

"I realize that," Jordanna replied. "But this time she's *really* over the edge."

Shep filled Jordanna's glass with iced tea. "She told me if she succeeds with the girls, she's starting a service to accommodate the wives."

Jordanna almost choked on her tea. "Huh?"

"Studs for bored women."

"No way!" Jordanna said, spluttering with laughter.

"She's quite serious. In fact, she asked me if I was interested in being on her books."

"Come *on*, Shep!"

"Honestly."

"I don't know why I'm surprised. She tried to recruit me too — said I'd make a shitload of money."

"You would."

They stared at each other and completely broke up.

"Can you imagine!" Jordanna exclaimed. "I'd like to see the face on one of Daddy's friends if I turned up at his door in a skimpy black lace teddy, carrying a whip. It could put him off sex for life!"

"Maybe not. Think about the vicarious excitement of it all."

"You're *bad,* Shep."

"So I've been told," he replied crisply, brushing a lock of blond hair off his forehead.

"Grant would be perfect if Cheryl starts a stud service," Jordanna mused. "Have active cock — will travel."

"Perfect," Shep agreed. "My mother's always had her eye on him. I'm sure if she could only pay for it, she wouldn't feel so guilty."

"Did she ever try to screw him?"

"When we were fifteen she came on to him one day after school. I told you about that, didn't I?"

"No, you certainly didn't. What did he do?"

"Refused to come back to my house for three years!"

"Grant must have been petrified — your mother's so . . . predatory."

"And needy."

"Is she?"

"There's no one more needy than an aging sex symbol."

"Poor Taureen."

"Her husbands get younger, she gets older, and the movie roles are almost nonexistent."

"It's so sad."

"Right now she's doing the nasty with an ex-bartender who thinks he's this generation's answer to James Dean."

"How old is he?"

"Barely older than me."

"Well . . . if it makes her happy." She sipped her tea. "How's *your* relationship with her now?"

"After ten years of therapy, I'm learning to accept her for who she is."

"And does she accept you?"

Shep turned away, not answering.

Jordanna knew better than to push. Parents. Who could understand them? Who really wanted to? She'd spent years in and out of shrinkdom, until she finally decided she didn't need help, she could deal with her own problems.

Am I doing that? she thought anxiously.

Yes, she decided, *I'm finally making a start.*

Bobby Rush sat at table number seven in Le Dome, surveying the scene. It was a good day — a power day. He'd already had a stream of people stop by his table as he waited for Mac Brooks to arrive. Something told him *he* was the movie star, he shouldn't be kept waiting. But so what? His ego wasn't out of control yet; he could handle it.

"Bobby!" Taureen Worth paused dramatically on her way to the back room, trailed by two short, hyper agents. For a woman in her early fifties, she was quite a knockout in a skintight white Montana suit and Walter Steiger stiletto heels.

Bobby jumped up and returned her enthusiastic greeting — even though the last time they'd met he'd had two lines in one of her movies and she'd barely acknowledged his existence. "You look wonderful," he said, with just the right degree of sincerity. He'd learned at an early age that in Hollywood you always complimented women and they always believed you, whether you meant it or not.

"I feel like a hag!" Taureen replied, knowing full well that she did indeed look wonderful. And so she should — she worked hard enough at it: liposuction, face peels, collagen injections, high colonics, punishing workouts. She hadn't resorted to plastic surgery — yet. "I've been working non-stop. You know how tiring *that* is."

Bobby nodded, wondering what she was working on.

"I'm so *proud* of you!" Taureen exclaimed, flashing her feral smile — big teeth and a curled scarlet lip. "To think I discovered you!"

What was the woman talking about?

"Now, Bobby," she said, leaning over his table, bending slightly so he couldn't miss her impressive trademark cleavage. "When you're casting your next movie don't forget it was *me* who gave you your first break. I'd love us to work together again."

He repeated his nod — it seemed that was all she required. He was saved by the two agents bobbing into view. Taureen did not introduce them. She pursed her lips and moved in for the kill, leaving sticky lip-gloss residue on both his cheeks. "Goodbye, darling." Meaningful pause. "You're looking very . . . sexy."

It's the hit movie that does it, he wanted to say. *Pulls 'em in every time.*

Taureen swept into the other room, her musky scent lingering behind.

What a town! Bobby thought. *When you're hot you're boiling. And when you're cold — lie down and die, asshole, 'cause even your exterminator won't speak to you.*

Mac Brooks hurried up to the table, full of apologies. "Trouble with my kids," he said ruefully.

82

"If you're single, Bobby, stay that way. Marriage leads to kids, and then normal life as you know it is over forever. I gotta have a drink." He wrinkled his nose. "That's a hell of an aftershave you're wearing."

"Taureen Worth."

"Is she doing that Elizabeth Taylor thing now?"

Bobby laughed. "Not yet. She stopped by the table. I'm sure she'll be back when she knows you're here."

"You heard about me and Taureen, huh? It was a location fuck. You know what that's like — six weeks of passion, and then you don't even remember each other's names. She's the worst actress I ever worked with. Never again."

Bobby decided to go the polite route. "It's a pleasure to finally meet you, Mac. I admire every one of your movies — especially *The Contract*."

Mac signaled the waiter. He really did need a drink, and a Scotch on the rocks would do nicely. "You too, Bobby. I had the studio screen *Hard Tears* for me — excellent work. As an actor you make interesting choices. You have an edge. I like that; keeps the audience alert."

Bobby felt suitably flattered. "Thanks," he said modestly.

"I almost worked with your father once."

"How lucky can you get."

Well, Mac thought, I guess we know where we stand on *that* issue.

"So," Bobby said, getting right to it. "Did you have time to read the script?"

"Read it. Loved it. That's why I'm here."

"Are you interested?"

Mac chuckled. "You don't believe in wasting time, do you?"

Bobby paused before answering. He'd gone over this meeting in his head for several days. Mac Brooks had a fine track record, but he hadn't had a moneymaking movie in several years, so choosing him for the project was a risk. However, Bobby was sure — in fact, he knew — that if they got along, Mac would be the perfect director for his film.

"You know what, Mac," he said slowly, measuring his words. "In the past I *have* wasted a lot of time — and now I'm taking the high-ticket ride." He stared directly at the Oscar-winning director, his blue eyes blazingly intense. "I need a fast answer, so let's cut out the bullshit. Are you in or out?"

8

"What's the matter?" Amber asked, as Michael and Quincy burst noisily into the house.

"It's not good news," Quincy replied, hurriedly taking her to one side as Michael ran to the phone. "Rita's not at her apartment, nor is Bella."

"Are they on vacation?" Amber asked, wondering why they both seemed so uptight.

Quincy shrugged, heading for the kitchen. "I doubt it. The place is neglected — looks like nobody's lived there in a couple of months."

Amber followed him. "So she's moved?"

"Don't think so," Quincy said, automatically reaching for the cookie jar. "All their stuff's there. Clothes, toys, everything."

She smacked a cookie out of his hand. "No," she said firmly.

"Amber!" he pleaded. "I'm starvin', woman!"

"You'll get fat," she retorted.

"One cookie?" he begged, snaking his arm around her waist. "C'mon, mama, one little cookie for one hungry man."

She ignored him. "How about her makeup?" she asked.

"What's that got to do with anything?"

"If she took her makeup, it means they're okay."

Women's logic. Quincy shook his head. "I don't know. She hasn't picked up her last two months' alimony checks. They're still in the envelopes."

"What does Michael say?"

"What *can* he say? Right now he's trying to reach her aunt in New York. She's Rita's only relative. He's hopin' she knows where they are."

"I'm telling you, check her makeup," Amber said, nodding wisely. "No woman goes anywhere for more than a day without taking her makeup."

"Yeah, yeah, we'll do that. We're goin' back to the apartment an' meeting a couple of cops I know. I'm gonna try an' get 'em to put out a missing persons report."

Michael slammed the phone down and marched into the kitchen. "I need a drink," he said, grim-faced.

"That's exactly what you don't need," Quincy said, remembering the bad times.

Michael managed a wry laugh. "I said I *needed* one, I didn't say I was going to have one." Opening the fridge, he grabbed a 7-Up and took a hearty swig. "There's no reply at her aunt's house."

"I have a feeling they're both fine," Amber said reassuringly.

Oh yeah, like she would know, Michael thought. If anything had happened to his kid . . .

No. It didn't bear thinking about. He would kill anyone who harmed Bella — blow their fucking brains out without a second thought.

Guilt was creeping up on him big time. He should have guessed something was wrong when

86

he kept on getting the answering machine. He was a detective, for chrissake. The moment he hit L.A. he should have run right over there, instead of waiting almost a week.

Taking two more gulps of 7-Up, he slammed the can on the counter. "Come on, Q, let's get back. I wanna talk to the woman in the upstairs apartment again. Maybe she's remembered something."

Stopping only to kiss Amber on the cheek, Quincy was right behind him. "We're on our way. See you later, hon."

"Lily," the fat woman said, then, lisping slightly. "My name's Lily Langolla." She was quite a sight to behold in stained yellow caftan and fluffy blue slippers, a pink bow stuck jauntily on top of her frizzy yellow hair.

At least she'd let them into her apartment this time. Michael had flashed his detective's badge, and she'd opened up immediately.

"So, Lily," Quincy said, keeping his voice nice and even. "When did you last see Rita Polone?"

"I don't spy on people," Lily said primly, throwing her huge bulk onto an old purple couch, from which the stuffing escaped in six different places.

"Nobody said you was spyin' by knowin' what's goin' on," Quincy said, continuing his soothing friendly bit.

Michael stared out the window. As far as he could see, the woman had a prime spot to watch everything that happened on the street. If there'd been any kind of commotion, there was no way

87

she could have missed it.

He turned toward her. "Lily," he said, speaking softly, "why did you call her a slut?"

"Not against the law t'call people names, is it?" Lily replied belligerently.

He used his charm, hitting her with a direct dark-eyed gaze. "No, Lily, I'm sure a smart woman like you wouldn't do anything against the law."

The heat of his gaze had the required effect. Reaching up, Lily patted the bow in her hair, suddenly aware that she might not be looking her best.

Michael knew he had her. Quickly he moved in, bombarding her with questions, taking her by surprise. "Was she noisy, Lily? In and out all the time? Did she have many visitors?"

"That's right," Lily agreed.

"What's right?"

Lily was flustered, but now she was determined to please. "Men. Comin' an' goin' at all times."

He felt a tenseness in his stomach, a knifelike feeling of doom. "How many men, Lily?" he asked, making a concentrated effort to keep his voice calm, because he knew exactly what she was alluding to. "One a night? Two?"

"Hey now, Mike, don't go thinking just because — " Quincy began.

Michael silenced him with a look.

Lily squinted, thinking about it for a moment. "First there was several different ones comin' an' goin' all times of the day an' night," she said, fidgeting with the bow in her hair. "Then there was just one. He visited her regular for a couple of

88

weeks, until one night he came an' got her an' they took off. I ain't seen her since."

"Was her little girl with her, Lily?" Michael asked softly.

"Maybe she was."

"What the fuck do you mean — *maybe* she was," Michael yelled, suddenly losing it. "Was she or wasn't she?"

"Okay, okay," Quincy said, hurriedly getting between them as Lily cowered back. "Let's take it nice an' easy here. Lily's doing her best to remember, aren't you, sweetheart?"

Lily was shaken. Jerking a cheaply bejeweled finger at Michael, she said, "What's the matter with *him?*"

"It's *his* kid, Lily," Quincy explained. "You can understand him being upset, can't you?"

"You *sure* he's a cop?" Lily asked, peering at Michael suspiciously.

"Just as much as I am," Quincy lied smoothly. "Now come on, Lily — let's try an' jog that memory of yours."

Poring over Bobby Rush's clipping file, Kennedy soon reached the conclusion that he was a driven workaholic, mightily striving to overcome the handicap of having a famous father. One of the things she took note of was that every time Jerry Rush's name came up, Bobby went on automatic response. Exactly the same answers kept appearing.

My father is a wonderful actor.
We're very different.
Jerry never helped me.

89

Yes, I've seen all his films. Growing up in the Rush household, they were required viewing.

We are not alike at all.

I don't know whether Jerry has seen Hard Tears *or not.*

No. We have no plans to work together.

Hmm, Kennedy thought, I wonder what a psychiatrist would make of Bobby's telling remarks. In fact, it wasn't such a bad idea to write the interview and intersperse Bobby's answers with a top psychiatrist's comments. That could be interesting.

Just as she was about to pick up the phone to contact Bobby's publicist, Rosa called. "Honey, you've got to do me a big favor," Rosa pleaded, sounding breathless.

Kennedy groaned. "Beware of friends asking favors," she said, wondering what Rosa wanted this time.

Rosa was at her most persuasive. "Don't be like that, sweetie. I really *need* you."

"For what?"

"Dinner."

"Why?" she asked suspiciously.

"Because Ferdy's best friend from Atlanta is visiting, and we want you to have dinner with us."

"Rosa," Kennedy said patiently. "Ferdy is a black, twenty-five-year-old basketball star, and much as I love you, I refuse to have dinner with his best friend. Cradle snatching is not my thing."

"I already promised Ferdy you'd come."

"That was foolish of you."

"He's going to think you're prejudiced if you don't show."

"That's ridiculous."

"So prove it."

"No, Rosa. I don't want to do this."

"*Pleeease!* I never ask you for anything!"

A lie, but Kennedy weakened. "Oh, all right," she said, knowing she was making a mistake.

"You're the best!" Rosa exclaimed. "The Ivy. Eight o'clock. Look sexy — it's his first visit to L.A."

"Rosa — "

Too late, Rosa was long gone. Oh, God! Why had she agreed to go?

Just lonely, I guess.

Lonely, ha! She was never lonely. She loved spending time by herself, taking long walks on the beach, reading, driving along the Pacific Coast Highway in her 1986 Corvette. In fact, she didn't even mind dining alone in a restaurant — something most people wouldn't consider under any circumstances.

Oh well, dinner at eight and out.

She called Bobby Rush's publicist. The magazine had already set the interview. Elspeth, his publicist, had set the ground rules. Now all she had to do was arrange a time and a place.

Elspeth spoke in short, sharp bursts. "Breakfast. The Four Seasons. Friday. He can only spare an hour."

"No," Kennedy replied pleasantly. "This is a major piece — a cover story. I need to spend a day with him. A couple of hours for the interview, and the rest of the time I'll follow him around and blend into the background."

"It won't fly," Elspeth said snappishly.

"I think you'll find it will," Kennedy replied, remaining calm. "I'm sure we all have the same goal in mind — plenty of coverage for your client, and I can't do that unless I spend time with him. Call me back."

Click. She was gone before the woman could argue.

Ferdy's friend, Nix, was six feet four inches of sinewy chocolate-colored muscle. He had tight curly hair, puppy-dog eyes, and a sweet smile. He spoke eloquently and intelligently. He was polite and charming. They had a terrific evening with Rosa and Ferdy, and when they'd finished dinner Nix overruled Ferdy's objections and picked up the check. Kennedy was impressed. Even more so when he insisted on following her home in his rented car to be sure she made it safely.

On impulse she invited him in for coffee, and they talked for two hours before ending up in bed. She hadn't expected it. Certainly hadn't wanted it; he was ten years younger than she. As it turned out, he was probably the most considerate lover, apart from her husband, she'd ever experienced. He left her totally breathless with his expertise.

"I'm a basketball player," he explained with a wide grin, when she questioned him on his prowess. "We have outstanding mind-body coordination."

"I'll say you do," she said, floating on air after two fantastic orgasms. It had been three months since her weatherman, and Nix was in the right place at the right time with the right attitude. He even carried his own supply of condoms.

He turned her over and began stroking her back with his long tongue, feathery strokes that immediately began driving her crazy.

"Not again," she murmured lazily. "I don't have your stamina."

"Oh, yes you do." He laughed, straddling her so she could feel his hard cock pressing insistently against her back.

And he was right. Suddenly her stamina level was rising, and when his large hands cupped her breasts and played with her nipples, she rolled over in a frenzy, just as ready as he was.

Nix was a technician. Orgasm number three, and she was purring.

Eventually they fell asleep, and when she awoke in the morning to the sound of the phone ringing, he was gone.

Groping for the receiver, she mumbled a sleepy "Hello."

"Well?" Rosa demanded, dying to hear everything.

"Well, *what?*" she said, stretching luxuriously.

"Details, Kennedy. I get off on details."

"I gave up kissing and telling years ago."

"You're no fun," Rosa complained sulkily.

She laughed secretively. "That's not what Nix says."

"So he *did* stay," Rosa said triumphantly. "Is he still there?"

"I'll talk to you later," she said, hanging up and wandering into the bathroom, where she found Nix had stuck a note on the mirror above the sink.

Thanks for a memorable trip to L.A. Can I call you next time?

She couldn't help smiling. A memorable trip indeed — for both of them. But no — there would be no repeat performances. It was a one-nighter — nothing more, nothing less.

Fifteen minutes and a long, warm shower later, she phoned Bobby Rush's publicist.

"Friday," Elspeth said, sounding as snappish as ever. "We'll meet at his office at the studio at ten o'clock."

"And do I get to spend the day?"

"He's very busy, but if you can assure me you'll stay in the background . . ."

"Once I've done the interview, he won't even know I'm there."

Sure, lady. Believe that, and you'll believe anything!

The Man rented a black car under an assumed name. Nothing fancy. Nothing memorable. Just a plain black Ford that allowed him complete anonymity.

He stopped by Sears and paid cash for a pair of black slacks, a long-sleeved dark shirt, and black running shoes. He needed shades, but vanity got the best of him — unable to settle for Sears sunglasses, he ended up buying expensive blackout Armani shades at the Fred Segal store in Santa Monica.

When he got home and was safely locked in his room, he tried on his new outfit and was satisfied.

Since he'd left prison his hair had grown longer. Carefully he slicked it back with gel, securing it with a rubber band. Then he stared at himself in the mirror for a long time, striking karate poses, taking his shades off and putting them on again several times, deciding that he bore more than a passing resemblance to his film idol, Steven Seagal. He'd watched all of Steven Seagal's movies over and over in prison, especially the one about vengeance.

Steven Seagal was a man who understood

about getting even.

Steven Seagal was someone to admire.

Not that The Man was into admiring people. It was weak to hero-worship. Better to hate everyone, and then there was no way anyone could ever get to you. He'd learned that important piece of information at a very early age. Unfortunately he hadn't always listened to his own counsel.

The Girl had been his downfall. The pretty Girl with the long silky yellow hair and the cornflower-blue eyes and the quirky little come-on smile.

The Girl had led him on. She'd encouraged him and tempted him in the thin see-through dresses she wore, her small tits beckoning him like beacons. She'd smiled and flirted and accepted his gifts — but when it came time to make the payoff, she'd acted as if he were some sex-starved stranger.

Bitch.

Whore.

Weren't they all?

He didn't like to think about The Girl, because it was her fault he'd spent the last seven years of his life in jail.

Angrily he banished her from his thoughts. She'd got what she deserved.

Sometimes he awoke in the middle of the night and saw her face before him. Those nighttime hours overpowered him, filled him with lustful memories, until he was forced to relieve the tension by his own hand.

He hated her for what she'd done to him.

He loved her. He always would.

The Man left his room, locking the door behind him.

The black housekeeper had a room on the premises. He suspected she spied on him. If she didn't stop he'd be forced to add her to his list.

His rented car was parked at the bottom of the driveway. He changed the license plates unobserved and got behind the wheel.

It was a long drive to Agoura Hills, and he didn't intend to be late.

9

They sat side by side in the beauty salon, Cheryl getting her legs waxed while Jordanna had a manicure. It was a weekly ritual, there was always maintenance to take care of.

"I'm having a party," Cheryl announced, adding casually, "You can come if you like."

"What sort of party?" Jordanna asked suspiciously. It was almost a week since Cheryl had announced her plans to become a Hollywood madam, and none of her friends had heard from her since.

"A get-together that will include a few of my girls and plenty of would-be clients," Cheryl said airily. "I've been on the phone all week."

"Thanks for the invite, but I don't think so."

"Grant's coming."

"I'm sure he is."

"I wish you'd support me in this."

"Why? We've done some crazy shit in our time, but this beats everything. You've lost it, Cheryl."

"Be like that."

"I will."

"I have some information you might be interested in," Cheryl said mysteriously.

Jordanna examined her nails. They were long

98

and shiny and strong. The good news was she'd finally managed to stop biting them — a minor triumph. "What information?" she asked curiously.

"It's juicy."

"So tell."

"Not here."

Sometimes — most times — Cheryl was an annoying pain in the ass. Since her new vocation, she was impossible.

"What's it about?" Jordanna asked.

"Your latest stepmother."

Jordanna buried a yawn. "What's she done now?"

"It's not what she's done *now*," Cheryl said, staring pointedly at the Puerto Rican woman diligently waxing her legs. "We'll talk later, in private."

Jordanna hated having to wait for anything — especially information. "Spill it, Cheryl," she said emphatically.

"This is *not* news for the *Enquirer*," Cheryl replied primly. "Learn to be patient."

"The last thing I am is patient."

"Don't I know it!"

"So?"

"So where did your father meet Kim?"

Shaking her head, Jordanna said, "Oh, like I know. Following his love life is not exactly number one on my agenda."

"Try asking her," Cheryl suggested. "See what she says."

"Why?"

"Just try it."

"And when I have this important piece of info you'll tell me all?"

"We'll have lunch tomorrow at Café Roma. One-thirty. Your check. I promise you it'll be worth it."

"Hi, Daddy."

Jordan Levitt looked up from his desk with an expression of surprise. "A visit. From my daughter. Who died?"

"Thought I'd drop by, check out how you're doing," Jordanna replied, ignoring his sarcasm as she flopped into one of the oversize leather chairs stationed in front of his massive oak desk.

"How nice of you to make the long trek from the guesthouse," Jordan said, removing his horn-rimmed reading glasses and smiling broadly.

God, he's handsome, Jordanna thought. *What is it with him? He doesn't get older, just more attractive.*

"I suppose your allowance is in need of a boost," he added, sliding open a drawer and removing his checkbook.

"No," Jordanna said, disappointed that he thought that was what she wanted. "Scoring more money is not the only reason I come to see you."

He placed his checkbook on the desk and picked up a gold pen. "That's reassuring."

She fidgeted uncomfortably. "I . . . uh . . . I guess I missed you." It was difficult for her to say, but she really wanted him to know how she felt. She craved his love and affection, but he was usually too busy giving it all to his current wife. It would be so nice if he responded to *her*.

Jordan looked pleased. "Missed me, huh?"

100

"Well, you *are* my father, and since you got married again . . ." She trailed off, not quite sure what she was planning to say. "By the way," she added, "where did you and Kim meet?"

"What a question!"

"Pretty normal."

"A mutual friend introduced us."

"How nice."

A critical tone entered Jordan's voice. "Since I married Kim we've invited you to the big house for dinner on countless occasions. You haven't shown up once."

"I've been busy."

His face turned stern. "Doing what?"

"Writing," she said defensively. "I'm writing a book." Hmm, not quite, but it was a good idea.

That stopped him. "A book? About what?"

It came to her in a flash. "Growing up in Hollywood."

He was silent for a moment. When he finally spoke, it was very slowly, making sure she understood every word. "Not about this family, I hope."

Why did they always end up fighting — because that's the way this conversation was headed, and they both knew it.

Jordanna thrust out her jaw, ready for battle. "Maybe. If I feel like it," she said in her best *don't you tell me what to do* voice.

"*No*, Jordanna," he said curtly.

Challenging words. "No what?" she said quickly.

"No revelations about this family. Do you understand me?"

She wanted to tell him to go screw himself. She was quite capable of telling anyone else — anyone except her father, who was still able to reduce her to a nervous twelve-year-old. "I've got a contract," she lied. "With a big publishing firm."

His left eye twitched, a sure sign he was severely angry. "Which one?"

"That's my business," she said, feeling like a defiant little girl.

"How much have they paid you?"

"It doesn't matter."

"I think you'll find it does."

"What does *that* mean?"

He stood up, glaring at her. "It means it better be enough to support yourself, because if you're writing a book about this family, young lady, you can get the hell out of my guesthouse and go live elsewhere."

Her eyes filled with tears, but with a supreme effort she managed to keep them in check. Couldn't let him see. Couldn't let him know he could still get to her.

"Fine," she said coolly, jumping to her feet. "I'll go pack."

"Do that," he said roughly.

Fuck you, Daddy, I will.

She rushed from the room, mission unaccomplished. All she'd wanted was to find out where he'd met Kim, and look where they'd ended up — fighting as usual. When was she going to learn that arguing with her father was a no-win situation? Now she was out on her own with nowhere to go.

She hurried to the guesthouse and called Shep.

"I need a place to crash," she said, speaking rapidly.

Shep sighed, he'd heard it before. "One night? Two?"

"This time it's permanent. I can't take his control shit anymore — I'm moving out for real."

"Sure," Shep said, not believing her.

"I mean it," she insisted.

"You always do."

"Can I come over or not?"

"I suppose so," he said, with limited enthusiasm.

She ran back and forth, piling her car full of as much stuff as it would take. Jumping in, she roared off down the long driveway.

From his study window Jordan watched her go. So beautiful, so unsettled, so like her mother.

Dammit, he wished there was something he could do for her, but the truth was he had no idea what Jordanna wanted. Materially he'd given her everything possible. A place to live, a new car of her choice every year, charge cards and a generous allowance. He'd never said no to her, how could he?

For a moment his mind wandered and he thought about Lillianne — his first wife, the mother of his children, and the one true love of his life. Certifiable. Everyone had said so. When he'd signed the papers to put her away in the private clinic, it was for her own protection. How was he to know she'd slit her wrists and die a miserable death, leaving him with two children to bring up on his own. Of course, he hadn't been on his own for long: marrying again had seemed like a good idea, except that the children had never taken to any of his wives — a shame, because he'd tried a few.

And then, as if he didn't have enough problems, his only son had killed himself — a boy with everything to live for.

The police said drugs had caused Jamie to jump from Jordan's New York penthouse. Jordan didn't know what to believe. His son was no drug addict; as far as he was concerned it was a terrible accident.

For a while Jordan was shattered. The press pounced on him, Jordanna had turned into a wild thing, and his life was a mess. But Jordan knew better than anyone how to survive. After all, he'd arrived in Hollywood as a sixteen-year-old runaway in 1948, with no money and no prospects. Over the years he'd built himself a formidable reputation. It would take more than a few tragedies to pull Jordan Levitt down.

Within the next few months he'd sent Jordanna off to boarding school in Paris, divorced his current wife, and produced two new movies.

Kim entered his study, interrupting his thoughts. Out of all his wives, Kim was the youngest and the most loving. She put him above all else, and it was damn refreshing to have a woman who cared so much for him. What did it matter that she was nearly forty years his junior? Age was irrelevant.

"Curtain samples," Kim announced, waving a swatch of fabric in the air. "I need your opinion, darling."

She was redecorating his house and doing an excellent job. It was costing, but whoever said women came cheap?

He stood up, towering over his young bride. "Come here, little one," he said, opening his arms.

Kim ran into his embrace, and they stood entwined while Jordanna zoomed down Sunset in her white Porsche, tears streaming down her face as Jimi Hendrix blasted full volume on the tape deck.

The next day a composed Jordanna Levitt sashayed into Café Roma — nodding at a few acquaintances, taking in the action, checking out the usual group of out-of-work Italian actors who gathered at a corner table, comparing testosterone levels, job opportunities, and how many girls they'd fucked.

Cheryl was already there, sitting at a table drinking coffee as she studiously wrote copious notes on a yellow legal pad.

"I'm not late, am I?" Jordanna asked, glancing quickly at her Cartier Panthere watch.

"Nope," Cheryl replied, putting down her pen. "I was here early. Had to interview a girl, a gorgeous blonde fresh in from Dallas."

"Christ!" Jordanna exclaimed. "You're even beginning to talk like a pimp. Did you inspect her teeth?"

Cheryl allowed herself a small smile. "Sensational teeth."

"I was being sarcastic," Jordanna said sternly.

"So what else is new?" Cheryl replied, adding

more Sweet'n Low to her coffee and stirring it vigorously.

Jordanna shrugged. "Nothing much. I moved out."

"*Again?*"

"This time for real."

"Well . . . ," Cheryl said. "I guess I have to tell you the big scoop."

Jordanna couldn't wait. "Yes?"

Without further ado Cheryl gave her the news. "Your stepmother was a whore," she said, relishing every word.

Jordanna blinked. "Excuse me?"

"Actually we don't call them whores," Cheryl added nonchalantly. " 'Party girls' is the politically correct way of referring to them."

Jordanna frowned. "Are you f-ing with me?"

"Would I do that?" Cheryl asked innocently.

"I certainly hope not. This is way too serious to joke about."

Cheryl began explaining. "I found her in Donna's files. Kimberly Anna Austin from San Diego. She worked for Donna a good six months, then she met your father and that was it, retirement city."

Jordanna was in shock, it was just too bizarre. "Are you sure it's the same girl?"

"Absolutely positive. Donna was very thorough. She kept a complete dossier on every girl who worked for her, including a photo."

Jordanna drummed her fingers on the table. "Can I see it?"

Digging into her purse, Cheryl produced a glossy photograph and handed it over.

Jordanna studied it. It was Kim, all right. Little Miss Sweetness and Light. Boy, had she gotten lucky, landing a man like Jordan Levitt.

"Yes, it's her," Jordanna said slowly. "Oh shit! What am I supposed to do — tell him?"

"Knowing your father, I have a feeling he wouldn't appreciate it," Cheryl replied. "Talk about a blow to the male ego."

"I can't *not* tell him."

"He'll find out eventually — let him do it on his own time. Believe me, you don't want to be involved, it'll only embarrass him."

"I suppose you're right," Jordanna replied, torn between the desire to reveal Kim's little game and a reluctance to hurt her father.

Why not?

Why yes? He's never done anything to intentionally hurt me.

Ah, but he has hurt you. In fact, he's just thrown you out.

"You're not going to tell anyone about this, are you?" she asked, knowing what a big mouth Cheryl had.

"I run a clean business," Cheryl said, very full of herself. "My clients are assured of discretion and privacy at all times."

"He's not your client," Jordanna pointed out.

"He could be," Cheryl replied knowingly. "Once Kim is history." Taking a sip of coffee, she added, "I have some really lovely girls, you know. If you come across any would-be clients, send them my way. I'll pay you commission."

"You're unbelievable!"

"Thanks for the compliment."

It was early in the morning when Mac Brooks picked up the phone and called Bobby Rush. He'd spent the previous evening arguing with Sharleen. She hadn't wanted him to call Bobby direct, she'd preferred him to do the dance of a thousand agents. But Mac wasn't in the mood for all that agent crap, half the time they caused deals to fail, and he wanted this one to fly.

He had a strong feeling *Thriller Eyes* was destined to be a winner, and he was definitely interested in directing it. The agents could get into it *after* he'd made a verbal commitment — that way they couldn't do too much damage.

Bobby answered his own phone — a good sign, because there was nothing worse than having to plow through an entourage every time you needed to reach the star.

"Hey, Bobby," he said. "It's Mac Brooks. Remember that high-ticket ride we were talking about? I've decided to take it with you, so all I need to know is — when do we get started?"

10

Michael had never felt more helpless in his life, and it wasn't a feeling he enjoyed. His gut instinct told him Bella was all right, but the reality was he couldn't find her, and it was making him frantic. When he finally reached Rita's aunt in New York, she knew nothing — she still had the same old address for her niece, with whom she was not close.

"How about her girlfriends?" Michael asked, referring to three big-haired Brooklyn blondes with loud mouths and bad attitudes, whose names escaped him.

Rita's aunt promised to try and track them down. Two days of silence, and he knew he had to do something fast before he went nuts.

He visited Lily again, taking her flowers, hoping the attention might loosen her memory.

It didn't. She still couldn't remember anything.

He went downstairs to Rita's apartment and sat on the couch for a while. He'd already searched the place thoroughly, looking for a clue — anything to help find her. He remembered that when they were married Rita used to hide things — money, her few bits of jewelry, letters from old boyfriends he wasn't supposed to know about. She'd always chosen odd hiding places, like ceiling light fixtures and the bottom of vacuum cleaner bags. He'd searched this apartment thoroughly, but now he decided to do it again for luck.

He started in the kitchen, graduating to the poky little bathroom, methodically sorting through everything, including a plastic bag full of dirty laundry.

Rita favored lacy lingerie, and there was a ton of it: push-up bras, thong panties, old-fashioned stockings, and panty hose in many colors.

Ah, memories . . . The first time he'd gone out with her, he should have known she was trouble, but somehow or other his hard-on had gotten in the way of rational thought, and all had been lost.

Michael Scorsinni had married Rita Polone on a cold December morning three weeks before Christmas. She'd worn a white satin dress studded with faux diamonds and cut way too low at the front.

He'd worn a dark suit and a dazed smile.

Rita was four months pregnant.

He was drunk.

Since she had no family, his had turned out in force. His brother, Sal, smirking proudly as he tried to cop more than a look down the bride's revealing neckline. His mother, Virginia, a thin, nervous woman who never stopped chain-smoking. His stepfather, Eddie, fat and old, plagued with arthritis. Plus a scattering of relatives and friends.

Michael remembered frantically dry-humping his bride in the rented limo on the way to their honeymoon hotel. He and Rita were so hot for each other they couldn't wait.

When his hard-on finally faded, he'd decided it was time to sober up. Rita no longer held the same fascination.

Now Rita had vanished with his kid, and he felt like he was drowning. No clues. Nowhere to look. And the cops had nothing.

Lighting up a cigarette, he blew smoke rings toward the ceiling and focused his mind.

Rita used to love dancing. Saturday nights she'd get all dressed up, and they'd hire a baby-sitter and hit the town. In his drinking days he'd made out pretty well on the dance floor. Once he stopped boozing he lost it.

"You won't take me, I'll go with the girls," she'd threatened, daring him to argue.

He was perfectly happy staying home in front of the TV watching a ball game while Bella slept peacefully in the other room.

Was Rita still dancing on Saturday nights?

If she was alive, she was still dancing.

The thought of foul play sent a chill through him. He had a daughter out there somewhere, and he was determined to find her.

Stubbing out his cigarette, he took one final look around and headed back to the Robbinses' place.

Kennedy was on time. She prided herself on always being punctual.

Bobby Rush was late. His publicist, Elspeth, an angular redhead in her forties, with too many freckles and a bad nose job, offered no excuses.

Kennedy sat on a couch in the outer office and steamed as an hour passed. At eleven o'clock she said, "Are you sure he's coming?"

111

"I can't do more than tell him," Elspeth replied in a not too pleasant voice. She'd been on the phone for most of the hour, conducting a low, angry conversation with someone who was obviously her husband or boyfriend.

"Yes you can," Kennedy replied. "I suggest you find out where he is and ask him."

Elspeth gave a put-upon sigh and made a couple of phone calls. "Apparently his assistant thought the interview was Monday," she said brusquely. "He's in Palm Springs."

"Oh, great," Kennedy said, waiting for an apology.

The woman didn't say a word. Picking up her copy of a Chanel purse, she hurried to the door.

Kennedy got up and followed her. "That's it, then? No Bobby Rush today?"

"I told you," Elspeth said, irritated at having to repeat herself. "He's in Palm Springs. Be here on Monday at ten." Clutching her fake Chanel, she walked out without waiting for a reply.

Unbelievably rude, Kennedy thought. There was nothing worse than publicists who thought they were as important as the stars they looked after. Bobby Rush must be stupid to employ such a person.

The day loomed ahead of her with nothing planned, and that really annoyed her, because she prided herself on being totally organized at all times. Phil used to call her Queen of the Lists — everything written down in an orderly fashion. He may have laughed at her organizational skills, but they'd sure accomplished a lot in their years together covering the world. They'd earned respect and kudos from the journalistic community *and* had a wonderful time. Now she was doing interviews with two-bit actors who couldn't even be bothered to turn up.

Damn Mason — he'd dangled the bait and she'd jumped. What the hell had happened to all her journalistic integrity?

Furious with herself, she left the office determined to talk to Mason and see if she could get Bobby Rush's cover dumped.

She marched down the corridor, buzzed the elevator, and waited impatiently. After a few moments she banged on the doors, sending an impatient message from the second floor. Of course, she could have walked down the stairs, but why should she? The way things were going, she'd probably trip and break her neck.

Just as she was about to hammer again, the elevator arrived, the doors opened, and a man in running shorts, a cutoff T-shirt, and a baseball cap stepped out. "Sorry," he said pleasantly. "Did I keep you waiting?"

"Yes," she replied, taking her bad mood out on him.

"You know what it's like," he said, smiling disarmingly. "Some guy grabbed me downstairs, and I couldn't close the doors."

"You should've gotten out," she said frostily.

As she spoke, the door closed again and the elevator took off.

"Damn!" she exclaimed.

"Sorry," he said apologetically. "Are you running late?"

"It's not my day," she replied, with a rueful

shake of her head. "I had an appointment with Bobby Rush, and he failed to show."

"You're here for the interview?"

"That's right."

"Then come on in, we can do it now."

"Mr. *Rush* is in Palm Springs," she said sarcastically. "Mr. *Rush* is too busy to do an interview today."

"Hey," he said, grinning. "Mr. Rush is standing right here, and I am in desperate need of an assistant, so let's go."

She raised an eyebrow. "*You're* Bobby Rush?"

His grin widened. "Guilty."

"I didn't recognize you," she said, stating the obvious.

It was quite apparent that he likewise had no idea who she was or the real reason she was there.

He was already on his way to his office. Turning around, he beckoned her. "Come on," he said, with an encouraging wink. "You can make coffee while I shower."

Oh, great, the little woman makes coffee, and the big man takes a shower. What a chauvinist! Was he going to come on to her, too? Sexual harassment would be a bonus.

Her adrenaline began to pump. This story had possibilities.

"I gave everybody the day off," he explained, as she followed him into his office. "Monday we start preproduction on my movie, they won't get another free day until we finish."

"What movie is that?" she asked.

"*Thriller Eyes*," he said. "If you get the job you can read the script."

Lucky me, she thought, as they moved through the outer office into his private domain.

Gesturing to a small bar, he said, "Coffee's in the fridge, coffee machine's over there. I take it black, no sugar." He opened a side door, and she caught a glimpse of his bathroom as he walked in. Hmm . . . what could be better than interviewing Bobby Rush when he thought *he* was interviewing *her.*

She looked around his office. It was light and airy, furnished in minimalist style. There were movie posters on the walls, a stack of scripts on his desk, and nothing much else of interest.

Opening the small fridge, she took out a packet of ground coffee and shook the right amount into the machine.

Over the sound of the shower, she heard a knock from the outer office. She went into the other room and opened the door.

An earnest young woman wearing owl-shaped glasses stood there. "Hi," the young woman said. "I'm Jenny Scott. I'm here for the interview with Mr. Rush."

"Oh, Jenny," Kennedy said, feeling guilty — but a story was a story, and she was on a roll. "Mr. Rush isn't available today. Can you be here Monday at ten?"

"Well, yes . . . ," Jenny said tentatively. "But I was told it was kind of urgent."

"Not that urgent," Kennedy said crisply. "Come back on Monday, he'll be happy to see you then."

The young woman left, and she went back to the coffee machine, poured two mugs of black coffee with no sugar, and sat down on the other side of his glass-and-chrome desk.

Bobby emerged a few minutes later, clad in faded jeans, a UCLA sweatshirt, and a big grin. His dirty-blond hair was wet and curly. "Jeez, that feels better," he said. "The only problem is I'm starving. How about walking over to the commissary?"

"Sure," she said, deciding he was much better-looking in person than on the big screen. He had these penetrating clear blue eyes and a certain energy about him. Sexually attractive definitely.

Who cared? Maybe her readers would.

"Okay, let's go," he said, already out the door.

She trailed him from the building, checking him out from behind. He had a confident walk and a tight butt.

Hmm . . . very nice.

Once outside, he covered his blue eyes with dark shades. She did the same.

"So," he said, as they strolled to the commissary. "I was expecting someone younger. This job is for a gofer, a kid who's prepared to do a lot of running around for me. You look like you passed that stage in your career."

"It's something to do," she replied.

He lifted his glasses and pinned her with his intense eyes. "Something to do for fun, huh?"

"That's right," she said, refusing to be sucked in by his movie star charm.

"I'm very demanding," he said, watching her closely.

"I'm sure you are."

"What I'm trying to say is, it may be fun for

116

you, but I expect the person I hire to be there at all times of the day and night."

"Day *and* night?" she asked quizzically.

"You get to go home to sleep."

"How reassuring."

"What was your last job?" he asked.

"I worked for a magazine in New York."

"Hey." He began to laugh. "You're not going to hand me your unfinished screenplay, are you?"

"No, Mr. Rush, I can assure you I'm not."

"Call me Bobby."

They entered the commissary. Bobby waved to several people as they made their way to his table.

As soon as they sat down, a middle-aged waitress was all over him. "Hello, Bobby. Are we bacon-and-egging it today, or is it the fruit thing?"

"The fruit thing, sweetheart," he said, patting his washboard stomach. "Gotta watch those rolls of fat."

The waitress giggled. "Not to worry, Bobby. If *you* don't watch 'em, every woman in America will."

"Hey — who cares about other women when you're around, Mavis," he said, giving her a friendly pat on the ass.

More giggles from the waitress, who was old enough to know better.

He picked up a menu. "What'll you have?" he asked Kennedy.

"An orange juice will do nicely," she replied.

"No muffins? No bacon and eggs?"

"Tell me . . . uh . . . Bobby, do you always buy breakfast for the people you interview?"

Now he was definitely coming on to her. "Only when they're as beautiful as you," he said, fixing her once again with the baby blues. "What did you say your name was?"

Halfway down the freeway, Michael realized that he hadn't been thorough enough in searching through Rita's dirty laundry. All he'd done was tip it on the floor, taken a cursory poke through it, and then stuffed it back in the bag. But Rita was devious, and he knew it. Something told him to turn the car around and take another look.

Driving off at the next ramp, he headed back to her place.

When he arrived, Lily was leaning from her window.

"You remember anything yet, Lily?" he called up to her.

"Still thinking, Mister Cop," she said coyly, fluttering her eyelashes.

"Don't forget, if you come up with anything at all you've got my number."

He entered Rita's apartment, went straight to the laundry bag, once again tipped everything onto the floor, and started a more methodical search. Picking up a pair of black panty hose, he noticed something stuffed in the foot. Investigating further, he discovered three Polaroids and a slip of paper with a name and a number written on it.

He checked out the Polaroids first. They were standard Rita, she'd always gotten off on having fun with a camera. In the first photo she wore nothing but a smile, a black lace garter belt, and roll-up stockings. The second one showed her minus the garter belt, smile firmly in place. And the third was of a greasy-looking man with an enormous hard-on pointed straight at the camera.

Michael quickly read the scrawl on the piece of paper, recognizing Rita's bad handwriting. *Heron Jones,* she'd written. *Club Erotica.*

Pocketing the information, he threw the clothes back into the laundry bag, dumped it on the bathroom floor, and hurried from the apartment.

11

Bobby Rush felt good. Breakfast with a beautiful woman did it for him every time. He'd enjoyed meeting Kennedy Chase; even though she wasn't right for the job, she sure was something.

He'd walked her to her car from the commissary. "*You're* the one should have been doing the talking, not me," he'd said with a rueful smile.

"Really?"

"That's usually the way it goes. I was supposed to be interviewing *you,* and you ended up asking all the questions."

"That's because I like to know what I'm getting into."

"Well, you sure found out. I think I told you my life story."

"It was interesting."

"Uh . . . Kennedy, I'll be honest with you. You're way too qualified for this job."

"You have no idea what my qualifications are."

"No, but I bet they're first rate."

She'd laughed. Great laugh, very throaty. "That sounds like one of those breakup lines where the guy says, 'You're too good for me, so I have to go find someone new.'"

He'd laughed too. "I have to admit I've used that one a couple of times."

"So you're into using lines?"

"Isn't everyone?"

"I'm not."

"That makes you very unusual."

He'd watched her drive off. Classy lady. He'd give it a day, send her flowers, maybe take her on a date, get laid.

Ha! He was starting to think like his father. God forbid!

Get laid, huh? It had been quite some time. Getting laid was not what it used to be. AIDS was out there now, and casual sex was a thing of the past.

He was well aware that because he was a movie star he could have almost anyone he wanted. But today that didn't mean shit.

He was on edge. Tonight was the big night — dinner with Jerry. Darla had insisted that the reunion take place at the family mansion, with both his brothers and their wives present. Great, and he didn't have a date. Maybe it was just as well — this way Jerry couldn't put a move on whoever he was with.

He was apprehensive about seeing his father after all these years, although deep down he was hopeful that Jerry might have changed, that maybe he'd tell Bobby he was proud of him and all his achievements. Wouldn't it be something to hear that from his old man?

Dream on. Jerry is a selfish sonofabitch; he's always been a selfish sonofabitch. Why would he change?

121

"Are we going to Cheryl's party?" Shep asked, pottering around his tiny neat kitchen.

"Why?" Jordanna replied, biting into an apple as she sat at the counter, flicking through the pages of *L.A. Weekly.*

"It might be amusing."

She put down the newspaper. "Amusing to mix with a roomful of hookers? I don't think so."

"Come on, Jordy, you used to be adventurous."

"You go if you want, but the thought of going to a party at Cheryl's while she pursues her new career as *the* Hollywood madam is not my idea of a fun night out."

"Okay, okay," Shep said. "Let's meet later at Homebase."

"You got it," Jordanna replied. She'd spent a restless day thinking about Cheryl's revelations and wondering if she should tell Jordan. After all, if Kim used to be a working girl, surely her father was entitled to know.

Maybe I'll tell him.

Maybe not. You want him to be even more pissed at you?

I don't care.

Oh, yes you do.

She called an actor friend of hers who was fun to be with and always had a great supply of pot. "Wanna cruise the clubs tonight?" she asked hopefully.

"I've got a new girlfriend," he said.

"Bring her along — I don't care."

"Sure, *you* don't care, but *she* probably will."

"Don't tell me you've hooked up with one of

those jealous little things?" she needled.

He sounded uptight, definitely pussy-whipped. "You could say that."

She hung up the phone. Men. They sure as hell didn't make good best friends. But hey — she didn't need a man to take her around, she could cruise on her own. In fact, hitting the clubs by herself allowed her more freedom.

After Shep left she watched a couple of movies on television, ordered a large pepperoni pizza from Jacopo's, and shortly before eleven pulled on her oldest jeans, a pair of motorcycle boots, a man's oversize shirt, and a Harley jacket.

Jordanna was ready to hit the streets.

Standing outside the house on Bedford brought back every bad memory. Bobby felt like a kid again, a stupid little kid whose father always put him down and told him he was useless.

Had to get his head straight. Had to remember he was not a kid. He was a successful businessman, producer, movie star.

Screw Jerry Rush. He was not afraid of him anymore. He was going to walk into the house like a man and be treated with respect.

The black barman who'd worked for the Rushes for twenty-three years opened the front door. "Mr. Bobby," the man exclaimed with a welcoming smile. "Good to see you again after all this time."

Bobby nodded. "Thanks, Jimmy."

He entered the house like a stranger. Darla had changed all the furniture. Hollywood wives had nothing much to do except redecorate and give great charity, and Darla was no exception.

123

He walked through the hallway, passing a familiar Picasso on his left and a glass-fronted cabinet of African artifacts on his right. He strolled into the main living room, trying to appear at ease.

Jerry sat in his favorite chair, nursing a Scotch on the rocks. As soon as he spotted Bobby, he put down his drink, got up, and threw open his arms. "Welcome home, son," he said magnanimously, as if playing to an attentive audience.

"Hello, Dad," Bobby said, hanging back.

Gathered in the living room were Darla, clad in a shocking-pink Valentino suit and tasteful diamonds; stepbrother Len, a florid-faced man with an aggravating wife called Trixie; and stepbrother Stan with his wife, Lana, a former *Playboy* bunny who'd put on thirty pounds since her glory days. From what Bobby had heard, Stan still fostered a major cocaine habit, and his wife was into pill popping big time.

"Hello, everyone," Bobby said, hoping he didn't sound as insincere as he felt. "Nice to see you all."

"Bobby." Darla floated over, greeting him warmly. "I'm *so* glad you're here. We're all delighted."

Trixie darted across the room. She was a pinch-faced woman with small beady eyes and a snub nose covered in too many freckles. "How would you like to speak at my ladies' lunch, Bobby?" she asked, never one to hang back. "We meet once a month to discuss politics and world affairs. We're quite a cultural group, and we'd love you to join us. Will you do it for me?"

"My schedule's full, Trixie."

She pursed her lips. "Too important for family now, is that it?" she asked peevishly.

It was starting already. "No, Trixie, just too busy."

He moved away from his annoying sister-in-law. Len came over and placed a hand on his shoulder. "Doin' pretty good, baby brother."

"Yeah, things seem to have worked out."

"Maybe we can talk about something for me?"

Christ! Nothing like getting hit on the moment he entered the house!

"So, Bobby," Jerry said in a booming voice. "When you gonna produce a movie for your old man to star in, huh? *Huh?* It's about time."

This evening was going to be twice as bad as he'd imagined.

By the time she reached Homebase Central, Jordanna was on a high. She'd stopped off at a couple of other clubs, talked to friends, done a little dancing, a little gossiping, smoked a little grass.

I thought your drug days were over.
They are. This is just recreational fun.
Bullshit.

Arnie was right up front, greeting her with a sloppy kiss on both cheeks. "How's it goin', Levitt?"

She sighed. "If you're going to call me anything, Arnie, call me Jordanna. It *is* my name."

He scowled, "Okay, okay. Don't go getting mad at me."

"Who said I was mad?"

"I know your moods."

125

No, you do not. "Is the gang here?" she asked restlessly.

"Nope. Your group hasn't arrived."

"They will."

Moving closer, he lowered his voice, speaking near her ear. "I understand Cheryl's going into business; she's asked me to find her girls."

"That should be easy for you."

"I'll want commission."

"Of course you will, Arnie."

"Can I buy you a drink?"

"No, that's okay."

Making a fast getaway, she wandered through the club, looking for someone she knew, or at least someone she might want to spend time with. The pickings were sparse.

As she passed Charlie Dollar's table, he waved at her. "Hey — come sit with an old man."

"That's an irresistible invitation," she said, strolling over.

"You're always in such a hurry," he said, with a crooked smile.

"Better to be in a hurry than to be left behind," she replied coolly.

He slid over in the leather booth, patting the spot next to him. "I know your father," he announced.

"Everyone knows Jordan," she said, sliding in beside him because she had nothing better to do.

"Knew your mother too."

"Hmm . . . you're a regular friend of the family."

"I've been watching you," he said, stoned eyes fastened on her.

126

"Why?" she replied.

" 'Cause you're different."

"I am?"

"You am."

Suddenly she was sitting there having a major flirtation with Charlie Dollar, a man old enough to be her father.

Oh, God, what are you doing, Jordanna?

Something that will really *piss Daddy off.*

Dinner was a nightmare. Bobby didn't know how he got through it. Fact of life. He'd grown out of his family, and he didn't have to take their crap anymore, especially Jerry's.

Darla tried to make everything all right, but she could only do so much. Jerry didn't apologize for the past — he didn't apologize for anything. He merely sat at the head of the table, guzzling Scotch and voicing his views on how the industry was falling to pieces because all they wanted to know about was hiring young talent.

"Movies today," Jerry pontificated, "got no point of view. They got nothing going for them. All you see are two-bit hookers flashing their tits, an' a bunch of muscle-bound assholes who can't act their way out of a sandbox."

Gee, thanks, Dad, Bobby wanted to say. But then he realized it didn't matter. He didn't need his father's approval anymore.

"I'm not talking about *your* movie," Jerry said, burping loudly. "Not that I've seen it, but I hear it's pretty damn good."

Screw you, Dad. How come you haven't seen it? How come everybody else in America has?

"Thought you'd run it for me," Jerry continued. "I'll come by the studio. Hear you've got offices there."

Oh, yeah, sure. I'll have you over to see my movie. No fucking way.

"I'll get you a print," he said. "You can show it in your screening room here."

"We don't use the screening room anymore," Jerry said. "Costs too much."

Oh, so now the great Jerry Rush was going to plead poverty?

"Don't be ridiculous," Darla interrupted, quite flustered. "I'll call the projectionist."

Jerry shot her a deadly look. "I'm not paying a fucking projectionist to come to my fucking house and charge me a fucking fortune to see a movie I can see in my son's screening room at the studio."

"We have our own screening room, it's stupid not to use it," Darla said, tight-mouthed.

"You miss our screenings, don't you?" Jerry sneered. "You miss all those freeloading friends of yours."

"Jerry, please!"

He was not to be stopped. "How many people did we have over every weekend? We fed 'em, showed 'em a movie, while they drank all my booze an' bad-mouthed me behind my back. Then they ran out on us when my fucking career stopped."

"That's not true." Darla's face was flushed. "Your career is fine."

Jerry laughed hollowly. "Isn't it nice to have a loyal wife."

"Please, Jerry. Don't start."

"Wake up, Darla. We don't get invitations anymore."

"I can show you a pile of invitations," Darla said defensively.

"For charities we gotta pay for. Big fucking deal." He picked up his drink, took a swig, and muttered, "I don't need their lousy invitations. Let 'em stay the fuck away. Who gives a rat's ass except you."

Later Darla took Bobby to one side. "Your father's getting old," she explained. "He doesn't like to go out anymore. He suffers with his hip. I know he hasn't said anything to you, but eventually, if it gets any worse, he may have to undergo hip-replacement surgery. Don't mention I told you."

Oh, Jesus — was she trying to make him feel sorry for the old man?

"Cash *is* a little tight, I'll admit that," Darla added. "But we do have a fine portfolio of stocks and investments."

What was she going to do now? Touch him for a loan?

"If it was up to me I'd sell the house and move to a condo on Wilshire. We don't need this big place now all you boys are gone."

Do what you like, Darla, he wanted to say. It has nothing to do with me. I've moved on. I don't have to put up with him anymore.

Before he was able to make a clean escape, Stan and Len cornered him, both canvassing for a job.

He tried to be nice about it. "It wouldn't pan out. Y'know, family working together — not a good idea."

They got nasty. "It's all right for you, Bobby," Stan said. "You've got plenty of money now. Big shot, huh? Don't want to help us."

They had short memories. Growing up in the same household, they'd treated him like a punching bag, never giving him any love or encouragement. He could remember numerous incidents from his childhood when they'd turned their backs rather than help him.

Screw this whole deal.

After thanking Darla for dinner, he made a fast exit, jumping into his car and roaring off into the night.

He needed a drink. His partner Gary had said to meet him at Homebase Central. He set off in the right direction.

"Why don't you come to any of my parties?" Charlie Dollar asked, watching her closely. "I know Arnie's offered to bring you up to my house."

"That's exactly why," Jordanna replied, sipping a Jack Daniel's to keep him company, although she really didn't like the taste.

Charlie chuckled. "Don't like Arnie, huh?"

"Would *you* like him if he was hitting on *you?*"

"Kiddo, you got a great look," Charlie said, still watching her with a half-lidded stare.

"Thank you."

"You got a touch of your mother, mixed up with the ballsiness of your father. Lethal combination, kiddo. Plus you're beautiful — an' that ain't bad."

"Is this a job offer or a come-on?"

He chuckled. "What d'*you* think?"

"Hmm . . . perhaps a come-on?"

"You an actress?"

She glanced restlessly around the club, wondering where Shep was. "I wanted to be, but my father didn't go for the idea."

"Jordan's right. You don't wanna be an actress; it's a shitty profession."

"You're an actor," she pointed out. "And *you've* done pretty good."

Running his tongue across his teeth, he eyed her contemplatively. "Like I said, it's a shitty profession. I happen to be in the fortunate position of being able to choose what I do, but most actors and actresses gotta eat crap, deal with asshole executives, not to mention the jerks, pricks, and motherfucking know-nothings who call themselves agents an' managers. There's times even *I* have to kiss ass."

"Oh, I can't imagine you doing that, Charlie," she murmured sarcastically.

Grinning slyly, he said, "I do it when I have to."

"And how often is that?"

He leaned back in the booth, and his grin broadened. "Not very often, kiddo. Not very often."

"I bet."

"So," he said slowly, "I hear you're a wild one."

"Who told you that?"

"Word's on the street, kiddo."

"*Your* image is not exactly Mister Clean."

"I'm an old guy. I can do anything I want an' just about get away with it."

"How nice."

He was giving her that stare again, that half-lidded insouciant stare.

"Wanna go back to my house tonight, Jordanna?" he drawled.

"Are you having a party?"

"Yeah, for two."

She didn't have to think about it; she knew what she was going to do. "Two, huh?" she said coolly.

"That's what I said."

"I think I can manage that."

"I'm sure you can."

Just as he thought he was lost forever, Bobby spotted a discreet sign saying *Homebase Central*.

He pulled his car up to the valet and got out. "Thought I'd never find this place," he grumbled.

"Some people have a problem," the valet replied, handing him a ticket. "This your first time here?"

Bobby nodded.

"Hope you got connections," the valet said, obviously not recognizing him. "They're pretty tough on who they let in."

"I have a feeling I'll make it," Bobby said dryly.

The bouncer outside recognized him, and by the time he got through the front entrance, Arnie Isaak had been summoned and was duly standing there waiting to greet him. "Bobby!" he exclaimed, as if they were old friends.

"Do I know you?"

"Arnie. Arnie Isaak."

"Oh, yeah — right," Bobby said, vaguely recalling the man's name but not his face.

"Welcome to Homebase," Arnie said, full of

genial-host attitude. "Perhaps you'd care to join me at my table?"

"Uh . . ." Bobby glanced around. The place was jammed, the music blasting, and he couldn't see Gary anywhere. "I'm meeting Gary Mann."

Arnie frowned. "Gary Mann, Gary Mann . . . not sure I know him. Why don't I show you to a booth, fix you up with a drink?" He sidled closer, bringing his voice down to a suggestive whisper. "An' anything else you'd like." A quick wink. "Know what I mean?"

"Hey, I'm cool," Bobby said, knowing exactly what he meant. "Find Gary for me, that'll be enough."

Arnie liked having stars in his debt. "You sure, Bobby?"

"Positive."

At that moment Charlie walked by with Jordanna. This stopped Arnie in his tracks. "Where're you going, Charlie?" he asked, his voice a petulant whine.

Charlie ignored him, focusing on Bobby. "Hey, Bobby, haven't seen *you* in a long time."

"Six years," Bobby said. "I had seven lines and one close-up in *Broad Street*."

"I remember. Knew you were goin' places."

Bobby laughed wryly. "*I* didn't."

Charlie patted him on the shoulder. "Congrats, you done good. I liked your movie."

"That's quite a compliment coming from you."

"I only hand 'em out when they're deserved. Call me, Bobby. Let's have lunch."

"I'll do that."

Charlie put his arm around Jordanna's waist and

133

pulled her forward. "You two know each other?"

Bobby stared at the girl with the long black hair and the wild look. She was unusually beautiful in an offbeat way. "No, I don't think we do."

"Bet you know her father," Charlie said with a wicked wink. "Jordan Levitt."

"Of course I know Jordan," Bobby said quickly.

"And I know Jerry Rush," Jordanna interjected, furious that Charlie was giving her billing.

Bobby sensed her anger and attempted to put things right. "Now wait a minute — " he began.

"How do *you* like it?" she interrupted. "Bobby Rush, Jerry's son. Got a ring to it?"

"I wasn't trying to piss you off."

Charlie chuckled. "What is this, a who-has-the-most-famous-father contest? Nobody gives a shit."

"Apparently *you* do," Jordanna said angrily.

"Get over it, sweetheart," Charlie said, tightening his grip on her waist. "Nice seein' you, Bobby. Don't forget to give me a buzz. C'mon, kiddo, we're outta here."

Arnie could not believe Charlie was leaving with the love of his life. "Is there a party tonight, Charlie?" he asked hopefully.

"Nothing I'm inviting *you* to, Arnie."

"Should I stop by later?"

"Nope."

"I don't believe it," Arnie mumbled, watching them leave.

"What?" Bobby asked.

"Charlie and Jordanna."

"She seems a little young for him."

"Nobody's too young for Charlie," Arnie said

bitterly, his mouth twitching with frustration.

"She's great-looking," Bobby remarked.

"Great-looking and out of her head," Arnie said sourly. "The last thing she needs is Charlie."

"Bobby!" Gary appeared, pulling a pretty girl behind him. "Thought you'd never make it. How was dinner?"

"Torture," Bobby replied, moving away from Arnie. "Pure and simple torture."

Charlie lived at the top of Miller Drive, in an enormous house with sprawling grounds, a vast swimming pool, and a professional tennis court. Jordanna had insisted on taking her own car — a clean getaway was her thing, she didn't like feeling trapped with no escape route. She followed his Rolls up the winding driveway in her Porsche.

"This doesn't seem like your image," she said, as they got out of their cars and stood side by side in the middle of his massive courtyard.

"What image is that?" he asked, amused.

"You know — you're kind of like the wild man of Hollywood. I didn't expect to see you behind the wheel of a Rolls."

"Comfort is everything, kiddo. When you grow up you'll find out."

"I can see that," she said, as they entered his house.

Two large dogs raced over to greet him, a chocolate Labrador and a black Doberman. "Scared?" Charlie asked, as if secretly hoping she was.

"*Me?*" Jordanna replied scornfully. "I'm not scared of anything." She bent to pet the dogs, rubbing their necks the way dogs enjoyed.

"You know what? I'm beginning to like you more and more," Charlie said, leading her into his large living room, comfortably furnished with oversize brown leather couches; colorful paintings hung on every wall. Going straight to the bar, he poured two healthy shots of Jack Daniel's, adding ice. "Whaddaya say? Wanna share a joint?"

"Just what I had in mind," she replied, noticing his two Oscars casually placed on a bookshelf. "I wasn't around in the sixties, but I'm so glad pot has made a comeback."

He chuckled. "Well, kiddo, *I* was, and as far as I'm concerned, it never went away." Opening a silver box, he extracted an already rolled joint. Then he picked up a packet of book matches, lit it, drew deeply, and handed it to her. "This is primo stuff. Enjoy."

"I'm really surprised," she said, with a hint of sarcasm. "I thought you'd have lousy shit."

"Ha! Funny."

She drew the smoke deeply into her lungs, inhaling slowly. Getting stoned wasn't as bad as doing coke, although if he'd suggested coke she probably would have done *that*.

What the hell happened to all my good resolutions?

Tomorrow, tomorrow.

"Wanna see the rest of the house?" he drawled lazily.

"Tours are my thing," she replied.

He reached out, gently touching her long black hair. "I do like you," he said.

"I'm so flattered," she murmured, determined not to act like some dim-witted star fuck.

136

He took her hand, and they walked up a curved staircase to his bedroom, an untidy room with an insane view, dominated by an enormous circular bed covered in fur throws.

"Very luxurious," she said, in spite of the fact that the room was incredibly messy, with newspapers scattered on the floor and stacks of magazines on every surface. "Do you have music?"

"You want music?"

"That's why I asked."

He opened a closet, revealing a bank of expensive stereo equipment. After he'd pressed a few buttons, Mozart flooded the room.

"I'm not into classical," she said.

He touched her hair again. "What *are* you into?"

"Madonna. Prince. Bobby Brown. John Coltrane."

"That's quite a mixture."

"How about Madonna's 'Bad Girl'?"

"Remind you of yourself?"

"Of course."

He looked at her quizzically. "You're cute."

"I've never been called cute before."

"There's always a first time."

"Yes, Charlie, there's always a first time," she said, shrugging off her Harley jacket.

"How old are you?"

"Young enough to be your daughter."

"Twenty?"

"Twenty-four."

"An old broad, right?"

"Right."

Picking up the phone, he spoke into an internal intercom. "Anyone in the house got Madonna, Prince, or Bobby Brown CDs? Make it snappy."

"What do you have, a staff of invisible popular-music fans who stay up all night?" she inquired, imagining the help scrambling like crazy to accommodate their famous boss.

He smiled faintly. "Something like that."

"How about Coltrane?"

Indicating a Lucite box stacked with CDs over in the corner, he said, "Check it out, maybe we'll get lucky."

Oh, you'll definitely get lucky, she thought, feeling decidedly horny.

She riffled through his collection of CDs, finding nothing she liked. Then she started wondering what his body was like. He was old, fifty-something at least, and older men were not into working out and keeping it all together.

"Do you have a gym?" she asked casually.

He knew exactly what she was getting at. "Nope," he said, "but I do have a few rolls of middle-aged spread you might be interested in."

She couldn't help smiling. "Oh, boy, you sure know how to turn a girl on."

That same crazed grin. "The truth is, kiddo, I've never found it to be a problem."

"I *bet* you haven't."

He sat down on the edge of the bed and patted the space beside him. "Come over here."

She strolled over, cool to the end, and stood in front of him.

He put his hands around her waist and pulled her close, then he unbuttoned her shirt and began licking her bare stomach, eventually sticking his tongue into her navel. It was, strangely, incredibly sexy.

She shrugged her shirt off, letting it fall to the floor.

"You taste like honey," he said, pausing for a moment. "Sweet, sweet honey."

It was a nice compliment, to which she had no flip reply. The combination of Jack Daniel's, pot, and Charlie Dollar was making her very mellow indeed.

He touched her breasts, fingering her nipples with stubby fingers.

A disembodied voice boomed through the room. "Mister D., Madonna and Prince are outside your door."

"Holy shit!" Jordanna exclaimed, jumping back startled.

"Calm down," Charlie soothed. "It's only the intercom. I guess you got your music."

"Wow! That's really service."

"Kiddo, you ain't seen nothin' yet."

By the time Madonna was on the stereo, singing "Bad Girl," Jordanna was ready to rock 'n' roll. Charlie was lighting another joint. She was already stoned — who needed more?

She wandered around the room half naked and began swaying to the music, mouthing the words. Madonna was a hell of a songwriter; how come she was never acknowledged for that part of her talent?

"You really like this stuff?" Charlie asked.

She wasn't sure whether he was referring to the grass or Madonna. "I love it all," she said, cleverly covering every base.

He stared at her long and hard, drawing deeply on the joint. "Take the rest of your clothes off."

"No," she replied sharply. "*You* take *your* clothes off."

"It's not a pretty sight."

"Turn off the lights."

He offered her the joint. She took a long drag and threw herself onto the bed. "I feel good," she said, expelling a thin stream of smoke.

"You'll feel even better in a minute," he said, moving on top of her.

She sighed, she'd heard it all before. "Don't make promises you can't keep, Charlie."

He was amused. "Is that a challenge, kiddo?" he asked, fiddling with the buttons on her jeans. " 'Cause I've never had any complaints."

"Are you sure you're up to it?" she asked mockingly.

He grunted. "Jesus — you got a smart mouth. Show a little respect for the movie star."

Rolling out from under him, she pulled off her boots and wriggled out of her jeans.

"No underwear, huh?" he said, raising extravagant eyebrows.

"Too restricting," she said, kneeling on the bed totally naked and staring at him. "Your turn."

He began to laugh. "You got a great bod, kiddo."

"Thank you, Mister Movie Star," she said, reaching for his belt and expertly unbuckling. "Can we get this train moving?"

"Got no reason to stall, babe."

"How about a condom?"

"How about I don't take a shower with my boots on?"

"How about safe sex?"

"How about I just took a test and got the all clear."

"How about I see the certificate?"

"How about shutting up?"

She acquiesced. She believed him. Besides, she was too stoned and too horny to argue.

Charlie Dollar was a terrific lover — surprisingly so. He wasn't in great shape, but he wasn't falling to pieces either. He knew all the moves and then some. He knew how to take her almost there and then stop seconds before the moment of no return. Timing. He had it down.

They made love a long time before either of them climaxed, and when they did, it was a mutual release of such exquisite pleasure that Jordanna found herself crying out — unusual for her. Charlie let out a yell so loud she almost jumped from the bed.

The downside was he fell asleep almost immediately. And he snored. Loudly.

She got off the bed, gathered her clothes, and went into the bathroom. Charlie's bathroom resembled a busy pharmacy — there were rows of bottled pills to cure every ailment; jars of vitamins in all combinations; potions and powders and creams and solvents. She decided this would be a good place to be sick.

After taking a shower, she hurriedly dressed and emerged into the bedroom. Charlie was still snoring.

Without disturbing him, she took off.

And so another one-night stand hit the freeway.

12

"Where are you?" Quincy asked, sounding annoyed.

"Across the street from Club Erotica on Hollywood Boulevard," Michael replied, stubbing out his cigarette as he stood at a pay phone.

"So what's goin' on I should know about?"

"I got a lead," Michael said. "Rita left behind photos."

"What photos?"

"Stop asking questions, and move your ass over here."

"I gotta do this?"

"For me, Q."

"Okay, okay — I'll be there."

"Club Erotica."

"Sounds like a nice classy place."

"Meet me at the bar," Michael said, hanging up the phone and crossing the street.

A burly man guarding the door announced it would cost him thirty bucks to gain entry to Club Erotica. He parted with the money reluctantly and entered the club.

Oh, yes, this was Rita's kind of place, all right. Dark and intimate, with plenty of weird-looking people in strange outfits and throbbing music blaring forth from multiple speakers.

A woman approached him wearing a peacock's mask and little else. "What's your pleasure tonight?" she asked in a deep, sultry voice.

"Huh?"

"Which room would you like to play in? Singles, group? Or perhaps the orgy room?"

It suddenly dawned on him that this was a sex club. Shit! He'd thought sex clubs were over in the seventies. "Hey, I just wanna get a drink. Is there a bar around here?"

"There's the selection bar."

"The *selection* bar?"

"Is this your first time here?"

"You got it."

"Okay, hon. You go sit in the selection bar, look around, and if there's anyone you care to be with, take them to the room of your choice."

"How much does this cost?"

"Club Erotica is not a clip joint," she said, quite indignant. "You paid at the door, and unless you require special services, you're covered."

"No special services."

"Suit yourself. The bar's that way."

He found the bar, walked in, and slid onto a high stool.

The female bartender approached him. She wore a short black leather toga, which barely covered her large bosom and ample ass. "Cocktail?" she said, eyeing him up and down. "I can make you the Club Erotica special."

He wasn't interested but asked anyway. "What's that?"

"Vodka, rum, and orange juice, with a touch

143

of Cointreau." She winked. "Guaranteed to keep your engine turning over."

"You got nonalcoholic beer?"

"I might be able to find one."

"Try hard," he said, surveying the scene. Several women were gathered at the bar, all on the lookout for a suitable mate. A fat businessman accompanied by a chubby blonde sat at one of the small round tables clustered at the far end of the room, and two young men in shirtsleeves and jeans hovered together over in a corner.

Oh, Rita, Rita — what brought you to a place like this?

Excitement. Rita was an excitement freak. Unfortunately he'd never been able to satisfy her cravings, although their sex together had always been hot — physically there'd never been a problem.

The black-leather-toga woman returned with his drink, placing it in front of him.

"I got a question," Michael said.

She leaned her elbows on the bar, her large breasts tipping toward him at an alarming angle. "Me too."

"You first," he said, taking a gulp of his non-alcoholic brew.

"What's a good-looking guy like you doing in a place like this?"

"My turn?"

"Shoot."

"You know anyone called Heron Jones?"

"You're kidding? Right?"

"Not kidding."

"Everyone knows Heron."

"You want to enlighten me?"

She licked her lips, viewing him speculatively. "You a cop?"

"Why would you ask that?"

" 'Cause you smell like a cop," she said, smirking, as if she knew something he didn't. "Now don't get me wrong," she added. "I got a yen for that cop smell."

Ignoring her knowing look, he kept going. "So how come everybody knows Heron Jones?"

" 'Cause he's famous."

"Not famous enough for me to have heard of him."

She threw back her head and laughed. "Heron Jones has the biggest dick in captivity. And he brings it here three nights a week and shows it off in the private room. Anybody wanting to use his . . . services pays big. But, honey, you don't look like you'd be interested in a *guy's* services."

He pulled out a picture of Rita — not the Polaroid, but a head shot he'd taken on their honeymoon. "You ever seen this woman in here?"

She took the picture and studied it for a while. "Y'know, honey, I honestly don't remember them unless they're like Heron and have something special to offer. Take a look around this place. . . . They come, they go, who cares?"

"So you don't recognize her?"

"Maybe she was here."

"How long ago?"

"She your girlfriend?"

"Ex-wife."

"Coupla months, I'm not sure."

He showed her the Polaroid of the man. "Is

this Heron Jones?"

"*Ooh, baby,* you could get arrested for carrying *this* around." She gazed at the Polaroid and began giggling. "Yeah, that's Heron, all right. The king of the monster cockadoodledo! He sure inherited *big.*"

"Is he here tonight?"

"You can catch him in the private room. I promise you — it's a real sight."

One of the women was edging along the bar toward him with a determined expression. She finally reached her destination. "I'm choosing *you,*" she announced, placing a well-manicured hand firmly on his arm.

"Excuse me?" he said, backing away.

She was all over him. "Tonight. You, me — a very . . . *sexual* experience."

"I'm on probation," he said, standing up.

She looked confused. "What?"

"It's complicated. Pick somebody else."

Quincy pulled up outside Club Erotica, wondering what Michael had gotten him into now. Amber was not pleased. They'd just been sitting down to get cozy and listen to a little Luther Vandross on the stereo when Michael had called.

"Gotta go," Quincy said, as soon as he'd hung up.

"Why?" Amber demanded, already looking mad.

" 'Cause Mike needs me."

"Can't he do anything by himself?"

"C'mon, sweet thing," Quincy said persuasively. "Me an' Mike got a lotta history between

146

us. His *kid* is missing. Be a little understanding, baby. Think about what *you'd* do if one of *our* kids was missing."

Amber was a soft touch, she'd caved without too much of a fight.

He'd kissed her, taken off, and now he was standing outside this sleazy clip joint.

The jerk at the door refused to let him in until he handed over thirty bucks cash. Thirty freaking bucks! Mike owed him big time.

Once inside, he went straight to the bar. Michael wasn't there. He approached the amazon in black leather who dispensed drinks. "Somebody leave a message for me?" he inquired.

"Blonde, brunette?"

"Male. Good-looking."

"Oh," she said. "You a cop too?"

How come they always remembered Michael? "Where is he?"

"In the men's room."

"Thanks."

Quincy entered the john just as Michael was zipping up. "This is some dump you dragged me to," he complained. "What's the story?"

"I came across some pictures and a note. She'd written down this club and the name of a guy. Rita's around somewhere, I got a feeling."

Shaking his head, Quincy said, "You an' your feelings — it always leads to trouble."

"I gotta find my kid, Q."

"I know."

"Rita's into something. I don't want Bella exposed to it."

"So why are we here?"

"We're waiting for Heron Jones to finish."

"Finish what?"

"Making out with a line of women. In case you hadn't guessed, this is a sex club."

Quincy let out a long, low whistle. "Jeez!" he said. "Just what I need to go home an' tell Amber. She'll go nutso."

"Not if you keep it to yourself."

"Amber an' me, we don't have secrets."

"Maybe now's the time to start."

Quincy wrinkled his nose. "So who's this Heron Jones — a male hooker?"

"The club pays him to perform here. He services as many women as will pay the hundred bucks to see him."

"What is he — Superman?"

"Kinda."

"And the story is we gotta hang out until he finishes?"

"That's it."

"Shit, Mike, nothin' with you is ever easy."

By the time Heron Jones emerged through the back entrance, it was past midnight. Michael and Quincy were waiting in the parking lot. They used the element of surprise, approaching him from either side.

"Let's talk," Michael said.

Heron eyeballed them, trying to decide whether to make a run for it or not. No way. He was sure they were cops, the fuckers had the attitude. Squaring his shoulders, he went for the innocent pitch. "Listen, guys, whatever ya wanna stick me with, I didn't do it — okay? Every time there's a freakin' robbery in this neighborhood you're on my case. I'm straight now, guys. I'm *screwin'* for a living — what more do y'want?"

"Whyn't we take it over here," Michael said, grabbing his arm and hustling him in the direction of a streetlight.

"Whaddaya want from me?" Heron grumbled, making an unsuccessful attempt to shake free. "I ain't done shit, man. Y'can ask anyone."

Michael thrust one of the Polaroids in front of his face. "You know this woman?"

Heron took a quick glance. "They all look the same in the dark."

"Take another look," Michael said menacingly. "You recognize her or not?"

"Dunno."

"Do you?" Michael said, pinning the man's arm behind him in a viselike grip.

"Yeah, I know her," Heron said sulkily. "So freakin' what?"

"Who is she?"

"Some bimbo used to come to the club."

"What happened to her?"

"Why?" Heron asked, his lips twisting in a sneer. "Is the douchebag dead?"

Michael spun him around. "You know something we don't?"

Heron threw up his hands. "Okay, okay. I don't know nothin' about her 'cept I got her a job in the movies."

"What movies?"

"Mary Poppins — what d'ya think?"

"Are we talking porno here?" Quincy interjected, waving his arms in the air.

"I didn't force her to do nothin'," Heron said

149

sullenly. "This broad got off on performin'."

Michael slammed him against the side of a brick wall. "Where is she now?"

"Man, you're hurtin' me," Heron complained.

"You listening, asshole? *Where the fuck is she?*"

"Dunno," Heron whined. "Who gives a shit? I don't — "

Before he could finish, Michael swung back and whacked him hard across the mouth.

"Aw, sweet Jesus," Quincy groaned.

"You feel like answering me now?" Michael demanded.

Heron reached up, gingerly touching his face. "She's livin' with a producer — only you didn't hear it from me."

"What's his name?"

"Some old guy calls himself Daly Forrest."

"Where's he live?"

"Look him up in the phone book. All those producer dudes are listed. I think you broke my freakin' tooth."

"When I find him, she'd better be there," Michael said threateningly. "Or we'll be back. And next time it'll be more than your tooth. Now get outta my sight."

Heron ran off to his truck without a backward glance. He might be a big man in the bedroom, but his balls didn't travel well.

"You're gonna get us in major trouble," Quincy said wearily. "You can't go around pretending we're cops. I got a private investigator business I gotta protect."

"What's the matter — you think he'll file a complaint?"

"No, Mike. I'm just saying we gotta be careful."

"All I'm interested in is finding my kid."

"I know that."

"Okay, so I do what it takes. Let's go run a check with the DMV, find out who this Daly Forrest is, and get his address."

"Sure, Mike."

"And after that we'll pay him a little visit."

Daly Forrest lived in an expensive high-rise on Wilshire. The porter at the desk stopped them in the lobby and asked who they were visiting.

"Daly Forrest," Michael said, flashing his badge.

The porter was duly impressed. "Fourteenth floor. Apartment fourteen-oh-three."

"Thanks," Michael said, adding as an afterthought: "Oh, and be sure you don't announce us."

The porter nodded, only too happy to oblige.

"Somebody's gonna bust our sweet asses," Quincy muttered as they marched through the marble foyer. "I'm telling you, Mike, we can't keep getting away with this crap. Bury that fuckin' badge of yours, it ain't legal here."

"It ain't legal in New York either, but so what?" Sometimes he got off on taking it to the edge, especially when he had a purpose.

They rode up in the elevator with a smartly dressed woman clutching a small Pekingese dog under one arm. She gave them an uptight rich-woman-being-gracious smile. Thin scarlet lips, white stretched skin, and capped teeth. She left them on the tenth floor.

"How come women always smile at you?" Quincy asked, poking his gums with a toothpick.

"Anyone ever told you you ask dumb questions?"

"It's 'cause you're such a handsome sonofabitch," Quincy mumbled enviously. "Me, I got the personality. You got the looks. Lucky asshole."

There were only two apartments on the fourteenth floor. Daly Forrest's had a red-lacquered door and a shiny brass knocker.

"Seems he had an urge to smarten the place up," Quincy remarked, rubbing the door with his thumb to see if the paint came off.

Michael pressed the buzzer, waited a few minutes, then pushed again.

When Daly Forrest finally appeared, he was not what either of them expected. He was an older, distinguished-looking man, with a shock of white hair, a snow-white goatee, and wire-rimmed spectacles. He wore a paisley silk robe with a tasseled sash and black velvet monogrammed slippers. He did not have the look of a man who produced porno films.

"Can I help you?" he said, speaking in a clipped English accent.

"Daly Forrest?" Michael asked politely.

"That's correct. I repeat, can I help you gentlemen?"

"We're investigating a case."

"Did something take place in the building?"

"That's right," Michael said. "We need witnesses."

152

"I've been home all evening," Daly Forrest replied. "I doubt I can be a witness."

"And your companion?" Michael asked, trying to see past him into the apartment.

"What companion?" Daly asked, standing firm at the door.

"Rita Polone."

"Miss Polone is not here," Daly said, stroking his goatee. "Furthermore, she does not live here. What gave you the impression she did?"

"The case we're investigating," Michael said, speaking slowly, "involves Miss Polone."

"In what way?" Daly inquired, not pleased with this intrusion on his privacy in the middle of the night.

"We need to talk to her," Michael replied, getting an uncomfortable feeling about this man.

Daly stared them down, cold as an Arctic winter. "I repeat — she's not here." His hand was on the door, ready to close it.

"So all we need is her address, and we'll be on our way," Quincy said, sensing this jerk was going to cause them trouble.

"Let me see your identification," Daly said, suddenly getting nasty.

Michael didn't take a beat. "Certainly," he said, reaching into his jacket and flashing his badge.

Daly Forrest was no fool. "That's a New York City detective's badge," he said sharply.

Still unfazed, Michael said, "Yeah, we're working on an out-of-state case."

Eyes steely behind his wire-rimmed spectacles, Daly said, "I wish to check with your captain, kindly give me his number."

Quincy was starting to get fidgety. "Tell you what, whyn't we come back," he said, cracking his knuckles — a nervous habit that drove Michael nuts.

Daly glared at them both. "I suggest you don't," he said, slamming the door in their faces.

"Goddamn it!" Michael said furiously.

"Let's get outta here," Quincy suggested, "before he calls the real cops."

"He knows where she is," Michael muttered, almost to himself.

"Yeah, an' he ain't telling us."

"He will."

"Not tonight."

"We'll see."

"Mike," Quincy pleaded. "Tomorrow is another day."

Michael turned on him angrily. "No shit."

Early in the morning, Michael was back without Quincy, who was busy working on a blackmail case for a studio honcho. He parked across the street, staking a prime spot that enabled him to watch all the comings and goings at Daly Forrest's building.

He'd slept fitfully, certain that today he was finally going to find out where Rita was. How he hated her for taking his kid and putting him through this. As soon as he found her, he planned on consulting a lawyer to see if he could get full custody of Bella.

Yeah, and how was he going to pay for it? He had to rent an apartment, hire a part-time nanny, and God knew what else.

Major priority — get a steady job. Quincy had offered him a partnership in his PI business, and it wasn't such a bad idea. They were a good team, and Quincy had assured him that working for the studios was nice and easy — nothing life-threatening, like their days in New York. He was considering it. After all, he had a year to make up his mind whether he wanted to go back to New York or stay in L.A.

I need a drink.

The thought nagged at his subconscious, forcing him to pay attention. Almost immediately he felt a dryness in his throat and the urgent desire to down something cold and alcoholic.

Christ! This was not good. He'd been sober almost four years, and he didn't need to be thinking about breaking the pattern of sobriety. Although he *did* think about it. Once in a while. When things got tough and he knew there was an easy answer to dull the pain.

The good thing was that the program had taught him to be smart enough to know it was the wrong answer and would eventually destroy him if he succumbed.

It hadn't been easy getting sober, and there was no way he was going to blow it — however strong the temptation.

Lighting a cigarette, he desperately tried to curb his subconscious, choosing to think only positive thoughts. Had to work the program again — he hadn't attended a meeting in months. He needed validation.

Daly Forrest emerged at ten forty-five and got into a chauffeur-driven Lexus.

Michael followed the car as it left the driveway and sped along Wilshire toward downtown.

Early in the morning he'd had a friend in the department in New York run a check on Mr. Forrest. He'd found out that Daly was a sixty-three-year-old naturalized American who'd lived in L.A. for fifteen years. During that time he'd written and produced a slew of soft-core porn films, moving into the real thing three years ago. He wasn't doing anything illegal, but he was dangerously close. Two years earlier he'd been arrested in a dramatic case involving an imported snuff movie, but the prosecution was unable to prove he was sufficiently connected, and he'd gotten off.

Daly Forrest had no wife and no family, and he was rich. That's all Michael knew. It was enough to scare him. Rita was a wild card; a wealthy man like Daly Forrest could persuade her to do anything.

He followed the Lexus all the way to Hancock Park, slowing down as he watched it pull into the driveway of a large house on a quiet side street. Daly emerged from his car, spoke to his driver for a few moments, then sent the car away. He entered the house with a key, slamming the door behind him.

Michael parked across the street and sat in his car for five minutes before getting out and approaching the house.

It was a beautiful morning, no smog, and the birds were singing. The front porch was alive with a breathtaking display of purple and orange bougainvillea. A skinny black cat slunk around the corner and vanished from sight.

Instead of approaching the front door, Michael decided to follow the cat to the rear, keeping an eye out for anyone watching him.

He had that gut feeling again, as if something was about to happen that he couldn't quite control.

The night he'd gotten shot, he'd had that same feeling, and what should have been a simple drug bust had ended up with him nearly dying. He'd never forget *that* night.

Moving stealthily, he reached the surprisingly large and well-landscaped back garden. Several swaying palm trees overshadowed him.

The door to the kitchen was open, and he could hear a child's voice.

His heart soared, he felt certain it was Bella.

He edged forward, getting closer to the open door. He thought he saw the back of a little girl.

Relief flooded through him. He'd found his daughter, and nothing would ever separate them again.

As he took another step forward, something smashed down onto his head, and he descended into blackness.

The last thing he heard was a child's scream.

The Man kept a scrapbook. Every so often he took it out and added to the contents. He'd bought scissors and double-sided tape at Thrifty's, and he worked on his scrapbook diligently whenever he had something new to add to his collection of clippings.

The woman in Agoura Hills did not rate as much newspaper space as he'd hoped, and that made him angry. He knew that to get the attention he craved he would have to start leaving a strong message, so they would know exactly who they were dealing with.

He thought about it for days. What would Steven Seagal do? How would the mighty movie star handle such a dilemma?

The Man honestly didn't know.

The other night, a woman living in the house had attempted to talk to him. He'd immediately tried to put a stop to her inane chatter, but it didn't seem to prevent her from accosting him whenever she could.

"I'm an actress," she informed him. "What do you do?"

"Writer," he replied, not looking her in the eye as they stood awkwardly in the front hallway.

"What kind of writing?" she asked.

He'd walked away from her without replying.

His rudeness didn't seem to bother her, because whenever she saw him she acted as if they were old friends. Yesterday she'd stopped him on the way to his car. "It's funny," she said cheerfully. "We live in the same house and I don't even know your name."

He was forced to reply. "John," he lied.

"John what?" she asked, edging closer.

"John Seagal," he replied, backing off.

She smirked coquettishly. "Don't you want to know my name?"

He had no desire to know her name, but she told him anyway. "Shelley. That's with an E Y. When I make it big, you can say you knew me when."

Would-be actresses. They were everywhere in Hollywood. They littered the streets. They filled the clubs. They drove on the freeways. Their hungry eyes watching . . . wanting . . . waiting . . .

If it weren't for that bitch of an actress who'd lured him with her tantalizing smile and her bouncy tits and her long yellow hair, he'd never have lost seven years of his life.

Pulling aside one of the blackout blinds that now covered his windows, he peeked out, watching the housekeeper as she trudged wearily down the path, carrying a heavy sack of garbage. She stayed away from him now. He had her trained not to go near his room.

His solitary existence suited him fine, as long

as he had everything he needed. A bed, a television, a VCR and a stack of movies, and his dreams of the future.

The future would be a better place when he'd dealt with the scum who'd so foolishly betrayed him. The female scum. They had to learn a lesson. A harsh lesson, perhaps, but there was no other way.

It was time to check off the second name on his list. Six women altogether. Five to go.

It was an exciting game, and he was enjoying playing it.

13

"No, Rosa, absolutely *not*," Kennedy said, cradling the phone under her chin. "I refuse to subject myself to one more blind date."

"But, Kennedy," Rosa pleaded, in her usual *you've got to do me this one big favor* voice. "Look what happened last time. You ended up enjoying yourself — I mean really enjoying yourself. What's so bad about that?"

True. Her one night with Nix had been memorable, but it was not something she wished to repeat.

"Nothing," she said. "I simply have no desire to do it again. Besides, I have to work."

"What work?"

"I'm writing the *Style Wars* piece on Bobby Rush."

Now she had Rosa's interest. "Did you interview him?"

"Sort of."

"What's he like?"

"He's okay," she said. "In fact, he's really a nice guy for an actor."

"Does he have a girlfriend?" Rosa pressed, dying to find out everything.

"We didn't get into his personal life."

Rosa was disappointed. "Why not? That's what all your women readers will want to know."

"Rosa," Kennedy said patiently. "You present the news *your* way, and I'll do my interviewing *my* way."

"So you won't come with us tomorrow night?"

"No. *Capisce?*"

"Your loss."

"According to you, it always is."

Once rid of Rosa, she called her father in the nursing home. He was cheerful as usual. Eighty-five years old, riddled with cancer, and yet he always managed to make her feel better.

"I'll drive out to see you on Sunday, Dad," she promised. "Anything you need?"

"Just your lovely face," he replied. "And a fine Havana if you can smuggle it past these damned nurses."

"I'll fly to Cuba."

"Dunhills will do."

She hung up smiling.

On Sunday, the long drive to the nursing home in Agoura Hills gave Kennedy plenty of time to think. With the Bobby Rush profile on its way to New York via Federal Express, she could now concentrate on the first big story she planned to write for *Style Wars*.

The movie industry was a tempting subject. Women on film. Women and violence. Women in Hollywood. Equality or sexism? Who's winning?

She'd been considering the women with power in Hollywood, and the two she most wanted to interview were Sherry Lansing, currently the boss at Paramount, and Lucky Santangelo, a woman with major clout who owned and ran Panther Studios. Under Lucky's ownership, the studio was producing some interesting movies depicting women as real people, instead of merely the girlfriend or the whore.

Kennedy knew there were many directions she could take. The battle of the sexes had been written countless times before, but never her way. Maybe if she wrote a powerful enough piece she could influence a few of the so-called Hollywood executives to change their sexist ways.

Ha! Extremely wishful thinking.

She decided to call Mason in the morning and discuss it with him. He had good instincts, and it was essential that her first real story for *Style Wars* make an impact.

Nurse Linford, a black woman in her forties with a huge bosom, a mischievous smile, and a crush on Kennedy's father, greeted her at reception. "Your daddy's an incorrigible flirtin' dog!" she said, beaming. "An' the truth of the matter is I enjoy every second of his bad-boy behavior!"

Kennedy had never considered her father to be either a bad boy or a flirt. It was obvious there was another side to the studious professor of literature she'd grown up with. He'd always been a wonderful and caring father, and even though she was an only child, neither of her parents had ever allowed her to feel lonely. Every summer they'd traveled extensively, exploring Europe and exposing her to all kinds of different cultures. At nine she was reading Dickens; at twelve Trollope and Dostoyevsky; and by fourteen she was into Henry Miller and Anaïs Nin. She'd certainly experienced a rounded education.

Nurse Linford led her into her father's room. He sat on top of the bed, a smile on his face, a pile of books on the bedside table, and a notepad balanced on his lap, pen poised. He was always jotting down notes, with the intention of writing another book. He'd already published three academic studies, and now he was planning a fourth.

Kennedy gave him a hug and a kiss. "How are you doing, Dad?" she asked warmly, thinking he looked thinner and more gaunt than last time she'd visited.

"How would *you* be doing if you were stuck in a nursing home?" he said, sounding cross but not really meaning it. He'd accepted his fate with as good grace as he could muster.

"Not as well as you," she replied.

"Take no notice of his complaining," Nurse Linford said, clucking her tongue. "He's a grouchy old boy today."

"I never complain," her father said indignantly. "If I did, you'd be the first to hear me."

"I'm sure about that," Nurse Linford replied, adjusting his bedcover. "How about taking a walk around the garden with your daughter? It's a beautiful day out there."

"An excellent idea, Nurse," he agreed. He wasn't bedridden, it was just that the pain was so intense that most of the time he was hooked up to a morphine drip to relieve his suffering.

"I'll set you up with your portable power pack," Nurse Linford said, fussing around him as she helped him off the bed. "That'll keep you going for a while."

"You keep me going, Nurse," he said, wincing as he straightened up.

Nurse Linford favored him with her mischievous smile. "You'd better believe it!"

Once outside, Kennedy and he strolled slowly arm in arm around the well-kept grounds.

"Tell me, dear, what have you been up to?" he asked.

"I abandoned the book I was working on. And since I needed money, I'm writing for *Style Wars* — you know, the magazine."

"Of course I know the magazine," he said irritably. "I may be in a nursing home, but I haven't stopped living."

"I didn't think it was your kind of literature."

"*Everything* is my kind of literature," he said gruffly. "That's what makes the world go round."

"You taught me that when I was five."

"I'm glad you remember," he said, with the glimmer of a smile.

"Anyway," she continued, "I have to write six celebrity profiles, and at the same time I get to write six other pieces, on any subject I care to cover."

"Sounds challenging."

"That's what attracted me to the assignment. I was considering writing an exposé on the way men treat women in the film industry. What do you think?"

"If you can make it fresh."

"Trust me, Dad, I can make it fresh."

He squeezed her hand tightly. "I'm sure you can, my dear. You can do whatever you set your mind to."

It was a good feeling, knowing her parents had always believed in her. They'd taught her well — infusing her with ambition, spirit, and energy. The result of their nurturing was that she'd grown up full of confidence. They couldn't have given her a greater gift.

"So what else has been going on?" she asked lightly. "Nurse Linford still chasing you around the room?"

"Nurse Linford is taking a self-defense course," he said with a chuckle.

"To protect herself against you?"

His gaunt face turned serious. "Actually, there was a murder in the neighborhood not too long ago."

"What happened?"

"A woman was strangled outside her house."

"I was under the impression this was a fairly crime-free area."

"It usually is, that's why everybody's alarmed. All the nurses are taking a self-defense course."

"I can't imagine anyone trying to attack Nurse Linford, she'd crush them like a bug!"

He laughed dryly. "Yes, she certainly would." He paused for a moment before adding, "That's what you should write about."

"What? Nurse Linford and her amazing strength?"

"No, dear. Write about the woman who was murdered."

"She's not news. The magazine wouldn't be interested."

Her father stopped short and gave her a withering look. "I'll pretend you never said that. Not news indeed! The woman was strangled outside her own home. What more has to happen to her before she becomes newsworthy?"

"You're right," she said, suitably chastised.

"I'm glad you think so. You should write about ordinary people instead of the rich and famous."

She hung onto her father's bony hand. "It's so good to see you, Dad. It always is."

"Make the most of it, Kennedy dear. When these old legs stop supporting me, I don't plan on staying around."

Sunday morning Bobby rolled out of bed, forcing himself to get dressed and go jogging. He'd had only a few hours' sleep, after hanging out at Homebase Central until three in the morning. Several beautiful girls had tried to persuade him that they were the perfect companion to take home for a night of passion. He'd resisted all advances.

Gary had tried to encourage him. "Go for it," he'd urged. "When it comes to pussy, *never* turn it down."

"I'm not interested in one-nighters," he said, and meant it. He considered himself past the *let's get laid just because I can* stage. There had to be more to life than sex with a stranger. He was looking for a meaningful relationship with a female who was not an actress. Most actresses were a

167

nightmare — insecure, narcissistic, demanding, fragile. His last two semiserious flings had been with actresses. Never again.

Jogging along the UCLA track, he worked up a heavy sweat. Then he went home, dove into his swimming pool, swam fifty lengths, got out, squeezed a glass of fresh orange juice, grabbed the *L.A. Times*, and lay out by the pool on a comfortable chaise.

It occurred to him that maybe he'd call the woman who'd come for the interview. What was her name? Ah yes, Kennedy something or other. Kennedy Chase, that was it.

He thought about her for a moment — cool, attractive, and very together.

It then occurred to him that he didn't have her number, so he phoned his secretary at home.

"Beth, did you preinterview Kennedy Chase?" he asked.

There was a long pause. "Uh . . . no," she said, sounding puzzled. "Should I have?"

"Sure you should. She's an attractive woman but not suitable for the job at all. By the way, what's her phone number?"

"I don't have it."

"Why not?"

"Bobby, Elspeth handles press, she *is* your publicist."

"What's Elspeth got to do with this?"

"Kennedy Chase," Beth replied patiently. "Your interview with her is now scheduled for ten o'clock on Monday."

"Beth, help me out here, I'm confused. I interviewed her on Friday."

"*You* interviewed *her?*"

"That's what you set up, isn't it?"

"No."

He was getting impatient. "If *you* didn't set it up, who did?"

"There's obviously some confusion here, Bobby. Kennedy Chase is the journalist from *Style Wars*. She's doing the story on you to go with the cover photograph."

"*Shit!*"

"According to your latest schedule, she's due to interview you Monday at ten A.M. And Elspeth has promised her she can hang in the background for the rest of the day, observing. I thought you agreed to this."

"I suppose I must have," he muttered, knowing he'd been taken.

"Do you still want me to get you her number? I can call Elspeth, I'm sure she'll have it."

"Don't bother," he said, hanging up.

Of course. It all made sense now, a case of mistaken identity, and Kennedy — good little journalist that she obviously was — had taken full advantage of the situation.

He couldn't wait until tomorrow morning. He would show Ms. Chase a thing or two. Oh yeah, *really.*

Kennedy drove home, thinking about murder and aging and disease and pain. All the good things. By the time she reached her apartment she was ready to call Rosa and yell, *Yes! Yes! I'm coming out with you. I don't care who he is! Bring him to me — naked and horny!*

Wisdom prevailed, and she didn't. Instead she heated a can of vegetable soup, sipped it slowly, took a leisurely bath, and got into bed with the latest Elmore Leonard novel — his wonderfully vivid crime books were her weakness. Thoroughly relaxed, she fell asleep dreaming of Florida con men and colorful losers.

In the morning she felt better. She had no intention of keeping her appointment to interview Bobby Rush — she'd already finished the piece and sent it to Mason. She also had no intention of informing his rude publicist, let the woman find out the hard way.

At ten-thirty her phone started ringing. She allowed the machine to pick up and listened in.

One desperate publicist.

Good.

The woman called four times between ten-thirty and noon. Finally she gave up.

Kennedy decided to go to the beach. After all, this was California, and it was a gorgeous clear day.

She left her apartment in a great mood. Putting the top down on her Corvette, she drove down the twisting curves of Sunset to the ocean.

When she got back, around four, there were several messages on her machine. Rosa, of course; Bobby Rush — that was a surprise; Mason, who said he had to talk to her about the piece; and last a sad-sounding Nurse Linford. "Kennedy dear . . . I don't know how to say this. Your father . . . he died late this afternoon. I'm sorry. I'm really sorry."

Kennedy gazed blankly at her answering machine and somehow or other fell back into a chair.

Her eyes filled with tears. Slowly they trickled down her cheeks.

Now she was completely and utterly alone.

14

"You *fucked* Charlie Dollar?" Cheryl exclaimed incredulously, as she and Jordanna strolled through Fred Segal, checking out the new Gaultier and Montana lines.

"It's not so difficult," Jordanna said huffily. "After all, he *is* a man."

"He's also on Donna's list of clients," Cheryl said, relishing the fact that she had inside information. "He orders up a little professional action once in a while."

Jordanna couldn't help feeling disappointed. "He does?"

"Two girls. Always blondes. Mister Movie Star is into watching."

Jordanna hated the fact that Cheryl now considered herself an expert on everybody's sex life. She wished she hadn't confided about her one-nighter with Charlie.

"So . . . what's he like in bed?" Cheryl asked curiously, grabbing a black leather bustier off the rail and holding it up against herself.

"Why don't you check it out with one of your blondes?" Jordanna replied tartly.

"Hmm . . . jealous?" Cheryl teased, posing in front of the mirror.

Jordanna narrowed her eyes. "It doesn't suit you."

"And being jealous doesn't suit *you*," Cheryl retorted, throwing down the bustier.

"I am *not* jealous," Jordanna said, furious that Cheryl thought she was. "Charlie can sleep with who he likes. I have absolutely *no* plans to see him again."

A sly smile slid across Cheryl's face. "Hasn't called or lousy fuck?"

"Neither," Jordanna said, closing the subject as they moved over to the shoe section. She picked up a Chanel black suede boot and pretended to study it while she thought about Charlie. How *did* she feel? She certainly hadn't fallen for him, if that's the impression Cheryl was under. But a man who liked watching women get it on together . . . Ugh . . . *major* turnoff. And she'd slept with him, just like that.

God, he probably considered her just another dumb star fuck. How humiliating.

A week had passed, and he hadn't called. Not that she wanted him to. Not that she'd given him her number.

Screw Charlie Dollar. The last thing she needed was a movie star in her life.

"Have you heard from your father?" Cheryl asked, picking up a Walter Steiger pump.

"No."

"Is he still paying your allowance?"

"The bank hasn't called. I'm sure they'd be throwing a shit fit if I was bouncing checks."

"Well . . . if you need a top-paying job, you know who to come to."

Jordanna stifled a giggle as she thought about it. Jordanna Levitt, high-class hooker. Daddy couldn't be *too* mad, after all, he'd married one.

Shep was in a pissy mood when she got back to his house. "When are you moving out?" he asked, lips pursed, a frown on his handsome face.

"Why? Am I bothering you?" she retorted defensively. " 'Cause if I am, I'll pack up and go."

"You assured me it would only be a few days," he reminded her.

"I told you — I'll move out now."

"You're so *messy*," Shep complained, gesturing at magazines littered on the floor, shoes and clothes scattered all around, and dirty ashtrays sitting on every surface.

"I'm sorry," she said tartly. "I didn't realize I was living with Mister House Proud."

Shep bent to pick up a magazine. "My maid only comes in twice a week," he said accusingly. "And instead of pressing my shirts and doing things for me, she's busy clearing up after you."

She'd heard enough of his complaining. "Okay, okay — I get it. I'm out of here," she said, wishing he'd shut up and leave her alone.

"You can go back to your own place," he suggested helpfully, reaching for another magazine thrown carelessly on the floor. "I'm sure Jordan will be glad to have you there again."

She hated it when anyone told her what she should do — especially Shep, who was so busy lurking in the closet he had no right to give advice. Without replying, she marched into the small guest room, grabbed a suitcase, and began stuffing it with her clothes.

Shep appeared in the doorway and stood there watching her. "You don't have to leave tonight," he said, managing to sound hurt.

Oh, yes, *fine*. He'd told her to get out, and now he was trying to play the concerned friend. Well, it was too late.

"Thank you, but I'd prefer to," she said frostily.

Shep was not into rejection. "Jordy, don't be mad at me," he said, trying to bring her around.

"I'm not," she said, continuing to throw things into her suitcase. "As a matter of fact, I was just about to tell you."

"Tell me what?" he asked anxiously.

Yeah, tell him what? She thought fast and came up with a good one.

"Charlie Dollar asked me to move in with him," she lied.

Shep's surprise was evident. "Charlie Dollar?"

"You got it."

So now she sat in her car with nowhere to spend the night. She refused to go home — no way would she give her father the satisfaction of seeing her return to the guesthouse. Quickly she checked off the alternatives. Staying with Cheryl was questionable, now that she was in the hooker business. Marjory had just moved back in with her father, on account of the threatening letters she'd been receiving. And Grant probably had hot and cold running girls all night long. Of course, she could always check into a hotel — but that seemed such a lonely thing to do.

On impulse, she drove her car in the direction of Charlie Dollar's house.

It was seven o'clock, and Mac Brooks knew it was time to go home because Sharleen had informed him early in the morning that there was an important charity event they were supposed to attend that evening.

The truth was he didn't feel like leaving the production office. He was perfectly happy sitting around with Bobby, Gary, and Tyrone, discussing script changes, casting, locations, and all the planning that went into the months of preproduction on a movie — in this case only six weeks, because they were on an accelerated schedule.

Casting was of paramount importance. Mac liked every role to be perfect, from the star to the extras; he needed the actor to be exactly right for the role. It was reassuring to find out that Bobby felt the same way. He was also adamant about hiring his regular crew — people he'd used on most of his movies. His cinematographer was available, and his first assistant. Plus the production designer he favored and his location manager. Soon all the other people would be in place, everyone from props to wardrobe.

He'd received bad news about the woman who usually headed his makeup team. She'd been murdered, somewhere in Agoura Hills near where she lived. Christ! The violence out on the streets today was lethal. He would miss Margarita, she'd worked with him on four movies. He'd sent a huge white wreath but did not attend the funeral. He didn't believe in funerals — when someone was gone that was it, keep only the sweet memories.

Having spent a week with Bobby, Mac was pleasantly surprised — he'd known Bobby was a professional, but he hadn't expected to like him as much as he did. Gary and Tyrone were great to work with too.

Making movies and having fun at the same time was the best experience you could possibly have. Who needed home life when work was all-consuming?

The phone rang, and Gary handed it to him.

It was Sharleen. Naturally. "Where *are* you?" she wailed, sounding upset.

"You know where I am," he replied patiently.

"We have to leave the house in twenty minutes."

"I'll meet you there."

There was a quaver in her voice. "Mac . . ."

"Yes?"

"It's black tie. I reminded you this morning."

"So?"

She was trying to be nice, in the hope that he'd come running. "So that means you'll have to stop home and change before you meet me."

"I know."

Nice wasn't working. She snapped — it didn't take much — "You sonofa*bitch!* You're not coming, are you?"

"I'll make it if I can." But he had no intention of doing so.

Slam. Down went the phone.

Christ! Women!

"Trouble?" Bobby asked casually.

"Nothing I can't handle," Mac replied. "You ever been married, Bobby?"

A big grin. "Hey — I might be an actor, but an idiot I'm not!"

When Charlie Dollar wasn't working on a movie he indulged himself, doing exactly what pleased him. Sometimes he didn't get out of bed until noon, and then he'd emerge from his bedroom and wander around the house in his black silk pajamas and white tube socks, playing ball with his dogs, reading a variety of books, eating tuna fish sandwiches, and watching videos of classic movies or reruns of *Taxi* — his personal favorite.

Around five he was into his receiving mood. Usually friends dropped by and hung out, smoking grass and drinking margaritas. Charlie got off on holding court, expounding his theories on every subject to anyone who'd listen. They all listened, because he was Charlie Dollar, superstar, and this was Hollywood. If you were lucky enough to be in the great man's inner circle, you listened good.

Jordanna turned up in the middle of one of his entertaining sessions. His housekeeper, Mrs. Willet, a brusque Welsh woman, answered the door, thought she was a fan, and attempted to get rid of her.

"Excuse *me*," Jordanna said, pushing past her with a determined expression. "Mr. Dollar is expecting me."

"Really?" Mrs. Willet said, in hot pursuit. "We'll see about that, young missy."

"Allow me to jog your memory," Jordanna said imperiously. "Madonna, Prince. Outside his bedroom door in the middle of the night."

Mrs. Willet knew when to retreat. Making a rude snorting noise, she stalked off.

"Old bag," Jordanna muttered, opening the door to the living room and marching boldly in.

Charlie lazed on the couch, smoking a joint. Arnie Isaak stood behind the bar, fixing margaritas. Melinda Woodson, Arnie's partner, sprawled on the floor, wearing black leather and wraparound dark glasses, her expression, as usual, sour.

The two dogs rushed over to greet Jordanna, sniffed her crotch, and quickly retreated when Charlie snapped his fingers. "Kiddo!" he exclaimed, beaming. "You don't believe in returning phone calls?"

"Huh?"

"Alexander Graham Bell. I've called you three times." He stood up, treating her to his slightly off-center crazed grin. "Rejection is not good for movie stars. We ain't used to it, kiddo. We get kinda pissed."

"I didn't know you called," she said, realizing that since she'd moved out of the guesthouse she hadn't checked her machine.

Arnie had been watching this exchange with a bitter expression, as the love of his life reentered Charlie's. Stepping out from behind the bar, he immediately said the wrong thing. "Levitt. You look tired."

She barely glanced in his direction. "Thanks, Arnie. You always know how to make a girl feel her best."

Charlie caught the friction in the air and knew just the way to defuse it. "Arnie and Melinda were on their way outta here," he announced.

179

Both looked at him with surprise — this was news to them.

Charlie took Jordanna's hand in his. "Come up to the bedroom, kiddo. I got something to show you I think you'll appreciate."

Melinda and Arnie exchanged looks. Charlie was usually so laid-back, it was unlike him to exhibit this kind of interest in a woman.

Arnie wasn't going quietly. "Thought you were coming to the club tonight, Charlie," he said in a whining voice.

"Maybe not," Charlie said mysteriously, and with that he led Jordanna upstairs.

She was flattered and confused — both unusual emotions for her. She certainly hadn't expected Charlie to be this pleased to see her, and yet it was nice that he was.

"How've you been, kiddo?" he asked, as they entered his chaotic bedroom hand in hand.

"Not great," she replied listlessly.

"How come?"

She shrugged. "Nothing important."

He turned her so that she faced him. "If it bothers you, it's important. Spill. I'm a very dedicated listener."

Sure. She was back in his life, and the first place he dragged her to was his bedroom. It wasn't listening he had in mind.

"I repeat, nothing important."

Swooping down, he picked up two Tower Records bags stashed in a corner and handed them to her. "Presents," he said with a big wide grin. "Thought I'd wasted my money — but here you are in person. See if I did good."

She peered into the first bag — it was jammed with every tape and CD Madonna and Prince had ever made. The second bag contained Bobby Brown and Coltrane. For a moment she almost lost it. This was thoughtful shit — she wasn't used to thoughtful, and it affected her. "Thanks, Charlie," she said softly. "I'll have to get my CD player back."

"From where?"

"My dad's guesthouse. I finally left home."

"Good move."

"Not so good. I moved in with a friend, who decided I was a slob and threw me out."

He raised his bushy eyebrows. "A slob, huh?"

"Yeah." She smiled and gestured around his untidy bedroom. "Kind of like you."

"You need a place to stay?"

She hesitated. "Well . . ."

"I got guest rooms comin' out my ass. You can move in here."

"I do plan on getting my own apartment," she said quickly. "But first I guess I have to find a job. So if I *can* stay here for a few days . . ."

"A few days, a few months . . . who gives a shit, as long as you don't bug me."

"I promise I'll leave you completely alone."

Grabbing her, he pulled her in for a big wet kiss. "Let's not get carried away, kiddo. I had an interesting time the other night, didn't you?"

"It was . . . memorable."

"So why didja sneak off before I woke up? Maybe I needed glowing reviews."

"I didn't want to disturb you."

"Hey . . ." He pressed her hand between his

legs. "You can feel how you disturb me, and it's a good thing — a *real* good thing."

"I'm not a blonde, Charlie."

He frowned. "What did you say?"

"Nothing," she said, sinking to her knees.

She knew exactly what he required, and she didn't mind obliging.

15

For over a week Michael lay in a hospital bed, drifting in and out of consciousness. When he finally opened his eyes for a sustained period of time, he had no idea where he was.

Trying to collect his thoughts, he realized he was connected to tubes, that his head ached like a sonofabitch, and that he was unbelievably thirsty. And then it suddenly came to him. He'd been shot. He'd been fucking shot!

As he struggled to remember, it all became clear. A drug bust. Two guys. One of them retreating. He'd known something was wrong, spun around searching for danger, and nearly got blown away.

He groaned. His head felt like it would bust wide open, and he'd kill for a glass of water. "Anybody around?" he croaked.

A nurse appeared at his bedside, an earnest little thing with cropped brown hair and sparkling eyes. "Mr. Scorsinni," she said. "I do believe you're with us again."

"Got shot," he mumbled.

"No you didn't," she replied gently, patting his arm reassuringly.

"Yeah, yeah, I got shot," he insisted.

"*No,* Mr. Scorsinni," she said, placing a cool

183

hand on his forehead.

"Gotta have water," he managed.

"Only if you promise to drink it slowly."

She fetched a paper cup half full of water and held it to his lips.

He sipped it slowly, savoring every welcome drop.

"I have to go call Mr. Robbins now," she said, withdrawing the cup. "I've alerted the doctor. He's on his way to see you."

"Quincy's here in New York?"

"You're in L.A., Mr. Scorsinni."

Yeah, sure, what did *she* know?

His head felt like a launching pad for rocket ships. Gingerly he reached up, touching his shoulder, knowing that's where he'd been shot.

There were no bandages — nothing. Goddamn it, they weren't looking after him properly. Had to get the hell out of *this* hospital.

After a few minutes the nurse returned to his bedside. "Mr. Robbins is on his way," she said. "He's very happy to hear you're awake."

"Where's my bandages?"

"What bandages?"

"I told you — I got shot."

"No, Mr. Scorsinni, you were in a car accident."

He attempted to sit up but couldn't quite make it. Falling back, he mumbled, "I know who did it. Been workin' this case for months. Where's the captain? I gotta talk to him."

"Please relax, Mr. Scorsinni."

Squeezing his eyes shut, he tried to remember more. Yeah, he and his partner had been working undercover when the shit went down. They'd met in a warehouse on Forty-second Street, and everything should have gone real smooth. But no, there was this one Puerto Rican guy who'd gotten suspicious and ducked out of sight. Sensing danger, he'd called to his partner to cover him while he went after the asshole.

And then the gunshot — so fucking loud, busting into his body, breaking it apart. And after that — unbelievable pain.

He remembered hitting the ground. The ambulance ride to the hospital. Frantic faces leaning over him.

Then he recalled waking up and somebody telling him they'd removed the bullet.

So why was he still in the hospital?

"Mr. Scorsinni. Delighted to see you're awake."

He focused on the doctor, a short, bald man with beady eyes.

"Where am I?" he asked.

"In the hospital."

"New York — right?"

"No. Los Angeles."

"And I got shot."

"No."

"You're telling me I *wasn't* shot?"

"No, Mr. Scorsinni. You're confused, concussion does that. You've been in and out of consciousness for over a week."

"No shit?"

"Yes. But it seems you're past the crisis point."

"Get these tubes outta me, Doc. I'm allergic to hospitals."

"All in good time," the doctor replied, leaning

over and shining a pencil-slim flashlight into his eyes. "You're fortunate," he commented. "No broken bones. Lots of bruises and a bad head injury, but that's about it."

Bella. The memory of his daughter's voice came crashing back. And then everything clicked into place. Rita. The photographs. Club Erotica. Daly Forrest.

He hadn't been shot, that was past history. He'd been following Daly Forrest when he'd gotten hit on the head. He'd been behind the house in Hancock Park, heard Bella's voice, and then . . . blackness.

Once again he attempted to sit up. "I gotta go," he mumbled urgently.

The doctor was Mister Authority. "You're too weak. We'll have to keep you here under observation for at least another forty-eight hours."

"I don't give a shit, Doc. I gotta leave."

"Not today," the doctor said firmly.

After the doctor left, the nurse returned and disconnected him from the tubes. "We'll have to help fatten you up," she said cheerfully. "I'm bringing you some nourishing chicken broth. Only liquids today. Tomorrow we'll start you off with scrambled eggs."

Fuck the scrambled eggs. By the time Quincy arrived he was ready to move, his strength coming back by the minute. "What happened? How'd I get here?" he demanded impatiently.

"You're asking *me?*" Quincy said, waving his arms around. "I was expecting *you* to explain it. Your car flipped over the side of Mulholland, and you got thrown out. They found you halfway down

186

the hill. You're goddamn lucky to be alive."

"I wasn't anywhere near Mulholland. I followed Daly Forrest to a house in Hancock Park. He went inside, and I made my way around the back. That's when I heard Bella's voice. I was about to go for her, when I must've gotten hit on the head."

Quincy looked skeptical. "You sure?"

"Course I'm sure."

"Then how do you explain the car wreck?"

"They wanted me out of the way. It was a setup."

Quincy scratched his chin. "Who's they? An' why would they go to all this trouble?"

He was already halfway out of bed. "That's what we're gonna find out when you get me outta here."

"They won't release you. I already checked."

"Get me my clothes. And my gun."

"You'll have to make a police statement."

"What'll I say? That I was driving up Mulholland and zipped over the edge by mistake?"

"Yeah, that's it, 'cause if you go with the other story nobody's gonna believe you."

"Find my clothes, Q. I told you, we're outta here."

Quincy knew better than to argue.

Getting past the downstairs porter in Daly Forrest's apartment building on Wilshire was no problem; by this time they were old friends.

Quincy trailed behind Michael, complaining all the way. "Shit! We should wait until morning, maybe bring in the cops. Jeez, Mike — you shouldn't even be walkin' around. Why didja have t'come out here? My life was — "

187

"Will you shut up," Michael interrupted. "I gotta find out what's going on here. I wake up in the hospital after some phony car accident — my fucking gun's been stolen — and this Daly bastard wanted me dead. Well, too bad — I survived. Tonight we're finding out the truth." He sprung the lock on Daly Forrest's front door.

"Aw, great," Quincy groaned. "Now we're breakin' an' enterin'. Fuckin' great!"

They slipped inside the front hallway, a silent place with marble floors and mirrored walls. Michael stood for a moment, getting his bearings before moving stealthily down the corridor. Quincy followed, albeit reluctantly.

Michael was like a cat, he had the ability to see in the dark, and it didn't take him long to find the bedroom. The room was in darkness except for the glow of a television. A movie played, the sound turned low.

Two people lay in the bed — a man and a woman. Both appeared to be asleep.

For a long moment Michael stood silently in the doorway, watching them. Then he hit the light switch, and the shadowy room was illuminated.

The man was Daly Forrest.

The woman was his ex-wife, Rita.

They had both been shot in the head.

16

Mason Rich flew out from New York to be with Kennedy at her father's funeral. It was a small affair, as most of her parents' friends had long since passed away.

Nurse Linford sobbed openly when the casket was lowered into the ground. "My father was very fond of you," Kennedy said, trying to comfort her. "He told me often."

"I loved that man," the nurse replied, tears rolling down her cheeks.

"I know," Kennedy said sadly. "We'll all miss him."

After the funeral, Mason insisted she accompany him to his hotel for a late lunch.

"I can't eat," she said listlessly, as the waiter led them to a table.

"You can and you will," he said firmly. "But first you need a strong drink."

She picked at a salad while he spoke about New York and mutual friends — inconsequential stuff. "You have to realize," he said at last, "that if your father was in pain, he's better off where he is now."

She sipped the vodka he'd made her order and stared at him. Mason had pointed features and a slick of smooth brown hair that some people thought was a rug. He dressed as if he were about to pose for a fashion spread in *GQ*. There was no way she could ever find him attractive, but she was well aware he lusted after her, even though he was very much married. "That's a cliché, Mason," she said flatly.

"What else do you expect me to say at a time like this?"

"I don't know." She paused for a moment before continuing. "It's just that when your second parent dies it makes you painfully aware of your own mortality. It's quite frightening. I feel very alone."

Mason signaled the waiter for another drink. "Your father was old, and you have to remember he lived an interesting life. In many cultures, if a person has lived a long and rewarding life, death becomes a celebration."

"I know. It's just that I feel as if I'm next in line. It makes me vulnerable."

"You're thirty-five years old; you're not going anywhere," Mason said with a dry laugh.

"I guess not." She gazed out the window, then glanced back at him. "Thanks for coming out here."

He pressed his hand over hers. "That's what friends are for."

Managing a wan smile, she said, "Isn't that a song title?"

"At least I can make you smile," he said, as the waiter brought him his second martini. "Now here's my suggestion," he said. "Take a few weeks off, fly to Hawaii, lie in the sun, and forget about everything."

"You know that's not my style."

"You have to mourn, K.C. It's a good thing."

Shaking her head, she said, "No, what I have to do is keep working. In fact, I'd like to talk to you about my first story."

"Didn't you mention the other day you were going to write about women in Hollywood?"

"I've changed my mind. I was thinking of writing about an ordinary woman who gets murdered outside her own home."

"Somebody I've heard of?"

"No, and I'm not even sure if I'll write it. I have to investigate further. It's still violence against women, but why must we always focus on the high-profile side of it?"

"If celebrities aren't involved, who's going to want to read it?"

"You'd be surprised."

Drumming his fingers on the table, he said, "Since we're talking about work, can we discuss your Bobby Rush piece?"

"What is there to discuss?"

"It's lightweight. You make him out to be too nice."

"He *is* nice."

"Maybe. But I need more heat. I thought you were planning on covering the father/son angle — stirring it up."

"I thought you gave assurances we wouldn't touch that angle."

Mason didn't care. "Do a rewrite," he said. "Expose nepotism in Hollywood, the shallowness of fame, and let's hear who he's screwing."

Kennedy controlled her anger. "Get yourself another hack."

"I'm not criticizing your writing," Mason said quickly. "It's a well-written piece, and I like the mistaken-identity angle."

"What *are* you saying?" she challenged. "That you don't want to run it?"

"Juice it up, K.C."

"I wrote Bobby Rush the way I saw him."

"Okay, okay, but don't soft-pedal your next celebrity assignment. I'm pretty certain we can get you Charlie Dollar."

Her interest perked up. "Yes?"

"He's executive producer on his new movie, so he's hot to promote. He doesn't usually do print, but a *Style Wars* cover story will suit him fine." He snapped his fingers for the check. "I have a plane to catch. You sure you're all right?"

"I'm certain, Mason. And once again, I really appreciate you flying out here. It means a lot to me."

"Anytime, K.C. You know you're my favorite," he said, planting a wet kiss on her cheek.

Rosa, who'd had to run back to the TV studio after the funeral, appeared at her apartment in the early evening. "I'm spending the night," she announced, dumping a huge Fendi travel bag in the hall.

"No you're not," Kennedy said firmly.

"Yes I am," Rosa replied, equally firm. "We'll talk, we'll eat, we'll have a girls' night in."

"You're useless at girls' nights in. If there isn't a guy around, you fall asleep."

Rosa looked at her with a hurt expression. "You're in a crisis, and I'm here for you. That's what friends are for."

"Jesus!" Kennedy exclaimed, rolling her eyes. "What *is* it with that corny song!"

As it happened, she was pleased Rosa was there, because she didn't relish being alone. They settled in the small kitchen, sent out for Chinese food, and sat around talking all night, covering most subjects, although whenever possible Rosa tried to steer the conversation in the direction of Ferdy.

"I mean, am I crazy or what?" Rosa asked, chewing on a spare rib. "He's younger than me, the wrong color, and yet I feel we have a great future together."

"You say that about every guy you've ever slept with."

"Maybe it's because I believe it."

"Keep on believing it and I'll *know* you're crazy."

Rosa shrugged, licking her fingers. "I'm not sure what I want a guy for anyway. Sometimes I think it's just for fantastic sex, because if I was truthful, I certainly have no desire to marry them and have their babies."

"You're sure about that?"

"I tried marriage twice, it didn't work either time. I'm not the maternal type; my career is too important. Anyway, where is it written you have to want kids?"

"I hear what you're saying," Kennedy agreed, although if Phil hadn't died she would have loved to have children, lots of them, and still pursue a career. It *was* possible.

"The thing is," Rosa mused, "that Ferdy wants babies. It's kind of a male pride trip."

Kennedy got up and began clearing the dishes.

193

"Are you *planning* on marrying him?"

"No."

"Then what's the problem?"

Rosa jumped up. "That's why I like you, Kennedy. You always make me feel better about things."

In the morning Rosa was in a rush. She commandeered the bathroom, perfecting her makeup, then she made six urgent phone calls before dashing from the apartment. "I'll call you later," she said, waving as she hurried to her car. "Catch me on the six o'clock news and take a look at the latest weather guy — I hear he's available."

What a matchmaker! The last thing Kennedy needed was a man. She needed space and time. She needed to throw herself into her work.

With that in mind, she went to the library and read everything she could about the woman murdered in Agoura Hills. Her father was right — why focus on high-profile Hollywood when there were stories taking place every day that affected people in a far more immediate way.

A woman had died violently, and she couldn't find much coverage — only two newspaper reports. The first featured a dramatic headline. She scanned the story:

WOMAN SLAIN OUTSIDE OWN HOME
Margarita Lynda, 37, was found strangled to death next to her car outside her house early this morning. There was no apparent robbery attempt, and rape is not suspected. A passerby spotted the body at 7:40 A.M. and summoned deputies.

Lynda, an Agoura Hills resident, was separated from her husband and had no children. She was a film makeup artist who had recently completed work on a Grant Lennon movie. Sheriff's officials are investigating.

The second story was even briefer.

Hmm . . . , Kennedy thought, *not much to go on.* But her journalistic mind was in action. Why had this woman been murdered? What was the motive?

It was her destiny to find out. She owed it to the memory of her father.

The Man trailed his soon-to-be-victim all day long. It gave him a perverse thrill to know he could follow her every move without her realizing it.

He knew his victim. He knew plenty about her.

Fact one: She was a lesbian.

Fact two: She lived with her mother.

Fact three: She had two cats and a small dog.

His victim spent a busy day. There was a trip to the dry cleaner and the photographic shop, a stop at the shoe repairer's, lunch with a friend, and then a movie. It was not a film The Man was interested in; it was a foolish love story. But he sat in the theater anyway — two seats behind his victim, who was not alone. She was with her friend from lunch, a younger woman in a yellow sweater and loose slacks.

Perverts, The Man thought to himself. He'd never understood how one woman could be attracted to another. It simply wasn't right.

After the movie the two companions shared a coffee and then went their separate ways.

The Man followed his victim home. He

thought about taking her then and there, before she entered her house, but it was still light out and he didn't want to run any risks. He had no intention of getting caught. There was no way he could ever go back to jail.

He parked his car in a spot where nobody would notice. He waited patiently, knowing that at nine o'clock his victim would emerge and walk her dog, as she did every night.

Sure enough, this occurred.

The Man left his car and fell into step behind her as she walked along the quiet side street in West Hollywood. After a few moments the victim sensed she was being followed and glanced behind her.

The Man did not hesitate, he approached boldly. "Do you have the time?" he asked politely.

She looked at him, a puzzled expression crossing her face. "Don't I know — ?"

The Man nodded. "Yes, you know me," he said, not allowing her to finish her sentence.

With one massive blow he knocked her to the ground, taking her by surprise. She fell silently. Her small dog began to bark and growl. He gave it a vicious kick, and it scampered off down the street, whimpering.

The Man squatted next to his victim, placed his hands around her throat, and slowly and methodically began to squeeze.

She struggled once, her body twitching uncontrollably, and then it was over.

There was one thing left to do. The Man reached into an inner pocket, producing a thin

strip of cardboard on which he had pasted —
with letters cut from newspapers — the words
DEATH TO THE TRAITORS. He placed it neatly
across her chest, took one last look around, and
returned to his car.

Then he drove off, humming softly to himself.

Victim number two disposed of. Four more
to go.

He was master of the game.

17

Living with Charlie Dollar was quite a trip. He was totally undemanding, not at all possessive, and he didn't care how much of a mess she made. The only drag was his stern housekeeper, who eyed her as if she were about to commit arson on a daily basis.

"Ignore the old witch," Charlie said with one of his crazed chuckles. "She's been with me fifteen years. Princess Di could move in and she wouldn't approve."

"But she watches me, Charlie — like I'm about to *steal* something."

"Are you?"

Jordanna stuck out her tongue and wiggled it at him. "Fuck you, asshole."

"Anybody ever told you you got a mouth like a truckdriver?"

She grinned. "Yeah, frequently."

"So clean up your dialogue, kiddo," he said good-naturedly. "It ain't ladylike."

One thing about their relationship — they were compatible, even if he *was* nearly thirty years older than her. Jordanna genuinely enjoyed his company, he was certainly more fun to be with than some Midnight Cowboy with a tight ass and an empty brain — and God knew she'd had enough of them to last two lifetimes. She didn't know much about his past love life, and she really didn't care. The word was that he'd been living with an actress up until a few months ago and they had a three-year-old child, whom he saw occasionally. Questioning wasn't her style. If Charlie wanted to tell her anything he would. As it was, she felt they were a couple, and it was a nice secure feeling.

Some of his habits drove her crazy. He played Sinatra and Tony Bennett on the stereo — full volume yet! He ate cornflakes in bed in the middle of the night. He was always stoned. And he liked her to give him endless head.

After several days she decided to go to her father's guesthouse and collect a few more of her possessions. Even though she slept most nights with Charlie in his bedroom, she'd staked out a nice big corner room in the house, and there was plenty of space for her things.

"You gonna tell your old man you moved in with me?" Charlie asked, a wicked glint in his eyes.

"Why would I do that?" she replied coolly, unwilling to get into a discussion about her father.

"Surely he's curious to know where you're living?"

Shrugging, she said, "Jordan has a new wife to worry about. He doesn't care what I do."

Charlie nodded wisely. "He will — when he gets a sniff you're living with me."

Was it her imagination, or did he seem to

want Jordan to know?

"You have your opinion, and I have mine," she said, thinking that she had no intention of telling her father. If she was lucky she could sneak back to the guesthouse, grab her stuff, and be out of there before anyone realized she was around.

Unfortunately it was not to be. When she arrived at the guesthouse she was confronted by Kim, standing at the door supervising a couple of maids and two moving men.

She watched in amazement as her favorite couch was carried out. "What the *hell's* going on?" she asked, outraged.

Kim hardly glanced in her direction. "Oh, it's you."

"Yeah, it's me, and what the *fuck* are you doing with my stuff?"

"I was under the impression you left," Kim said briskly. "That's what Jordan told me."

"Whether I left or not, you have no business messing with my things."

"I'm having everything put in storage," Kim said offhandedly. "We need the space."

"You've got enough space to accommodate a fucking football team!" Jordanna said furiously.

"We need more," Kim replied with a tight little smile.

"Why?"

Kim gave a long-drawn-out sigh, "I suppose you'll hear soon enough, so I may as well tell you — your father and I are having a baby."

The hooker was pregnant? *No fucking way.*

Jordanna caught her breath, desperately trying to stay in control. "Does Jordan know?" she blurted foolishly.

Kim threw her a withering look. "Of course he does."

"I wasn't talking about the pregnancy," Jordanna retorted sharply, determined to gain the upper hand.

"What *were* you talking about?"

She played her ace card. "Remember Donna?"

"Donna who?" Kim said, her pretty face masklike.

In for the kill. "Donna Lacey."

Kim didn't miss a beat. "I met her once or twice. Why?"

"Because she sure remembers you." Jordanna paused briefly before continuing. "Tell me, Kim, is Jordan aware of your past?"

Not a flicker. "I don't know what you're talking about."

She pressed on. "I think you do."

Kim's tone turned low and angry. "Why don't you leave us alone? Isn't it enough you're still taking money from him at your age?"

"That's none of your business," Jordanna said angrily.

"I'm making it my business."

They glared at each other.

"Your father's had a very difficult life," Kim said at last. "He doesn't need to listen to your lies about me."

"A difficult life indeed!" Jordanna snorted. "Like *you* would know."

"I know everything about Jordan — including how disappointed he is in you."

Kim's words stung. Was he really disappointed in her, or was Kim simply making it up to hurt her?

"The only thing you know is that you love every moment of being Mrs. Jordan Levitt," she fired back. "You sure moved in on him big time, didn't you?"

"Yes, I did," Kim replied defiantly. "And you're not spoiling it for me."

"I can try."

"Where's your proof? He'll never believe you."

"I'll *get* proof."

"I'm having his baby," Kim said triumphantly. "You don't have a chance."

"We'll see."

"Do what you have to do," Kim said with an exasperated sigh. "Because frankly, if it's a choice between you and me, I *know* who he'll choose." She turned around and marched down the path toward the big house.

"Don't bet on it!" Jordanna yelled after her.

Kim didn't look back.

Jordanna rushed into the guesthouse. Two Hispanic maids were busy loading up boxes with her possessions. "What are you doing?" she asked, grabbing a stack of tapes out of one of the women's hands.

"Mrs. Levitt — she told us to pack everything," the shorter woman said, her broad face expressionless.

"Please get out of here," Jordanna said wearily. "I'll take care of it myself."

The women exchanged glances and left.

So Daddy really wanted her out permanently. Well, that was fine with her. She certainly wasn't staying where she wasn't welcome, and there was no way she'd accept any more money from him either.

Grabbing the phone, she dialed information and got the number of a moving firm. They promised to have a van there within the hour.

By five o'clock she was packed and ready to split. There was no word from Jordan. Surprise, surprise. Should she go say goodbye, and casually throw into the conversation that she was living with Charlie Dollar?

Why not? May as well piss him off all the way.

She headed for the main house and was disappointed to find nobody around except Kim, who emerged from the kitchen and said a curt, "Yes?"

"Where's my father?"

"Oh, didn't I mention he's away on a location scout?" Kim said sweetly. "So . . . I guess your little talk with him will have to wait."

"It *can* wait, Kim. When you see him, tell him he can call me at Charlie Dollar's."

Kim raised an eyebrow. "Really?"

"Yes, *really*."

Licking her pink lips, Kim gave a small, venomous smile. "Do give *Charlie* my love," she said. "We're *old* friends."

Driving back to Charlie's, with the moving van following closely behind her Porsche, Jordanna couldn't help wondering about Kim's expression of triumph. *Give him my love.* Ha! Was Kim one of the blondes whom Cheryl had mentioned Charlie enjoyed getting it on with?

Easy enough to find out. She called Cheryl on the car phone.

"Where have you been?" Cheryl asked. "I haven't heard from you in days."

"I'll tell you later. Right now I'm after information."

"What information?"

"Remember you told me that Charlie Dollar was into like kind of a watching thing with blondes?"

"I *knew* you were jealous," Cheryl shrieked.

"Merely curious. Was Kim one of the blondes?"

"I'll have to look up his records."

"Do that for me, will you?"

"Are you still at Shep's?"

"I'll call back."

"You're being so mysterious."

"All will be revealed later."

Charlie's housekeeper took one quick look at the van loaded with Jordanna's possessions and scurried off to find her boss.

Jordanna issued instructions to the movers as they unloaded the truck.

After a few minutes Charlie wandered out to the front of the house, tucking his shirt into his pants. He stood on the top step, surveying the action. "I see you're moving in," he said at last.

"You told me I could stay."

"I didn't know you were bringing a vanful of stuff."

She hoped he wasn't going to be difficult. "Is it a problem, Charlie?"

"Nope. As a matter of fact, I'm kind of pleased."

"You are?"

"I said to make yourself at home."

"Thank you."

"The thing is, kiddo, we'll have fun while it lasts, but eventually you'll have to find your own place. And like you said, get yourself a job. 'Cause the truth of the matter is I ain't Daddy, and you gotta make your own spending money."

She narrowed her eyes, annoyed that he thought she was after his precious money. "Did I ask you for money, Charlie?"

"No, but I'm sure you're gonna want some, so I came up with a Charlie Dollar special-on-sale brilliant idea."

"What idea is that?"

"I scored you a job, kiddo."

"A job?"

"Yeah. I had lunch with Bobby Rush, an' whadaya know — he's looking for an assistant. I told him you'd fit right in."

"Thanks a lot," she said, not exactly thrilled at the prospect of working for Bobby Rush.

"Anything wrong with that?"

"I did that assistant thing once. It's boring."

"Correct me if I'm wrong, but wasn't it *you* who told me you wanted to act?"

"What's that got to do with anything?"

"It doesn't just fall into place, kiddo — you have to learn. It'll be good for you to be on a set, watching what goes on."

"I've been on a set since I was born," she said, exasperated that he was trying to fix her up without asking her.

"So you'll do it again. *I* started off shifting scenery. Got me an education before I went in front of the camera. It sure put *me* ahead of the game."

"Charlie — "

Now he was challenging her, his eyes watchful and amused. "Too tough a gig, huh?" he asked, staring her down.

"I *can* do it," she said defensively. "I just don't want to."

"You'll make your own money for once."

Finally it was getting interesting. "How much?"

Charlie chuckled. "I'll negotiate for you, kiddo. I'm a specialist when it comes to killer deals."

Cheryl searched through the books. Donna had used a code for important men, which she'd explained before leaving town. Movie stars were listed under special names. Cheryl checked for Charlie Dollar and found he was known as Big Money. She then looked over Big Money's preferences. It appeared he didn't indulge often, but when he did he had very particular requirements. Two big-breasted blondes with long hair and no inhibitions.

Rapidly scanning the names of girls he'd had, Cheryl ascertained that Kim was indeed one of them.

She immediately called Shep. "Where's Jordy?"

"How would I know?"

"Wasn't she staying with you?"

"Left a few days ago."

"Why?"

"Said she was moving in with Charlie Dollar.

I haven't heard from her since."

"Charlie Dollar? Are you sure?"

"That's what she told me."

"Hmm . . . giving it away for free again," Cheryl said disapprovingly. "I could make her a fortune."

"You're disgusting."

"Why's that, Shep dear?"

"Don't you realize what you're doing?"

"Fulfilling a need. One that *you* obviously don't have."

"*Excuse* me?"

"Oh, come off it. Everyone knows your preference."

A long silent moment, then — *"Bitch!"*

"Likewise."

She was about to call Arnie to get Charlie's number when a girl arrived for a prearranged interview. What a business! Pick the best prospects, send them out on a job, and pocket forty percent of the fee. There was no shortage of girls — they applied in droves, recommended by friends and acquaintances. And because this was Hollywood, they were usually pretty, with good bodies, all of them — with few exceptions — would-be actresses, singers, and models, out to pick up extra money.

The girl today was a voluptuous nineteen-year-old brunette with a Cindy Crawford look. She was perfectly lovely except for her crooked front teeth. Cheryl loved being in a position of power. Criticizing the girls was a definite highlight of the job, plus making big bucks and enjoying the special relationship she was beginning to develop with the johns.

Ah . . . the johns — what a mixed-up group *they* were. Donna had warned her about their idiosyncrasies, but jeez — some of these guys were into *major* weird.

One client requested girls dressed as nuns; another required every hair on their bodies to be shaved; and a certain Arab prince ordered up dozens of bottles of Cristal and endless cans of Beluga caviar, so he could eat and drink off the girl of his choice. Cheryl's personal favorite was the big action star who got off on being scolded, while three girls dressed in green leather elf uniforms led him around the room on a choke-chain leash.

Cheryl felt true power for the first time in her life. In fact, she felt so in control that she'd stopped her twice-weekly visits to her shrink. Being a madam was better than therapy any day. She finally felt fulfilled.

She often thought about what would happen if her illustrious and socially connected parents ever found out what she was doing now.

They would hang themselves in the middle of Chasen's, that's what would happen. Her mother, so proper and Nancy Reagan–like, when she wasn't rolling around drunk. And her father — Ethan, Mister Big Studio Owner, with his two mistresses stashed in matching apartments at either end of town. What a hypocrite *he* was, she was surprised she hadn't found him listed in Donna's fat black book.

Fortunately she didn't have to seek their approval anymore, she'd made it on her own.

Idly she wondered if Shep was right and Jordanna *had* moved in with Charlie Dollar. Shacking up with a dissolute movie star old enough to be her father was pure Jordanna.

"How much can I expect to make a week?"

Cheryl was jolted back to reality by the lovely girl with the crooked front teeth sitting in front of her.

"Uh . . . it all depends," she said. "If the client likes you, return engagements can be quite frequent."

"I'm only doing this because I need the money," the girl said. "And my friend told me I'll meet men who might help my career."

Cheryl nodded. How naive these girls were. Did they honestly believe anyone was going to help them? The truth was they'd get royally fucked for a year or two, make a lot of money, and hopefully go home to the little town they came from and marry the boy next door.

"We'll have to get your teeth fixed," Cheryl said bluntly.

The girl's hand flew to cover her mouth. "I can't afford it," she muttered guiltily.

"I'll give you an advance, it'll be deducted from your fees."

Another fifteen minutes of conversation, and Cheryl sent the girl on her way with a dentist's appointment and a rendezvous with Grant that evening.

Grant was her front man, sleeping with the girls on a trial basis and later giving her a full report so she was sure they knew what they were doing. He performed this service for free. Hardly a favor, since sex was the main thrust of his life as he strove to keep up with his father's legendary reputation. On one level it saddened Cheryl that Grant was prepared to do this. But at least it kept them close, and she'd always liked having him around.

The phone rang. It was the head of development at one of the major studios. They exchanged pleasantries for a few moments before he announced the real reason for his call. "We got a French actor in town, totally nuts. He requires two girls — one Eurasian, one good old American white trash. He's into that Guess girl look — the one with the big silicone tits and the straw in her hair. His hotel, eight o'clock tonight." A slight pause. "Oh, and honey, have your girls bring the coke. My connection's taking a trip."

"No problem," Cheryl replied calmly, although this was the first time she'd been asked to supply drugs, and it didn't give her much of an opportunity to decide whether she wanted to or not.

After putting the phone down she called Grant and asked if he could help out. Grant didn't have to think about it, he offered to supply her with whatever she needed. "My friendly neighborhood dealer will be happy to oblige," he said. "Don't worry about it."

Things were moving faster than she'd expected. Too fast, maybe?
No. Never.

18

Weeks passed, and Michael couldn't find a lead of any kind. It was driving him insane. He had a daughter out there somewhere and nobody knew what had happened to her. It was almost as if Bella had never existed.

Rita was dead. Murdered. So was Daly Forrest. The lovers had been shot execution style and — the kicker — with his gun. The gun Quincy couldn't find when they'd checked out of the hospital had turned up in Daly Forrest's apartment, and Michael immediately became suspect number one. Now he was sure he'd been set up. They'd knocked him out, taken his gun, and used it for the double killing. And he had no idea who "they" were. The cops had experienced no trouble tracking the gun to him. He'd purchased it as soon as he'd arrived in California, acquired a legal permit to carry — and now this.

The detective on the case had hauled him in for questioning, and he wasn't released until it was established that he'd been with Quincy since leaving the hospital and therefore couldn't have done it.

Within hours the media jumped on the case. It was a hot one. A good-looking redhead and a rich older man, discovered in bed together in a luxurious apartment. He'd produced porno movies. She'd starred in one. And her ex-husband had discovered the bodies. Juicy stuff. The TV newsmagazines went to town.

The detective handling the case let out the information about the missing child and the father searching for her. Suddenly Michael was big news and found himself pursued by the press. To Amber's fury, they gathered outside the Robbins house, waiting to pounce.

After forty-eight hours of this inconvenience, Michael moved out and went into hiding in a hotel. The press tracked him down. He moved to another hotel, and hours later they were staking a spot outside, still begging for an interview.

"Maybe you *should* do something," Quincy suggested. "Somebody out there watching might know where Bella is. Whyn't you talk to Rosa Alvarez on the local news? A friend of mine knows her boyfriend, so let's see if we can set it up an' make sure she treats you right."

Michael nodded. He was getting desperate. "Go ahead, arrange it."

After all, he had nothing to lose.

The events of the last few weeks were a horrible blur. After dealing with the police and finally convincing them he'd had nothing to do with the killings, he'd set off on a quest of his own to get to the truth. Nobody seemed to remember Bella, although they all remembered Rita — she'd cut quite a swath.

The first thing he'd done was revisit the house in Hancock Park to which he'd followed Daly Forrest. The door was answered by an ancient care-taker, who informed him the house was unoccu-pied and had been for several years. Michael didn't believe him, but what could he do?

He checked out the back garden, peering through the kitchen window. From what he could see, the room looked dusty and unused — maybe the old man *was* telling the truth, and he'd gotten the wrong house. Since being hit on the head he'd been suffering from the occasional blinding head-ache — Christ — what if he was losing his fucking memory?

His next move was to go after Heron Jones, only to discover that Heron had taken off, leaving no forwarding address.

Quincy and Amber had somehow gotten him through it. "We're gonna find your kid," Quincy assured him daily. "If she's out there we'll find her."

In the meantime he continued to pursue every lead, getting exactly nowhere. He talked to busi-ness acquaintances and employees of Daly For-rest's, he even tracked a scattering of the movie crew who'd worked with Rita on the one movie she performed in. And performed was the right word. He'd seen it — a soft-porn exploitive piece of crap, with Rita in a small role making all the appropriate moves.

It saddened him that she'd thought appearing in that kind of low-life film was going to get her anywhere.

The police put out a Missing Persons report on Bella, informing him that's all they could do.

Meanwhile the investigation of Daly and Rita's

murder reached a dead end. There were suspects involved with the porn industry, but nobody they could pin anything on. It was frustrating, but Michael refused to give up.

Rosa Alvarez arrived at his hotel with her crew. She was warm and sympathetic. "I'm so sorry, Michael, to hear about your little girl," she said, pressing her hand over his.

"Look," he informed her. "I'm uncomfortable doing this, but I need to put out a message in case anybody knows anything. You'll show Bella's picture on camera, right?"

"Just tell me your story," Rosa said soothingly. "And I'm sure we'll see results."

He shrugged. "It's a short story."

"Somebody must know something," Rosa said, taking a quick peek in a hand mirror and fluffing her hair. "And if they do, this interview could persuade them to come forward."

"Yeah," he said, still not fully convinced he was doing the right thing.

"Now, Michael, try to relax," Rosa said, sitting down in a chair. "Just pretend it's you and me talking."

"You make it sound so easy."

"It will be if we take it nice and slow."

The soundman began attaching a small microphone to the lapel of his sports jacket. The thought of this interview frightened the shit out of him. Michael Scorsinni, who'd faced up to guns, drug dealers, and God knew what else, was scared and yet at the same time hopeful.

When the interview started he was dry-mouthed and found himself mumbling. But Rosa knew her stuff, she dealt with him gently, drawing him out until he told his story as clearly as he could.

When it was over she seemed pleased. She handed him her card. "Call me. We're sure to get a big response."

He pocketed the card. "Thanks. I appreciate this."

"I'd like to do a follow-up — maybe in a couple of weeks? Perhaps we'll have good news. What do you think?"

"What do *I* think? I think I'm gonna find my daughter, and then we'll see."

"I've caught you a live one," Rosa announced triumphantly as she and Kennedy worked out.

Kennedy was on the treadmill, reaching the end of a vigorous thirty-minute stint. "How many times do I have to tell you," she said, out of breath. "Nix was positively my last blind date."

"No, no," Rosa said, lifting light hand weights. "You don't understand."

"Oh, yes, I understand perfectly."

"This guy is the one," Rosa said, working on her arms. "And handsome too. He looks like a movie star. If I wasn't with Ferdy I'd grab him for myself. But since I'm such a generous friend, I'm handing him your way."

Kennedy slowed the treadmill. "Thanks, but no thanks."

"Let me tell you about him," Rosa said, full of enthusiasm. "He's an ex–New York detective. In fact, he's *the* ex-detective, the one who's been all over the news. You know, with the missing kid."

"Great! Now you're bringing me a guy with problems, on top of everything else."

"No, no, this problem will get solved. I have no idea what the outcome will be — it doesn't sound good, but who knows?" She paused for a moment before adding, "There's something about Michael — I know you'll love him."

Kennedy stepped off the treadmill, grabbed a towel, and slung it around her neck. "I will *not* love him, because I am *not* going to meet him."

Rosa put down the weights and took a breather. "Did you see my interview with him? The response was amazing, we got over *three hundred* letters from women. Can you believe it? And what's more, forty-three of them proposed marriage!"

"That's good. He can find himself a lovely wife, go off, and live happily ever."

"What's the matter with you lately? Don't you have any heart? I'm offering you this great-looking guy that forty-three women want to marry, and you're turning him down?"

"Rosa, English is your first language — right?"

"Yes."

"Then why don't you understand me? I do *not* wish to be fixed up."

"You used to be willing to take chances."

"I still do — in my work."

"So now you're becoming a nun?"

Kennedy ignored the comment. "By the way," she said, "I've been meaning to ask — do you know anything about the woman who was murdered in West Hollywood a few weeks ago?"

"What woman?"

"Her name was Stephanie Wolff. She was strangled — the same MO as Margarita Lynda."

"Really?"

"Two women, both strangled for no apparent reason, neither of them raped or robbed."

"Hmm . . . I'll get the news division to look into it."

"I wish you would. I've tried calling the police to see if the murders are connected in any way, but I got nowhere."

Rosa stretched and picked up the weights again. "What are you writing about these women for anyway? They're not famous."

Kennedy laughed dryly. "You sound like my editor. If somebody gets murdered, does she have to be famous before anybody pays attention?"

"I thought celebrity interviews were your thing. When does your Bobby Rush piece appear?"

"It'll be on the stands this week."

"Did you hear from him after your interview?"

"No. He tried calling me a couple of times. I never returned the calls."

"Why?"

"Because I didn't want to explain myself. Better he reads the interview. I think he'll like it."

"I'm sure he will," Rosa said with a sigh. "And if he does and he calls again, will you date him?"

"No."

"No, huh?" Rosa shook her head. "You're a strange one."

Amber deposited her children with a girlfriend and spent two days traipsing around until she found Michael an apartment — a perfectly nice

218

furnished one-bedroom on Riverside Drive in the Valley.

"Don't know what I'd do without you," he told her gratefully as she helped him settle in.

"Somehow I've got a feeling you'd manage," Amber said, organizing the tiny kitchen. "You're a survivor. You keep on proving it."

He caught her in a hug. "That's 'cause I've got good friends who are always around to support me."

She looked at him for a moment, her eyes full of sympathy. "We care about you, Michael. Underneath that tough-guy exterior lurks a very special friend."

Her words touched him, but it wasn't enough to jolt him out of a deep depression.

After she left, he sat on his rented couch in his new apartment and thought about having a drink. A double Scotch. With ice.

Oh, Christ — he could fucking smell it, taste it, feel the strong liquid burning a path down his throat.

Why not? he asked himself. *Why the fuck not?*

Because he had to stay sober to find his daughter. There was no chance if he was out of his head. And that's how alcohol affected him. It turned him into a crazy man. It turned him into his fucking stepfather. Uncontrollable.

I am powerless over alcohol, he thought. *Totally powerless.*

He'd never forget the night before the day he'd sobered up. What a bad trip that was! Rita and he got involved in one of their usual fights about money and her extravagant spending habits. She

219

screamed at him that he was no good, exactly like his real father.

"You don't know my real father," he yelled at her.

"I don't *have* to," she yelled back. "Sal told me all about him, and you're just as bad. A loser. A nothing. A down-and-out bum!"

He stormed out of their apartment and went to a bar, where, after two hours of heavy drinking, he allowed himself to get picked up by a tall, sexy blonde in a miniskirt and tight sweater.

Drinking was his curse, when he drank he became a different person — someone he hated — but once he started he couldn't stop.

The blonde was persistent, and he wasn't resisting. They ended up in a cheap hotel room off Times Square, with a bottle of tequila and their hands all over each other. She gave him head and he grabbed her tits.

Memories were blurred up until then, but he'd never forget what happened next. Everything flashed into sharp focus when the sexy blonde dropped her short skirt and lace panties and showed him her penis and balls.

Goddamn it! He was with a fucking transvestite!

He beat the crap out of "it," and her/his screaming could be heard for blocks. Then he pulled his gun and wanted to blow the pervert's brains out. Fortunately the cops got there in time, before he killed the motherfucker. And he would have. Oh yeah, no doubt about it.

The next day Quincy had gotten him into rehab for a grueling four weeks. After that he started attending AA meetings.

He'd never looked back. His past was too scary.

He realized now that he needed to work the program again, start attending meetings before it was too late.

God grant me the serenity to accept the things
I cannot change, courage to change the things
I can, and the wisdom to know the difference.

He remembered the AA Serenity Prayer and immediately felt calmer.

The truth was he was in a slump because he honestly didn't know what to do next. He was a detective, for chrissake, he knew how to solve cases — but he couldn't get anywhere with finding his own daughter, and it was breaking him up.

He'd loved Rita once, she was the mother of his child, but there was no way he could summon up any grief about her demise, he felt only anger that she'd deprived him of his little girl.

Quincy was working on a case involving a series of threatening letters being sent to the daughter of a television magnate. At first he'd assisted Michael in his investigation of Rita's murder and Bella's disappearance whenever he could, but work beckoned, and when they'd encountered a series of leads that took them nowhere, he finally had to back off.

The morning after Michael's move, Quincy called and insisted he come for dinner that night. On the way over, he stopped off at a meeting. It was a worthwhile move and calmed him considerably.

Amber had cooked meat loaf, mashed potatoes, and crisp fried onions. Comfort food. They sat around the kitchen table, enjoying each other's company.

Amber decided he needed the company of a woman. Quincy decided he needed to get laid. They were both on his case, until he finally acquiesced and agreed to go out on a date with a friend from Amber's salsa dance class.

"I don't know her well," Amber explained, "but she sure is pretty. I showed her your picture, and she's willing to meet you."

"The bad news is she's a would-be actress," Quincy interrupted, grinning. "I got a look at her the other night when I met Amber after class. Nice legs — get her in the sack an' wrap 'em around your neck, Mike, you'll be a new man!"

Amber tut-tutted. "Is that the only thing you can think of — sex? It's companionship he needs at a time like this."

Quincy's grin broadened. "Yeah, sure, honey — companionship, an' a little pussy to go with it!"

"You're so crude," Amber said crossly.

"It's part of my charm, sweet thing!" Quincy said, throwing Michael a knowing wink.

They met in the bar of the Hyatt Universal Hotel.

"Shelia?"

"Michael?"

They circled each other like wary soldiers on either side of the battlefield. She was California pretty, with the requisite toned and tanned body, deep-dish tits exhibited in a low-cut short dress, and long, sexy legs.

"Shall we go into the restaurant?" Michael asked, surreptitiously checking her out.

"Good idea," she replied. Sliding off the barstool, she exhibited a dangerous amount of creamy thigh.

A hostess escorted them to a table. Michael ordered his usual nonalcoholic beer, while Shelia settled for vodka tonic.

When her drink arrived she held it with both hands, toying suggestively with the stem of her glass. "Amber tells me you and Quincy were detectives together in New York," she said.

His eyes dropped to her breasts. "And she told me you're an actress."

"I've done one *Murder She Wrote*, two lines in a Clint Eastwood movie, and seven commercials. My agent says I'm almost ready to break through. Lately I've been thinking about hiring a manager, it's the smart thing to do."

He tried to look interested. "Really?"

"My nutritionist has a client who hired a manager, and her career took off immediately. It's worth the extra ten percent."

"It is?"

"Yes, Michael. How much do you know about show business?" Her long fingers continued to rub the stem of the glass.

Jesus! Did she know she was turning him on? "Not a lot."

"I look at it this way, I either hire a manager or I take it all off for *Playboy*. Now that's a *real* attention getter. Kim Basinger did it and never

223

looked back. So did Joan Severance."

"Who's Joan Severance?"

"Hmm . . . ," she said, frowning. "I guess it didn't have as much impact as she'd hoped, although she's on TV a lot."

He'd forgotten what dating was like. Two people out on a crap-shoot. It wasn't for him.

"I've done some *Playboy* test shots," she said.

"Yeah?"

"They loved my body."

He really wanted to be with a woman who stripped down to nothing for some jerk-off magazine.

"They said my breasts were perfect," she announced proudly.

It was obvious Shelia knew nothing about the double murder and his missing child. That was fine with him, because he had no desire to discuss it with a stranger — especially this stranger.

Dinner seemed interminable. Shelia continued to drone on about her career, while he listened, trying to pay attention, but nevertheless he couldn't help thinking about his little daughter and where she could possibly be. Thoughts of Bella consumed him. It would be that way until he found her.

Shelia ate a hearty meal, polishing off a shrimp cocktail, a large pepper steak, and a huge dish of apple pie. After dinner she ordered a brandy and finally got around to asking him a couple of questions about himself.

He answered briefly. Crass as it might seem, he wasn't out on a blind date to start a relationship. Quincy was right, he was out to get laid. Period.

And it shouldn't be too difficult. He'd never had any trouble getting women into bed; in fact, it was only too easy — his good looks did it every time. Women were suckers for handsome, they took one glance and simply couldn't resist. Sometimes it saddened him. Didn't they care about the person inside? He was so much more than just a glossy exterior. He had so many cravings, and yet there'd never been a woman who satisfied him emotionally.

Outside the restaurant Shelia said the magic words. "Would you like to come back to my place for coffee?"

Translation: *How about a fuck?*

"Yeah, that'd be nice," he said.

She lived in a small one-bedroom apartment on Fountain Avenue with two angry-looking cats named Arnold and Sly, who prowled restlessly around the apartment, glaring at him with steely elongated eyes.

"I recently ended a steady relationship. How about you?" Shelia asked, handing him a cup of instant coffee in a colorful Superman mug.

"Divorced," he said, taking the coffee and sitting on the couch.

She sat down beside him. He took a gulp of the hot liquid, put the mug on the coffee table, and slid his arm around behind her, pulling her in for a long kiss. After a few moments of heavy kissing activity she got to her feet, took his hand, and pulled him silently into the bedroom.

It wasn't until they fell on top of her bed, locked in a steamy embrace, that he unhooked her bra and realized that what he'd thought were magnificent breasts were actually silicone implants. Easy enough to tell — they felt unreal, like a couple of solid plastic beach balls. If he weren't so horny he would've lost his hard-on. As it was, he hadn't gotten laid in months, so there was no stopping him now.

She thrust a hard nipple into his mouth. He sucked for a moment before groping for his wallet and removing the condom he'd been carrying for a while.

Shelia was already going for his zipper, pulling it down with an expert's touch.

He handed her the rubber. "Here, sweetheart, you put it on," he suggested in what he hoped was an encouraging fashion.

To his dismay she tossed it carelessly to one side. "I hate those things. We're both safe — who needs it?"

Oh, shit! This AIDS thing had him very nervous. "Uh . . . I'd feel happier," he mumbled.

"*I* know how to make you feel happier, baby," she crooned, and with that her mouth descended on him, going to work like a dentist's suction tube.

Christ! She wasn't giving him time to enjoy it. He came so fast he felt like he was back in grade school!

As soon as it was over he wanted out, but Shelia had other ideas. Throwing off the rest of her clothes, she lay back spread-eagled on the bed and commanded, in an *I take no prisoners'* voice, "Eat me, baby, eat me!"

He stared at her muff, a neat little strip of brown pubic hair shaved into submission. Whatever happened to good old bushy triangles?

"The . . . uh . . . the shrimp," he said vaguely. "I got a feeling it disagreed with me."

"What?"

He was already zipping up and getting off the bed. "We'd better finish this another time. I'm not feeling good."

She wasn't pleased. In fact, she was furious.

He made a daring escape, reached the street, and sat in his car for a moment, leaning his arms on the steering wheel. Sometimes he understood why paying for it was a sought-after alternative. You didn't have to buy them dinner, listen to them talk, and you certainly didn't have to give them head.

Even more important, if you wanted to wear a condom there wasn't a hooker on earth who would argue with you.

19

Bobby received an advance copy of *Style Wars*. His photograph on the cover was arresting. He'd allowed their star photographer to capture him stepping naked from the shower — although of course you couldn't see the goods because he was emerging from a frosted shower door and his pertinent bits were hidden. However, it was quite obvious he was bare-assed naked. The photographer — a manic woman with frizzed red hair and a seductive personality — had talked him into it. She'd been so persuasive and full of positive energy he'd agreed. After all, Sly had posed naked for the cover of *Vanity Fair*, and Demi Moore made a habit of it. He'd wanted the photo to make a statement. Boy, did it make a statement!

Seeing it in full color on the front of a national magazine was somewhat startling. He almost laughed aloud — it was a kick. At least his body looked buffed and ready for anything, all that jogging and working out had paid dividends.

The caption on the front of the magazine read in bold red letters: BOBBY RUSH — BODY OF THE YEAR. And underneath, in smaller print: *"Bobby Rush moves in and muscles Dad straight out of the picture,* by Kennedy Chase."

228

That didn't thrill him, his publicist had assured him there would be no mention of his father.

He picked up the intercom and buzzed his secretary. "Beth, get me Elspeth on the line," he said, drumming his fingertips impatiently on the desk.

"She was around earlier, Bobby, shall I try to page her?"

"Do that. Have her come straight to my office."

"ASAP."

With a certain amount of trepidation, he opened the magazine and turned to the article. There were six more pictures. He studied the photos first, steeling himself to read the copy because he'd had a feeling that it was not going to be flattering.

Giving interviews to the press was a treacherous path to travel at the best of times, with this devious lady it was probably a minefield.

Okay. So now he was going to read it. Take a deep breath, get past the headline and see what she has to say.

Bobby Rush — a paler clone of Big Daddy, Jerry — thinks he's hot stuff, and he struts it all the way around the studio he acts like he owns. This is about the only time Bobby acts, because baring it all seems to be his skill de jour. What a great tight ass! And don't we all know it. Daddy would be proud.

It got worse.

Why is Bobby Rush a star? Could it be that Big Daddy used his considerable clout in a town so open to a touch of creative nepotism to get him where he is today?

He groaned and threw the offending magazine across the room, just as Beth popped her head around the door. "Something wrong, Bobby?"

He attempted to make light of it, although he was churning up inside. "No. I've just been portrayed as asshole of the year — why should anything be wrong?"

Beth looked suitably sympathetic. "I'm sorry."

"*You're* sorry. Where the hell is Elspeth?"

"She's on her way."

It was unfair. The entire interview was an unfounded attack on his integrity as an actor and as a man. Kennedy Chase intimated that the only reason for his success was his famous connections, and she carried on endlessly about Jerry and what a fucking icon he was.

She should only know the truth. That he, Bobby Rush, was a success because of *his* hard work and nobody else's. That Jerry would have been happier if Bobby'd stayed in his shadow forever.

But no — Kennedy Chase wasn't interested in the truth. She'd tricked him into being interviewed and hadn't given him a chance.

He felt so betrayed. As far as he could remember, he'd behaved perfectly decently toward the woman, and yet for some unknown reason she'd decided to trash him.

Elspeth entered his office with tightly drawn lips and a ferocious expression. She was carrying a copy of *Style Wars*, which she waved in his face. "I read it," she said, before he could utter a word. "I will *never* work with this magazine again. I am furious!"

She was furious! How about him? He was supposed to be the star around here.

"Elspeth," he said evenly, "how did this happen? I was under the impression we had assurances that they were not going to mention Jerry. That's why I cooperated on the pictures and gave them a day of my valuable time."

"Do I know?" said Elspeth, as if it had absolutely nothing to do with her. "Did you see what that bitch said about *me?* She described me as unprofessional."

"I don't give a shit what she said about you," he snapped. "You're supposed to be in control of the press. What happened here?"

"I am *not* unprofessional," Elspeth said heatedly. "Do you think I can sue?"

"Concentrate on the subject at hand, which is me," he said pointedly. "Everybody in town reads this magazine. I look like a total jerk."

"It's not *my* fault." Elspeth shook her head as if to convince herself. "I fixed up the first interview, and you failed to show."

"I failed to show because *you* failed to tell me about it."

"Whatever," Elspeth said vaguely. "Kennedy Chase was supposed to come back and spend the day with you."

"I told you what happened — you should have followed through. I knew when she didn't return my calls she was going for a kill."

"I contacted the magazine," Elspeth said. "They assured me she had all the information she needed."

"Sure she did," he said bitterly. "She combed through my clippings file, picked out everything negative, and decided the father connection was the way to go."

"It's done now," Elspeth said flatly. "Too late to change anything."

"Is that all you have to say?"

"You can't always have good press, Bobby."

He was fast losing patience. "I'm not getting through to you, am I? I went on your word, you let me down."

"It won't happen again," she said tightly.

He had a strong urge to fire her, but he hadn't yet learned how to be ruthless, even though, growing up, he'd watched his father do it plenty of times. The great Jerry Rush got off on firing people.

Can him — he's an asshole.

Give the dumb broad two weeks' money and throw her out.

Prick — get rid of him.

Yeah, Jerry was pretty good at booting people out.

Bobby closed the magazine and pushed it to the side of his desk. "Okay, Elspeth, I guess there's nothing I can do."

"I guess not," she said flatly.

He wanted her out of his office before he lost it. She didn't really give a shit, all she was concerned about was the way she'd been portrayed.

It had been a long day. In the morning he'd

232

gone on a location scout. Later that afternoon they'd had a production meeting, followed by two hours of final casting. The casting process always wore him down — he wanted to give every actor and actress who came in the job, because he remembered only too well what it was like going on auditions and suffering rejection. God, it was the worst! Walking into a room full of people who looked you over with weary eyes because they'd been checking out other actors all day long. Then that awkward moment of silence before the casting woman announced your name. And after that you had to try and make a lasting impression in a three-minute interview. It was pure shit.

Unfortunately he couldn't give every actor a job, had to be choosy. But he and Mac thought alike, and they'd put together a stellar cast. They started shooting in a week, so it had better be right.

The good news was that working with Mac was turning out to be a pleasure.

The bad news was they had yet to cast the lead role of Sienna, although they had several actresses on the short list. Mac had wanted Winona Ryder or Julia Roberts, but both actresses were committed on other projects. Bobby hadn't seen anyone who struck him as right, and since they were so close to a start date and the role was pivotal, he was getting nervous. He'd talked to his production manager and instructed him to schedule Sienna's first scenes as far into the shoot as possible.

Sometimes it happened this way in movies — you edged right up to the starting line, and then miraculously everything fell into position. This movie meant a lot to him, every detail had to be right.

Style Wars would hit the stands within days. If there had been a decent article to go with the pictures he could have lived with it, but as it was, he looked like the town fool standing there in his birthday suit while Ms. Chase thoroughly trashed him. Just exactly who did she think she was?

Beth knocked tentatively and put her head around the door. "Don't forget you're meeting Mac and his wife tonight. Morton's, eight o'clock. I'm leaving now."

"Hey," he called after her. "Thanks for caring." Beth had been with him almost two years. She was loyal and efficient. He wished he could find a set assistant as smart as she was. The girl he'd hired followed him around like an obedient dog, he had to tell her everything, she possessed no initiative. Once he started shooting, he knew it wouldn't work out.

There was an alternative. Jordanna Levitt.

Yeah, sure, what a trip *that* would be. Spoiled Hollywood brat who thought she owned the world. He knew her type backwards — he'd grown up surrounded by them.

Jordanna had gotten hired because of Charlie Dollar. Who could say no to Charlie? He was the best actor of his generation — a true original. And whatever Charlie wanted Charlie got. When he asked Bobby to give Jordanna a job, he'd said yes immediately.

He'd hired her, but he hadn't seen her. Instead he palmed her off on Gary, who'd given her a tiny office in the downstairs production offices, helping out in casting. Feeling generous, Bobby had also arranged jobs for both his brothers — Len in development and Stan in accounting. If they screwed up they were out, but at least he'd given them a chance — which is more than Jerry Rush had ever given him. Still, he shouldn't complain. Jerry's total lack of interest had toughened Bobby up and filled him with an unbeatable desire to succeed.

Score a major touchdown. He was exactly where he wanted to be.

Morton's was crowded as usual. The same old mix of studio heads, stars, producers, and agents. The wannabes hovered at the bar, waiting for a table, knowing they hadn't a hope in hell of getting seated anywhere near the front of the exclusive restaurant. The maître d' juggled his customers with his usual aplomb, guiding Bobby to a side table — near the front, of course — where Sharleen and Mac waited.

Sharleen was on producer alert — primed and glossed and shimmering with steamy sensuality. She wore a clinging dress, dangerously low cut, and her pale-red hair was piled casually atop her head, a few loose curls escaping around her pretty face.

"Bobby," she murmured in a low, husky voice. "How nice to see you again."

"Nice to see you too, Sharleen. You're looking sensational."

She sat up a touch straighter, flashing a megawatt smile and plenty of cleavage. "Thank you, Bobby."

"Hey," Mac said, greeting him with a wave. "Don't know about you, but I'm beat."

"Same," Bobby said.

Sharleen pouted. "I can see you two will be great company," she said. "I suppose I'll have to entertain myself."

"That'll be the day," Mac said with a dry laugh, already fantasizing about the drive home.

"So," Sharleen said brightly. "I understand you're having a problem casting Sienna."

"We'll find someone," Mac said quickly, hoping to shut her up. They were consumed with the movie all day, at night he wanted to sit back and forget about it.

Sharleen concentrated on Bobby. "I love the script," she said, her almond-color eyes burning with intensity. "I read so many, but I couldn't put this one down. The characters are beautifully fleshed out, so full of anger and pain and real sexuality. It's very . . . European."

"Yeah, it's a good script," Bobby agreed.

"Not good — devastating," Sharleen said passionately. "And I have a sensational idea that will make it even better."

Mac was surprised. "You do?" he said, wondering what Sharleen was cooking up now.

"Yes, I do," she said, still concentrating on Bobby.

Bobby waved at a couple of agents across the room. "What's your idea, Sharleen?" he asked casually.

She leaned across the table, and he couldn't keep his eyes off her very impressive breasts.

"How old are you, Bobby?" she asked, running

her tongue across her lips.

He laughed. "How *old* am I?"

She sat back. "It's a simple question."

"Thirty-two."

"Hmm . . . we're the same age."

Yeah, give or take a year or two, Mac thought. His darling wife was thirty-five, soon to be thirty-six. She was an actress. There would be no cake with tell-tale candles.

"Really?" Bobby said.

"Yes, really," Sharleen replied. "And we look pretty damn good together."

Mac had a horrible feeling he knew what was coming next. He wasn't wrong.

"Bobby," Sharleen said intently. "Think about it. *I* could play Sienna. I'm perfect. And what's more, I'll do it because I love the script, even though Spielberg is interested in me for his next movie."

Mac wanted to smack her. How dare she embarrass him this way. "For fuck's sake, Sharleen — " he began.

"That's okay," Bobby said easily. "Sharleen's right, we'd look great on the screen together, and maybe in the future we'll come up with a script tailored for us. A comedy, perhaps. I bet you're terrific at comedy, Sharleen, and nobody ever sees beyond your spectacular body. Am I right?"

Sharleen realized that somehow this conversation had veered off in the wrong direction. "Well . . . uh . . . yes, Bobby. I've always wanted to do a comedy. Kind of a Marilyn piece; we share the same timing. But about *Thriller Eyes* — "

"Wouldn't work," Bobby said firmly. "Sienna

has to be in her early twenties or the plot falls to pieces."

"But I thought — "

"So I'll put the idea out there, Sharleen," he said smoothly, interrupting her. "You and me together in a comedy. It'll be a blast." He clicked his fingers for a waiter. "Hey — can we get a menu? I'm starving."

They rode in silence, the powerful Rolls belting around the winding curves of Sunset full speed ahead. Mac couldn't hold back any longer — blow job or not, he had to say what was on his mind. "That was a cunty stunt to pull."

Sharleen took the innocent route. "What stunt?"

"That shit about you and Bobby looking so great together and being the same age and all. The same age, my ass!"

"I'm three years older than him. That's nothing."

"*I'm* the director of *Thriller Eyes*," Mac said sharply. "The fucking director, for chrissake. How do you think it looks when my wife starts canvassing the star-producer for the lead role and I'm sitting there like Joe Schmuck comes to Hollywood?"

"I'm sorry," Sharleen said, not sounding sorry at all. "But I knew if I mentioned it to you there was no way you'd consider it."

"Damn right."

"So you can't blame me for trying. It's a wonderful psychotic role. I'd be fantastic in it."

"You'd also be at least ten years too old."

"Nonsense. A few adjustments to the script would take care of that minor problem."

"Minor problem, Sharleen? I don't think so. The script hinges on the fact that the girl is so young."

She pursed her luscious lips. "You're being difficult, Mac. You don't want me in the movie because I'm your wife."

"I'd have nothing against it if you were right for it."

"I don't believe you."

"Why not?"

"Because you wouldn't want to watch me naked in bed with Bobby Rush."

"I'm a professional, Sharleen. When I'm on the set nothing else matters except the movie."

"Easy for you to say now," she taunted, still using her low, sexy voice. "When there's no way you'd consider me for the part."

"I'd consider you if you were right."

"It's a hot script. All those explicit love scenes, the sex, the nudity . . . And the ending is so intensely emotional. No" — she shook her head knowledgeably — "you couldn't take it."

"Yes, Sharleen. I could."

"So test me for it. Let's see if it *could* work." As she spoke, her hand descended on his thigh and very slowly crept up to his crotch.

Oh yeah. Instant hard-on. She did it to him every time.

"What do you think, sweetheart?" she murmured, unzipping his fly.

"I . . . think . . . you're . . . a . . . very . . . exciting . . . woman."

239

"Good. Because I'm about to excite the hell out of you." And with that she sprung him free and bent her head.

Dreams do come true. Sunset Boulevard. Sharleen giving him a blow job. He was one lucky man.

Just as he was about to come, a police siren blasted them from behind, lights flashed, and a deep male voice boomed through a loudspeaker. "Pull over to the side. Do it now!"

Oh shit! Instead of an explosion, it was a mere fizzle. Talk about a disappointment.

Swearing under his breath, he swerved the Rolls to the curb, while Sharleen sat up, took out her compact, and began applying fresh lipstick. Nothing fazed Sharleen.

The police car pulled up behind them, and a good-looking cop emerged.

Everyone is good-looking in L.A., Mac thought sourly, stuffing himself back into his pants. They all came to town with the intention of becoming movie stars. Too bad hardly any of them made it.

The good-looking policeman strolled over cop fashion and shone a flashlight into Mac's face, almost blinding him. "Step out of the car, sir. And, lady, you too."

"Officer," Mac said, trying to sound authoritative, even though he was sitting there totally unzipped and feeling somewhat insecure. "Can you please tell me what the matter is?"

"Driving in two lanes will do it every time," the cop drawled. "Your car was zigzagging all over the place. I'm going to have to ask you to take a Breathalyzer test. Please exit your vehicle."

Satisfied that her makeup was once again perfect, Sharleen spoke up. "Officer," she purred, "I'm Sharleen Wynn."

His flashlight zoomed in her direction and hovered on her face. "It's our wedding anniversary," Sharleen continued in the same sexy tone. "And perhaps it was indiscreet of me, but I was merely giving my husband . . . how shall I say it? An early anniversary present. I'm *so* sorry if I got carried away, causing him to become . . . overheated. Next time I'll wait until we're home. Promise."

The officer was in love. Boy, did he have a story to tell the guys! "Uh . . . Miss Wynn," he managed. "That's . . . uh . . . not the smartest way to behave."

"I know, Officer," she said, fluttering her eyelashes in an age-old flirting stance. "And I won't do it again. I promise. Can we go now?"

He was almost speechless, though not quite. "Uh . . . Miss Wynn, maybe you'll give me an autograph?"

"Certainly," she said, taking his pen and magnanimously signing the back of his notebook with a flourish. "Thank you for being so understanding. I really do appreciate it."

"Don't mention it, ma'am. You be careful now."

"Oh, I will."

Mac started the car and they took off.

"Turn up Stone Canyon," Sharleen said urgently.

"It's the wrong way — "

"Now!"

241

He turned right onto Stone Canyon.

"Pull into that driveway over there. The dark one," she ordered.

"Sharleen — "

He heard the rustle of silk as she began to divest herself of her clothes. This was one crazy broad and he loved it!

Quickly he pulled into the darkened driveway and stopped the car.

"Get into the back," she whispered, peeling off her panty hose.

She didn't have to ask twice.

By the time they arrived on the back seat, Sharleen was completely naked, and they started going at it like a couple of horny teenagers. "Ohh, Mac, you're the best . . . the crème de la crème . . . the absolute best . . . ," she murmured heatedly, her hands roaming over his chest.

Sharleen had a knack for saying exactly the right thing at exactly the right moment.

Then she climbed on top of him, riding him like a stallion, her fine tits in his face, her musky scent all over him.

This time when he came, it was a monster.

Marriage to Sharleen was never dull.

20

"It's a crock, Charlie," Jordanna complained, screwing up her face. "I never *see* Bobby Rush. How can I be his personal assistant if I'm stuck down in casting, sorting through boring actors' résumés and photos?"

Charlie yawned and stretched. "Hey, kiddo, it's a job. Do you have any idea how many poor schmucks are out of work?"

"Give me a break," she said, jumping out of bed, angry that Charlie wasn't taking her seriously.

"C'mon back here," he said, half serious, half joking. "I got a hard-on that could crack ice."

"So go crack some," she called over her shoulder as she headed for the bathroom. "I can't be late for work."

She marched into his bathroom totally naked and considered her reflection in the full-length mirror. Lately she'd been suffering from the blond-hair big-tits syndrome. Usually so confident about her offbeat slender beauty, for the last few weeks she'd been inundated with big-breasted blond actresses traipsing in and out of the downstairs casting office like a parade of prize cows. Too bad Cheryl wasn't around, she'd recruit them by the dozen!

It irked her that she'd been hired as Bobby Rush's personal assistant and yet she never saw him. He was giving her a runaround like she was some new kid on the block, and she didn't appreciate it.

Growing up in Hollywood she'd met the biggest and the best. Bobby Rush failed to impress her, although his two partners seemed like okay guys. She sensed that one of them, Tyrone Houston, was on the verge of asking her out, obviously he didn't know she was currently living with Charlie Dollar.

Tyrone was very black and very sexy. If he asked, she'd definitely be tempted — only tempted, though, because now she was in a monogamous relationship, and she wanted to see if it could work.

Of course, Charlie wouldn't care — he was that kind of guy. Yesterday she'd arrived home to find his ex-girlfriend and his three-year-old child in residence. "You know Dahlia, don't you, kiddo?" he'd asked, stoned as usual. Then he'd gestured to his son. "An' this is Sport. They'll be stayin' a couple of weeks, while their place gets painted."

No, she didn't know Dahlia, but she certainly knew of her. Dahlia Summers was a regal-looking, forty-year-old talented actress, with long straight hair and a stern expression. Gossip had it that she and Charlie had been an on-off item for ten years, and when she'd pressured him to marry her he'd promptly bought her a house and moved her out.

"Hello," Dahlia had said, not cracking a smile.

"Hi," Jordanna replied, thinking that this was

244

a strange situation but one she could cope with.

They'd all eaten dinner together in the big, dark dining room. It was an odd setup, and not one she'd particularly enjoyed. If Dahlia stayed longer than two weeks she was definitely going to get restless.

"How about breakfast?" Charlie yelled from the bedroom. "I'm ordering bacon and sausages. Want some?"

"No," she shouted back. "I don't eat pigs."

"You could've fooled me," he chortled.

One thing about Charlie, he had absolutely no ego.

At the studio, she sat in her cubbyhole office sorting through endless photographs and résumés, shuffling them from one pile to another, cross-eyed with boredom. It was noon when Florrie Fisher, assistant to Nanette Lipsky, the casting director for Rush Productions, put her head around the door. Florrie was in her thirties, plump and cheerful, with braces on her teeth — placed there fifteen years too late — and a crush on every man in sight.

"You're summoned," Florrie said. "I've got an awful toothache, and I have to run over to see my dentist. There's fifteen actors coming in this afternoon, and Nanette needs plenty of help."

"What kind of help?" Jordanna asked, alarmed.

"You'll do what I do. Meet and greet. Then read through the sides with the actors, unless they're on a look-see."

"A look-see? What's that?"

"You know," Florrie said a trifle impatiently. "When you want to just take a look and see if they've aged ten years or put on twenty pounds. Oh yes, and watch out for love scenes, some of the actors can get quite carried away, and it's embarrassing. I once had an actor practically crawl up my skirt. No kissing either."

"Do I have to do this?" Jordanna groaned, not liking the sound of it at all.

"Yes," Florrie said. "It's fun, and at least you'll be in the same room as Bobby. You've been bitching you never see him, now's your chance to impress."

Impress. No way.

Nanette Lipsky was one of those small, sharp-faced women who'd been in the business for a hundred years and knew it all. She had thinning carrot-colored hair, a permanent twitch in her left eye, and a perennial cigarette dangling from parched lips.

"You know what to do, I hope," she croaked to Jordanna as they headed upstairs to the interview room.

"Sure," Jordanna replied, wondering if anyone was aware of the fact that she was Jordan Levitt's daughter. Probably Bobby hadn't bothered telling them — which was okay with her. Anonymity was next to godliness. She kind of liked it.

"Bobby and Mac are very particular," Nanette continued, puffing on a cigarette. "They do not like to be kept waiting, so get the talent in and out, in and out. No hanging around — whoever they are. When the interview is over, move 'em fast. You got it?"

"I think I can manage that."

Ah, if only Nanette knew how many actors

she'd had in and out, in and out. She stifled a wild giggle.

"Did I say something funny?" Nanette demanded, her left eye twitching out of control.

"Not at all," Jordanna replied, thinking that this was a double whammy, not only would she get to be face-to-face with Bobby but she'd see Mac too. She recalled that he'd been sensational in bed, although she'd only been seventeen at the time and not nearly as experienced as she was now.

Jordanna Levitt. Expert on men.

Stifling another giggle, she followed Nanette upstairs.

Two hours later she was really into it. She felt important and useful, and most of all, she was enjoying herself, and she wasn't even stoned!

They were a team. Bobby, Mac, Nanette, and herself. They were focused on the final casting of *Thriller Eyes*, and nothing else mattered.

Jordanna led the talent in, read a scene or two with them if it was required, and then ushered them on their way. She soon picked up the rhythm of how to do it without hurting anyone's feelings.

Middle-aged actresses were the worst to shift — especially if they had a half-assed name. They came in with plenty of attitude, the best part of their physical anatomy on show, and a yen to greet either Bobby or Mac with a big wet kiss.

Jordanna quickly learned how to circumvent that little piece of activity. She stationed herself between the couch, where Bobby and Mac sat, and the chair in the middle of the room, where the talent parked themselves. She did not move until everyone was settled.

"Very clever," Mac said admiringly, when she'd done it a couple of times. "You learn fast."

She knew that after fifteen minutes she had Bobby's attention. Good. It was about time he realized she existed.

Reading through scenes with the actors and actresses was fun. She got to play a variety of characters — male and female. Her only regret was that she hadn't taken the time to study the script beforehand. It seemed to be an interesting piece of material — but then Mac had a knack of making the right choices. His movies might not all be box office winners, but they were always intriguing and on the edge.

The last interview of the day was a long-haired young actor in ripped jeans and cowboy boots. He was reading for the minor role of a security guard. The scene took place between him and the character of Sienna.

It was a short, seductive piece, and Jordanna gave it her all, enjoying the twists and turns of the cutting dialogue. When they were finished, Mac and Bobby conferred for a few minutes, then requested they read the scene again. Jordanna and the actor obliged.

Another conference. Another repeat performance.

They must like him, Jordanna thought, taking another glance at the young actor. He did have a certain charisma that was quite sexy.

When she led him from the room he was vibrating with nervous energy.

She eyed him up and down. "Pumped, huh?"

He cracked his knuckles. "You got it! They had me read the scene three times, they must've thought I was good."

"I guess so."

"You *guess?* Can't you tell?"

"Hey — I'm new at this."

"How about finding out what they say and meeting me for coffee at the place across the street?"

What did she have to lose? She was in no rush to go home on account of Charlie's houseguests.

"Sure," she said. "See you there in fifteen minutes."

"I'll be waiting," he said, flashing a Midnight Cowboy smile. Nice teeth. An even better butt.

She hurried back into the interview room. "That's it," she said. "He was the last one."

Bobby, Mac, and Nanette were all staring at her.

"What? What have I done?" she asked anxiously, sure that she'd screwed up in some major way.

"Jordanna," Mac said at last, "have you ever thought about taking up an acting career?"

"You'll never amount to anything. Do you understand me? You're nothing — a roach — lower than a roach — you're a fucking roach turd. Do you understand me?"

Yes. He understood his father. He was ten years old, and he understood that he deserved his father's eternal rage. He didn't know why. It was merely a fact of life. Something he took for granted.

His mother never sprung to his defense. She merely nodded sadly, as if every word his father uttered was the truth and nothing but. She nodded in agreement and stared at him with mournful eyes. And when his father went out she held him to her bosom and crooned old love songs to him in a low, shaky voice.

Before she married his father she'd been a Las Vegas showgirl, and she hung on to her show business memories as if she were Marilyn — sometimes telling tales of her great triumphs with men.

The Man didn't know much about feelings. Women were whores, he knew that. Bitches and whores.

This was what his father had to say about

women: "Never, never, let 'em get to you. They're all cheap hookers, an' don't you forget it, 'cause if you do, they'll screw you into an early grave an' leave your heart in fuckin' ribbons. They got makeup on their faces an' witchcraft in their two-timing cunts. Remember what I told you, son, an' you'll never go wrong."

Yes, Dad.

And Dad was right. Women were the betrayers. Women had to be punished. And he was doing an excellent job as he drove down the freeway, heading for his third victim.

Of course, if he'd listened to his father he'd never have gotten involved with The Girl. She'd lured him with those blue eyes and that quirky innocent smile, pulling him closer, tempting him, encouraging him. Until one day he'd accepted her invitation to be seduced . . .

Well, he'd shown her. He'd shown everyone.

Sometimes it puzzled him that he was punished for doing what any sane man would do. He'd put his hands around her soft white throat and choked the breath out of her. Squeezed tight until she flopped in his arms like a useless rag doll.

She'd deserved it.

Bitch.

Whore.

A white van, driven by a thin-faced youth with a wasted blonde draped all over him, passed by on the inside lane. The girl leaned over and honked the horn, then the van cut in front of The Man, causing him to apply his

251

brakes sharply. The van speeded up and took off, its occupants doubled over with laughter.

The Man didn't carry a gun. Perhaps he should. If he'd had a gun he could have killed scum like the two people in the van. He could have blown them away. Sent them to join The Girl in the place where she rested, repenting her sins.

Ha! If he had a gun he could do a lot of things.

He put it on his shopping list.

The off-ramp beckoned him, telling him he was near his destination. Pasadena. A peaceful place. When his list was taken care of, he would have to find somewhere decent to live. Pasadena wouldn't be bad. The tree-lined streets were wide and pleasant enough. He could see himself living there.

He drove down the street full of confidence, because he knew exactly where he was going. Previously he'd checked out the house where his victim lived in a downstairs apartment. He'd even gained access and looked around at his leisure while she was out at work. She was a bank officer. No more dreams of Hollywood and stardom, she'd gotten out of the business seven years ago, right after the trial. Sensible girl. Hollywood was nothing but a bargain basement filled with secondhand talent. A cesspool of out-of-control egos.

He should know. He'd seen the things that went on.

Seven years ago he could have become a star if things had gone as planned. He could have been as big as Steven Seagal.

But no, it wasn't meant to be. The Girl had ruined everything, and the traitors surrounding her had helped.

But they were paying for their bad behavior. One by one they were paying.

21

"There's a case I want you to come in on," Quincy said as they jogged through the park.

"I got things to do," Michael replied restlessly. "People to talk to."

"Yeah, things to do. Meanwhile how you gonna pay your rent? Listen, Mike — if *you* don't join me, I gotta hire somebody else."

He knew Quincy was right, he had to work — if just to occupy his thoughts with something other than Bella. "So what are you offering — a partnership?"

Quincy threw up his arms. "Don't let's get carried away. First you'll work with me a couple of weeks, see if you like it. Then we can talk partnership."

"I won't like anything until I find my kid."

"I know that," Quincy said, already out of breath. "We'll keep doing our best." He almost tripped. "Jeez — can we stop? I'm bustin' a gut here."

"You're out of shape, Q."

"I'm older than you."

"No excuse."

"I'm gonna be fuckin' fifty!"

"All the more reason to stay fit."

They rested by a tree. Quincy doubled over, groaning and catching his breath.

"Okay, so I'm in," Michael said, making a fast decision.

Quincy straightened up. "Jeez! It's about time you said yes."

"Tell me about the case."

"There's this daughter of big-shot billionaire, Franklyn Sanderson. He owns TV stations across the country. You've probably heard of him."

"I know who he is."

"Anyway, the girl — Marjory — she's been receiving a series of letters threatening to slit her throat or kill her in some god-awful way."

"How many?"

"One or two a week for the last few months."

"Has Sanderson contacted the police?"

"No publicity. This is strictly low key. That's why he brought me in."

"What do you have?"

"Not much. The letters are postmarked from all over the city. The girl's frightened."

"How specific are the letters?"

"Look, I gotta go see her later today. She moved back home with her old man. Come with me, I'd like your take on it."

Michael agreed. He had to do something to keep himself busy.

The Sanderson estate, set way back off Sunset Boulevard, was impressive. Two guards manned the ornate heavy gates, while three fierce-looking rottweilers patrolled the grounds. Quincy stopped his car and produced identification before they gained entry.

"This is like fucking Fort Knox," Michael remarked as they drove up a long winding driveway through acres of immaculately kept grounds. Passing an elegant fountain in the forecourt, they glimpsed the house up ahead, a slightly smaller version of a stately European palace.

A valet ushered them from the car, while a formally dressed butler waited at the front door.

"This way, sir," said the butler in a clipped and very precise English accent.

Michael tried to appear at ease as he entered the mansion, but he couldn't help thinking to himself, *Holy shit! If the guys from the neighborhood could see me now. How people live in California!*

They followed the butler into an enormous living room, tastefully furnished with French period furniture and ornate antiques.

"Kindly take a seat," the butler said, looking down his nose at them.

Michael roamed around, taking in his surroundings, marveling at the opulence of it all. He whistled softly. "Some place!"

"Yeah," Quincy replied. "You get used to it after a time — most of the big shots live this way."

"They do?"

"It's one of the perks of bein' in the movie and TV biz."

"I couldn't imagine living like this."

"Fortunately, my friend, you'll never have to."

"Yeah, remind me."

A thin, plain girl entered the room. Dressed all in white, she had long fair hair and downcast eyes.

Quincy got up and went over to greet her. "Marjory, how you feeling today?"

"I received another letter," she said, in a barely audible voice.

"Do you have it with you?"

She glanced nervously at Michael. "Who's he?"

"My colleague. Michael Scorsinni. He's helping out."

Her pale-blue eyes stayed fixed on Michael. "Does Daddy know?"

"I spoke to him, told him I was bringing somebody in. Michael and me were partners in New York."

She thrust a piece of paper at Quincy. "This is the latest."

Michael watched her closely. Boy, she was agitated, she couldn't keep still. Her hands, in constant motion, pulled at her hair, her dress, anything she could get hold of.

Quincy read the letter, scrawled in red ink on a lined page torn out of a school notebook. The handwriting was barely legible. He handed it to Michael, who scanned it quickly.

Rich Princess, You will die soon. Your money can't save you.

"Where's the envelope?" Quincy said.

"I have it," she replied, her eyes darting around

the room. Fishing in the pocket of her dress, she passed a crumpled envelope to him.

Quincy took it, weighing it in his hands. "Your father here today?"

She shook her head. "Daddy's out of town."

"So you're by yourself?"

"There's eight servants and two guards on the premises," she stated blankly.

What a way to live, Michael thought, staring at the skinny little thing. No wonder she was scared, obviously she had not grown up in the real world, and the letters came as a rude shock.

"When do you think you'll find this man?" Marjory asked with a frightened expression.

"I'm working on it," Quincy said confidently. "Building up a profile. You know — handwriting analysis, putting together where the letters were sent from, all that stuff. It takes time, but we'll nail the sonofa— I mean, the perpetrator — eventually. The good thing is you're safe as long as you're here. And if you need anything at all, I'm only a phone call away."

"Thank you, Mr. Robbins. That's very reassuring."

Later that day Michael met with Rosa. She'd called and invited him down to the television station to sort through some of the letters they'd received after his interview.

"This is it, Michael," she said, leading him into her office and indicating a huge sack full of letters. "Your fan mail. I thought you'd want to take a look through it."

"Fan mail?" he asked with a note of surprise.

"I told you we had a fantastic response to the program."

"Any information that could help me?"

"I really don't know. A couple of kids in the office read them. Whether there's anything pertinent is up to you to find out."

He was daunted by the big sackload of letters. "I'll take 'em home," he decided.

"You know, I've been thinking," she said, moving around her desk. "Isn't it about time you got out and had some fun?"

He laughed dryly. "You sound like my best friends. They're always after me to do just that."

"I have a suggestion. My girlfriend, Kennedy Chase, is smart, attractive, and available. She writes for a magazine, and it occurred to me you might make an interesting couple. How about I fix the two of you up?"

"How about *not*."

"Huh?"

"I'm not into blind dates. In fact, right now I'm not into dating at all."

"It wouldn't exactly be a blind date. I've told you what she looks like."

"Thanks, but I'm not going out right now."

"Hmm," Rosa said thoughtfully. "That makes two of you."

"What do you mean?"

"I told her about you, she doesn't want to go out either."

He laughed. "So what are you trying to promote here?"

She smiled back. "Apparently nothing."

"Listen," he said, thinking she was a very attractive woman. "I appreciate your concern."

"Ah," she said wistfully. "If I was single, Michael, I'd be more than concerned."

"You're married?" he asked lightly.

"Taken," she replied, wishing for a moment that she weren't.

"Sounds serious."

"I'm hoping."

They smiled at each other, and Rosa decided that Kennedy had made a big mistake turning this one down. He was a great-looking guy with a very sexy edge. Not to mention his mouth — full lips . . . sensual lips . . .

"Michael," she said, pulling herself together, "it's time to do a follow-up piece on you before people forget. This is my suggestion, take the letters home, read through them, then give me a call by the end of the week and we'll set up another appearance."

He was unconvinced. "If you think it'll help."

"I'm sure it will," she said, very positively. "People love watching real-life dramas, and your story is extremely appealing. The more attention we can bring to it the better. You should feel fortunate you've got this opportunity to be on television. Actually," she added playfully, "you should be kissing my ass."

"Rosa, if I was in a better mood, I'm sure there's nothing I'd like better."

She laughed flirtatiously. God! She must be crazy to let this one go. "Ohh, Michael, I bet you can be a bad one."

They exchanged smiles again and he left, stopping at a small Italian restaurant he frequented for dinner. He sat outside at a table for one and ordered a simple plate of pasta.

The pretty waitress was all over him. "Alone again, Michael?" she asked, a definite come-on in her voice.

"That's the way I like it," he replied, thinking that there would be no women. His experience with Shelia had made him realize that unless it was meaningful it simply wasn't worth it. And how could anything be meaningful until he'd found Bella?

Or her body . . .

The thought that his daughter might be dead haunted him. It lurked in the shadows of his mind and refused to go away.

He ate his pasta and drove home to his apartment, stopping at the supermarket for a carton of milk and two bottles of fresh orange juice.

Once home, he took the big sack of letters and tipped them out onto the floor, staring at them for a while before sorting them into neat stacks.

Somewhere in one of the piles of envelopes there might be valuable information. He could hope, couldn't he?

By seven o'clock he was reading.

22

Jordanna was in a state of shock. Mac Brooks and Bobby Rush were actually considering testing her for the role of Sienna in *Thriller Eyes*. It was like one of those insane dreams come true.

She would never forget the look on their faces when she walked back into the room. The three of them sitting there staring at her — Bobby, Mac, and Nanette.

And then Mac came out with the famous words, "Jordanna, have you ever thought about taking up an acting career?"

"Who, me? No way," she replied, flip as ever, although of course she had.

"You're good," Bobby said. "You're really good."

She barely glanced in his direction. "Hey, I was just following the actors," she said, gathering up photos and résumés, trying to appear uninterested.

"Here's the thing, Jordanna," Mac said. "We're searching for someone to play Sienna. It's a challenging role, and so far we haven't come up with the right actress. You could be her."

"I could?" She gulped.

"Yes, you could."

"What we thought," Bobby said, joining in, "is that we should run a test on you."

"Test *me?*"

"I don't see anybody else in here."

"Well, yeah, sure," she said, attempting to sound nonchalant, although her stomach was jumping butterflies. Dammit — she was probably coming across like a total idiot. What was it about Bobby that made her completely lose it?

Mac nodded seriously. "It's worth a shot. After all, you come from a talented family."

That was the trouble — her talented family. Like Jordan always said, how could she live up to the great Levitt reputation? On-screen her mother, Lillianne, had been an incandescent presence, a beauty who made grown men drool. And a wonderful actress too.

"Uh . . . let me think about it," she mumbled.

"We'll do the same," Mac said.

She left the office as fast as she could, full of mixed emotions. She almost forgot about Midnight Cowboy waiting across the street, but he hadn't forgotten her. He was right there, waving anxiously, when she drove out the studio gates.

"What did they think of me?" he demanded.

"They . . . uh . . . they liked you very much."

"Did they think I was good? What did they say about my reading?"

"They loved it," she lied, not wanting to tell him it was her they were interested in.

His words were tripping over each other. "Have I got the part? I know it's only a small role, but Mac Brooks is an ace director, and I'd sure get

263

off on working with Bobby Rush. Who's set for the girl?"

"Beats me," she said vaguely.

She had a coffee with him while she mulled things over. Should she tell Charlie? Or her father? What if her test was terrible and they hated her?

Oh, God, what had she got herself into? This was ridiculous.

Midnight Cowboy was on a roll, talking about himself. He told her he'd come to California four years ago, done some modeling, then a few one-liners in movies. He stated that he wanted to be as big as Clint Eastwood. "And I will be," he said, actually believing it. "One of these days."

Sure, baby, she thought, *And Clinton will grow flowers out his ass and boogie down Main Street.*

Eventually he made his pitch. Normally she would have said yes, because he was real hot-looking, with the requisite tight butt. But wasn't she supposed to be improving her life?

Gotta stop sleeping with actors. Especially the tight-butt brigade.

She jotted down his phone number, told him she'd call him later, and drove back to Charlie's.

The place was buzzing. Charlie was entertaining. He sat in the middle of his old brown couch, smoking a joint, surrounded by hangers-on. His son, Sport, crouched at his feet, playing with an electric train set. Dahlia lingered at the bar sipping Perrier, her face long and mournful.

"I didn't know you were having a party tonight," Jordanna said accusingly, thinking he could have warned her.

Charlie smiled dreamily, his eyes on a space

264

trip. "Hey, kiddo, it's only a little celebration —
for Sport."

"He's three, Charlie," she pointed out.
"Shouldn't the guests be younger?"

He chuckled and offered her a drag on his joint.

She declined. She'd been dying to tell him her
news, and now he was too stoned to care.

"I'm going up to my room," she said. Like he
gave a shit. He was too busy playing genial host
to a roomful of drugged-out freeloaders.

Once in her room, she slammed the door, put
on a CD of Madonna singing "Bad Girl," and sat
back on her bed.

Opportunity knocks. Was she going to open the
door or not?

Picking up the script of *Thriller Eyes*, she started
reading.

The role of Sienna was wild. In fact, if Sienna
hadn't turned out to be a psychotic killer at the
end of the piece, she would have been a lot like
Jordanna.

Reaching for a yellow marker, she went through
the script again, highlighting certain passages, saying the words aloud, getting deep into the character.

Wistfully she thought it would have been nice
if Charlie was around to read with her, but no
— he was too busy partying, and she had no desire
to join in.

Madonna gave way to Prince, singing "Cream."
The music drowned out the noise coming from
downstairs. She glanced out the window and observed that the party was getting bigger. Valet
parkers were shuttling cars back and forth, and

there were now two catering trucks parked around the side.

Charlie should have told her he was planning a party. She did live there, after all.

Around midnight she decided to venture downstairs and check out the action.

There were people everywhere, spilling out onto the terrace, crowding the bar, hanging out around the swimming pool. The smell of pot was heavy in the air. A skinny girl — star of a TV sitcom — sat cross-legged on the floor, popping pills, while a well-known country singer in snakeskin boots and matching vest snorted cocaine from a side table. Belly dancers undulated their way through the crowd, and the noise was deafening.

She didn't know anybody except Cheryl, who held court on the big leather couch, surrounded by two bimbo-type blondes, an underage redhead, and several attentive men. Charlie was nowhere to be seen.

She went over. "What are *you* doing here?"

"Hi," Cheryl said vaguely. "I wondered where you were."

"Conducting a little business?" Jordanna asked, indicating the girls gathered around her.

"Socializing," Cheryl replied, sipping a tequila on the rocks. "It's good to socialize."

"So I see."

"Is it true you're living here now?"

"Yes."

"Thanks for telling me. I had to find out from Shep."

"I never see you anymore, Cheryl, you're always too busy."

266

"Business comes first."

"I guess business is booming."

"In this town, always," Cheryl said, attracting the attention of a waiter. "Another tequila rocks," she said tersely, before turning back to Jordanna. "You seen Grant?"

"Is he here too?"

"Over by the bar."

She had no intention of hanging around Cheryl and her merry band of hookers, so she fought her way through to the bar, where Grant had a Chinese girl pressed up against the wall. They were exchanging tongues.

"Grant," she said, tapping him on the shoulder.

He stared at her with a foggy expression.

"Jordanna," she said, adding a sarcastic "Remember me? We grew up together."

A stupid grin spread across his face. "Yeah, Jordy . . . How's it goin'?"

He was stoned out of his head, and when Grant was stoned he was bad news. A couple of years ago he'd had a serious heroin problem. His father had found out and forced him into rehab. When he got out he'd been fairly straight. Now he was obviously back on the merry-go-round.

The Chinese girl pulled him back toward her, wiggling her tongue in his face. "C'mon, honey baby, let's get into it," she crooned.

"See ya, Jordy," Grant said, his stupid grin firmly in place.

She wandered around the party, searching for Charlie. Where the hell was he? And why did he want all these stoned people in his house?

She poked her head around the kitchen door. Chaos reigned as the caterers did their stuff. Mrs. Willet was nowhere to be seen, she'd probably taken off the moment the party started.

Back in the front hallway, she was just in time to see Arnie arrive, accompanied by another batch of hangers-on.

"Levitt!" Arnie exclaimed, hardly able to believe his luck.

"Arnie," she replied coolly.

"Where's the man?"

"He's around."

"Haven't seen you in the club lately. You've missed some radical nights."

"I've been working."

"*You?*" He chortled with laughter. "Working? I don't believe it."

"Fuck you, Arnie."

Arnie turned to his friends. "You see," he said proudly. "She loves me."

Jordanna stalked away and headed upstairs. She was about to go to her own room, when she changed her mind and decided to wait for Charlie in his bedroom. Eventually he'd stagger upstairs, and then she could talk to him about her test, maybe even read through some key scenes with him. That's if he wasn't too out of it.

She entered his large, untidy bedroom. It was dark, but she could hear noises. "Charlie?" she said, switching on the light.

His head was between Dahlia's legs, eating her pussy like he'd been on a starvation diet. He came up for air, completely unembarrassed at being caught. Dahlia lay there without moving, her face a study in stoicism.

"Oops," Charlie said, his half-crazed smile at full mast. "I guess you caught me with my mouth in the cookie jar!"

She stared at the two of them. Her heart was beating very fast, but she managed to remain calm. "Yes, I guess I did," she said quietly.

"Wanna join in, kiddo?" he asked, raising an extravagant eyebrow.

She shook her head. "No, thank you, Charlie." And with that she turned the light off and left the room, closing the door behind her.

It was definitely time to move on.

Midnight Cowboy got a call at one A.M. He was asleep. "Who's this?" he mumbled.

"Jordanna. Remember me? I read with you at the casting session today."

"Hey, yeah, Jordanna — what time is it? Have I got the part?"

"Oh, like I'd be calling you at one A.M. to tell you that you got the part," she said edgily. "I gave you a good recommendation, can't do more than that."

"So what's up?"

"Thought I'd drop by."

"Now?"

"No, tomorrow morning."

"Yeah, yeah, yeah — come by now. It's cool."

"Where do you live?"

"Venice."

"Shit."

"What?"

"You mean I've got to drive all the way to Venice?"

"You don't gotta do anything."

"Okay, give me directions."

Throwing a few things in an overnight bag, she took off, her Porsche zooming all the way down Wilshire to the beach. She felt let down and hurt. Okay, so she hadn't been foolish enough to imagine Charlie was a long-term relationship, but she also hadn't expected to find him in bed with his ex-girlfriend while she was still living in the house. Men. They always let her down. That's why she was better off with one-night stands. Hit and run. Make out on *her* terms.

Rule number one — never stay around long enough to get hurt.

Midnight Cowboy's tumbledown house was situated in a rough neighborhood near the boardwalk. She left her car on the street, hoping it wouldn't get vandalized or stolen.

He greeted her in Levi's and nothing else. Great body. Great sex. And he didn't mind using a rubber. At least she made *that* concession to good behavior.

In the morning her Porsche was still there, untouched by human criminal. She drove back to Charlie's, took a shower, and changed clothes.

Mrs. Willet was sipping tea in the kitchen. "Are you moving out, dear?" she asked, quite cheerful for a change.

"Haven't made up my mind yet," Jordanna replied, grabbing an apple from the fruit dish. "Sorry to disappoint you."

"I thought with Miss Dahlia and Sport moving back in . . ."

"That's a temporary arrangement."

"No." Mrs. Willet was adamant. "Mr. Dollar assured me they'd be here on a permanent basis."

"Well, good for Mr. Dollar," she said, biting into the apple as she walked over to the door. "Tell you what, Mrs. W., if I *do* decide to move, you'll be the last to know."

The hatchet-faced housekeeper glared at her.

At the studio, there was a message for her to report straight to Bobby's office. She lingered in the ladies' room first, studying her reflection in the mirror. She looked good. Bright-eyed. Too enthusiastic? No. When it came to scoring a role in a major movie, there was no such thing as too enthusiastic.

Bobby Rush threw her off balance. He knew all her secrets, so to speak. He'd lived the same experience and come through unscathed. It was unnerving. *He* was unnerving. She couldn't quite get a beat on him, he seemed so together, and yet she — better than anyone — knew how difficult it must have been growing up with Jerry Rush as your father.

She also found Bobby undeniably attractive, even though he wasn't her type. Oh no, not at all. She liked them young and hungry or old and successful. Bobby didn't fit into either category.

They were waiting for her when she entered the office. Bobby sat behind his desk, while Mac paced around the room. "Take a seat," Mac said. "And for chrissake relax."

Easy enough for him to say. She was uncomfortable, excited, filled with trepidation. Oh, God, it was so unlike her to be nervous.

271

"So," Mac said. "Have you given our idea some thought?"

"Yes," she said, trying to sound cool and in control. "If you still want me to test, I'll do it."

"Did you mention it to your father?" Mac asked, chewing on his thumbnail while watching her intently.

"Why would I do that?" she snapped.

"I thought — "

"Mac," she interrupted heatedly. "I don't even *live* there anymore — why would I tell Jordan?"

Bobby got up, came around his desk, and stood in front of her. "Your mother was an actress, wasn't she?"

"Yes," she said, beginning to feel really uptight.

"So how come you never wanted to try it before?"

She decided to be honest. "Because my father told me I'd have too much to live up to."

He burst out laughing. "That's *exactly* what I heard from my old man, and look at me today."

Yeah, look at you. I saw Style Wars, she wanted to say, but she curbed her tongue for once. This was her chance to do something she'd always wanted, and she wasn't about to blow it.

"We'll test you today," Mac said. "Bobby'll test with you."

"When?" she asked nervously.

"This afternoon."

Her stomach churned. "I can't do it that soon."

"Why not?" Mac asked, quite reasonably.

"Because . . . because I need more time," she stammered, unable to come up with a better excuse.

"Don't worry about a thing," Bobby said, patting her on the shoulder in what she considered a patronizing fashion. "You'll go over to wardrobe now, then we'll sit down for a couple of hours and read through the test scenes." He fixed her with his incredibly intense blue eyes. "Jordanna, trust me. It'll be okay."

Sure. For him it would be okay, for her it would be a fucking nightmare.

She returned downstairs in a daze.

The good news was that she was going to test. The bad news was that now, everybody knew who she was. Somehow word had leaked.

Florrie greeted her with a frown and a sharp "Why didn't you tell us who you were?"

"What was I supposed to do? Take out an announcement in the trades?" she fired back.

"No," Florrie said, with a hurt expression. "But you could have confided in *me*."

Oh, yes, confiding in Florrie would be like buying a full-page ad in *Variety*.

Jordanna noticed that people were treating her differently. The kids around the office, who'd once been so friendly and nice, were now either distant or fawning all over her.

Nanette called her into the main casting office and gave her a vigorous pep talk. "Listen, dear," she said, squinting while dragging hungrily on her cigarette. "You might be able to pull this off, or maybe you won't. The camera loves some people, hates others. Nobody knows until you get in front of it." She expelled a stream of lethal smoke into Jordanna's face. "I'm sure you're aware they wanted Winona Ryder for this role."

273

Oh, great, make me feel really secure.

Over in the wardrobe department, a bossy woman in ill-fitting dungarees tried to talk her into wearing a short red low-cut dress for the test.

"No," she said, going on instinct. "My character wouldn't wear this, it's too cheap-looking."

"*I* know what the character would wear better than you," the wardrobe woman said, ready for a fight.

She refused to be swayed. "I won't test in that dress," she said, searching through several racks of clothes until she came across a simple white silk suit. "Sienna doesn't flaunt her sexuality, she's more subtle," she explained, holding the outfit up against herself. "This'll be perfect."

The wardrobe woman made a face and reluctantly agreed she could wear it.

Reading through the scenes with Bobby was painful. She wished she had a joint. She wished she were stoned. She wished she weren't there.

Oh, Charlie, where are you when I need you?

Bobby was pleasant enough, but he got impatient if she didn't do things his way, and that made her even more edgy. As she got into the character, she could feel the vibrations of Sienna. *I know this girl,* she thought. *I know her very well. She's real fucked up. And if it wasn't for the fact that I'm a survivor, she could've been me.*

"What are you thinking?" Bobby asked, placing his script on a table.

"About the character and her hang-ups," she said, hesitating for a moment. "I understand her psychology. Sienna's a little crazy, like me."

He raised an eyebrow. "*You're* a little crazy,

274

Jordanna?" he said, teasing her.

"You know what I mean, Bobby. I'm sure your life hasn't always been easy."

Their eyes met, and for a brief moment there was a strong connection.

"Right," Bobby said, breaking the look as he picked up the script again. "Let's read the second scene one more time."

The two scenes they'd chosen were quite different. One took place at the beginning of the movie, when Sienna was supposed to be naive and innocent. The second happened near the end, when her madness finally manifested itself.

Jordanna enjoyed reading the second scene most, playing psychotic was easy.

After they'd rehearsed awhile longer, Bobby got up and said, "That's it — you're on your own. Get yourself over to hair and makeup, and I'll see you on the set." He took her hand and squeezed it. "Good luck."

No flip reply came to mind. What was happening to her?

"Thanks," she mumbled. "I'll . . . uh . . . I'll try my best."

23

When Kennedy saw *Style Wars* she went into a fury. They'd taken her piece on Bobby Rush and totally reworked it, adding a whole load of material about his father and his hang-ups, all the stuff Mason had wanted. And her name was on the interview. *Her name!*

She called Mason in a white-hot rage. He blamed it on an overzealous copy editor. She told him exactly what he could do with his job. He pleaded with her to reconsider. She didn't know what to do, this had never happened to her before and she felt utterly betrayed.

Rosa came over and calmed her down. "You need a good lawyer," she advised. "Stay with the magazine and get a legal document stating that in the future, they can't change a word or you'll sue their ass. Why blow a good gig?"

Angry as she was, Kennedy agreed it was an excellent idea.

Rosa sat on the floor in the living room, performing leg lifts. "There's been another murder," she said.

Kennedy snapped to attention. "When?" she asked.

"A few nights ago, in Pasadena."

"Who was the victim this time?"

"Another woman, strangled in her apartment. She lived with her boyfriend, but he was out of town." Rosa stretched her legs to the left. "Here's the kicker: *exactly* the same MO. She wasn't raped or robbed, and the killer left a 'Death to the traitors' sign on her body. It's not public knowledge, but one of our news guys is tight with the county sheriff's department, and they got a report of the murder on the teletype. The sign matches one left on the woman in West Hollywood."

"What do the police say?"

"Nobody's releasing any statements."

"That's three women strangled within a couple of months."

"I know."

"What did this one do?"

"She was an officer at a bank."

"Hmm . . . ," Kennedy said thoughtfully. "Did you know the other two both worked on movies? Margarita was a makeup artist, and I found out that Stephanie Wolff was a script supervisor."

"That could be coincidence. It's certainly not enough to connect them."

"I know. But surely somebody should be investigating other than me?"

"You're right."

"Who's in charge of this case, Rosa?"

"The problem is that all the murders took place in different counties, so there's several investigating officers. I'll see what I can find out."

"Do that."

The next morning she attempted to call Bobby Rush, anxious to apologize. It was no surprise when he failed to take her call. She sat down and wrote him a letter explaining what had happened. At least it made her feel better.

Detective Carlyle was an overweight slob who ate doughnuts for breakfast, smoked cheap cigars, and was saving up for a hair transplant. He'd been on the force too long to care about anything much, he had too many personal problems.

First, there was his wife — she wanted him to retire and go live in Montana. Second, there was his mistress — *she* wanted him to divorce his wife and move in with her. Mostly Detective Carlyle was lucky to make it through the day.

When Kennedy Chase requested an interview, he turned her down. Obviously the woman had connections, because an hour later his captain called him in and informed him that he had to see her.

"What I gotta talk to a magazine writer for?" he grumbled.

"She's doing a story on that woman who got herself strangled. You'd better make sure our department comes out of this looking good."

"Okay, okay," Detective Carlyle said, agreeing reluctantly.

When Kennedy strode into his office he got a shock, he wasn't expecting a classy-looking blond broad with a sensational body. He perked up considerably. "What can I do for you, honey?" he asked with his best *I'm a stud* smile.

"You can stop calling me honey for a start," she said briskly, taking a seat on the other side of his desk and crossing impressive legs.

Another uptight feminist. Whatever happened to the days when you could compliment a woman without getting a snotty put-down?

"What can I do for you, *Miz?*" he asked, heavy on the sarcasm.

She chose to ignore his attitude. "I'm writing a piece on three women who've been strangled in L.A. over the past couple of months."

"Yeah, yeah," he said dismissively. "The one in West Hollywood's the only one concerns me."

"Why's that?"

" 'Cause she's the only one where the crime took place in my division."

"But isn't there a feeling that the cases might be linked?"

"Where'd you hear that?" he asked cagily.

"It doesn't matter where I heard it."

"It matters to me."

"I'd like all the information you have."

He cleared his throat. Snotty broad — who did she think she was? "The only information I can give you is that we have no proof of anything as of now."

"How can you say that?" she said forcefully. This guy was verging on being a moron. "The murderer left a 'Death to the traitors' sign on the last two victims, there *has* to be a connection."

Carlyle shifted in his seat, he was dying to let a fart, but this uptight drill sergeant would probably complain. "Rest assured we're investigating," he said, fed up with being grilled.

She uncrossed her legs and rose to her feet. "When you have something, I'd appreciate it if you'd give me a call."

She handed him her card and left.

As soon as she got home she reviewed her files. She'd interviewed several people who'd known the first victim, Margarita Lynda, and they'd all spoken highly of her. According to her neighbors, she was a hardworking woman with plenty of friends.

She'd also found out that Margarita was divorced and had lived by herself, with no current boyfriend. The ex-husband was not a suspect, he'd died in a car accident six months ago.

According to her best friend, Margarita used to enjoy going to country-and-western clubs Saturday nights. It was an interesting lead. Maybe Margarita had met someone there: a man who'd followed her home . . . a stalker who preyed on women living by themselves.

The second victim, Stephanie Wolff, was a different case. A lesbian, with a tight circle of friends, she'd lived with her elderly mother, and her only interest had been her work.

The only thing the two women had in common was that they'd both worked in the movie industry.

Gerda Hemsley, the third victim, didn't seem to tie in.

Kennedy hadn't questioned anyone about Gerda yet, but she planned on doing so.

Later she called Rosa. "How about going line dancing one night?"

Rosa hooted with laughter. "*Line* dancing?"

"You'll love it," she assured her.

"Are there men there?"

"Cowboys."

"Okay, count me in."

"I knew I could."

"By the way," Rosa added, "I keep on forgetting to tell you."

"What?"

"I talked to Michael the other day."

"Michael?"

"You *know*, that incredibly good-looking ex-detective I wanted to fix you up with?"

"Oh yes, another one of your fabulous blind dates."

"The funny thing is he doesn't want to go out with you either."

"Wow," Kennedy said dryly. "I'm really heart-broken."

Rosa laughed. "Hmm . . . What can I tell you? You're probably perfect for each other."

"Too bad we'll never find out."

24

Jordanna had never had such a feeling. Standing in front of a camera with a crew watching her every move, being the center of attention, becoming another character. It was the most dizzying, amazing, awesome experience. She felt important — really important — for the first time in her life. Never mind that she'd grown up on film sets, been surrounded by movie stars at home; *this* was the real thing, *this* was magic.

Bobby seemed pleased with her performance, so did Mac. They did several takes on both scenes, and then all too soon it was over.

"What happens next?" she asked Mac as they strolled from the set.

He threw his arm around her shoulders. "We'll see how you come across, and if it works we'll show the test to the studio guys who'll make the final decision."

"What do *you* think?" she asked hopefully. "Have I got a chance?"

"This is a new you," he replied affectionately. "You actually sound vulnerable."

"Sure I am," she replied seriously. "Why wouldn't I be?"

" 'Cause all I've ever seen is the other side of

you. The tough biker-chick image, with hot and cold running guys."

"I'm changing my life, Mac," she said earnestly. "I moved out of the poolhouse. I don't take money from Jordan anymore. I'm finally getting it together."

"That's good to hear. You know, Jordanna, I've always had a special feeling for you."

She tried flirting in a jokey way. "Special enough to put me in the movie?"

Shaking his head, he laughed. "Hey, c'mon, you know it's not up to me."

She left the studio in a daze, trying to be cool but filled with great expectations. God! What would everyone say if she got the part. Jordan, Charlie, her friends, a legion of Midnight Cowboys with tight butts and hungry eyes. Wow! It would really blow everyone's mind.

And if she did get it, her life would change. She'd have a career, a reason to get out of bed in the morning. She would be somebody in her own right, not merely Jordan Levitt's daughter.

It occurred to her that because she *was* his daughter, they might not take her seriously.

No. Had to think positively. She had a fair chance. Look at Bridget Fonda, Laura Dern, Anjelica Huston. Plenty of Hollywood kids made it, you just had to be prepared to try harder to prove your own worth. And she was ready to do that. She was *really* ready.

"Hey, kiddo." Charlie was happily ensconced in front of his giant-screen TV in the den, while

Sport played at his feet with a selection of toy soldiers. Dahlia was nowhere to be seen.

"Hi, Charlie," she said evenly, wondering if he felt even the tiniest bit guilty about their last encounter.

He threw her a quizzical look. "Mrs. W. tells me you didn't spend the night."

"That's right."

As if on cue, Mrs. Willet bustled into the room, picked up Sport, and said, "Time for this little man's dinner."

"Good," Charlie said, waiting until she was gone before returning his attention to Jordanna. "Where were you?" he asked, using the remote to click off the TV.

"I had an appointment with sex."

He chortled. "You're pretty out there, kiddo." A beat. "Anyone I know?"

"Not your generation, Charlie."

He scratched his head. "A young one, huh?"

She wanted to hurt him as much as he'd hurt her. "Tight butt, hard dick. I needed to jog my memory."

He took a longer beat before replying. "Sorry if you've got an attack of damaged feelings, but I never promised you fidelity."

"I know."

"So why are you upset?"

"Because . . . because . . ." Why *was* she upset? Could it be that she'd expected something from him that he wasn't capable of giving? Could it be that she *had* expected fidelity? "Because I thought . . ."

"Yes?"

"That we had something special."

"We do."

"What?" she asked, genuinely puzzled.

"Friendship. I *like* you, Jordanna. Don't you like me?"

"Yes, Charlie."

"Then drop it. Dahlia's back. She doesn't mind you being around. See if you can feel the same way about her."

"I can't," she said honestly.

"Too bad."

"I'm moving out."

"Where to?"

"I'll find a place."

"Do you need money?"

She'd sooner work for Cheryl than take money from him. "No, thank you. I'm fine."

"Well, kiddo, you know you're welcome here anytime. My door is always ajar. Give it a kick and come back in whenever you want."

She didn't know where to go, she knew only that she had to get out. She couldn't go home to Daddy anymore. Shep was hardly likely to welcome her again. Cheryl was probably knee-deep in girls. And Grant was wasted.

That left Marjory. Even though she was living at home, the Sanderson estate was bigger than a hotel, and Franklyn Sanderson spent most of his time on his private jet. Yes, Marjory seemed like a good idea, so she went upstairs and called her.

Marjory was happy to hear from her and insisted she come right over. She packed a couple of bags and left a note for Mrs. Willet, saying she'd send for the rest of her stuff.

One of these days she had to find a place of her own, this was getting ridiculous.

Maybe if she got the part in the movie . . .

Don't even think about it, she told herself sternly. *Do not get your hopes up.*

She left the house with no regrets. And once more it was a girl and her Porsche against the world.

Marjory seemed to be in a lively mood.

"How come you moved home again?" Jordanna asked, settling into one of the lavish guest suites.

"Daddy insisted," Marjory replied, pulling at the hem of her pink cashmere sweater. "Because of the letters."

Jordanna frowned and began unpacking one of her bags. "You're not still getting them?"

"Regularly."

"Where do they come to?"

"He *was* sending them to my apartment," Marjory said, fiddling with her long pale hair. "But now they're coming here."

Jordanna opened a bureau drawer and threw in some T-shirts. "That's creepy," she said. "Like he's watching you."

"I know," Marjory agreed.

"What's your father doing about it?"

"He's hired a private detective."

"You've got to be careful."

"I am."

For a moment Jordanna thought she might confide about the test. Then she changed her mind.

Wait and see, a little voice warned her. *Don't go announcing something that might not happen.*

286

Later she fell asleep missing Charlie, but knowing for sure she'd made the right move. Charlie was a talented man with a big heart, but when it came to relationships, he was totally insensitive.

In the morning she reported for work as usual, hoping to hear something — anything — even if they didn't like her, she'd sooner know than not.

Nobody said a word. She was stuck in the casting cubicle, sorting through photos as if nothing had happened.

At the lunch break Florrie entered the room, perched on the side of her desk, and came out with a halfhearted apology. "I suppose it was smart of you to keep who you are a secret," she said, chewing on a breath mint. "Sorry I let it out."

"It wasn't that I kept it a secret," Jordanna explained carefully. "I simply didn't advertise."

"*Why* are you working?" Florrie demanded rudely, as if it were her right to know. "You must have tons of money."

"It's not *my* money, it's my father's."

"Isn't that the same thing?"

Jordanna decided there was no point in carrying this conversation further. "Uh . . . Florrie," she said, attempting to sound nonchalant. "What's happening upstairs?"

"Same old same old," Florrie replied, obviously about as sensitive to the situation as a plank of wood. "Actors in, actors out. Oh, and that girl from TV came in — Barbara Barr. The one from that big-deal nighttime soap. Y'know, she's always in the tabloids. Anyway, she read for Sienna."

Jordanna felt her heart jump. "Was she good?"

"They're putting her on video."

Now her heart was pounding. "Really?" she said, trying to sound as if it didn't matter.

"After lunch."

"Did you hear anything about my test?"

"Nope," Florrie replied, picking at her nail polish. "But it doesn't matter, does it? It's not like you're a proper actress or anything. I expect they were getting desperate when they tested you. There's two more Siennas coming in this afternoon, and three videos of New York actresses."

Jordanna managed to remain expressionless as Florrie rattled on. She didn't think the girl was being mean or even bitchy — merely thoughtless. Everyone imagined that if you had a famous parent, it was enough, you didn't need anything else — certainly not a job. In a way, she could understand Cheryl's delight at becoming a successful Hollywood madam. She'd made it in her own right, not because of Daddy and his studio.

"I'm not eating lunch today," Florrie confided, removing her big butt from Jordanna's desk. "I have to lose three pounds by Saturday. I've got a date with that cute guy over in promotion, the one with the new Acura Legend."

Three pounds won't cut it, Jordanna thought. *Try fifteen.*

Florrie wandered off. Jordanna sat still for a moment, considering her next move. Should she go and badger Mac, or sit tight and wait to see what happened next?

Sit tight. Stay cool. Do not get panicked.

But I am panicked. Totally. I want this part more

than I've wanted anything in my entire life.

Chill out.

Fine.

Midnight Cowboy called the casting office in the afternoon. Her luck she answered the phone.

"Any news?" he asked, sounding as agitated as she felt.

For a second she thought he was asking about her, then she remembered she hadn't mentioned her test to him. "Uh . . . no. But if there is, the casting director will contact your agent."

"Fuck!"

"What?"

"I hate this waiting-to-find-out crap."

"I know exactly what you mean."

"Fuck!" he repeated, as if it were her fault. "Can't you go in and *ask?*"

Nice of him to tell her what a wonderful time he'd had the night she'd driven over to his place and given him the best sex he'd probably ever experienced.

Nice of him to be so solicitous and charming and concerned.

If he knew she'd tested for Sienna he'd throw a fit!

She almost told him, but changed her mind. "I gotta go," she said. "Work beckons."

"Call me as soon as you hear?"

Don't hold your breath.

The rest of the day dragged. She caught a glimpse of Marcy Bolton, another young actress who arrived to read for Sienna, accompanied by her manager.

She's too short. Her face is pointed, like a ferret's.

And she's wearing too much makeup.

When Florrie emerged from the interview room on her way to the bathroom, Jordanna grabbed her. "What was she like?" she demanded.

"What was who like?" Florrie replied vaguely.

"Marcy Bolton. Did she read? Was she good? How did they react?"

"Mac seemed enthusiastic."

"And Bobby?"

"He was okay with her."

Tell me she stunk, Florrie. Tell me they hated her!

"Has anyone else read for Sienna?"

"They're viewing the New York tapes now."

Jordanna wished she could burst into the office and watch with them, get an eye on the competition. "How's your tooth?" she asked Florrie, hoping that maybe she'd have to go back to the dentist.

"It's all right," Florrie replied, moving her tongue around her mouth. "If ever you need a good dentist . . ."

No, Florrie, I do not need a good dentist. I need answers, and I need them now!

Mac came down to see her at five-thirty. She stared at him expectantly, waiting for the good news. He cleared his throat, looking everywhere except at her.

"So?" she said at last. "What's the verdict?"

"Sorry," he said, rubbing the bridge of his nose. "I fought for you, but the studio won't go for it. They say you don't have any experience — which unfortunately is true, but in my opinion we could have made it work." He patted her on the shoulder. "If it's any consolation, you came across like dynamite."

The disappointment that enveloped her was so overwhelming she could barely breathe. "Who's got the part?" she managed to get out.

"Barbara Barr."

She's totally wrong. Doesn't anybody realize that?

"Is . . . is Bobby happy?"

"Between you and me, he's not ecstatic — after all, she's TV. But this is an important movie for him, and he wants to please the studio. They've decided that since we can't get a star at this late date, it's prudent to go with Barbara. She has an enormous TV following and garners front-page publicity. They think it'll work."

"Do you?"

"I wouldn't agree to cast her if I didn't."

So that was it. Big opportunity out the window.

Normally something like this would have set her off on a self-destruct course. Drinks, drugs, Midnight Cowboys. But lately she'd been feeling more centered, and the never-ending cycle of trying to cure things with transient remedies had to stop.

I can handle it, she told herself. *I can and I will.*

She'd handled the Charlie situation when he'd screwed around on her. Okay, so she'd run to the actor in Venice. Big deal. It had made *her* feel better, she hadn't gotten wasted, and she *had* used protection. Score one for a change of direction.

The truth was she'd finally realized she was responsible for her own life. No more brooding about

Jordan and his series of wives, they were his business, not hers. At last it was becoming clear. No more punishing herself.

"So that's the end of my brilliant career," she said ruefully.

"You're taking it well," Mac replied, obviously relieved.

"I'm a big girl," she said, full of false bravado, because she'd learned early on that the best way to survive was to hide your true feelings.

"And a smart one," Mac said. "Bobby's giving you a shot as his personal assistant. He'd like you to go up to his office."

From movie star to PA in one minute flat. Quite a leap. "Sure, Mac."

"Oh, and Jordanna?"

"Yes?"

"We're going to have fun making this movie. That's a promise."

She smiled wanly, still hiding her disappointment. "Okay, Mac, if you say so."

"Good morning, Mister President." The Man cleared his throat and tried again, lowering his voice to a macho growl. "Good morning, Mister President."

The Man stared at his naked reflection in the mirror and repeated the greeting twice more.

If circumstances were different, he could have been the President of the United States. It was possible. The great American dream was always attainable. Look at some of the men who'd made it. Carter — a peanut farmer. Reagan — an actor. Kennedy — a womanizer.

Ah . . . what it must have been like in the days of Kennedy, when the media were not snooping around every corner, photographing every move. President Kennedy had gotten away with plenty.

The Man decided to add President Kennedy to the list of men he admired. Of course, the dead President would not knock Steven Seagal from the top spot, because Steven Seagal was a true hero. Unbeatable.

The Man continued to study his reflection in the mirror. "Good morning, Mister President," he said in a whispery female voice à la Marilyn

Monroe. "How ya doin', Mister President?"

It occurred to him that there was a certain similarity between Monroe singing "Happy Birthday, Mister President" to President Kennedy and Barbra Streisand crooning one of her mournful love songs to President Clinton.

The truth was that all Presidents were whoremongers. He knew that. America knew that. It didn't seem to make any difference. In America, looks were everything, and the best-looking scored the most points.

I am very good-looking, *The Man thought smugly.* I am very handsome. I could have been a famous movie star if the breaks had been different.

A knock on his door startled him. How dare anybody disturb him. How dare they interrupt his precious solitude.

"Who's there?" he called out.

"Shelley."

Shelley? He didn't know anybody called Shelley. In fact, he didn't know anybody at all. He was alone, and that's the way he liked it.

"You must remember me," Shelley said hopefully. "I live in the house. We bump into each other sometimes. My mother sent me a homemade fruitcake, and I'd like to offer you a piece."

"No," he said abruptly.

"Please," she wheedled. "Yesterday was my birthday."

He didn't wish to arouse her suspicions. "I'll be out shortly," he said gruffly.

"Come to my room — it's by the pool."

He wondered if Shelley wanted him to fuck her. That's what most of them were after. Most of them except The Girl, who'd led him on, and then, when he'd tried to consummate their relationship, she'd treated him like a stranger.

On reflection, he was glad he'd killed her, even though he'd been forced to accept the harsh and unfair punishment.

AND THE TRAITORS SHALL DIE FOR GANGING UP AGAINST ME. EVERY ONE OF THE BITCHES AND THE WHORES.

He remembered meeting The Girl for the first time. So pretty and beguiling — it had not been difficult to fall in love with her.

But she'd made one fatal mistake. She'd rejected him. She should never have done that.

He dressed quickly, unlocked his door, relocked it behind him, and went looking for Shelley.

He found her in a large room overlooking the old tile swimming pool.

Though her door was open, he did not enter immediately but stood hesitantly on the threshold.

"At last," she said, rushing to greet him. "I thought I'd never get you here."

He entered the room, hovering awkwardly in the middle of the floor.

"I can offer you herb tea, apple juice, or wine," she said.

"Nothing."

"You know, John — you don't mind if I call you John, do you?"

John? And then he remembered he'd told her

his name was John Seagal, which of course was a lie. "No," he said flatly.

"What do you do all day?" she asked curiously. "I never see you around. You seem so . . . lonely."

"I told you, I'm a writer."

"Do you write screenplays?" she asked excitedly.

He noticed that her hair was the same color as The Girl's. Natural yellow, not dyed like most of the hussies in Hollywood.

"Books," he said.

Now she was even more impressed. "That's serious. What kind of books?"

"Vendettas."

"Vendettas?"

"Revenge. If somebody does you wrong, then you must see they get their comeuppance."

"Oh, you mean like **Death Wish.** I love those movies where Charles Bronson walks around blowing the bad guys away. Why don't you write a movie like that?"

"I told you — I don't write movies."

"Shame. You could've written one for me, and when I'm a star you could've written all my movies. Then I could tell everyone, 'No, sorry, I only work on John Seagal films, he's my closest personal friend.' " She hesitated a moment before rushing on. "And actually you are, because I don't have any friends in L.A. I hardly know anybody."

He found it hard to believe that a pretty girl like Shelley knew hardly anybody.

It occurred to him that maybe his uncle had been talking to his mother and they'd arranged to put the girl in the house to spy on him. Nothing they did would surprise him.

Thought for the day: If she was a spy he'd have to kill her.

"How come you're here?" he asked.

"A friend borrowed the place from a girlfriend of hers, and she kind of passed it on to me."

"You told me you didn't have any friends," he said accusingly.

"She's just a girl I met at acting class."

"You go to class?"

"Yes."

He wished he could go to acting class, but it was impossible. Had to keep to himself. People were treacherous, and the less he mixed with them the better.

"I'm moving soon," Shelley revealed. "My acting teacher is going to Europe for three months, and he's asked me to house-sit."

"Where's that?" he asked, not really interested.

"Way up Laurel Canyon," she said. "It's a lovely small house, completely secluded. Perhaps you'll visit me."

He nodded.

"Let me get you a piece of cake," she said, moving across the room. "I'm from Utah," she called over her shoulder. "Where are you from?"

There seemed no harm in telling her. "New York."

"You won't believe this," she exclaimed, "but I've never been to New York."

She was wearing shorts and a skimpy T-shirt, and as she moved back toward him, carrying a plate, he noticed her small breasts bouncing up and down beneath the thin material.

He'd not had a woman in a while. That initial rush of whores when he'd first left jail had sated his sexual appetite, but now . . .

What if he decided he wanted to fuck Shelley? Would she allow him to? Or would she react the same way as the one with the yellow hair and start yelling and screaming and kicking until he'd been forced to put his hands around her soft white throat and squeeze tightly until he'd shut her up.

Shelley handed him a piece of fruitcake on a blue plastic plate. "Taste that," she said, licking her fingers. "It's delicious." She paused for a moment, then blurted out, "Can we go to a movie one night?"

He considered her invitation. "No," he said.

"Why not?"

"I'm on a deadline."

"Is that why you're always locked in your room?"

"Yes."

"I never hear a typewriter."

"I write in longhand."

She looked impressed. "Oh, you're a real writer. That's so exciting." A pause, then — "If you're ever lonely, John, you can knock on my door, because I'm always here. We could listen to music."

He tasted the cake. It was sticky and sweet.

He imagined Shelley without her clothes.

Soft skin . . . sweet skin . . . sticky skin . . .

He knew he had to leave immediately. It wouldn't do to get aroused in front of her.

He took another bite of cake and walked to the door.

"Are you going?" she asked, sounding disappointed.

"I have to."

"Don't forget," she said hopefully. "Drop by anytime."

"I won't forget."

He returned to his room, closed and locked the door, stripped off his clothes, and resumed his pose in front of the mirror.

Now he could allow himself to be aroused.

He stared at himself so long and so hard that his own reflection came back at him, and he felt exactly as if he were staring into the soul of another being. It was an eerie feeling.

After a while he began stroking and caressing himself until the moment was upon him, and when he climaxed he stifled a cry of pure anger, stuffing his fist against his mouth to stop the sound from escaping.

Later that night he slipped quietly from his room.

It was time to deal with victim number four.

25

The late Gerda Hemsley's boyfriend was a big man with rugged features, crew-cut red hair, and a worried expression. He was the manager of a sporting goods store. Kennedy came to see him at his place of work. He wasn't happy when she introduced herself and told him she was writing a story.

"I'm trying to put this behind me," he said, agitatedly glancing around. "Gerda was a fine woman. We lived together a year, and then . . . this. Now everything's gone crazy. I had to move out of our apartment yesterday. I can't stay there without her."

Kennedy made an instant evaluation and crossed him off as a suspect. She always trusted her immediate reaction when it came to people, and she sensed this was an ordinary guy caught up in a bad situation. "Have the police questioned you?" she asked.

"Yes," he said grimly. "As if they had a right to. It isn't enough my girlfriend gets murdered, now *I* become a suspect." He paused for a moment. "You know what's happening in this country, don't you?"

"What?"

"It's the criminals that get treated right," he said heatedly. "The innocent people are the ones that end up with no justice."

She nodded. "I'm sure you're right."

"I *know* I'm right," he said forcefully.

A sales clerk came up with a request for him to sign off on a check. He did so.

Kennedy took out her notebook. "Can I ask where you and Gerda first met?"

He frowned. "Are *you* questioning me too? Do *you* think I'm a suspect?"

"Of course not," she said, realizing what a strain he must be under. "I'm writing about several other women who've been murdered in the same way. Two of the women worked in the movie industry, Gerda in a bank. Can you tell me what she did before that?"

"She was a bookkeeper at an accountant's office."

"And prior to that?"

"Her mother knows. She can tell you."

"Do you happen to have her number?"

He wrote the mother's number down on the back of a receipt and handed it to her.

"Thanks," she said. "I'll leave you alone for now, I can see you're busy."

He nodded abruptly and walked over to the cash register.

She made her way to the front of the store and stood outside for a moment before crossing the parking lot.

He caught her before she reached her car, startling her. "Sorry," he said, out of breath. "But you must understand — this isn't easy for me."

"I *do* understand," she said sympathetically.

"Look." He hesitated, having trouble talking. "I'm glad you're trying to do something. You have no idea what it's like when somebody close to you is murdered." He paused before continuing, choking back his emotions. "If they ever catch the guy who did it, I'd like to personally hang him up by his balls."

Kennedy nodded understandingly. "If it were up to me I'd make sure you could."

She called Gerda's mother from the car. An answering machine picked up, so she left her name and number and requested a return call. Then she set off to meet Rosa for lunch.

The restaurant was crowded, and Rosa was excited, her brown eyes sparkling. "Listen, Kennedy," she said. "I'm about to suggest something, and I insist you say yes, because it's a *fantastic* idea."

Oh, God, Rosa never quit. "If it's a man . . . ," she began.

"*No.*" Rosa interrupted quickly. "It is *not* a man. It's business, pure business — okay?"

She sighed. "All right, tell me about it."

Tapping her long scarlet fingernails on the table, Rosa said, "The situation with these murdered women is getting out of control, and since the police are not exactly active, my station has decided to adopt it as our story. We're all very excited. And I came up with a *brilliant* idea. *You're* going to appear on camera and talk about it on the evening news."

Kennedy almost laughed aloud. Rosa had really lost it this time. "*Me?* On television? You've *got* to be kidding. I don't even watch it, let alone appear on it!"

"I am *not* kidding. You'll do it," Rosa said, eyes flashing.

"Why would I?"

"I'm telling you, there's a serial killer out there. It's time the police formed a task force, and we can make them. The power of TV is awesome. You'll see."

"I'm sorry, there's no way I can do it."

Rosa wasn't listening. "Don't worry — you'll be great."

"Says you."

"My news director's joining us for coffee. If you haven't said yes by then, he'll talk you into it. And no, Kennedy, *do not* get turned on, he is *not* available."

Kennedy began to laugh. "Finally, a man who's *not* available. And this will be the one I'll want — right?"

Rosa laughed too. "Yeah, *right*."

Kennedy was apprehensive. It was all happening so fast. She should have said no and listened to her gut instinct, but Rosa and her news director had been very persuasive.

She sat down and wrote an editorial, then she went over it with the news director, who was enthusiastic.

Rosa advised her on how to behave in front of the camera. "It's easy. Sit still and get a fix straight into the camera. When the monitor rolls, you'll see your words come up on the TelePrompTer. All you have to do is read 'em. It'll look exactly like you're talking directly to the viewers."

"Are you certain this is going to help?" she asked tentatively, not sure at all.

"Positive," Rosa guaranteed.

"Then why don't *you* do it?"

"Because they're used to me. They see me on the news every night. You're a big-time journalist. Our viewers will love it."

"I *am?*"

"Yes, you *am.* Your *Style Wars* cover story on Bobby Rush is pretty controversial. *USA Today* did a piece about it. You're hot right now, and we'll use that factor to boost ratings."

"I am not responsible for that story."

"Think about it this way, you'll be doing some good. If we can get the chief of police to put together a task force, then we'll have done our job. Remember the Hillside Strangler, a few years back? This is beginning to be just as bad."

"Okay, okay, I'll do my best."

They did a run-through. What an ordeal! She stumbled and stuttered, feeling like a complete fool. Later she went into the makeup room, where they proceeded to put too much blush on her, and a deep-green eye shadow she hated. "I can't stand all this makeup," she complained.

"TV lighting washes people out — especially blondes," Rosa explained. "This way your features will come across."

Next the hairdresser teased and sprayed her hair. "Oh, God! I look like a Barbie doll," she moaned, peering in the mirror.

"No, you do not. You look magnificent. Stop having a fit."

By the time she got back in front of the camera, she was nervous. *Really* nervous.

The news team began taking their positions. Rosa and her co-anchor — a black man with crinkly hair and a deeply reassuring voice — sat at the center of a curved desk, while the other regulars gathered around them.

Kennedy's mouth was so dry she didn't know whether she'd be able to say anything. Who *needed* this kind of stress!

Finally the cameras started to roll. She watched Rosa slip easily into her anchor role and felt slightly better. If Rosa could do it, so could she.

By the time the studio manager gave her the signal to start speaking, she was like a greyhound at the starting gate — ready to win.

Taking a long, deep breath, she began to speak.

"So," Kennedy said after the show, feeling quite elated. "I've done my part, now it's your turn — we're going line dancing."

"Are you certain this is a good idea?" Rosa asked unsurely, as they left the studio.

Kennedy got behind the wheel of her Corvette. "Whether it is or not, we're doing it."

"Maybe we should have brought Ferdy with us."

"I have a feeling he'd stand out," Kennedy said dryly. "Somehow I don't think these country-and-western dives are exactly crawling with six-foot-four black basketball players."

Rosa agreed. "I suppose he isn't exactly unobtrusive."

They drove to Boots, on Pico Boulevard, pulled

into the large parking lot, and got out of the car. Rosa immediately began worrying about her appearance. "Is my ass too big for these jeans?" she said anxiously. "I'm sure people are going to be pointing at me, saying, 'There's that anchorwoman with the big fat ass.'"

"Oh yes, that's what they come here for — just to spot celebrities with big butts."

"You'd be surprised. This is Hollywood, babe. Celebrity spotting is what it's all about."

"You've got it wrong — people come to these places to learn to dance. They're into this whole cowboy thing."

"Bullshit," Rosa replied succinctly. "They come here to get picked up."

"Margarita wasn't the type."

"Every woman's the type if she's available."

"I don't think so. Take me as your prime example."

"Oh, *you*. You're hardly normal."

"Thanks a lot."

The place was packed. Would-be cowboys abounded, circling the vast round bar that took up the entire center of the huge space. There were a few booths against the wall, and several standing stations, where you could place your drink and survey the action that took place on a large dance floor, where groups of people indulged in two-stepping and line dancing. Good old country togetherness.

"Jeez!" Rosa exclaimed. "Am *I* in the wrong place! This is Americana City. I bet I'm the only Hispanic here. I'll probably get beaten up in the parking lot!"

"Calm down," Kennedy said. "We'll have a drink, take a look around, then we're out of here."

"I don't believe these guys," Rosa exclaimed, checking out the passing parade of men. "Look at 'em. Cowboys by night, accountants by day."

"How do you know?"

"Hey — you think real cowboys would walk around like that, with their ten-gallon hats and sassy attitude. Honey, I can *assure* you, they *ain't* real cowboys."

"So now you're an expert on cowboys. I thought basketball players were your thing."

"Do me a favor — buy me a beer and let's make this short."

They approached the bar. "Howdy, little ladies," greeted the barman, confirming all their worst fears.

"I suppose a martini's out of the question?" Rosa said, perching on a barstool.

He chortled happily.

"Two beers," Kennedy said.

"This your first time?" the barman asked, with a gap-toothed leer.

"How *did* you guess?" Rosa drawled sarcastically.

"You can have a real blast if you leave your cares on the doorstep."

Rosa's eyebrows shot up. "You got that out of a fortune cookie at Trader Vic's — right?"

His face was blank. "Trader who?"

"Forget it."

"I suppose you get a lot of regulars here?" Kennedy asked, leaning her elbows on the bar.

" 'S'right," he replied. "Regular as clockwork.

They come in, dance four or five hours, then go home happy. That's our motto at Boots — put a smile on your face and a spring in your step."

"Oh, *please*," murmured Rosa.

"Will you shut up," Kennedy whispered. "I'm trying to make contact here."

"Make contact, my ass," Rosa said. "Ooh, there goes a cute one." Her attention was taken by a blond hunk in a plaid shirt, jeans, and a brown Stetson.

They made eye contact, and he swooped. "Care to take it to the floor, ma'am?" he asked politely.

"Why not?" she said, winking at Kennedy.

"Little lady's gonna fit right in," the barman remarked as Rosa hit the floor with the hunk.

"My friend Margarita used to come here," Kennedy said, showing him a picture. "Do you remember her?"

"I know a lotta people, but names ain't my strong point." He squinted at the photograph. "Naw, don't recall her."

"You might have read about her," Kennedy continued. "She was murdered a couple of months ago."

"Was she murdered here?" he asked matter-of-factly.

"Here?"

"I'm not supposed to say this." He leaned across the bar, speaking confidentially. "We had a coupla rapes in the parking lot."

"You did? When?"

"The last one was a few weeks ago. Course, they've beefed up security since then."

"Margarita wasn't raped, she was strangled. It's

possible she might have been followed home from here."

"Really?" he said thoughtfully. "You a relative?"

"No, I'm a writer," she said, handing him her card. "If you come up with anything, give me a call."

He peered at her card. "Kennedy. That's a funny name for a girl."

"What's *your* name?"

"Brick."

"Oh, that's much more sensible . . . for a boy."

Before he could react, she took her bottle of beer, moved away from the bar, and stood at the edge of the dance floor, where she watched Rosa make a complete fool of herself as she tried to two-step with the young stud, who had his arms all over her. Trust Rosa to get right into the spirit of things.

"Okay, folks! Time for a little line dancing!" the disc jockey announced through his microphone. "We'll start you off with the Tumbleweed — follow that with a sexy dose of smooth Black Velvet — an' then we're divin' straight into the Achy Breaky." A cheer went up.

Rosa's cowboy for the night escorted her off the floor. "We're going over there to practice," Rosa said, her cheeks flushed. "Billy's teaching me to line dance."

"Billy, are you a regular here?" Kennedy asked, stopping him before he whisked Rosa off.

"Yes, ma'am — come here all the time."

She took out her photograph of Margarita. "Do you know her?"

Tipping his Stetson back, he stared at the picture for a moment. "Can't say I do, ma'am."

"She used to come here every week."

"Reckon she hung out on different nights to me."

"Reckon she did," Kennedy replied.

"Maybe you should ask one of the bouncers. They know everythin' happens around here."

"That's a good idea. Thanks."

She'd noticed several bouncers roaming around the place, dressed in black cowboy hats, black shirts, and the de rigueur tight blue jeans. She approached one standing by the door, a shiny silver sheriff's badge gleaming on his shirt.

"Do you remember this woman?" she asked, showing him the picture of Margarita.

He glanced at the photo. "What do I get if I do?"

"What do you want?" she replied, going along for the ride.

This one was not shy. "A date," he said.

"I have a feeling my husband wouldn't appreciate it."

"Aw, shit! All the best ones are taken."

"*Do* you remember her?"

"Yeah. Good-lookin' lady. She used to come here every Saturday night. Fancy little dancer."

"Did she hang out with anybody in particular?"

"Nope. Sometimes she'd be with a couple of girlfriends, never saw her leave with a guy."

"You've got an excellent memory."

"It's a trick of the trade."

She was surprised he didn't tag "little lady" on the end of the sentence; he seemed to be the type.

"Okay, thanks," she said, brushing back her hair.

"Too bad you're taken," he said, winking suggestively.

It was obvious she was getting nowhere fast. She looked around for Rosa and found her in the practice area, learning some kind of intricate two-step with the very attentive Billy. Oh boy, if Ferdy could only see her now!

"We're going," she said.

"We are?"

"Sorry to drag you away."

Rosa waved at her new conquest. "See ya, cowboy."

He tipped his hat. "See ya, pretty lady."

"Stop baby snatching," Kennedy scolded. "You've got one juvenile at home, isn't that enough?"

Rosa giggled. "I may be taken, but I'm not dead!"

26

Mac Brooks couldn't sleep. Something was on his mind, and there was no way he could shake it. He watched *Nightline* for a while, until Sharleen complained that the glow from the television was bothering her.

"I need my sleep, honey," she murmured. "I'll have bags under my eyes in the morning if you keep this up."

He switched off the television and lay flat on his back in the dark, his mind racing this way and that.

Something was horribly wrong, his past was coming back to haunt him, and it wasn't a good thing.

When he'd heard about Margarita Lynda's murder, he'd thought of it as random violence, one of the many perils of living in L.A. But recently he'd found out about Stephanie Wolff's demise, and he'd known — without a doubt — that their murders had to be linked. Then tonight, on the early news, they'd reported the brutal murder of actress Pamela March.

He'd gone cold inside. There was no doubt now, he *knew* who was committing the murders.

After dinner he'd gone to his study, hoping for

some peace and quiet so he could think things through and decide what action he might take.

Sharleen had followed him in, leaned over the back of his chair, and began ruffling his hair. "Let's go to a movie in Westwood," she suggested. "And if you're very, *very* good, we can make out in the back row. How does *that* grab you?"

"Not tonight, sweetheart."

She was in a flirtatious mood. "Why not, pussycat?" she asked, playing with the top of his ear. "I promise you I'll make it worth your while."

"Because I don't feel like it."

"You're so boring when you're working," she said, pouting.

"So are you," he retaliated.

"I could've been in this movie," she said petulantly. "Bobby and I would've had sensational chemistry, *and* you know it. It's so silly you're jealous — "

"Sharleen, I've told you once, I am *not* jealous."

"Yes you are."

"No. I'm *not.*"

"Oliver Stone wants to meet me."

"Good. I hope he meets you, loves you, and hires you. Several months in Vietnam will do you a power of good."

"He's not doing another Vietnam movie."

"Whatever," he said shortly, wishing she'd leave him alone.

Now he was lying in bed unable to sleep, with Sharleen beside him, breathing deeply, her eyes closed, her luscious mouth slightly open.

All he could think about was the murdered

313

women. How long would it take before the police connected them?

How long before they realized that all three had worked on *The Contract?*

He knew he had a responsibility to speak up, but if he did so it would only drag the whole nightmare back into the headlines.

Seven years ago a murder had been committed on his movie set. Ingrid Floris, a beautiful young actress, had been brutally killed by the actor portraying her ex-boyfriend. He'd dragged her from her trailer in front of several witnesses and, after a violent struggle, strangled her.

Margarita Lynda had run screaming for help, while Stephanie Wolff and Pamela March had hovered in the parking lot, watching the entire incident, both of them transfixed with horror. Jordanna Levitt, Cheryl Landers, and Gerda Hemsley had seen everything from the window of the production trailer.

By the time Margarita returned with a couple of burly drivers, it was too late to save Ingrid. She was already dead.

All six women were called as witnesses at the trial.

All six helped put the killer away.

The name of the actor was Zane Marion Ricca. He was the nephew of Mac's godfather, although nobody knew it — including Zane, who thought it was just pure luck that he'd gotten such a big break in an important Hollywood movie.

Mac knew better. Mac had done his godfather a favor, because when asked he was smart enough not to say no.

The truth was that nobody said no to Luca Carlotti.

Christ! Mac realized that Zane must be out of jail. And the horrifying reality was that he could be systematically killing every one of the women who'd testified against him.

Everyone except Jordanna, Cheryl, and Gerda. Maybe they were next.

He sat bolt upright in bed, sweat beading his forehead.

"Wassamatter?" Sharleen mumbled sleepily, throwing her arm across him.

"Go back to sleep, baby," he said, surprised to hear his voice so soothing and calm.

"Hmm . . ." She turned over, and he noticed the voluptuous outline of her breasts through her silky nightgown. Too bad he wasn't in a better mood, although they rarely had sex in the bedroom — that was too normal for Sharleen.

He slid out of bed and went into his dressing room, where he put on jogging pants, a sweatshirt, socks, and Nikes. Then he went downstairs. There was no point in trying to sleep, this problem wasn't going away.

He hurried into his study, shutting the door behind him. The blinds were open to the patio, so he pulled them down, then crossed the room and removed a small Picasso from the wall next to the fireplace. Behind the expensive painting, embedded securely in the wall, was a safe.

He entered the combination, and the steel door clicked open. This was his safe. Sharleen had her own. Only in California.

He paused for a long moment before divesting

315

the safe of its contents. It wasn't often he took the bittersweet memory trip — some things were best left unremembered.

First he removed a large brown envelope. Opening it, he took out the photographs it contained and spread them across his desk.

Memories came flooding back. Mac Brooks aged three, balanced on the shoulders of his father, a tall, lanky man with curly brown hair and a carefree expression; Mac at six with his mother, Priscilla, a gorgeous blonde in shorts and a halter top; Mac at twelve, a dirty-faced villain with a crooked grin and larceny in his heart; and Mac at fifteen, standing next to his godfather, Luca Carlotti.

Mac stared intently at the photo. Luca Carlotti, a short man with deep-set hooded Valentino eyes, full lips, and slicked-back patent-leather hair. He wore a cobra's smile and excellent tailoring.

Luca Carlotti had been the most feared man in the neighborhood. He'd also been the most loved.

Luca Carlotti could make dreams come true, or he could crush you underfoot. He was a powerful force, and Mac's father was his right-hand man.

As Mac grew up, he realized why the great Luca Carlotti was his godfather. It was because Luca was fucking his mother and his father didn't have the balls to object.

Luca Carlotti and Mac's parents went everywhere together, until one night when they visited an after-hours club in Harlem to hear a famous jazz singer. It was past two in the morning when they left. Mac's father exited the club first to signal their driver. As the sleek limousine pulled up, Luca and Priscilla emerged from the club.

A car cruised slowly by. Luca stopped, began to say something. At that exact moment a hail of bullets came at them. Luca dropped to the ground, dragging Priscilla with him, while Mac's father took a bullet straight through the heart — a bullet meant for Luca. Mac was sixteen at the time.

Luca was not an ungrateful man. From that day on he was actively involved in seeing that Mac got everything he wanted.

He wanted to be a boxer.

Luca paid for a trainer and arranged a series of amateur fights.

He wanted a car.

Luca bought him a red Mustang.

He wanted to be a film director.

Luca fixed it so he could go to film school.

He wanted to be employed on an actual movie.

Luca arranged for him to work as third assistant on *New York Nights*, a film some of his "friends" had invested money in.

The experience thrilled Mac. He knew he had found his true vocation.

The director of *New York Nights* was William Davidoss, a forceful man with a loud voice and a flamboyant style. His daughter, Willa, was the key to Mac's golden future.

Shortly after the movie wrapped, Mac and Willa ran off to Las Vegas and got married. Within three years he was directing his first movie.

Luca Carlotti and his mother had wished him luck when he'd moved to Hollywood. They'd respected his decision to distance himself from his New York connections. Luca understood things like that, he was a very understanding man.

It wasn't until years later, when Mac was prepping *The Contract*, that Luca phoned him. "I need a favor, son," he'd said, as if they'd spoken yesterday.

Mac hated it when Luca called him "son." Even though Luca was still in bed with his mother, it didn't give him the right to call him "son."

"Whatever you need, Luca," he replied smoothly, because it suited him to stay on his godfather's good side.

"I got me this nephew wants t'be an actor," Luca said. "Not a bad-lookin' kid. Give him a part in one of your movies. I promised my sister I'd do this."

"It can't be a starring role," Mac said curtly.

"A coupla scenes, that's all I ask."

"It's done."

Mac remembered their conversation well. And then he remembered Zane Marion Ricca.

From the moment Mac set eyes on Zane Marion Ricca he got bad vibes. Zane had an attitude problem — he thought that just because he'd been cast in a major movie he was a star, and he behaved accordingly.

Mac did not appreciate such behavior on his set. He expected everyone to respect one another and get along, but with Zane around it was not to be.

Because of his promise to Luca, Mac was stuck with the little jerk. He'd interviewed him briefly, had him read for the small but pivotal part of the ex-boyfriend, and hired him, much to the disgust

318

of his casting director, Nanette Lipsky.

"He has no experience," Nanette complained. "Why, Mac? You're usually so particular."

"Because he's got a look," Mac replied stubbornly. "It'll work for the character."

Zane did have a look. Flat gray eyes narrowed like slits in a pale, thin face. A blank expression. Black hair, slicked back like his uncle's.

Zane wasn't handsome, he wasn't ugly, he was merely . . . nothing.

His nothingness would enhance the role. Mac felt he could live with it.

He was wrong. Zane was the worst pain in the ass he'd ever come across. He hit the set like he thought he was Tom Cruise. He insulted the makeup person straight off. Margarita ran to Mac in tears, complaining bitterly. Then Zane proceeded to alienate everyone else connected with the movie.

Mac felt helpless. What could he do? If it was any other actor, he would have fired him. But he'd promised Luca this favor, and he felt duty bound to deliver.

Ingrid Floris was an incandescent beauty, young and innocent, with a pure virginal grace. Mac felt sure she had a big career in front of her. He'd given her a small part in his previous movie, and now she had a larger role in *The Contract*. She did not disappoint him, her performance was just right. She had a special quality, similar to a young Grace Kelly.

Mac was so impressed that he didn't even try to hit on her, as was his habit. It would have been difficult, because at the time he was still married to Willa, and he was also sleeping with Jordanna, who, at seventeen, was a wild thing. He felt guilty about sleeping with Jordanna for about five minutes. But she was so determined — if she wanted something she went for it. And she wanted him, it was hardly like he chased her.

He lived in fear that her father — a friend of his — would find out and kill him. But Jordanna merely laughed when he expressed his thoughts.

"Jordan couldn't care less what I do," she said lightly. "He's too busy getting married again . . . and again . . . and again!"

"You're going to be a very exciting woman one of these days," he told her.

She grinned. "What am I now — a dog?"

"Yeah, that's exactly what you are — a cute little mutt."

Their affair lasted exactly six weeks. After that she got bored and turned her attention to one of the extras, who rode a Harley and surfed. Mac was relieved, her energy was zapping every ounce of his.

Ingrid had almost completed her role in the movie when she started to work with Zane. Her disposition was as sweet as her looks, she was such a pleasure to be around that even Zane began to behave himself.

This was good, because by this time everyone on the set couldn't stand the sight of him.

The scenes between Ingrid and Zane were quite powerful. Zane might be jerk of the year, but it worked for the role he was playing, because that's what her ex-boyfriend in the movie was supposed to be, a total jerk-off.

Mac had no idea that off the set Zane was coming on to Ingrid — propositioning her, inviting her out, bombarding her with gifts and flowers. His attention was unwelcome, Ingrid had a boyfriend. She told Zane, who refused to accept it, and continued to pursue her full force.

On the day they were due to shoot the rape scene, Ingrid was extremely nervous. She confided in Margarita while sitting in the makeup chair.

"Do you want me to talk to Mac?" Margarita asked. "I will if it'll make you feel more secure."

Ingrid shook her head. "I'm sure Zane doesn't mean any harm. He's confused, and it's almost as if he thinks I *am* the character I'm playing, and he *is* my ex-boyfriend. It's weird, but I suppose it works for him."

"Don't worry, we'll all be on the set, watching out for you."

Rape scenes were hard to shoot at the best of times, but with Zane the experience was tougher than usual. He was taking all his frustrations out on Ingrid — treating her roughly in rehearsal — in spite of Mac's warnings to hold back.

When it came time for the first take, Zane really let rip.

"Cut," Mac yelled.

Zane was on top of Ingrid, shoving his mouth down on hers, ripping at her clothes.

"Fucking *cut!*" Mac screamed when Zane failed to stop.

Still he kept going.

"Crazy bastard," Mac shouted, running forward and personally hauling Zane off Ingrid, who was genuinely petrified. "You dumb motherfucker!" Mac bellowed. "What the hell do you think you're doing?"

Zane's eyes were flat and cold. "I'm acting," he said. "Isn't that what you wanted?"

"When I call 'cut,' you goddamn jump. This is *my* film, *my* set, and you go by *my* rules. Now get the fuck outta my sight." He bent to assist Ingrid to her feet. "You okay, sweetheart?"

She nodded, attempting a weak smile. "It'll work for the scene, won't it?" she asked hopefully.

"You bet," Mac said. "Print it!" he called out. "I'm not putting you through that again."

Later that day Zane went to Ingrid's trailer. Thinking he had come to apologize, she let him in. They began to fight verbally — even Ingrid had a limit to how far she would allow herself to be pushed. When Zane tried to force himself upon her — claiming she'd been leading him on — their fight turned physical, and they burst out of her trailer in full combat.

It all happened so fast.

One moment they were struggling, and the next, Ingrid lay dead on the ground.

A promising young career was over, and Mac felt completely and utterly responsible.

"Honey, what are you doing?" Sharleen stood in the doorway of his study, wrapped in a pale-peach peignoir, the outline of her full breasts disturbingly visible.

"Sharleen," he said patiently, "go back to bed. It's three in the morning."

"I know," she said, shivering as she entered the room. "That's exactly my point."

"I'm studying the script," he said.

"No you're not."

"Yes I am."

"Come to bed," she said temptingly. "I'm lonely."

"Don't do this to me, honey. I need time by myself."

She spied the photographs, and before he could stop her she reached across his desk and picked one of them up. His luck it was the one of him at fifteen, standing next to Luca Carlotti.

"Who's this?" she asked curiously. "Not your father?"

"No, that's not my dad."

"Well, who is it?"

"A friend of the family."

Sharleen gazed at the picture. "He looks very . . . gangsterish."

Mac laughed uneasily, moving casually around his desk and plucking the photo from her grasp. "Gangsterish! What kind of word is *that?*"

She grabbed for the photo. "Let me see again. How come — "

He held her wrists lightly and shut her up by pressing his lips firmly down on hers.

Sharleen responded immediately. After all, they weren't in the bedroom, why wouldn't she?

Peeling off her peignoir, he bent her back against the edge of his desk and roughly lifted the skirt of her nightgown.

"Sweetheart," she murmured huskily. "The kids . . . they might come in."

"Everyone's asleep," he assured her, touching the tangle of hair between her legs. "Besides, I thought you got off on a little danger."

As he said "danger," he thrust himself inside her. She was not quite ready, which added to the excitement.

"Mac — "

He reached for her breasts, covering them with his hands as he began to make love to her.

She threw her head back and sighed deeply.

Soon they were in perfect sync.

27

Working with Quincy was about to keep Michael very busy indeed. Apart from the Marjory Sanderson case, there were several other things Quincy was into, such as trailing an errant husband on behalf of a jealous wife, and damage control on a drugged-out female TV star.

"Our job is to keep her outta the papers," Quincy said. "So every time this girl goes out, gets stoned, hits somebody, or creates a riot in a club, we gotta pay people off an' make sure it doesn't headline the scandal rags."

"Sounds like a full-time job," Michael said, swigging nonalcoholic beer from the bottle.

"She has a bodyguard with her at all times. He reports to me every morning. If there's any damage control, I take care of it, an' get paid plenty for doing so."

"Who picks up the tab on this one?"

"Orpheus Studios. She works for their TV production company. Orpheus picks up the tab on a lot of things, you'd be surprised."

They were sitting in front of the television in Quincy's house, half watching a ball game. Amber had cooked them a fried-chicken-and-mashed-potato dinner and then gone up to bed, as she,

Quincy, and the kids were leaving on a weekend skiing trip to Big Bear early the next morning. Michael had volunteered to house-sit.

"Remember Rosa, that TV reporter?" he said, settling back on the couch. "I met with her the other day, and she handed me a sack of letters. I've been reading through them. Mostly they're from women."

Quincy's eyes didn't leave the television. "Yeah? What do they say?"

Michael shrugged and shook a cigarette loose from a pack of Camels. "Y'know the kind of thing," he said, slightly embarrassed. "They wanna marry me, take care of me, have my babies."

Quincy chuckled loudly. "You mean they want to jump your bones — right?"

"Very funny," Michael said, lighting up his cigarette.

"But true, huh?"

"There were a couple of interesting letters that might be worth following through."

"What makes you think so?"

"I know it's probably crap, but I gotta do something. The cops have come up with exactly nothing — I call 'em every day." Reaching into his jacket pocket, he pulled out two letters and handed them over. "Here, take a look."

The first letter was written on scented notepaper with raised flowers printed around the top. Quincy scanned it quickly.

Dear Mr. Scorsinni,
I watched you on TV. I can be of great help to you. To make contact, take an ad in the per-

sonals of 213, the weekly Beverly Hills mag-
azine. Be prepared to pay ten thousand dollars
cash for information. It will be worth it to find
your child.

A friend

"What do you make of it?" Michael asked.

"Someone trying to scam you for money."

"You think?" Michael said, expelling a stream of smoke.

"Yeah, I think," Quincy said, shifting on the couch. "Jeez, Mike, if Amber saw you smokin' in here she'd have a freakin' fit."

"One more drag and it's history."

"I should hope so. What's the other letter say?"

"Read it."

Quincy opened the scrawled note written on plain paper with no signature.

Heron Jones is in Las Vegas.
He knows where your baby is.

"What you gonna do?" Quincy asked, putting the letter down. "Go running to Vegas to search for Heron Jones?"

"Rosa Alvarez has asked me to do another TV interview. Maybe I'll do that and see what happens."

"The more you're on television, the better it is for business. You know what they say in Hollywood — there's no such thing as bad publicity."

"Jesus Christ, Q, I never thought I'd hear you quoting Hollywood expressions."

"You gotta go with the flow when you live here."

"Jerk."

Quincy grinned. "Thanks!" He got up from the couch, walked into the kitchen, and helped himself to another can of Heineken. "You've got the number where we'll be this weekend, right?" he said, strolling back into the living room.

"Yeah, yeah."

"And if there's any emergency — "

"I'll call."

"You should've come with us, but no, you gotta stay here and brood."

"You make it sound like I'm doing this for fun. I can't get on with anything until I find Bella."

"I understand. Look, if Marjory Sanderson calls, you sure you can handle her?"

"C'*mon*, Q."

"Y'know, I don't get it — the guy hasn't phoned or attempted to see her. There's no payoff for him. The letters come at random, all mailed from different locations. All we can do is keep an eye on the situation, make sure she's okay. She's . . . uh . . . kind of neurotic."

"I noticed."

"That's it, I think. Oh yeah, I had a call from my connection at Orpheus Studios, asking me to meet with Mac Brooks, the director."

"What does he want?"

"Don't know until we see him. We'll visit the set first thing Monday."

"You mean I get to watch a real live movie being shot?"

"Exciting, ain't it?"

They looked at each other and broke up.

Quincy, Amber, and the kids left early in the morning. Michael rolled out of bed and decided to call his mother. He'd spoken to her twice since Rita's murder. Naturally he'd told her about Bella's disappearance, but she hadn't bothered to phone back to check on developments or see how he was holding up. Big surprise.

She answered on the first ring, which was a relief because it meant he didn't have to speak to Eddie.

"Hey, Ma, how's it going?" he asked, falsely cheerful.

"The same, Mikey," she said with a weary sigh. "Always the same."

"That's good."

"You're not coming back, are you?"

"No, Ma. Can't do it. Gotta stay here till I find Bella."

"That's right, you gotta stay there," his mother repeated, not sounding too concerned.

"How are you?" he asked. "Eddie keeping his hands to himself?"

"Eddie's all right, Mikey. He works hard. You always talk bad about him, but he's only doin' what he has to do. It gets him through the day."

Gets him through the day, my ass, Michael thought sourly.

"He's an old man now, Mikey," Virginia added, her voice quavering. "An' I'm an old woman."

"No you're not, Ma."

"I get heart flutters, an' my blood pressure's shooting way up."

"C'mon, you'll outlive us all."

"Don't want to," she said sourly. "I've had enough."

"Do you need money, Ma?" Not that he had any to spare, but as long as he could make his rent he was happy to send her what was left.

She cheered up considerably. "If you got some, Mikey. I havta take pills now, they cost plenty. We could use some help."

How come she needed his money? He'd heard from one of his friends in the neighborhood that his brother had come into plenty of bucks. Apparently Sal was now involved in small-time racketeering and drove around in a flashy gold Cadillac with his wife of eighteen months, Pandi, a hard-faced bottle blonde who ran an escort service. He'd also bought a house — things must be going well. The last time Michael had seen Sal was at his wedding to Pandi, and they'd gotten into a big fight over Rita.

"Rita's the fuckin' best, how come ya treat her so bad?" Sal had demanded, like it was any of his business.

"Don't lecture me on how I should treat my wife," he'd replied, stifling a murderous urge to smash Sal in his big fat face.

"You wouldn't know how t'handle a woman if ya tripped over her in a dark place," Sal sneered. "Rita's a fuckin' queen, an' you're lettin' her go. Don'tcha have no sense?"

"Rita's moving to California because she wants to. We're getting a divorce."

"Y'know whatcha are, Mikey?" Sal taunted. "You're a dumb fuckin' cop, an' that's all you'll ever be."

They'd almost gotten into a fight, but Eddie had prevented it, placing his bulk between them, telling them they were killing their poor mother. Never mind that Eddie was the one who beat the crap out of her whenever he thought he could get away with it.

Sal's words had infuriated him. They'd brought back every bad memory of his childhood. Eddie whacking him, screaming in his ear, "Ya nothin', Mikey, ya take after ya old man, an' he was nothin'. Two fuckin' split peas."

Every day he was told he was useless. Every single day until he got the hell out.

After Sal's insults at the wedding, he'd made up his mind never to go out of his way to see his brother again. And Sal obviously felt the same, because when Michael was shot and lying in the hospital, Sal had not bothered visiting.

"I'll send you what I can," Michael said, waiting for his mother to say something nice — anything to show she at least cared a little bit.

Nothing. He got nothing.

So what else was new?

Staying the weekend in the Robbinses' house was nice; it gave him a sense of family. He often found himself wondering what it would have been like if things had worked out with Rita. He'd tried. When he got off the booze he really tried, but by that time it was too late, although Rita didn't think so; she dragged him to a marriage counselor, and they sat in the office of a total stranger for two hours, while Rita bitched about him.

He's selfish. He never shows his love for me. He

331

doesn't compliment me. He's never there for me.

She didn't mention that he paid all the bills and worked nonstop, and that as a provider he gave her nothing to complain about.

Shortly before they left the counselor's office she said something that still bothered him. "I know he had it tough growing up — who didn't? But so did his brother, Sal, and Sal's a terrific guy."

He was really startled by her words. Since when did Rita think Sal was such a terrific guy?

Out in the car, he tackled her about it. "What's with this Sal-is-terrific shit? Since when were you and he so close?"

"Don't forget he introduced us," she reminded him. "I should've married *him* instead of *you*."

And of course that had started another fight.

He didn't remember only the bad times. Sometimes he recalled Rita at her best, when they were first together. She'd been so fun-loving and full of life, now she was just another crime statistic. A pretty girl chasing a big career, who'd ended up on a slab in the morgue.

He slept fitfully, first dreaming about Rita and Bella, then waking early and lying in bed thinking about the two letters he'd shown Quincy and wondering if he should do anything about them. If Heron Jones was in Vegas, how would he find him? It shouldn't be too difficult tracking Heron if he was still performing.

He decided that maybe he'd hop a plane next weekend, take a little trip. It was worth following every lead.

In the morning he got up late, cooked himself bacon and eggs, and enjoyed the luxury of watching ball games uninterrupted all day long.

At seven-thirty he sent out for pizza, then settled back on the living room couch to watch the first part of *The Godfather*. Amber had bought Quincy the trilogy for his last birthday, and if Michael was lucky he'd get to watch all three *Godfather* movies. What a treat! Al Pacino, James Caan, Marlon Brando, Robert Duvall — each actor better than the next.

He was mesmerized, so much so that he almost didn't hear the phone. He grabbed it just in time. "Yeah?"

A whispery female voice. "May I speak to Quincy, please."

"Who's this?"

"Marjory Sanderson."

"Hey, Marjory . . ." He pressed the pause button on the remote. "This is Michael Scorsinni, Quincy's partner. He had to leave town this weekend, but he told me if you need anything at all to let you know I'm here for you. What's up?"

"I . . . I don't feel . . . safe," she said hesitantly.

He sat up straighter. "What do you mean? Did something happen?"

"No. I'm at the house, and the guards are here and the dogs and everything . . . but I have this bad feeling."

"What do you want me to do?"

"Can you come over?"

He stalled for a moment. The last thing he felt like doing was driving over the hill into Bel Air. "Uh . . . sure, Marjory, if it'll help you out."

"Please."

"Okay, I'll be there soon as I can."

Goddamn it! Just when the movie was getting to the best scene — the hospital setup where Al Pacino has to guard Marlon Brando all by himself.

He thought about calling Quincy, but decided against disturbing the family on their weekend vacation. He was quite capable of calming Marjory.

He had on jeans and a work shirt, but why change? After all, it was Saturday night. What would she expect — a suit?

Too bad if she did. He turned off the TV and set off.

The guards at the gate of the estate waved him through. He wasn't sure if they'd been apprised of the situation, so he didn't bother stopping to discuss it. He drove straight up to the main house, parking outside the massive oak front door.

The butler led him into the fancy living room, where he took a seat and waited . . . and waited . . . and waited.

Thirty-five minutes later Marjory made her entrance.

"I'm so sorry," she said. "I was on the phone to my father."

Michael was not used to dealing with Hollywood. He was pissed, and it showed. "Yeah, well, you don't even have a magazine in this room," he said curtly. "I don't appreciate waiting around with nothing to do."

She fluttered around the room. Was it his imagination, or was she naked under her sheer white dress? He could make out the outline of her erect dark nipples, not to mention the faint shadow of her bush.

"How about a drink, Mr. Scorsinni," she offered, her thin face flushed.

"Call me Michael," he said, averting his eyes from the obvious show she was putting on.

"Very well . . . Michael," she said, her voice almost a whisper. "Can I fix you something?"

"Uh . . . I don't drink."

"What a coincidence. Neither do I."

She was seriously pissing him off. He'd driven over here because she'd sounded upset and panicked, and now she was calmly offering him a drink like nothing was going on. "This isn't a social call, Marjory," he said tightly. "I came here because you asked me to. You said you were upset. How about telling me what happened?"

She lowered her eyes. "He phoned."

"Is this the first time?"

"Yes. He's never called before."

"What did he say?"

"The same things he wrote in the letters. That he's going to kill me . . ." She trailed off, too upset to continue.

"What did his voice sound like? Was it muffled? Young or old?"

"It was . . . muffled."

"So you couldn't figure out his age?"

"Maybe . . . maybe in his thirties."

"That's good, Marjory. That's a start. Black, white, Hispanic?"

"American."

"So after you hung up, you called your father — is that it?"

"I . . . I contacted you. Then my father phoned to see if I was all right."

335

"Why? Did he know about the call?"

"No, he phones most evenings. I told him you were on your way over. He was pleased."

"Okay, Marjory, this is the next move. I'm going to put a machine on your phone line. It'll tape all your conversations, so the next time he calls we'll be able to tape him — hear what he sounds like, maybe even trace the call."

"My private conversations?"

"I'll show you how to activate the tape. If it's private you can turn the machine off."

"I understand."

"I'll set it up Monday, when I can get the equipment. In the meantime — you got a friend who can spend the night?"

"My girlfriend is staying here now."

"That's good. Where is she?"

"Working on a movie. She won't be back until later."

"Any idea what time?"

Marjory shook her head.

"Is she an actress?"

"No. She's Bobby Rush's set assistant."

"Sounds like fun."

"It does?"

"Yeah, anything to do with the movies must be fun." He wondered if he could light up a cigarette in this mausoleum. "Do you work, Marjory?"

"I help out on charity committees. It's very time-consuming."

"I bet," he said, not believing her. As far as he could tell, this girl was in desperate need of a life. "Okay," he said briskly, ready to make a move. "You got the guards, you got me on the phone if you need me, you got that butler guy — he lives here, right?"

"Not in the main house, he has an apartment in the servants' building."

"How about if he moves into the main house for the night?"

"I wouldn't feel secure," she said anxiously. "I'd sooner you stayed."

This was a new one. "You want *me* to stay?" he asked, genuinely surprised and not thrilled.

"Yes. Quincy said if I needed him to spend the night it would be okay."

Fine for Quincy to say that, he'd pissed off on a skiing trip. "He did, huh?"

"Yes."

"Uh . . . y'know, Marjory, I didn't come prepared."

"All our guest rooms are fully stocked with anything you might need. You can sleep in the room next to mine."

"It's kinda inconvenient."

She fixed him with accusing pale-blue eyes. "He threatened to kill me. I can't stay here alone."

Michael sighed, there was no backing out of this one. "Yeah, that'll do it every time," he said wryly, rubbing his stubbled chin. "Okay, Marjory, if it'll make you sleep easier, I guess I can stay."

She looked suitably grateful. "Thank you."

"Don't mention it."

"Have you eaten?"

"I had a pizza. When you called I was watching *The Godfather* on tape — that's some movie."

"My father has a complete library of films. I'm

sure we have it here if you'd like to continue watching it."

"That wouldn't be a bad idea."

"I'll watch it with you."

Not exactly what he had in mind, but he could hardly say no.

"Come," she said. "Let me show you the library."

He followed her down a vast hallway into an enormous wood-paneled room. Floor-to-ceiling shelves on one wall were filled with probably every movie ever made, stacked neatly side by side.

"Now let's see," she said. "It will either be under *G* for *Godfather*, or sometimes he has them filed under directors. Was it Scorsese?"

"Nope."

"I know," she said triumphantly. "Francis Ford Coppolla."

"Very good."

She started searching through the tapes and finally found it. "We could watch it in the screening room. It's set up for video."

He shrugged. "Suits me."

"And then I can have the guards send out for pizza."

"I didn't say I *wanted* pizza, what I said was I'd already had some."

"Whatever you like . . . Michael."

He had an uneasy feeling. There was something in the air he didn't like. Was she coming on to him? Please, please, don't let it be so. But Michael had an antenna for these things.

How was he going to explain this one to Quincy?

28

Watching Bobby Rush in action was quite an experience. Jordanna really got off on his dynamic energy, he never stopped. Not only was he the star of *Thriller Eyes*, he was also the executive producer, so if he wasn't in the shot, he was busy looking over Mac's shoulder or conferring with either Gary or Tyrone about budgets and schedules.

Suprisingly, Jordanna found the work invigorating. He was extremely fast, and the real challenge was anticipating his needs before he asked. Not that she planned on making her life's work gofer to a movie star, but it was interesting, and as Charlie had said, being on the inside track and watching everything up close was an education.

When she'd worked on *The Contract*, she was a kid of seventeen who'd only been hired because of her father's influence, so there hadn't been much for her to do. This time she was next to Bobby constantly, and felt very much a part of the great moviemaking experience. Mac was right, it *was* fun.

Bobby was friendly but kept his distance. She did the same. She didn't want him to think of her as Jordan Levitt's daughter. She wanted to prove herself and show him that she could be there for him, giving him the kind of support he needed.

His secretary visited the set every day, so did his publicist. Jordanna couldn't help noticing how both women fussed around him. It aggravated her, the way they hung on to his every word as if they didn't have anything better to do. So he was Bobby Rush, movie star. Big fucking deal.

Three days into the shoot, he said to her, "You know, Jordanna, I'm kind of surprised."

"Why's that, Bobby?"

" 'Cause I figured I'd have to fire you after one day."

"Thanks a lot!"

"Hey — this is a demanding job. But I gotta tell you — you're doing real good."

"Is that a compliment?"

He smiled lazily. "I guess so."

He had the bluest eyes she'd ever seen, and a sensational body. Not a Midnight Cowboy body, but a great one all the same.

The one area Jordanna had always had complete confidence in was her relationships with men. Sex was easy. She'd known from an early age she could have anybody she wanted.

Bobby was different. Whenever she thought of him in a sexual way she got a strange shy feeling. This so confused her that she couldn't even bring herself to flirt. It was ridiculous. And yet . . . why did she find herself thinking about him all the time?

Well, of course I think about him. I'm working for him. I'm with him seventeen hours a day. Why wouldn't I think about him?

Could this be love?

No way.

Neither Mac nor Bobby ate with the crew. They took their meals in their respective trailers, sometimes together so they could get into one of their heated discussions.

Bobby was a vegetarian, although he sometimes ate chicken.

"Don't you ever feel like a great big juicy steak?" she asked him.

"No."

She rolled her eyes. "I couldn't go without it."

"I'll take you to a slaughterhouse one day — that might change your mind."

"Oh, come on, Bobby, you wear leather shoes, don't you? And jackets and gloves?"

"But I don't eat it — there's a big difference."

Usually she had the caterer prepare him a plate of vegetables or pasta, but Saturday night he decided to have dinner with the cast and crew. He strolled over to the catering truck, getting into line behind a couple of the grips. She stood next to him.

"How's Charlie?" he asked.

"Charlie?" she answered blankly.

"Charlie Dollar."

"Oh, Charlie. Um . . . I'm sure he's fine. I haven't seen him for a while."

"You haven't?"

"We were hanging out on a temporary basis."

"Really?"

"Yes, really."

"Hmm . . ."

"What does *that* mean?"

"I got the impression — "

"That we were fucking?" she said boldly, wanting to shock him. "Yes, that's right, we were, until he moved his ex-girlfriend back in. Satisfied, Bobby? Is that what you wanted to know?"

He began to laugh, which infuriated her. "Slow down," he said, still laughing. "I'm not the *Enquirer*. I don't care what you do."

Now she felt really foolish. Why had she come out with all that stuff? It wasn't his business.

"If you don't need anything, I'll take my break," she said tightly.

"Go right ahead."

She skipped out of the line of fire, thought about visiting Mac in his trailer, but he'd been in a strange mood all day and she didn't feel like bothering him.

Just as she was turning the corner to hang out in the makeup trailer, she bumped into Tyrone.

He grabbed her arm. "Hey," he said. "You're working so hard I never got a chance to tell you how great your test was. If it had been my call, I'd have hired you right then."

"You would?"

"Oh yeah."

"Thanks," she said, smiling broadly. There was nothing like praise to put her in a good mood.

"You eating from the truck? Or you want to catch a bite at this little Chinese place I know around the corner?"

"You're tempting me," she said, thinking he looked like Denzel Washington with a Magic Johnson build — not a bad combination.

"Let's go."

"Hmm . . . maybe I should tell Bobby, just in case he needs anything."

"And she's diligent too. I like that in a woman."

They found Bobby sitting at one of the trestle tables, surrounded by admiring females.

"I'm kidnapping Jordanna," Tyrone said. "I'll have her back within the hour."

Bobby barely glanced up. "See that you do," he said, "or I'll dock her pay."

Tyrone laughed. Jordanna didn't, she was too busy trying to figure out who all the women were. A couple of them were part of the production, but there were at least three others she couldn't place.

"Who's the cast of female talent?" she asked casually, once they were in Tyrone's car.

"Huh?"

"The women all around Bobby. It seems like he has a traveling fan club."

"He does. They trail him everywhere, slipping him their phone number, telling him how much they loved his last movie — or hated it. Anything to grab his attention."

Tyrone seemed like a pleasant enough guy. But Jordanna made a conscientious effort not to come on too strong. There was no way she was about to jump into bed with him. The new Jordanna reigned supreme. No more one-night adventures. Although a joint would have been nice — she kind of missed running the clubs and getting high.

No. That was the old Jordanna. Now she had this whole new image to live up to. Jordanna Levitt, working girl. Could've been an actress, but it didn't work out.

When they arrived back at the location, Bobby was in deep conversation with Barbara Barr.

"What's *she* doing here?" Jordanna asked Tyrone, irritated that Barbara was on the set. "She doesn't start until the end of next week."

Tyrone shrugged. "She's probably dropping by to meet everyone. Bobby encourages a family atmosphere."

"It's not the crew she's meeting," Jordanna pointed out, unable to hide her displeasure.

Tyrone threw her a quizzical look. "You're not interested in Bobby, are you? 'Cause if you are, let me know and I'll back off."

"Who, me?" she said indignantly. "Interested in Bobby? Oh, *please!*"

"Just asking. I don't like to run second."

"Ask away, because it's the most ridiculous thing I've ever heard. I am working for him, and I respect his work, but as far as going out with Bobby Rush — *me?* C'*mon,* give me a break."

"Okay, so you don't want to go out with him. How about me?"

"How about you what?"

"How about you and me going out?"

"We just did. That Chinese meal was great."

"I can offer you more than a Chinese meal."

"Yeah? What?"

A smile spread across his face. "Probably not anything you haven't seen before."

"Ooh!" she said flirtatiously. "I don't know about that."

"Let me see," he said. "We're working all weekend, and then Tuesday's a day off. Dinner Tuesday night?"

"A deal."

Barbara Barr stayed far too long, which really pissed Jordanna off as she watched from afar. No way was Barbara Barr right for Sienna, her doll-like prettiness didn't work for the role. Her long raven hair was obviously dyed and did not suit her sallow complexion. She was too short, and her eyes were too close together.

Bobby, however, seemed quite taken — typical male — just because Barbara was giving him her full attention, as if he were the only man on earth. Corny shit. Jordanna had given up doing that at sixteen. Bobby let Barbara sit in his director's chair, chatted to her between takes, and generally took no notice of anybody else.

Jordanna was there when he needed her, running and fetching and doing. Suddenly the glow was off the job. She felt like she was nothing more than a glorified errand girl.

Barbara ignored her. That was okay, Jordanna ignored her back.

Mac was in a vile mood. It was unlike him to be testy with the actors, but he was short with everyone.

All in all it wasn't a scintillating night, and she was delighted when they packed up at one A.M. Jumping into her Porsche, she drove back to Bel Air playing Shabba Ranks full volume on her stereo. Shooting by the guards at Marjory's, she pulled up behind a gray Ford, entered the house, and was surprised to find the butler standing in the front hall. "Isn't it past your bedtime?" she asked.

"Miss Marjory is in the screening room with a . . . friend," he said disapprovingly.

"What friend is that?"

"The detective gentleman."

"Are they watching a movie?"

"I'm not sure, Miss Levitt. May I get you a drink, or something to eat?"

God, living at Marjory's was just like being in a luxury hotel with twenty-four hour room service. "No, thanks. I'll wander in and say good night."

"Yes, Miss Levitt."

She opened the door to the screening room and stood at the back, watching the final scene of *The Godfather* play out. She was silently transfixed until the credits began to roll, and then she exclaimed, "I *love* this movie! I try to see it at least once a year."

Michael turned around as Marjory switched on the lights. He saw a beautiful young woman with long tousled dark hair and a devastating smile, wearing a battered leather jacket, faded jeans, and combat boots.

Jordanna saw an incredibly good-looking man in his thirties with thick jet hair, intense eyes, an athletic body, and a dangerous edge.

"Hi," she said with a friendly smile. "You must be Mister Detective."

"Michael Scorsinni," he said, getting to his feet.

"A nice Italian boy, huh?" she said, still smiling.

"You got the Italian right," he replied. "Nice and boy — hey, I'm not so sure."

She laughed.

Marjory was agitated. "Why are you back so

early?" she questioned. "I thought you were night shooting."

Jordanna glanced at her watch. "It's nearly two — isn't that late enough for you?"

Marjory edged closer to Michael. "I'm fine," she said, placing a possessive hand on his arm. "Michael's taking excellent care of me."

"Good," Jordanna said, getting the message that Marjory did not want her around. "I'll . . . uh . . . leave you two alone then."

"Hey," Michael said quickly, turning to Marjory. "Since your friend is home, perhaps it's not necessary for me to stay over."

"You promised," Marjory said, fixing him with a hurt expression.

"What's going on?" Jordanna asked, looking from one to the other.

"I had a phone call from the psycho," Marjory said, "the one who's been sending me letters. He threatened to kill me tonight."

"Oh, great. Now I'll really sleep well," Jordanna said, only half joking.

"If it'll make everyone feel better, I'll stay," Michael said.

"Do you pack a big gun?" Jordanna asked teasingly.

"Big enough."

"Then *definitely* stay over."

"You got it," he replied, thinking that Jordanna was quite something, but had *Trouble* emblazoned on her forehead in big red letters.

She tilted her head. "Is that a New York accent I detect?"

"Brooklyn."

"And what's Brooklyn doing in Bel Air?"

He shrugged and made a face. "Beats me."

Marjory was getting even more agitated. "Excuse me, Jordanna," she said. "Can I have a word with you?"

"Yeah, sure. What's up?"

Marjory steered her into the corridor outside the screening room. "He's *mine*," she hissed, red in the face.

"Excuse me?" Jordanna said blankly.

"He's mine," Marjory repeated. "He's here for *me*, not you."

"What *are* you talking about?"

"Michael — I'm talking about Michael. You're flirting with him. You flirt with everybody. You think you can have anybody you want, but this one is mine."

Jordanna threw her hands up. "Oh, sorry . . . I didn't realize I was stepping on your territory. I thought he was your detective, not your lover. By the way, what *is* that you're wearing? Are you aware it's see-through?"

Marjory blushed an even darker shade of red, the color rising in her cheeks. "Michael likes me this way."

"I didn't realize it had progressed this far. How come you haven't mentioned him before?"

"You don't know everything about me."

This was true, Jordanna reasoned. Even though they'd grown up together, Marjory had always been a loner — keeping to herself, never joining in the outrageous things that Cheryl and Jordanna got up to. Grant used to call her sexless, and Shep claimed she was quietly crazy, but somehow she'd

348

always been part of the Hollywood Five.

"Look," Jordanna said, yawning. "I'm tired. I've had a tough day, and I can assure you I am *not* trying to put a move on your guy. I'm going to bed. I'll see you in the morning."

"Thank you," Marjory said tightly.

Jordanna turned at the end of the corridor. "Hey — I hope you *are* getting laid, it's about time."

Before Marjory could reply, she was out of sight.

Marjory returned to the screening room.

Michael feigned a yawn. "I'm beat. We should call it a night."

"Oh," Marjory said, disappointed. "I thought we could watch *Godfather Two*."

"Tempting offer, but I gotta get some sleep. And so should you."

"I suppose so," she said reluctantly.

"Don't worry, I'll be right next door if you need anything."

"Yes . . . Michael."

Gotta keep this on a very impersonal level, he thought to himself. This girl could go way over the edge — and he did not want to be the dumb schmuck at the receiving end of her obsession.

Since leaving prison he'd killed four women. Five if he counted The Girl who'd started it all. She was totally responsible for the deaths of these four women. It was her fault. He refused to take the blame.

Although he had to admit there was something extraordinarily pleasurable about doing away with these women.

He thought about their necks a lot, their soft white necks. Squeezing the life out of them was a very civilized way to kill.

There were two more women on his list. Two more females who had to be punished. Cheryl Landers and Jordanna Levitt. He'd purposely left them for last because they might not be as easy as the other four. They lived different lives.

When he was working on The Contract, Cheryl and Jordanna had been regarded as nothing more than a joke. Two teenage girls with rich fathers and no experience. Yet they'd managed to stand up with the others and accuse him. They'd managed to say that they'd seen him kill The Girl.

Fortunate for him his uncle had connections.

The best lawyers were hired to defend him, and he'd gotten away with manslaughter. If it had been up to those six women who testified against him, he would have been jailed for life — he might even have drawn the death penalty.

Tracking each of the women had been easy. He still had in his possession the original crew and cast list from **The Contract.** Margarita Lynda and Stephanie Wolff had both lived at the same addresses. Gerda Hemsley had been a little more difficult to find, but he'd tracked her. The post office had supplied him with Pamela March's new address.

He had home addresses for Jordanna Levitt and Cheryl Landers, and over the next few days he planned on making sure they were both still in residence.

The only problem was he could not decide which one to deal with first. He remembered Cheryl as a sour-faced girl, always complaining. And Jordanna was the restless one — marching around the set as though she owned the world.

He hated them both. He hated them so much more than the other four women, because Jordanna and Cheryl came from the kind of privilege he would have liked to have had, and for that they would be punished.

Today he would begin the tracking. Watching a victim days before the event was almost as exciting as the moment of finality.

He had plans for both Cheryl and Jordanna. Strangling them was too easy, they deserved to suffer as he had suffered.

Yes, he had big plans.

He spread the cast and crew sheet on the table, studying it carefully. Cheryl Landers lived in Bel Air. Jordanna Levitt's home was in Beverly Hills.

Bel Air or Beverly Hills — where to start?

He realized this was not going to be so simple. Those big fancy mansions had security systems and guards. He was not naive about the fact that people who lived in large expensive houses took more precautions.

But nobody could outsmart him. He'd done his time in prison. He'd endured countless acts of vile degradation and hadn't complained — the humiliations he'd put up with had made him strong. Stronger than most.

He tossed a coin to see where he would start. Bel Air or Beverly Hills. Which would it be?

29

Michael escaped from the Sanderson estate on Sunday morning by saying he had work to do — which was no lie.

When she saw that he was leaving, Marjory acted distressed. "But what if I receive another call?" she asked plaintively.

"Soon as I get hold of the tape equipment I'll be back," he promised. "On the way out I'll stop and speak to the guards, tell 'em what's going on."

"No," she said vehemently. "Daddy doesn't want anyone to know. If this got into the press it could be very harmful."

"How's that?"

"Daddy shuns publicity — especially about me. He's always been nervous about kidnapping."

"The guards *should* be alerted, Marjory."

"They're always alert."

"Then you have nothing to worry about," he said, silently reminding himself to ask Quincy if he'd met the father, because in his opinion it was crazy if the guards weren't apprised of the situation.

Back at Quincy's house there were several messages. He punched on the machine and listened while he fixed himself a cup of coffee.

The first message was from the bodyguard of the young TV star. "Trouble," the bodyguard said. "She punched out another girl in front of Club Sirocco a few nights ago. I got her out of there in time, but somebody should pay a visit to the bouncer, 'cause I've heard he's tryin' to sell his story."

The second message was from Quincy's mother, inquiring after her grandchildren.

The third was a long complaint from Amber's girlfriend Shelia. Michael listened to her message with amusement. "Hi, this is Shelia. Just thought I'd touch base. I dated that friend of yours, Michael. Haven't heard from him since. Men are such bastards, they take you out, lure you into bed, and that's the last you hear. Anyway, I wouldn't mind going out with him again — he *was* cute. Give me a call."

The final message was from Quincy, who sounded extremely pissed. "*This* you ain't gonna believe. Me and a tree got very intimate — it's called a broken arm. I won't be back tomorrow. Where are you anyway? Hell of a house-sitter you turned out to be."

Michael called him back immediately.

"I'm a one-man business, Mike — what am I gonna do?" Quincy complained.

"You're not a one-man business anymore," Michael reminded him. "I'm your new partner."

"Can you handle things until I get back?"

"Yeah, I'm kind of getting used to it. I spent the night at Marjory Sanderson's. You forgot to tell me we baby-sat too. Oh, an' there's a message from the guy who looks after your bad girl TV star."

"Trouble?"

"Nothing I can't take care of."

"And you'll go see Mac Brooks tomorrow?"

"You got it."

"We're drivin' back on Tuesday. Check my red appointment book on the desk an' you'll find everybody's numbers listed — connections at the studios, all my clients."

"Relax — okay? And the next time you go skiing be more careful."

"Careful? *Shit!* You think I did this on purpose?"

"Yeah, that's what I think."

"Asshole."

"Putz."

Bobby Rush knew he'd made a mistake. After shooting late on Sunday he'd taken his soon-to-be-costar, Barbara Barr, back to his house and back to his bed, where they'd indulged in two hours of very physical sex.

Now it was six A.M. Monday morning, and he was regretting every minute of it. She didn't start work on the movie for another two weeks, and he'd already compromised himself. Not that she wasn't pretty and talented, with a sexy body. But getting involved with his costar was a negative; it always led to big trouble, and he'd promised himself he would never do it again. Barbara was also overly demanding. He couldn't quite place what it was, but there was something about her that set off warning bells in his head.

He had another problem. Should he wake her and send her home? Or should he go to the studio, leaving her alone in his house? There were papers and personal things all over the place, and he hardly knew her, it wasn't a comfortable situation.

He made the decision to wake her.

"What time is it?" she sighed, stretching languorously.

"Late," he lied. "Time to get up."

She rolled across the bed. "You were hot last night, Bobby. A real hot fuck."

Reviews were always interesting. "I was?" he asked, not averse to hearing raves.

She sat up, and the sheet slipped, revealing her ample breasts with their extended nipples. "I wouldn't say it if you weren't," she murmured, throwing her arms around his neck and pulling him close. "I have *never* enjoyed giving head to anyone like I do to you. Your cock really turns me on."

His sudden hard-on suggested that rushing to the studio didn't seem quite so important. He began touching her nipples with the tips of his fingers.

"Don't do that unless you mean it," she moaned. "I can't get through the day filled with the thought of your cock. I need it, and I need it now." Her hands began feverishly unzipping his pants.

He forgot about it not being a good idea and fell on top of her.

She spread her legs. He began pounding into her fast and rough, the way she seemed to like it.

It was raw sex, very basic.

"You're the best fuck I ever had!" she exclaimed after a noisy climax.

Not exactly the perfect way to be described: flattering on the one hand — but not so flattering on the other. What did she think he was? A screwing machine with no feelings?

Now that it was over he started regretting it again. Sneaking a quick peek at his watch, he decided he just had time for another shower, then he had to get out of there if he didn't want to be late for his call.

She trailed him into the shower, naked and sweaty.

"Enough!" he said sternly, when she joined him under the running water and went for his cock again.

"It's never enough for me," she said, getting on her knees while the water cascaded over her head.

Backing out of the glass door, he reached for a towel.

"What's *your* fucking problem," she yelled after him.

You're my fucking problem, he wanted to answer.

When she emerged from the shower it took her forever to dress.

"I'll drop you home," he said, when she was finally ready.

"Goody," she replied cheerfully. "That'll give me time to change and eat breakfast before I meet you for lunch."

Who invited her to lunch? Certainly not him.

"Today's a bitch," he said quickly. "I won't have time for lunch."

"Then I'll sit and watch."

"Uh . . . I'm not crazy about people on the set when I'm shooting an important scene. It blows my concentration."

She regarded him coolly. "Do I feel rejection in the air?"

Jesus, why did he get himself into dumb situations? "Are you nuts?" he said calmly.

"I hate rejection. It pisses me off."

Something told him this one was a clinger. The sooner he cooled it the better.

He drove straight to her apartment and pulled up outside.

"How about I cook you dinner and have it waiting when you come home?" she suggested brightly — a woman of many moods. "Do you want to give me your key?"

No, I do not want to give you my key.

"I have a business dinner tonight," he said, trying to sound suitably disappointed.

She threw him a penetrating stare. "I'm beginning to think you regret what we did last night and this morning."

His reply was smooth as silk. "How could I possibly regret being with you?"

Even as he said it, his words rang horribly false. Maybe that's what Kennedy Chase had nailed him on. Maybe he *was* nothing more than a charming jerk with an excellent line in bullshit.

Oh, great — nothing like putting oneself down to start the day.

"When *will* I see you?" she persisted.

"I'll call you later," he promised.

"You'd better," she said, half joking, half not. "Or I'll have to punish you in a really bad way."

At last she got out of his car. He watched her enter her building. When was he going to learn? No actresses.

They were shooting in the Ambassador Hotel. He drove there fast, Sade on his stereo to soothe him on his way.

When he arrived, Mac was standing by the catering truck, getting breakfast. "Morning," Bobby said. "How was your night?"

"What night?" Mac said sourly. "We didn't finish until one."

Bobby yawned. "Yeah, you're right; it was a tough one. But I think we got some good stuff, don't you? Can't wait to see dailies."

"Are you eating?"

"No. Gotta go straight to makeup. See you on the set."

He sat in the makeup trailer, staring at his reflection. It was a well-known fact that Jerry Rush had nailed every one of his leading ladies. Was he turning into his father? He did not want to be known as Bobby Rush, movie star and major cocksman.

On the other hand, what was he supposed to do? There was nothing wrong with having a fast one-nighter if he felt like it.

She's an actress, his inner voice warned.

Yeah, well, I'm an actor — so what?

Jordanna tracked him to the makeup trailer and handed him a cup of coffee. "You look like you had a long, hard night," she said amiably. "You've got bags under your eyes I could pack clothes in."

He glared at her. "When I want your personal critique I'll ask you."

"Yes, *sir,* Mr. Rush."

"Where's my script?" he asked irritably.

"In your trailer."

"Can you get it?"

"But of course . . . sir."

Jordanna had a smart mouth. She'd be a good assistant if he could only survive her attitude.

"Do me a favor," he called after her. "Bring my portable phone too."

She hurried to his trailer and picked up the script and the phone. On her way back she bumped into Mac. "You feeling okay?" she asked, stopping for a moment.

Did she know something? Jordanna had always been extremely intuitive. "Why? Don't I look well?" he said warily.

"You always look well, Mac — for an old guy."

"Very amusing, Jordanna."

"I'm trying to put a smile on your face. I haven't seen one there lately."

"I've got a few personal problems."

"Sharleen?"

"No, not Sharleen," he said guardedly. "My wife and I are very happy."

"I'm thrilled to hear it."

"You really *are* a smart-ass."

"I'm *really* fed up with hearing that."

"Then stop acting like one."

"You know what the problem is, Mac? I say what's on my mind. I don't hang back. So if that makes me a smart-ass — too bad."

He shook his head and walked away. He was not in the mood for Jordanna's shit; he was too worried about Zane and what he might do next.

He wondered if he should warn Jordanna to be exceptionally careful. If anything happened to her, he'd never forgive himself. . . .

No, nothing would happen to Jordanna. Besides, he was meeting with the private investigator later, everything would be taken care of.

When Jordanna and Cheryl were called to testify at Zane's trial, Jordan Levitt and Ethan Landers had tried to fix it so they didn't have to appear in court. But both girls had been adamant — they'd absolutely insisted on testifying. Foolish decision.

At the time, Mac had been in constant touch with Luca Carlotti. "I can't afford to be connected to Zane in any way," he'd warned his godfather. "I must be kept out of this. I gave an actor a job — that's all I know."

Fortunately Luca agreed with him. "Zane has no idea who you are," he said. "I never even mentioned we knew each other."

"Good. It's imperative we keep it that way."

"Personally," Luca ruminated, his words quite chilling, "I'd like to kill the dumb motherfucker. What kinda crazy bastard does a thing like that? In front of witnesses too."

"He's *your* nephew, not mine."

Mac had always harbored the thought that Zane should have been sent to the gas chamber. Too bad he wasn't.

Now he had to find out if Zane was on the loose. He could have called Luca, but he didn't care to do so. The less he had to do with Luca

Carlotti, the better.

A production assistant stopped Jordanna on her way back to the makeup trailer, handing her several new script pages. She took them to Bobby, who flipped through them before asking her to attach them to his script. She sat in the corner doing so, while he activated his portable phone. She pretended not to listen, but of course she did.

He called Barbara, knowing he had to ease out of the situation he'd gotten himself into as quickly and cleanly as possible. He decided it was best to be truthful and tell her their one night of sex was a mistake.

"I'm sorry if you thought I rushed off this morning," he said, speaking close to the receiver. Pause. "Yeah, I had a good time too. Lunch tomorrow?" Another pause. "Sure. I happen to have the day off."

Lunch was good. It would give him an opportunity to convince her that getting involved was a bad move for both of them.

As soon as he hung up, Jordanna was by his side. "Shall I book you a table at Le Dome or Cicada?" she asked, Little Miss Efficient.

"Beth will take care of it," he said shortly.

Hmm . . . Jordanna thought, *that means he doesn't want me to know. That means he's having lunch with Barbara Barr. That means he took Barbara home last night and probably fucked her senseless.*

Was he nuts? Barbara Barr had a reputation for being a maniac, any idiot knew that.

Jordanna was filled with an unfamiliar feeling of dismay.

She couldn't be jealous, could she?

No way. Why would I be jealous of Barbara Barr?
Because you like Bobby.
I do not!
Oh, yes you do!
She hurried from the makeup trailer, dashed straight over to Kraft Service, and wolfed down three sugar doughnuts and two cans of *7-Up*. Then she felt sick.
Satisfied, dear?
Screw you.

He tried not to look impressed, but Michael had never visited a film set before. Oh, sure — he'd seen plenty of movies being shot on the streets of New York, but now he was in Hollywood, and this was the real thing. It was kind of exciting.

Unfortunately they were not shooting at a studio — the location was the Ambassador Hotel on Wilshire Boulevard. He drew into the parking lot and left his car alongside a line of trailers. Then he walked toward the building, stopping to ask a guard where the filming was taking place.

"You'll find them inside the grand ballroom," the guard said, waving his newspaper in the general direction of the hotel.

Strolling through the spacious grounds, Michael marveled at the old hotel — it was quite something. Way back, he'd read, it was the hangout of all the big stars of the thirties and forties — Clark Gable, Joan Crawford, Lana Turner. What a time that must have been!

When he reached the set they were in the middle of shooting a scene. He hovered on the periphery, fascinated by the activity.

Looking around, he recognized Mac Brooks from pictures he'd seen of him with his wife, Sharleen Wynn Brooks, the very sexy movie star. Lucky guy.

As soon as Mac called "Cut," Michael started over to him.

His path was blocked by a young black production assistant with dreadlocks and a sharp attitude. "Can I help you?" she asked officiously.

"I got a meeting with Mac Brooks."

"Is he expecting you?"

"Yes."

"Your name?"

"Michael Scorsinni . . . uh . . . from the Robbins Agency."

"Wait here. I'll see if I can get his attention."

She went and conferred with Mac, who glanced over and waved. When she came back she was slightly more friendly. "He'll be finished with this shot shortly. Grab a seat and hang out — there's a few empty ones over there."

He sat in a high canvas director's chair and wondered what it must be like to be an actor. All that attention. All that money. All that power.

Not that he'd ever had any ambitions in that direction, although in high school the acting coach had always been after him to join the drama group.

Bobby Rush hit the set movie star style, surrounded by an entourage. Michael immediately recognized the dark-haired girl he had met at Marjory's. He waited until they started blocking the scene, then got up, made his way over, and tapped her on the shoulder. "Remember me?"

She turned and looked at him with surprise.

364

"Hey — Brooklyn!" she exclaimed.

"Hey — Bel Air!" he responded.

"What are you doing here?"

"I've got a meeting with Mac Brooks."

She grinned. "I see you survived your night at the mausoleum."

"You feel the same way about that house as I do."

"I'm only staying there on a temporary basis until I get my own place. Marjory's been a friend for a long time. We were at school together."

"Really? She seems kinda . . . neurotic."

"I wasn't going to be the one to say it, but . . . uh . . . yeah, I've always thought she was slightly crazy."

"What do you make of these letters she's been getting?"

"I don't know. What do *you* think?"

"I haven't formed an opinion."

"Look — if her father's paying, you may as well stick with the gig. She likes having you around, make the most of it."

"What's *that* supposed to mean?"

"Hey, c'mon, Brooklyn — get real. You're a good-looking guy, Marjory will inherit everything when Big Daddy slides off. You could be on easy street here."

He did not appreciate her thinking he was only around to take advantage of Marjory. "I'm working for her," he said tightly. "That's *all* I'm doing."

"Sorry," she said blithely. "Forget I said anything."

"I will."

They stood in silence for a moment, watching the rehearsal.

"Okay, Brooklyn," Jordanna said, genuinely curious. "Give me the juice. What are you seeing Mac about?"

"Private business."

"I bet I know. He's discovered Sharleen's having an affair and wants her followed."

"You've got some imagination."

"Are you like the private detectives in those cool Raymond Chandler novels? Do you leap out at people brandishing a Polaroid when they're in the bedroom making out?"

"You're behind the times. If I was going to do that I'd have an electronic camera embedded in the ceiling."

"Ooh, very high-tech."

"Quiet, please!" the first assistant yelled. "We're going for a take. Everyone settle down."

Michael watched them shoot a scene between Bobby and Cedric Farrell, the actor playing his father. They repeated the scene five times, until Mac was satisfied, then he conferred with his cinematographer, walked over to Michael, shook his hand, and said, "Glad you could make it, Michael. Quincy comes highly recommended. Where is he today?"

"A skiing accident."

"So you guys are partners?"

"Yeah, we were detectives on the force back in New York. Now we're together again."

"What I have to say today is confidential," Mac said. "*Very* confidential. I don't want to read about myself in the *Enquirer*."

"We got a reputation to protect. You can trust us."

"Let's go to my trailer."

They left the set, walking through the empty hotel and all the way outside, until they reached Mac's luxurious trailer.

"Take a seat," Mac said.

Michael sat down on the built-in couch. "So," he said, "why don't you tell me what's on your mind?"

"I've been in this business a long time," Mac said, pacing around. "Made a lot of movies."

"I know. I've seen most of them. You do great work."

Mac liked the fact that this detective was smart enough to have seen all his movies — or at least most of them. "Did you see *The Contract*?"

"Yeah — powerful movie."

"It was, wasn't it?"

"That ending was really something. Had me on the edge of my seat."

"Do you remember the story that hit the press while I was making that film?"

"Uh . . . I don't recall anything."

"A murder took place. A young actress was strangled by one of the actors working on my film. We tried to keep it low profile, but it made head-lines."

"Now that you mention it . . ."

"I recast both roles — never used Ingrid or the actor in the movie. There was a trial, and he was sent to jail. As far as I was concerned, that was the end of it."

"So?"

"During the trial six women gave evidence against him. All six of them witnessed the murder."

"I'm listening."

"In the last couple of months three of those women have been killed."

"Excuse me?"

"You heard me correctly. Three have been murdered."

"Is the actor still in jail?"

"That's what I want you to find out. Zane Marion Ricca got fourteen years for manslaughter."

"Fourteen years ago?"

"No, seven. But I'm almost sure he must be out."

"That's about right. In California his sentence would be automatically halved. Have you told the cops?"

"Why do you think *you're* here? No more headlines. I can't be involved in this. You'll find out if he's been released, and if he has . . . we have to protect the other three women. Because if he has a list, believe me — they're definitely on it."

30

The last thing Kennedy felt like sitting through was an interview with Charlie Dollar. Especially since a new murder had taken place and she was anxious to investigate further.

Her appearance on TV had garnered quite a reaction. "We're stirring 'em up," Rosa assured her. "I've heard the chief of police and the mayor's office are finally getting into it. We're forcing 'em into action. They'll have to make an announcement soon, or there'll be a public outcry."

"That's great," Kennedy said, delighted that something was happening.

"My news director wants you to appear again. He sees this as an ongoing story. In fact, he'd like you to be on once a week until they catch this maniac."

Kennedy agreed. Anything to help nail the killer. She knew that somewhere up there Phil and her father were watching her. Hopefully they were proud she was working on something worthwhile.

In the meantime she was stuck interviewing another movie star. This time the lucky victim was Charlie Dollar — a man who picked up his own phone. She'd actually gotten to speak to him when arranging the appointment, an unusual occurrence when dealing with a celebrity. He'd given her directions to his house and told her he'd expect her at noon.

When she arrived, she was surprised that he answered the door himself. "Hey, lady journalist — come on in," Charlie said, greeting her warmly. Two big dogs sprang to attention. "Take no notice of the killers," he said, leading her through to the living room. "I got 'em trained — they only bite other actors."

He had the wildest smile she'd ever seen, and glittering stoned eyes. Even though he was slightly balding and a little paunchy, he was definitely attractive in his brightly colored Hawaiian shirt, pale-beige chinos that had seen better days, and scuffed white sneakers with no socks.

"Sit down," he said, waving toward the couch.

She checked out her surroundings, deciding she liked his house; it was lived in and comfortable, not designer decorated to the last inch like most Beverly Hills homes. Obviously he'd surrounded himself with things he loved. The old brown leather couch was worn and welcoming; there were interesting paintings on the walls; the dogs wandered around as if they owned the place; and Charlie seemed perfectly at ease.

"Let's start by taking a detour an' going off the record," he said with an endearing grin.

"Sure," she agreed.

"Y'see, I got this raging desire to smoke a joint, but not if it offends you. Oh yeah, an' don't mention it in your story — that's all I ask."

Didn't he know he was stepping on dangerous territory? His opening line was almost too good *not* to write about.

"Can I trust you, Kennedy?" he asked, fixing her with his crazy seen-it-all eyes.

"I suppose so," she said reluctantly.

"Good," he said, lighting a joint and taking a deep drag.

This was a new one, an actor who dared to get stoned in front of a journalist. She admired his balls.

"You really did a kill on Bobby Rush," he remarked, offering her a drag.

She shook her head. "It wasn't me, but I guess I have to take the blame."

Unperturbed, Charlie took another long pull. "What happened?"

"My copy was changed and expanded. I feel bad about it. Trust me, it will never happen again."

"I hope not."

"Don't worry — you're completely protected. I now have a contract that precludes them from changing a word."

"Bobby's an okay guy," Charlie said, through a haze of smoke. "It's a bum rap growing up in this town with a famous parent. He's doin' good."

"I would say having a famous parent makes life easier. Money, privilege . . . anything you wish for."

"I never fight with lady journalists, but you're wrong."

She decided to change the subject. "You have a little boy, don't you?"

A pleased grin spread across his face. "Sure do. His name is Sport, and he's the greatest."

"On the record, are you planning to marry his mother?"

Charlie chuckled again. "You'd better ask Dahlia whether *she's* planning on marrying *me*. I simply do what people ask me to. If I make it through the day, then I'm a happy movie star!"

Charlie had an extremely seductive, easygoing manner, his charm was addictive.

"Do you mind if I use a tape recorder?" she asked, reaching into her purse and extracting a small Sony cassette machine.

"Show me yours, I'll show you mine," he replied with a stoned smile.

"*You* want to tape *me?*"

"I'm sure neither of us would appreciate the inconvenience of being misquoted."

He got up and came back with a portable Panasonic recorder, which he placed on the table in front of them. "We're even," he said.

"Hmm . . ." Kennedy said. "And I never had you tagged as suspicious."

They exchanged a long look.

"*You* are one good-looking broad," Charlie said at last.

"Broad?" she said with a mixture of amusement and contempt.

"Uh oh, I smell a feminist in the room."

She smiled coolly. "Sweet talk will get you absolutely nowhere." She activated her tape. "Can we discuss your movie?"

He leaned forward, clicking on his machine. "I would deem that a great favor. All people usually care about is my personal life." He paused, then waved his arms dramatically in the air, taking on a Shakespearean stance. "Who do I fuck — that is the question," he emoted, sounding more like a grand stage actor than his usual self.

"Are you going to answer it?"

"People aren't interested in the essence of an actor, all they want is this personal shit. Tabloid to the max, that's America today."

"I've seen you in the tabloids."

"Can't avoid it. Wish I could."

"Let's start with that. What do you think of the stories that appear about you?"

"Fairy stories." He snorted disdainfully. "The unfortunate reality is that people believe 'em."

"You really think so?"

"Talk to any of the maids and everybody's mother. They'll come at me waving a paper, sayin', 'Did you see what Michael Jackson did?' Or Marlon Brando. Or Jack Nicholson. Like, baby, they are *true* believers."

"Is everything written in the tabloids lies?"

"Sometimes there's a micron of truth. But them there hacks got a column to fill every week, so they're inclined to make things up. An' if they don't invent, they *embellish*. What a word — embellish!"

He seemed to have a habit of veering off track. She tried to lure him back. "Let's talk about your movie," she said. "Why did you decide to produce it yourself?"

His eyebrows shot up, giving him an even more crazed look. "Why not? When I'm in a movie I kinda get off on making my own decisions. Wouldn't you?"

"Is this a new trend for you? Do you think that

in the future you'll produce all your films?"

"Haven't made up my mind yet." He took a long beat. "So you were married to Philip Chase."

She was startled. "Uh . . . yes. How did you know?"

" 'Cause I followed his work. Yours too. Liked that piece you wrote on Anita Hill. And the stuff you got into about the Bush administration was admirable. But my favorite work of yours and Phil's were the pieces you did together for *National Geographic*. His pictures were outstanding. Lady, you two sure got around."

"Yes, we did," she said quietly, impressed that Charlie knew who Phil was.

"I was real sorry to read that he died."

Inexplicably her eyes filled with tears. It was still so painful to talk about Philip.

Charlie observed her discomfort. "Hey — I got me an idea," he said, jumping to his feet. "We'll drive down to the beach for lunch. I'll treat you to crab cakes at Ivy on the Shore, order you an exotic drink, and we'll pretend we're on vacation. How about it?"

It sounded good. Why resist? "If that's what you'd like to do," she said, feeling uncharacteristically vulnerable.

He grabbed her hands, pulling her up from the couch. "C'mon, sweet green eyes, follow me. I'm the king of how to forget your worries an' stay happy. Let's do it!"

Cheryl Landers was on a power trip. She had the attention of some of the most important men in town. All of a sudden she was a major player.

No longer known as just Ethan's daughter, she was finally free. And making mucho bucks. What an exhilarating high!

Her girls were the best. Once she'd taken over Donna's list, she'd weeded out the druggies and troublemakers and solicited some fine new talent. First-class service all the way was her motto. You pay top price and you get top pussy. Everyone was happy. Especially Grant — who not only tried out new girls for her and supplied the drugs that quite a few clients requested, but also did an excellent recruiting job, bringing her would-be talent on an almost daily basis.

Cheryl found there was another advantage to being *the* Hollywood madam. Men. They all desired her approval, and she could play with them the way she'd always wanted.

She and Grant had started a regular Saturday-night late party at her house, and it was a hot ticket. The guest list was exclusive and exciting — beautiful girls who got paid for their services, and horny powerful men who seemed to get off on shelling out big bucks. Several movie stars were regular attendees; an English rock superstar who went through the girls by the dozen; producers, studio executives, and a scattering of Eurotrash.

She kept her Arab clientele separate. They paid for their own parties, and she made sure they paid double.

Grant was seriously considering dropping out of the agency business and becoming her partner. "Your entire operation could be bigger and better," he said, trying to persuade her. "We'd send girls all over the world — maybe even work out a franchise. The possibilities are limitless."

She'd been paying him a commission for the girls he found, and since business was so good, why not bring him in — not as a full partner, but allowing him to collect a percentage wouldn't bother her. As long as he didn't get too stoned, he would certainly be an asset. He could take over many of her responsibilities, and she'd enjoy having him around on a more permanent basis.

He was sulky when she told him her plan — he wanted fifty percent of her take or nothing.

"Okay, nothing," she bluffed.

He agreed to twenty-five percent and quit the agency.

Cheryl was delighted. Nobody knew it — not even Jordanna — but growing up, she'd always harbored a secret crush on Grant. It started when she'd hit puberty, and continued over the years. She'd never told anyone because it was painfully obvious bimbos were his women of choice. Grant always went for the exterior — the big-breasted, long-hair, fat-glossy-lips look. He'd never second-glanced her — she wasn't pretty enough, her breasts were too small, and besides, he'd always regarded her as one of the boys — and although they'd had fun together, it had never gone any further.

Over the years Cheryl had sat back, watched, and waited. Now she was in an excellent position, she was about to be his boss, and total control would be hers.

Cheryl had decided that if you wanted something badly enough you *could* have it. And she wanted Grant. She'd waited almost twelve years, wasn't that long enough?

Charlie was an interesting man, he did not try to charm — he just did. That he seemed totally oblivious to his fame made him even more attractive.

People loved Charlie. They waved at him from their cars as he sped down the freeway behind the wheel of his black Rolls, grinning his maniacal grin, playing Sinatra, swigging from a flask of something he assured her was distilled water, although she suspected it was pure vodka.

"I wouldn't expect you to have a car like this," she said, fingering the expensive leather seat.

He creased his forehead, genuinely puzzled. "Why do people always say that?"

She gestured vaguely. "I don't know. It's — it's too . . . grown up."

He chuckled. "Surprise, surprise — I *am* grown up."

"How old *are* you?" she asked curiously. Reports varied, pegging him as anything from forty-nine to fifty-five.

"Mentally twelve. Physically a hundred and twelve. Spiritually fifty-three. It's a bitch, but it's better than the alternative."

"Which is?"

"Dead," he said flatly. "I lost a lot of loyal buddies in Vietnam."

"Were you there?"

He lowered the volume on Sinatra. "Sure I was. Where do you think I learned the valuable lesson that to get through each day you gotta start off stoned?"

"College?" she said facetiously.

A hollow laugh. "Naw. Never went. Dropped outta high school at fifteen an' hit the road. That's a whole loada higher education right there."

"I'm sure."

"How about you, green eyes? Give me the story."

"High school. College. The entire process."

"Sounds conventional."

"I met Phil in college, we got married and traveled the world together. He was a very special man."

"Ain't it a bitch — it's always the good ones that go first. You must miss him a lot."

She didn't know what to say. How did you put into words the unbearable pain of losing someone close to you? It was impossible. "I do," she said quietly.

Charlie swerved across three lanes of speeding traffic and just about made it to the Santa Monica exit.

"Driving's not your greatest skill," she gasped, bracing herself against the dashboard.

"The trick," he said with a perverse smile, "is never to hit anything — an' *never* to have anything hit you. That's my philosophy. Think about it; it's sure worked for me."

Their lunch together was enjoyable. She couldn't remember laughing so much in a long time. But there was a seriousness lurking beneath Charlie's lighthearted exterior. Apart from being one of the greatest film actors of his generation, he was an extremely complex and interesting man. When he suggested dinner the next night she readily agreed. Wait until she told Rosa about *this* one!

After lunch, Charlie drove her back to his house, where she picked up her car and headed straight for the television studio. Rosa and the news director were waiting for her. They spent the afternoon going over material for her appearance that night. She got the facts on Pamela March, the latest murder victim. Pamela had been strangled late Friday in West Hollywood — Detective Carlyle territory. She was a small-time actress, divorced, with no children. Thirty-one years old, she had been walking her dog when she was attacked. Exactly the same MO as Stephanie Wolff. Only this time there was no "Death to the traitors" sign left on the body.

"But it has to be the same killer — right?" Kennedy questioned, still scanning the information.

"Unless it's a copycat murder," Rosa replied. "Sometimes that's what happens."

This time Kennedy fought against makeup and hair. She insisted on doing her own, applying a smoky brown eye shadow and a deeper lipstick. Then she brushed her honey-colored hair until it casually framed her face.

Going over her copy, she felt surprisingly calm. It read well; she was pleased with what she'd written.

Before the broadcast she wandered into the green room, picked up a chocolate chip cookie, and nibbled on it.

Rosa entered a few minutes later. "Everything okay?"

"This is a cinch," she replied, not feeling at

all nervous. "I think I'm getting used to it."

"Told you you'd grow to love it!" Rosa exclaimed, grabbing a bottle of Evian on her way out. "See you on the set. We've got a busy show. Oh, and by the way, if you bump into Michael, do me a favor and try not to insult him."

"Michael who?"

"Scorsinni. The New York detective with the missing kid. Remember? He's on again tonight."

"What a coincidence," she said, shaking her head.

"I told you — you're safe, he's not dating and has no desire to, just like you."

"*Sure.*"

Rosa laughed. "Honestly," she said, vanishing out the door. "One of these days you'll learn to believe me."

Kennedy perched on the edge of the couch and glanced through her notes again. Four women. Brutally murdered.

There was a strangler on the loose, and she had to help stop him before he claimed a fifth victim.

31

After leaving Mac, Michael drove over and talked to the doorman at Club Sirocco about the badly behaved TV star, but his mind was elsewhere. The meeting with Mac Brooks was really bothering him. Women were getting killed, Mac thought he knew who was doing it, and he'd only now decided to say something. Didn't these Hollywood people have a fucking social conscience?

From the studio, he'd called a contact in the LAPD and asked him to run a check on Zane Marion Ricca. Phoning back an hour later, he received the information that Zane had been released from jail three months ago. At the main library, Michael scanned newspaper reports on the murdered women. He came across a fourth victim, Gerda Hemsley, and wondered if she'd also worked on Mac's movie.

He couldn't believe that this insane guy was somewhere out there running riot and nobody was doing a goddamn thing.

He reached Mac on the set. "I've got news," he said tersely.

"Just remember I'm speaking on a cellular phone," Mac said warningly. "I have people all around me."

Is that all he cared about? That someone might hear him? "The party we spoke about is on the loose. What do you want me to do about it?"

Now that he knew for sure, Mac panicked. He had to reach Luca and tell him. "Nothing," he said.

"Nothing," Michael repeated.

"For now."

"By the way," Michael added, "does the name Gerda Hemsley mean anything to you?"

"Yes. Why?"

"Add her to the list. She was strangled two weeks ago."

Mac was bad-tempered with everyone. So much so that Bobby came to him at the end of a setup and said, "What's your problem?"

"It's personal," Mac replied shortly. "I'll work it out."

"Something to do with Sharleen?"

Why did everybody always think it was Sharleen?

"Everything with Sharleen is fine," he said irritably. "This is nothing for you to concern yourself with."

Bobby stared at him for a moment, trying to decide whether to push it further. "Okay, okay — I'm not concerned," he said at last. "But try and take it easy on the crew, they're about ready to mutiny if you don't lighten up."

At the lunch break, Mac shut himself in his trailer, ready to make the call.

A million and one excuses not to came to mind. Luca might not be home. He could be busy. Maybe he was out of town. It was also unwise to conduct this particular conversation on a cellular phone. People listened in for sport, it could be dangerous.

That convinced him. He left his trailer and went back to the hotel, making his way into the offices at the front, where a pretty secretary asked if she could help him.

"I'm Mac Brooks, the director of *Thriller Eyes*," he said, giving himself billing. "Is there somewhere I can make a private call?"

"Certainly, Mr. Brooks," she said, impressed.

He followed her into an empty office, where she assured him he would have complete privacy.

Waiting until she closed the door behind her, he punched out Luca's number.

A guarded male voice answered the phone.

"Let me speak to Luca Carlotti," Mac said, keeping his voice low just in case the secretary had X-ray ears.

"Who wants him?"

"Tell him Mr. Brooks from California. He'll know."

"Hold on."

He began picking at a hangnail, tearing at his skin until it throbbed. Sweat beaded his forehead. Why was this phone call agitating him so?

Because he was dangerously close to being exposed as Luca Carlotti's godson — and if the truth came out, it could ruin his career. Even Sharleen didn't know.

He wondered what she'd say if he confessed. *Hey, Sharleen sweetheart — there's something I haven't told you. My godfather is one of the most notorious mob guys in New York. What do you think of that?*

Sharleen would probably say, So what? She wouldn't understand the ramifications. Besides, she had the attitude that nothing mattered unless it directly concerned her.

Luca's unmistakable raspy growl. "Mac?"

"Hey — how ya doin'?" Automatically he slipped into his old Brooklyn accent.

"Doin' good," Luca replied. "What's kickin' with you? Still out on the Coast?"

He cleared his throat. "There's a problem," he said hoarsely.

Luca chuckled. "So what else is new? Problems I'm here t'solve."

"This is your problem too."

"Spit it on the table."

"Your sister's kid — he's out."

"Yeah," Luca said calmly. "That ain't news t'me."

He was amazed. "You mean you *knew?*"

"The fucker's been out three months."

"Why didn't you tell me?"

"I gotta report in to you?"

Mac felt the fury building inside him. Luca was treating him with no respect, and that was one thing his father had instilled in him. *Get people to respect you, and you'll never be less than a man.*

Sure. It had done his father a lot of good. Luca had respected the shit out of him while screwing his mother. He'd never forgive Luca for that.

"You should've told me," he said angrily. "You should've fucking told me."

Luca's voice hardened. "I shoulda done what

384

I think is right — an' I did. I gave instructions to that shitfaced cocksucker t'stay put on the West Coast. He ain't welcome back here. I sent him money. Gave him a place to live. What do I care, as long as he stays outta *my* life."

Mac was incredulous. "And you thought that was it? He'd take the money and leave everyone alone?"

"He'd better, unless he's a dumb fuckin' moron."

"Well, I've got news for you, Luca — he *is* a moron. A dangerous one. I think he's systematically murdering each of the women who testified against him at his trial. Four of them are already dead."

There was a long, ominous silence. He waited for Luca to say something. His hands were trembling. He didn't want to be involved in this, but he *was,* and there was nothing he could do about it.

Luca finally spoke. "You sure about this?"

"Who else could it be?" he replied evenly. "Four of them killed within the last couple of months. Strangled the same way Ingrid was strangled. And there's two other girls who gave evidence — they could be next."

"Do the cops know?"

"They'll put it together eventually."

"Shit!" Luca said furiously. "That motherfucking dumb-ass prick!"

"Where is he?" Mac didn't really want the information, but he was unable to stop himself from asking.

"L.A."

"I realize that, but where in L.A.?"

Luca ignored his question. "I'll tell you what I'm gonna do, son," he said slowly. "I'm gonna take care of this one myself. I'll be on a plane first thing tomorrow."

Don't call me "son," Mac wanted to scream. "What do you mean, you'll take care of it yourself?" he asked.

"Not on the phone. We'll talk when I get there."

"How about the other girls? Shouldn't they be warned?"

"When was the last murder?"

"A few nights ago."

"And before that? How long between attacks?"

"A couple of weeks. I'm not sure."

"It looks like he's workin' to a pattern. They're safe."

"How can you possibly know they're safe?" Mac exploded.

Luca did not take kindly to being yelled at. "You want my help or not?" he said coldly. "Because it'd be just as easy to call the cops and bust this whole deal wide open."

"Yes, I want your help," Mac said, calming down.

"I'll be there tomorrow."

Mac left the office with a heavy heart.

"Can I do anything else for you, Mr. Brooks?" the secretary asked with a bright *I could be a star* smile.

"No, no. Uh . . . charge the call to the studio."

"That's okay, Mr. Brooks — compliments of me. And if you're ever looking for a girl to play a secretary, how about using the real thing?"

His mind was elsewhere. "Yeah, yeah . . . sure."

Luca Carlotti was always impeccably dressed. He favored pin-striped Savile Row suits made by his personal tailor, who flew to New York from London every two months to confer with him. His shoes were handmade — also in London, at an exclusive shop on Jermyn Street. His shirts were the finest silk, and his sweaters and overcoats pure cashmere.

Once every two weeks Luca had a facial to keep his sixty-four-year-old skin smooth. He favored Erno Laszlo products. Every other day he had a full body massage, and once a week he indulged in a mineral mud bath. One room in his home had been converted into a tanning parlor, so that he always had a nice deep tan. Luca believed in pampering himself. With his slicked-back hair and hooded eyes, Luca Carlotti was quite the dandy.

Mac's phone call disturbed him. His sister's idiot son was the bane of his life. He should have ordered a hit on the kid while he was locked up, but out of the kindness of his heart he'd allowed the boy to live. Big mistake.

"There's no way he's comin' back to New York," he'd warned his sister, Phyllis, when Zane was first released from jail.

"But he's my baby — " Phyllis had started to say.

"He ain't your baby — he's a murdering bastard who'll stay in California, outta the family's way. I got a house I can put him in. Don't worry,

I'll send him money."

Phyllis didn't object too vigorously. She'd recently divorced her first husband, who was doing time in Attica, and she was now married to her second: a schmuck called Petey (Wild Man) Borosin. Petey was fifteen years younger than Phyllis, and Luca couldn't stand the sight of the punk, but at least he kept his sister happy.

Now, according to Mac, his stupid sonofabitch nephew was running around killing people.

Luca decided not to tell Phyllis, better she didn't know. Women had big mouths. They couldn't help it, information leaked from them like sieves.

He called his personal travel agent and booked an early-morning flight to L.A.

Michael picked up the tape equipment he needed to bug Marjory's phone and drove over to the Sanderson estate late in the afternoon.

Marjory greeted him like a worried wife. "You promised you'd be here this morning," she said, biting anxiously on her lower lip.

What was it with her? "I never said what time I'd be back," he said, attaching the equipment to her phone.

"I feel so . . . alone," she said, wringing her hands.

This was one hysterical woman. "You're not alone, Marjory. I'm here now."

"Can you stay?"

He made sure everything was in place. "No, I have too much work to do."

"What if I get another call?"

"It's hardly likely. The guy's been sending you

letters for months now. The first time he phoned was Saturday, he won't make a habit of it."

"How do you know?" she asked accusingly.

"If he phones again, you'll contact me and I'll be here. This time we'll have him on tape. Here — let me show you how to work this."

When he was satisfied she had it down, he said, "I gotta make a phone call. Where can I be alone?"

"Is it to do with my case?"

"No, it's something else I'm working on."

Her mouth tightened. "Very well," she said. "You can use this phone."

"Thanks."

She stood near him, staring.

He waited for her to shift, she didn't. "Uh . . . Marjory, this is private."

"I won't listen."

"I'm sure you won't, but you wouldn't appreciate me discussing *your* case in front of other people, would you?"

"I'll be outside," she said, marching stiffly from the room.

He reached Mac on location. "Did you decide what you want me to do?"

"I told you — nothing for now."

"The smartest thing would be to bring the cops in. They'll put a trace on Zane — probably pick him up within twenty-four hours."

"Let me think about it."

"While you're thinking about it, the other two women could be in danger."

"I'll make a decision. In the meantime, is there any way you can place security around Jordanna

Levitt and Cheryl Landers?"

"You mean bodyguards?"

"That's too extreme. I wouldn't want to alarm them. Maybe they can be watched from a distance without them knowing."

"Jordanna Levitt — isn't she Bobby Rush's PA?"

"Yes. How do you know?"

"She's staying with Marjory Sanderson, and I happen to be working on a case for Marjory's father, so I can easily watch her. Quincy's back tomorrow, he'll take care of Cheryl Landers. All we need is her address."

He put the phone down on Mac, still feeling uneasy. If he had a choice he'd go straight to the cops, but he had to talk this out with Quincy before doing anything.

It was a bitch of a situation, and he didn't have an answer.

In the room next to the library, Marjory listened on the extension until she heard Michael hang up. Then she hurriedly replaced the receiver.

What was going on? The man on the other end of the phone had sounded worried. And who was Zane?

She felt excited, part of something. If only Michael would confide in her.

The annoying thing was that Jordanna was involved in some way and Michael had to protect her. At least that meant he'd stay around more.

Growing up with Jordanna and Cheryl, Marjory had always felt like the outsider. She knew she was pale and insignificant compared to them —

390

almost like their mascot — and though they'd included her in everything, along with Grant and Shep, she'd always been the invisible one.

If only she could grab a good-looking man like Michael, wouldn't that show them all?

Of course, he was only a detective, and her father would object strongly, but so what? She was over twenty-one, she could do what she liked.

She exited the room, catching Michael on his way to the front door.

"I gotta go," he said. "I'm late for the studio."

"What studio?"

"I'm on TV tonight."

"Doing what?"

"My four-year-old daughter is missing. I'm making an appeal."

He had a daughter! Did that mean he was married? She'd checked his wedding finger, and there was no band.

"I . . . I didn't know, Michael. I'm so sorry. Will your wife be appearing with you?"

"My wife is dead."

"Oh." A brief pause. "Would you like *me* to come with you?"

"That's okay," he said, consulting his watch. He was running late, and Rosa had particularly asked him to be on time. "When will Jordanna be home?" he asked as he reached the front door.

"They might be working late again."

"Well . . . uh . . . maybe I should spend the night. I'll be back when I finish at the studio."

"I'd like that, Michael," she said, lightly touching his arm. "What's your favorite food?"

He backed off. "Huh?"

"I want to cook for you."

"No way, Marjory. Pizza'll be fine."

"I'll send out to Spago."

"Where?"

"Don't worry. You'll love it."

Michael made it to the TV station in time. A production assistant met him at the door and rushed him into makeup.

"I can't stand all this crap," he complained, sitting reluctantly in front of the mirror as the makeup woman went to work.

"Just a touch of powder to take away the shine," she insisted, dabbing away. "We'll soon be done."

Being in the studio was nerve-racking. The last time, Rosa had done the interview at his apartment, and it had been far less stressful.

"We have a busy program tonight," the production assistant said. "Kennedy Chase is appearing again. Do you know her?"

The name sounded vaguely familiar. "No. Who is she?"

"A journalist. She's doing a piece on the L.A. strangler. Our station is trying to alert the chief of police to form a task force."

"Really?"

"There's been a series of these murders in L.A. over the last couple of months. Kennedy will be on any minute. Come into the green room and watch her."

The girl led him into the green room, where he grabbed a cup of coffee in a Styrofoam cup and sat down in front of the TV set. Rosa was on camera, reporting on a small plane crash. When she was finished she turned to her co-anchor, a smooth-looking black man. They exchanged a few words, and then he proceeded to do a story on an armed robbery in Orange County. When the camera zoomed back to Rosa, she flashed her best professional smile and began to speak. "Last week, journalist Kennedy Chase talked about the murders of several women in Los Angeles over the past two months. I am sad to report that since then the police have taken no emergency action. Recently another woman met her death at the hands of this sadistic strangler. We are all at risk. Kennedy — over to you."

The camera switched from Rosa to Kennedy. Michael's interest was immediately aroused.

Kennedy stared gravely into the camera and began to speak. "Good evening," she said. "Or is it?" A short but meaningful pause. "How many more women are going to lose their lives before the chief of police and the mayor decide to act? How many more female victims will be murdered before the conclusion is reached that what we have here is a serious state of emergency?"

Michael found he couldn't take his eyes off her. She was appealing and articulate. She was also incredibly attractive.

Was this the woman Rosa had tried to fix him up with? At the time he'd said no, but she sure had his attention now.

Kennedy continued to speak eloquently. She seemed to know plenty about the murders. Maybe it wouldn't take long before she discovered that seven years ago the victims had all worked on the

393

same movie — Mac's movie. And that a killer had walked among them.

Before she was finished, the soundwoman bustled into the green room and began hooking him up to a microphone. He stood up as she fitted the power pack onto the back of his belt.

"Not nervous, are you?" the soundwoman asked.

"No, this is the second time for me."

"I saw your first interview. It was quite touching."

"Thanks," he said, breathing deeply, preparing himself for his on-camera appearance.

Whenever he thought about Bella he felt depressed and helpless. He had to face the fact that she could be dead, or involved in child pornography. Both thoughts made him go cold inside.

As he was leaving the green room he bumped into Kennedy, coming from the studio.

"That was a very effective speech," he said, stopping to speak to her.

"Thank you," she replied, barely glancing in his direction.

"I'm Michael Scorsinni."

"Nice to meet you, Michael," she said, turning to talk to one of the associate producers.

He was used to a more positive reaction from women, but she seemed distracted, in a hurry.

"I think Rosa might have mentioned you to me," he added, determined to attract her attention. "She tried to set us up on a date."

Kennedy turned back to him with an amused expression. "Ah . . . Rosa and her setups. She's always trying to fix me up, and I'm *always* saying no. Did she do the same to you?"

He scratched his chin. "Yeah — as a matter of fact she did."

"Hmm . . . Rosa has a dating obsession. Take no notice."

"I didn't. But now that we've met, I *would* like to discuss the murders with you."

Finally he had her attention. "Do you have information?" she asked, regarding him with serious green eyes.

"I used to be a detective in New York. Worked a couple of serial-killer cases over the years. Maybe we can have a drink later and talk about it."

"I'm on my way home."

"Another time?"

"If you have anything to add, yes. Rosa has my number."

"Okay, Michael, it's show time," said his production assistant. "They're waiting."

"I'll get your number from Rosa," he said, allowing himself to be led away. "And I'll call you — soon."

She nodded and watched as he was escorted down the corridor. For once Rosa was right, Michael Scorsinni was a great-looking guy. But she was not in the market for great-looking guys. She was not in the market for anybody.

All the same, she found herself lingering in the green room, waiting to watch his interview.

He came across as sincere and sympathetic. Once she heard his story, she felt genuinely sorry for him. What a nightmare situation, not knowing where your child was.

When he came back to the green room she was

still there. "Changed my mind," she said casually. "I think I will have a drink."

He smiled ruefully. "Feeling sorry for me, huh?"

Her eyes met his. "Exactly."

"Is there a Michael Scorsinni here?" somebody yelled from one of the offices.

"That's me."

"You have a phone call. Press extension three and pick up."

He hurried over to the phone sitting on a corner table. "Yeah?"

A muffled female voice. "Michael Scorsinni?"

"That's right."

"I saw you on TV."

"Yes?"

"I can help you find your kid, but it'll cost."

"Who is this?" he asked urgently.

"It doesn't matter who I am. Listen good — I *know* where your kid is, an' if you want to see her again you'd better come up with ten thousand in cash. I'll be in touch."

"No — wait a minute! We can talk about the money, but first I need proof she's alive."

"Try this for proof."

He heard a scrambling on the other end of the line, and then a child's voice, "Daddy! Daddy!"

Oh, Jesus, it was just like the last time. He was almost positive it was Bella.

32

They sat in a bar across the street from the TV station. Kennedy sipped a vodka martini and Michael had his usual nonalcoholic beer in front of him, although right now he yearned for something stronger.

"I'm not the greatest company in the world tonight," he admitted, rubbing his chin, thinking to himself that he was incredibly attracted to this woman. It wasn't so surprising — she was coolly beautiful, with a subtle sex appeal.

"You don't have to be," Kennedy said, wondering why she felt so drawn to this man she hardly knew. Was she merely sorry for him? Or was there a genuine attraction? "If I were in your position I'd be insane by now."

"It's the not knowing that's such a bitch. I think of Bella all the time. It's like a constant ache. I think about where she is, what she's doing, or — even worse — if she's dead. Because if she is, it would almost be better knowing."

"The strain must be unbearable."

"It is. No leads. Nothing on who killed my ex-wife and her boyfriend. I call the detectives working the case every day — they're understanding, but they've got nothing to go on. And

397

then I get a call like this, and I imagine I hear her voice . . ."

Impulsively Kennedy placed her hand over his. "You can't be sure it was her on the phone. It could be somebody trying to get money out of you."

"Yeah — fine chance! Where would I come up with ten thousand bucks?"

"I don't know what to say, Michael."

"Hey." He paused. "It's enough that we're here talking. It makes a difference. Quincy, my partner, he's away right now." Another pause. "Besides, you're great to talk to."

She moved her hand away and smiled. "I missed my vocation. Maybe I should have been a bartender." She picked up her drink and sipped it slowly. "Where's your family, Michael?"

"New York. I got one brother — a real loser. And my mother has her own problems."

"How about your father?"

"He took off when I was a kid. My stepfather brought me up. Eddie Kowlinski — a real jewel of an asshole."

"Do you see them often?"

He laughed dryly. "Not if I can help it."

"Hardly *Little House on the Prairie*, huh?"

"Hey — you're pretty good at this."

"What?"

"Asking questions. Getting things out of me."

"It's my job."

"Do you mind if I smoke?"

"As long as you don't blow it in my face."

He lit a cigarette and squinted. "I noticed your ring. You married, Kennedy?"

398

"My husband died," she said quietly.

"I'm sorry."

"He was a great guy."

"If he was married to you I bet he was," he said, regarding her seriously for a moment. "So here we are, sitting in a bar, and the funny thing is I don't even drink."

"Never?"

"I used to be a crazy man. AA saved me. I've been dry for several years now."

"Me, I'm a social drinker," she said. "If there's a glass of wine I'll drink it — if it's not around I don't miss it."

"You're lucky. One drink puts me over the edge."

"I'm glad you're not over the edge, Michael."

"And I'm glad we're sitting here having a drink together."

She smiled. "Wouldn't Rosa be surprised?"

He smiled back. "It's hardly a date, but I guess she'd be pleased, huh?"

"Ecstatic! Let's not tell her."

"You got it."

He took a pull on his cigarette. "So how did you get involved in this murder investigation?"

"I was deciding what to write for the magazine I work for. My father was sick, and a woman was murdered near the hospital. One of the things my father said to me before he died was, 'You should write about ordinary people instead of the rich and famous.' And you know something? He was right. So I started to investigate the first murder and discovered there were others that might be connected. The police weren't interested, so Rosa

399

talked me into appearing on TV to see if we could light a fire."

"She's good at that."

"You mentioned you worked on a couple of serial-killer cases in New York. What do you make of this one?"

What was he supposed to say? That he knew who was committing the murders? That right now he couldn't do anything about it? Jeez, she'd really respect him for that.

"To tell you the truth, I haven't been following it," he said, avoiding her eyes.

"Maybe you should. I'd appreciate your input."

He waved for the check. "Y'know, it's late. I gotta go, I'm working on a case. There's this rich girl who's being stalked . . ."

"Really? Think it could be related?"

"I doubt it. But I'll let you know if anything develops."

"Do that, Michael."

"How about we try this again?"

She laughed wryly. "What — tell each other our troubles?"

"I could buy you dinner tomorrow night."

"I'm busy tomorrow."

"Then can I call you?"

She looked at him very directly. "I think I'd like that."

Bobby awoke Tuesday morning regretting that he'd agreed to have lunch with Barbara Barr.

When he arrived home from location the night before, she'd been waiting in his bed, incense burning, a mound of caviar piled in a glass dish, and a matching mound of cocaine on the bedside table.

He was furious. "How did you get into my house?" he demanded angrily.

"I broke in." She giggled, jumping out of bed stark naked and throwing her arms around him. "I knew you'd be hungry, so I brought you caviar. It's a gift from me to you. So's the coke."

"I don't do drugs, Barbara," he said, trying to extract himself from her clinging embrace.

"You don't? Why not?"

" 'Cause it screws up your head. So put on your clothes, take your coke, and get out of my house."

"Sorry," she said, with a sarcastic twist to her mouth. "I didn't realize I was dealing with Mister Clean."

"I don't appreciate your breaking in, Barbara."

Her eyes glittered dangerously. "I could suck you off, Bobby. Or I could fuck you good. How about it?"

The way she said it scared him. There was something way off about Ms. Barbara Barr.

"We'll have lunch tomorrow and talk," he said, trying to stay calm. "Right now I'm going to sleep."

Somehow he'd managed to get her out of his house and into her car.

Because she was about to star in his movie, he was caught in a trap. Before lunch he had Beth check her out, and she came up with a pile of lurid headlines from the tabloids. Bobby felt foolish, he should have known that Barbara Barr was trouble about to happen.

Over lunch she regaled him with stories of her exploits. "I've got this reputation for being out of my head," she said, with an uncontrollable giggle. "Queen of the rags! I don't know why. If somebody insults me, like this tramp did the other night outside a club, I smash 'em in the face. Wouldn't you?"

"No, Barbara, that's how you get sued."

"Nobody's going to sue me, I can assure you of that," she said boldly. "I have two brothers who'll break their fucking balls one at a time."

Oh, shit!

"Can we have dinner tonight?" she asked, playing with a silver crucifix hanging around her neck on a long black cord.

"No."

She crinkled her forehead. "What do you mean, no?"

"It's not a good idea."

"Why not?" she demanded, pouting.

"Barbara, back off."

"Back off?" she said, her voice rising. "Back off? What's with you, Bobby? I'm not the kind of girl you can fuck and then run. You'd better remember that."

"I didn't say you were."

"Good." Her eyes glittered dangerously. "As long as we understand each other."

After lunch he couldn't wait to get away. He knew that casting her as Sienna had been a grave mistake, and there was only one solution.

He had to figure out a way to get them out of the commitment and Barbara off the movie before it was too late.

Luca Carlotti flew to California with two of his henchmen — Reno Luchesi and Bosco Nanni. Both good guys. Both men he could trust.

Trust and loyalty meant everything to Luca. As far as he was concerned, without trust and loyalty you were deader than a dog in a ditch.

Reno Luchesi was Luca's crown prince. At thirty-nine, Reno was tall and manly-looking, with light-brown hair that fell casually onto his forehead, long, sweeping eyelashes, and an innocent expression. His expression belied his true personality.

Reno was a killer — there was nothing he liked better than beating a man to death.

Bosco Nanni was a short, rotund man with pop eyes, hairy hands, and no chin. He was nicknamed The Pig because of his excesses with women. Bosco could never get enough pussy, and because of his less than perfect appearance he tried harder in bed. It worked every time. Most of the women he slept with claimed he was the best lover they'd ever had.

They made an odd trio, but as far as Luca was concerned the three of them were totally compatible.

The flight to Los Angeles was uneventful, although Bosco managed to screw one of the stewardesses in the cramped toilet. "Whaddaya want from me?" he said with a shrug, after he had returned to his seat with a sly smile. "She's a neighborhood girl. I owed her a favor."

They arrived shortly before noon on Tuesday. A limousine with a handpicked driver met them at the airport and drove them directly to the St. James's Hotel, where Luca had reserved three separate suites.

As soon as Luca was settled he requested a manicure, a pedicure, and a massage. It wasn't until he'd received all three that he called Mac, reaching him at home. "I suggest we meet," he said. "It's been too long. Drop by the hotel."

"If you think it's necessary," Mac replied stiffly.

Luca was not happy with his response. "We agreed you was gonna live your life," he said. "But sometimes, I gotta tell you, your attitude surprises me."

"I'm not a kid, Luca," Mac said hotly, feeling like one. "Don't speak to me like I'm a goddamn kid."

"Be here at four o'clock."

Bosco was already on the line in the living room of Luca's suite, busy finding out where the action was. "L.A.'s got the best-looking hookers in the world," he informed Luca. "Better than Vegas."

"Vegas hookers are shit," Luca commented, inspecting his manicure. "They got no class."

"Not in my opinion," Bosco answered, ready for a lengthy discussion. "I almost married a Vegas dancer once. She gave the greatest head I ever had."

"You wouldn't know a good hooker if she sat on your face." Reno snickered, picking up a handful of nuts and tossing them into his mouth one by one.

Bosco threw him a disgusted look.

"Me, I've *never* had to pay for it," Reno boasted,

brushing out a crease in his pants. He aspired to Luca's sartorial perfection, but didn't quite cut it.

"Then you don't know what you're missin'," Bosco said, with a wink in Luca's direction. "You get a classy-lookin' broad, pay her to do whatever you want, an' the best thing is she don't give you no grief. You don't even havta buy her nothin' — not even dinner, not even a friggin' drink! She just fucks the shit outta you an' goes home."

Reno shook his head. "I've never paid for it," he repeated. "Never have. Never will. Never needed to."

Luca started to laugh. Reno and Bosco were about as opposite as two people could get. Watching them together was like having his own entertainment channel.

"I found out there's a new place runnin' the best call girls in town," Bosco announced. "Primo pussy. You want I should order one for you, Luca?"

Luca considered the question. If he was going to deal with Zane he would certainly feel horny. Violence always made him horny. "Yeah," he said. "Why not? Get me a short one, big tits, red hair, and a nurse's uniform."

"A nurse's uniform?" Reno said. "What're you — sick?"

"Didn't I tell you about the time I was in the hospital when I was sixteen?" Luca said. "Some crazy bastard busted my leg with a baseball bat. There was this nurse took care of me, a real looker — gave head like she was suckin' the chrome off a 1969 Cadillac! Yeah, get me a fuckin' nurse."

They all laughed.

Sitting out by the pool reading *Variety*, Jordanna stopped at Army Archerd's column because she spotted Jordan's name. She read the few lines quickly and her heart jumped.

Friends of Jordan Levitt's will be pleased to know the abdominal pains he suffered recently were nothing serious, and after an overnighter in Cedars he's now home.

She read it twice, furious that no one had called her. Then she realized, how could they? Neither Jordan nor Kim knew where she was.

The time had come to make her peace. What if anything had happened to him?

Since she'd moved out of Charlie's and started working, she felt pretty good about herself. Good enough to forget about her differences with Kim and make peace. Yes, she decided, it was definitely time to resolve matters with Jordan — time to let go. Whatever Jordan had done in the past, it was *his* life, and now she'd finally realized it. So Kim used to be a call girl. Big deal. At least she was making Jordan happy. Maybe that was all that counted.

She drove over to her father's house, zooming her Porsche up the driveway. She knew he was home because his Bentley was parked outside.

Jumping out of her car, she ran up to the front door. "Hi," she said to the Filipino houseman who let her in. "Is my father around?"

"He's in his study, Miss Levitt," the man said.

"Thanks," she said, entering the house and heading for Jordan's study. "Surprise!" she exclaimed, flinging open the door.

He glanced up from behind his desk. "Where *the hell* have you been?" he said gruffly.

She wrinkled her nose. "That's a nice greeting. And I thought you were supposed to be sick."

"I'm serious, Jordanna," he said sternly. "Where *have* you been? Don't you think I worry about you? You take your things and run out of here, leaving no forwarding address. I don't appreciate that kind of thoughtless behavior."

"I'm not a little girl, Daddy."

"You behave like one."

Oh, God, were they destined to fight straight off?

"Look," she said sensibly. "I came here today because I wanted to tell you that I have a job, I'm looking for an apartment, and I don't need your money anymore — I'm making it on my own. I hoped you'd be proud of me."

He continued to frown.

"*Are* you proud of me?" she persisted.

"I've heard all kinds of rumors," he grumbled. "I *even* heard you were living with Charlie Dollar, but I knew that couldn't be true, he's almost the same age as me, for chrissake."

"Of course I'm not living with him," she said, adding a silent "anymore."

He stood up. "I'm relieved."

"So am I," she said. "I read you were in the hospital."

"Gas."

"Charming!"

"One fart, and they let me out."

"You're disgusting!"

"Merely truthful, my dear."

She giggled. "Anyway," she said warmly, "I came to congratulate you — I heard about the baby."

"Who told you?"

"Kim did when I collected my things. I'm really happy for both of you."

He was waiting for the catch.

There wasn't one.

"Do you need a check?" he asked suspiciously.

"No. I told you — I have a job. And I'm not writing a book. I'm working on Mac Brooks's new movie as assistant to Bobby Rush. I'm learning about the business, just like you always told me I should. Hey — maybe one day I'll even be a producer like you."

"Jordanna, are you sure you're feeling all right?"

"You know what, Daddy? I've never felt so good. I think it's because I've finally found out being independent works for me."

He held open his arms. "Come here, skinny bird."

"Don't *call* me that," she said, not really cross at all.

"Come *over* here."

She walked up to him, and he wrapped her in a big hug. "I've missed you," he said, holding her close.

"I've missed you too," she replied, feeling a rush of emotion. "I was so worried when I read you were in the hospital."

At that moment a breathless Kim entered the room. "What's going on?" she asked in a strained voice.

"We're having a father-daughter reunion," Jordan said, beaming.

"Hi, Kim," Jordanna said in full friendly mode. "How are you feeling?"

"Fine," Kim said uneasily, waiting for her to ruin everything.

"I'm glad to hear that."

"So here we are," Jordan said, unaware of the tension. "All my girls together. This is wonderful. We should go out and have a celebration lunch."

Kim chewed on her bottom lip. "*Can* we call it a celebration?" she said, staring meaningfully at Jordanna.

"Yes, Kim," Jordanna said quietly. "We certainly can."

"Nice of you to make it back," Michael said, greeting Quincy at the door.

"Can you believe it?" Amber said, lugging the baby inside, while the toddler trailed behind, clinging tightly to her skirt. "I *told* him he was a lousy skier. But did he listen? Oh no, Mister Big Sports Star Robbins just says, What you worryin' 'bout, baby? An' then promptly skis into a tree!"

Quincy managed to look sheepish. "I didn't *see* that tree, honey. It came outta nowhere."

"Don't you *honey* me!" she scolded. "I'm putting the kids down for a nap, and I am *not* cooking dinner tonight, so don't you be expecting any."

"I'm a wounded man," Quincy said plaintively. "I need sympathy an' lovin' care."

"Get it from Michael, 'cause *this* store is closed."
She vanished upstairs with the children.

"Ain't marriage grand." Quincy sighed, walking into the living room and flopping down on the couch.

"Seems like she's pissed," Michael said.

"Dunno why. *I'm* the one with the broken arm."

"Okay," Michael said. "Let's get serious. There's been plenty going on while you've been away."

"There has? Why didn't you call?"

" 'Cause I figured it could hold until you got back."

"Do me a favor — get me a beer from the kitchen."

"How long you gonna be in the cast?"

"The doc said six weeks."

"Jeez!"

"I know."

Michael went into the kitchen and grabbed a can of beer from the fridge. He couldn't stop thinking about Kennedy. He'd never met a woman like her before. Beautiful *and* smart — a killer combination. He was looking forward to seeing her again.

"Where's my beer?" Quincy yelled.

"Coming."

He took Quincy his beer, sat next to him on the couch, and began filling him in.

After lunch Bobby drove over to the screening room at the studio, just in time to view the dailies with Mac. He turned to Mac when the lights went up, expecting praise. Instead Mac glanced at his watch and muttered a fast, "I've got to go."

"What did you think of the scenes we just saw?" Bobby asked.

"They're good. Cedric Farrell's giving a fine performance as your father. He's a real pro."

Just what an actor longed to hear — praise for another actor. Bobby couldn't help feeling hurt, he needed praise too.

"We have to talk," he said. "There's a major problem about to happen."

Mac looked at him sharply. Did Bobby know? How could that be? "Later," he said, halfway out the door. "I have a meeting."

"This is important, Mac."

"So's my meeting."

"Then you'd better come by the production office later."

"I'll try," Mac said, running out of there like he had a rocket up his ass.

Bobby hurried across the lot to the office, where the first person he ran into was his brother Stan, now working in the accounts department.

"Bobby!" Stan exclaimed happily. Since scoring a job he'd cheered up considerably.

"Hey, Stan, how's it going?" Bobby said, hoping he wasn't about to be trapped.

"Couldn't be better," Stan replied. "Everything's under control."

"Good," Bobby said. "Let's keep it that way."

Stan was still around, but Len had gotten canned after the first week because he'd come to work drunk three days in a row. Len's wife, Trixie, had been trying to reach Bobby to complain about

411

the firing, but so far he'd managed to avoid her calls.

Bobby made a fast escape upstairs to his office; he simply wasn't comfortable around Stan.

Beth greeted him with downcast eyes. "I have really bad news, Bobby."

"What?"

"Cedric Farrell's wife just called. He had a heart attack."

"Oh, Jesus! Is he at Cedars?"

"No," Beth said quietly. "He died an hour ago."

"God, that's terrible."

"I know."

"How old was he?"

"Seventy-two."

"Can we do anything?"

"His wife said she'll let us know the arrangements."

It was shocking news. One moment Cedric was walking around perfectly healthy, and the next gone. He couldn't believe it.

When the news sank in he began to realize they were in a crisis situation. Cedric had been in almost every frame for the last two days, now they'd have to recast and reshoot. This would put them behind schedule and over budget.

"Try and get hold of Mac," he said, thinking fast. "We'll need him. And call Nanette Lipsky pronto. Get everyone up here as soon as possible."

Beth couldn't reach Mac, since he'd failed to leave a number, but she did manage to locate everyone else.

They gathered for an emergency meeting: Nanette and Florrie, Gary, Tyrone, and several of the production staff. They sat around the office, trying to come up with a solution.

"I got it, Bobby," Nanette Lipsky said at last, flicking thick cigarette ash on the floor. "It's a helluva idea — but knowing you, you'll probably spit in my face."

"Let's hear it," Bobby said. "I'll try not to spit too hard."

Nanette took another long pull on her cigarette, inhaled deeply, and said, "Your old man."

"My old man?" he repeated blankly.

"Jerry Rush. He's your father in real life — what could be better?"

"Jesus!" Bobby said, slapping his forehead. "Don't even suggest it."

Nanette's expression was inscrutable. "You want to spit now or later?"

But the seed was planted. And Bobby knew in his heart that Jerry would be perfect for the role.

Somehow or other Jerry's name slipped out of the room and reached the studio honchos. One of them called to offer his congratulations. "Bobby, this is the best piece of stunt casting I've heard in a long time. Will Jerry do it?"

"We haven't made a decision," Bobby said edgily. "I'll have to talk to Mac, he's unreachable right now." And then he came up with a brilliant idea. "Tell you what," he added. "If I hire Jerry Rush to play my father, can we work out a way to pay off Barbara Barr? I feel strongly that she's not right for the role, we made a bad choice. Plus I got this strong hunch she'll cause us nothing but trouble."

"You saw the story in the tabloids too, huh?"

"What story?"

"Apparently she had a fight with a girl outside a club, and now the girl is suing her for ten million bucks."

"I'm telling you, if we can pay her off and come out of this clean, we'll be better off."

"So we'll cut a deal, Bobby. You get us Jerry, and we'll let you go with who you want for Sienna."

"Sounds good to me."

The Man had been busy. Tracking Cheryl Landers was no mean feat.

First he'd visited the address he had for her in Bel Air. He'd watched and waited for two days, but there was no sighting of her.

On the third day she'd appeared at lunchtime, driving a silver BMW. Shortly after arriving she left again — with a woman in the passenger seat who looked like she could be her mother.

He followed them to the Bistro Gardens on Cañon, where they had lunch.

When they were through there they went shopping. He trailed them to Saks and Magnin's. Rich women idling away the afternoon — how he loathed them both.

Eventually Cheryl drove back to the Bel Air house. She dropped off her mother and drove away, heading back to Beverly Hills.

The Man was right behind her.

She stopped at Thrifty's on Cañon Drive. He parked his car and followed her into the large drugstore — eyes covered by his blackout Armani shades, hair neatly scraped back in a ponytail.

Cheryl would never recognize him. Even if they came face-to-face in one of the aisles she would not know who he was.

He liked that. It made him feel powerful. He knew who she was, and yet he was able to remain totally anonymous.

Taking a basket, he filled it with a few items as he trailed Cheryl around the store.

She wheeled a cart, throwing in boxes of Kleenex, packets of candy, a bunch of magazines, cartons of cigarettes, condoms, and several cans of bug spray.

Next she went over to the liquor section. She filled the cart with three giant bottles of margarita mix and two bottles of tequila.

He stood in the checkout line behind her and observed as she paid with a gold credit card. Then he followed her out to the parking lot, where he watched her load her car.

Go home, bitch! *he thought to himself.* Go home so I can find out where you live.

When she set off, he was right behind her as she drove up Benedict Canyon, turning on Beverly Grove Park Road.

She drove up into the hills and turned into a private driveway. He parked and waited a few minutes, then he left his car and scurried up the driveway on foot. He was in time to see Cheryl at the front door of a country-style house, unloading her shopping bags, being helped by a Mexican maid.

Now he knew where she lived.

Plans. He had to make plans. Because it was not going to be so easy for Cheryl Landers. She would suffer before the final cleansing — just as he had suffered in jail.

Soon he'd have to move out of the house. The last check he'd received from one of Luca's companies had been for six thousand dollars. He'd carefully changed the amount to sixty thousand and deposited it in an account he'd opened with a phony name. Over the next few days he'd withdrawn the cash. Once his uncle found out about the check he'd be after him.

He'd already starting making preparations for the future. A week ago he'd purchased several guns — one of them an Uzi automatic — and a good supply of bullets. Now he had money and weapons. It made him feel invincible. Nobody could touch him ever again.

Driving back to the house, he was suddenly overcome with bad vibrations. Something was amiss. In prison he'd developed an antenna for trouble, it never let him down.

Before entering the driveway he parked on the street, and once more he made his way carefully up the driveway on foot, staying near the shrubbery.

Parked outside the entrance to the house was a long black limousine. Leaning against it, puffing on a fat cigar, was Bosco Nanni, one of his uncle's associates.

The Man felt a shiver of fear. Did this mean that Uncle Luca was somewhere in the vicinity?

Had he found out about the check?

It was more than likely.

The Man edged back down the driveway

until he reached the safety of his car. Then he drove a block away and parked, keeping the entrance to the house in sight.

He was mad at himself. He should have moved days ago. Bad timing on his part.

He'd wait until they left, collect his things, and never come back. He could outsmart his uncle any day.

Where to go? That was the question. He pondered, thinking hard. Several days ago he'd found a note from Shelley stuck on his door. She'd written that she'd moved and would love him to come and see her. She'd included her new address.

He'd stuffed the piece of paper in his shirt pocket, thinking nothing of it. Now he removed the note and read it through again.

Shelley was about to have a visitor.

33

Michael filled Quincy in and got his input. Once Quincy heard the Mac Brooks story he wanted immediate action. "We have to do something about those other two witnesses," he said.

Michael agreed with him.

"You can watch the Levitt girl," Quincy said. "I'll keep an eye out for Cheryl Landers."

"How'll you do that?" Michael asked, shaking loose a cigarette. "In case you've forgotten, your arm's in a cast."

"I can handle it," Quincy said. "I'll drive over to her house and sit outside in the car. Tomorrow I'll put a guy on it."

Michael lit up and took a drag. "What if anything came down?"

"Relax, it's my left arm. Besides, I'm carryin'. And put that cigarette out — you know Amber doesn't allow it."

Michael took another drag and searched for an ashtray. "The smart move would be to alert the detectives working this case," he said.

"No way," Quincy said sharply. "A private investigator has a privileged relationship with his clients, the same kind of confidentiality psychiatrists have with their patients. We can't break it. The business wouldn't be worth shit if we did."

"So we gotta sit back and let this go on?"

"If what you tell me about Kennedy Chase is true, the cops'll figure it out soon enough. They'll break the case without our help."

"I hope so."

"In the meantime, take my beeper. Give the number to Marjory and the Levitt girl. Tell her she might need to reach you on account of Marjory."

Michael headed back to the Sanderson mansion. Marjory was thrilled to see him. As soon as he walked through the door, she presented him with a gift-wrapped package.

"What's this?" he asked uncomfortably.

"A small present for taking such good care of me."

He frowned. "I can't accept it, Marjory."

"Why not?"

"Because I'm getting *paid* to take care of you."

"I know. But I can do something nice, can't I?"

He opened up the package. It was a special presentation set of the *Godfather* movies. "That's very thoughtful," he said warily. "But I told you — I can't accept it."

"Yes you can," she insisted. "And tonight I hope you'll have dinner with me."

He thought about Kennedy. She'd said she was busy, but he decided he'd call her anyway. "What time will Jordanna be back?" he asked, switching subjects, not even acknowledging her dinner invitation.

"You're always asking me about Jordanna," she said snippily.

"Since she's staying here, I've gotta know her movements," he explained.

"I have no idea, and quite frankly I don't care."

"Are they working today?"

"I'm not the production office."

She was a big help. "You know what? I'll be back later," he said, and much to her annoyance, he took off.

Luca had not visited the house he owned in California for many years. He'd bought it twenty-five years ago as a secret hideaway for a Hollywood actress who at the time was his West Coast mistress. She lived there until he'd flown in unexpectedly one day and discovered her in bed with a brawny stuntman. First he had them both beaten up, then he had them thrown out.

After that the house stood empty for a while, until a friend who was going to L.A. asked if he could use a room there. Luca said yes. Then the friend asked if another acquaintance could take up residence. Luca agreed. And somehow, over the years, it had become a crash pad for friends and acquaintances.

Luca had always intended to do something about the big empty house, but he'd never gotten around to it. And when Zane came out of prison, it seemed to be the perfect place to stash him.

When Luca entered the grounds he frightened the shit out of the old Japanese gardener, who leaped to attention. "Mr. Carlotti," the gardener exclaimed, eyes bugging with surprise. "You remember me?"

Luca stared at the weathered old man, who he could swear he'd never set eyes on before. "Yeah, yeah," he said cordially. Always be nice to the little people — you never knew when you might need them. "It's Juan . . . or Chico — right?"

"Tiko, Mr. Carlotti," the gardener said, beaming through his wrinkles, thrilled that the owner of the big house was actually paying a visit.

"Yeah, right. I'm gonna take a look around, Taki, check out you been doin' a good job."

The old gardener's head bobbed up and down. "I do the best for you, Mr. Carlotti. Always."

"Glad to hear it, Toko. How many people we got livin' here now?"

"Only one, Mr. Carlotti. There was a young lady staying, but she left a few days ago."

"Only one, huh?" His voice hardened. "Where is he?"

The gardener pointed at the house. "In the back room."

Luca nodded and entered the house, Reno close behind him.

"You want me to take him out soon as we see the prick?" Reno asked, impatiently cracking his knuckles.

"No, not here," Luca replied. "Not in my house. We'll take him for a ride."

"Will he give us trouble?" Reno asked, always hopeful.

"No chance," Luca replied confidently. " 'Cause *I'm* the one handin' him money. *I'm* the one supportin' the fucker."

Eldessa approached, lugging an ancient vacuum cleaner behind her. She stopped as soon as she saw them.

"Where's the guy that's livin' here?" Luca demanded.

She pointed to Zane's room, a few feet away, her face impassive. "It's locked," she said. "He don't allow nobody in there."

"You got a key?"

"No, sir."

"This is my house," Luca said. "You know that, don't you?"

"You been payin' me twenty-five years."

He reached into his pocket and slipped her a hundred-dollar bill. "I was never here today."

"I din't see nobody," she said, taking off, dragging the vacuum behind her.

Luca turned to Reno. "Break down the fuckin' door."

Reno inspected the door. "I need tools," he said, scratching his head. "This is a heavy-duty lock."

"Shit!" Luca said.

"If I have tools I can do it."

Luca stomped down the hallway, found a side door, and walked outside.

He peered into Zane's room from the garden. There were iron bars on the window, precluding entry.

"The cocksucker ain't home anyway," he said, turning around and strolling over to the swimming pool. He studied his reflection in the water. "This is a nice house," he remarked. "It occurred t'me I gotta renovate it. Put it on the market instead of it sittin' here empty."

Reno nodded his agreement.

"Let's go," Luca decided. "We'll come back tomorrow. The prick ain't goin' nowhere."

On their way out he stopped to talk to the gardener, slipping him a hundred bucks as well. "I wasn't here. Ya didn't see nothin'," he said gruffly.

The old man nodded as he pocketed the money.

Luca got into his limousine. It was nice to have loyal employees.

Mac was reluctant to visit Luca. He hadn't seen him since his mother's funeral, three years before, when he'd flown to New York. At that time he thought he'd never have to see him again.

He'd always been angry that Luca never made an honest woman of his mother. The two of them had been together for so many years, and when Luca's wife passed away ten years ago, Mac quite expected them to marry.

But no, they'd continued to maintain separate residences. Priscilla stayed in her Park Avenue penthouse, while Luca still resided in his Long Island mansion.

Mac had asked her about Luca once.

"Why would I marry him and spoil everything?" she'd said, as if it was the last thing she wanted.

His mother had been very beautiful, very remote, and completely loyal to Luca.

It pissed Mac off. Growing up, he'd never had her full attention.

The lobby of the St. James's Hotel was Art Deco and rather stylish. It seemed a strange choice for

424

Luca, but then he was always full of surprises. Mac hesitated, trying to figure out what he was doing there.

He had on his dark shades, but the woman behind the reception desk recognized him anyway. "Good evening, Mr. Brooks," she said with a touch of the deference famous film directors merited. "And what can we do for you this afternoon?"

"I have a meeting with Mr. Carlotti," he mumbled, not happy she'd recognized him.

She called Luca's room and pointed him toward the elevator. "Mr. Carlotti's in the penthouse suite. I certainly enjoyed your last film, Mr. Brooks."

"Thank you."

He took the elevator up.

Luca greeted him at the door, looking as dashing as ever. "Mac — good to see ya," he said, patting him on the shoulder, as Mac entered the luxurious suite. "How long's it been? Two years? Three?"

"My mother's funeral," Mac replied dourly.

"Ah, yeah. Priscilla's funeral — may she rest among the angels. She was some great lady."

I hardly knew her, Mac wanted to say. *She never had time for me. It was always you. You were the center of her universe. You were everything to her. Even my father was pushed into second place.*

"What'll you drink?" Luca asked, gesturing expansively toward the bar.

"Scotch on the rocks," he said, feeling uncomfortable.

"Help yourself."

He walked over and poured himself a healthy

dose of Scotch, adding several ice cubes. "You know, Luca," he said, settling on the couch, "it wasn't necessary for us to meet."

Luca did not take offense. "What — you didn't wanna meet with me?" he said good-naturedly.

"We made a decision when I came to Hollywood that our lives would be separate. I find this awkward."

Some of Luca's good humor slipped away. "Oh, you find it awkward, huh?"

Mac was silent.

"You didn't find it so awkward when you called to tell me about Zane."

Mac took a gulp of Scotch. "I told you because I felt I owed it to you." The ice cubes in his glass jangled noisily.

"Don't give me that bullshit," Luca snapped. "You told me 'cause you don't want it gettin' out you're in any way responsible for him bein' on your fuckin' movie."

"*I* wasn't responsible," Mac said sharply. "*You* were."

"You got a shitty attitude," Luca said. "An' I ain't too fond of it."

Mac held his glass so tightly it almost shattered. He got up, walked over to the window, and shrugged. "If you don't like my attitude, I can always leave."

"No, you can't fuckin' leave," Luca said, his hooded eyes angry. " 'Cause there's somethin' I gotta tell you. Somethin' I shoulda told you a long time ago, only your mother wouldn't let me."

"What?"

"You ain't gonna like it. Or maybe you will."

The room was full of the smell of Luca's potent aftershave, he hadn't changed it in twenty-five years. Mac found it brought back every bad memory of the day his father was gunned down. He remembered that fateful day so vividly. Luca had given him the bad news. Embracing him tightly, he'd said, "Kid, your old man's gone, but he's probably in a better place."

And that had been that.

Ever since then, the smell of Luca's aftershave had made him queasy.

I am a grown man, he thought to himself. *I am a world-renowned film director. I have won an Oscar. I don't need to sit in this room and be intimidated by the likes of Luca Carlotti.*

"So," Luca said. "This is the deal, son."

"Do me a favor," Mac interrupted sharply. "Don't call me 'son.' " It was the first time he'd said it out loud, and it felt good.

Luca adopted a pained expression. "I always looked after you, didn't I?" he said. "I always made sure you had the best."

Mac nodded. He couldn't deny that Luca had done everything he could. Only sometimes everything wasn't enough.

"Whatever you asked for you got," Luca continued, throwing his arms wide. "Was there anythin' I didn't do for you?"

Including fuck my mother, Mac wanted to say, but he refrained from doing so.

"No, Luca, you were always good to me," he said levelly. "It's not that you weren't. But we moved on to different lives, and as the years have passed I've realized I can never forget that my father got shot with a bullet meant for you."

Luca began pacing up and down. "I understand," he said. "An' that's why it's about time
you listened to the truth."

"What truth?"

"There ain't no easy way t'say this," Luca said,
suddenly standing very still and staring at him.
"So I'll try an' give it t'you straight." A long silent
beat. "Your old man was never your old man."
Another beat. "*I'm* your real father."

The glass shattered in Mac's hand, slicing into
the soft skin between his thumb and forefinger.
Ice cubes and Scotch spilled onto his pants, along
with a stream of blood.

Luca said nothing. He walked into the bathroom, returning with a towel.

Mac wrapped the towel around his wounded
hand. He was stunned. "I — I — don't believe
you," he finally stammered.

"I don't care whether you believe me or not,"
Luca said, his smoothly suntanned face impassive.
"I hadda keep it to myself all these years outta
respect for your mother. Y'know, Priscilla an' me,
we was always in love, ever since we was kids."

"Then why didn't you marry her?"

" 'Cause we had a dumb fight an' didn't talk
for a coupla years. During that time I married
a rich broad whose father helped finance me —
put me into business, so to speak. By the time
Priscilla an' I got back together, she was married
too. We made the best of a bad situation. I hired
her husband — the man you thought was your
father — an' the three of us started hangin' out.
My wife was sickly, she stayed at home most of

the time." He took another long beat before continuing. "When your mother got pregnant she hadn't slept with her husband in over a year. He wasn't into sex — not with her anyway."

"What does that mean?"

"You want I should spell it out? It means he was a fag. A pansy. A pretty boy."

Mac was so shocked he could barely speak. "Why are you telling me now?" he managed at last.

" 'Cause I'm a rich man, a powerful man. I got a sister dumber than shit. She's got a kid who's a murdering cocksucker. An' the only real relative I got is you." He sighed. "I'm sixty-four years old, Mac. If anything happens to me, it's all yours."

"I don't want it," Mac said forcefully.

Luca's chuckle was totally humorless. "Whether you want it or not, you got it, son. Oh, yessiree — you got every single red cent."

By the time she left her father and Kim, Jordanna felt really good about things. She finally understood him, and by understanding him she could accept him. It was all so easy.

She decided to drop by the production office before she went home to prepare for her date with Tyrone.

At the office, Florrie was running around looking frantic, carrying stacks of photographs under her arm.

"What's going on?" Jordanna asked. "I thought we were off today."

"Emergency meeting," Florrie said, full of her

own importance. "Didn't you get a call?"

"No, I haven't been home. What happened?"

"Cedric Farrell died. He had a heart attack."

"That's awful."

"We have to find a replacement immediately."

"Is everybody upstairs?"

"No, the meeting just finished. We're bringing in a couple of actors tomorrow morning, but the word is we might hire Bobby's father, Jerry."

"Would Bobby go for that?"

"Dunno, but it'll be great PR for the movie."

Jordanna ran upstairs and burst into Bobby's office. He was sitting behind his desk, looking tired and drained.

She stifled a strong desire to put her arms around him and hold him close. "I'm sorry, Bobby," she said softly. "I only just heard."

"Hey — it's one of those things."

"Cedric was a sweetheart. Everyone liked him."

"Yeah, we'll all miss him."

"You look exhausted. Can I get you anything?"

He laughed dryly. "How about a new life?"

Smiling ruefully, she said, "I'm good at a lot of things, but a new life might present a problem."

Drumming his fingers on the desktop, he said, "You heard the news, I suppose. They want me to hire Jerry Rush."

"Florrie mentioned it. Are you going to?"

"Don't want to, but I can see where it would work for the movie."

She brushed back her long dark hair. "What comes first, Bobby? Your feelings or the movie?"

He shook his head. "You got me there."

"Guess where I was?" she said.

"I'm not in the mood for guessing games."

"I visited my dad. Made a peace pact."

"You did, huh?"

"I read he was in the hospital — nothing serious, but it freaked me out, so I went to see him." She paused for a moment. "Y'know, Bobby, we've never discussed it, but we both grew up in Hollywood with famous, powerful fathers, so I guess we shared a few problems. I decided to resolve mine."

"And did you?"

"Today was the first time I've seen Jordan without wanting anything from him. God, it felt good!"

"Why are you telling me?"

"Because you should do the same."

"I haven't wanted anything from my old man in a long time."

"Are you sure? Think about it. Love. Acceptance. Respect. It doesn't all revolve around money."

"You've been spending too much time at your therapist's."

"I don't go to a shrink anymore," she said earnestly. "I worked this out by myself. For years I was sitting in my father's guesthouse — not paying rent, collecting an allowance I thought I was entitled to. The result was I resented him. I thought everything he did reflected on me personally. Every time he got married I took it as a direct hit. But today I woke up and let go. He's him, I'm me. It's pretty damn simple. Now why are you so hung up about *your* dad?"

431

He looked at her quizzically. "You got several weeks to discuss it?"

"Bobby," she said fervently, "I wish I could explain it. Your father is probably a pain in the ass, but he's nothing to do with you. You're a grown-up, you don't have to answer to him anymore, you've proved yourself. And if it works for the movie, why *not* hire him?"

She was making sense, but he wasn't prepared to admit it. "Ever thought about appearing on TV, doing one of those inspirational programs? You'd be a smash," he said lightly.

She grinned. "Thanks. I always wanted to be a life enhancer."

"Okay, so you've convinced me. I'll go see Jerry."

"Want me to come with you?"

"You think I need the support?"

"Maybe."

"It's a deal. If I find myself weakening I'll look to you for inspiration."

"Whenever you're ready."

He stood up. "First I've got to reach Mac. I can't make this decision without him. There's also no guarantee Jerry will want to do it."

"C'*mon*, Bobby — when was the last time he worked?"

"Jerry was a huge star."

"Every star makes its descent. *You're* the huge star in the family now. Believe me, he'll be thrilled."

He walked around the desk and stood near her. "You've got a lot to say, haven't you?"

"Right now, yes — 'cause I'd really like to

get through to you."

"You would, huh?"

They locked stares until Bobby broke it by walking back behind his desk. "Uh . . . Beth's been trying to reach Mac for the last couple of hours. It might be a good idea for you to take over."

She nodded. "Sure, I'll get right on it."

"So I'll see you later."

"Yes, Bobby."

She ran downstairs and tried Mac's home number.

"How many times must I tell you people," Sharleen said irritably. "Mac is *not* home. When he gets here I'll have him call back."

"It's urgent."

"I gathered."

Jordanna hung up just as Tyrone put his head around the door. He tapped his watch. "I'm supposed to be picking you up in half an hour. What are you doing here?"

Oh, God, she'd forgotten all about their dinner date. "I'm sorry, Tyrone," she said sheepishly. "I can't make it tonight."

"You can't make it tonight," he repeated blankly.

"Nope," she said, hoping he wasn't too mad.

"That's too bad."

"Sorry."

"I'm *very* disappointed. I had everything planned."

"What did you have planned?"

"That's for me to know and you to find out next time."

"I'll look forward to it."

He shook his head. "You're a difficult one."

She smiled winningly. "Makes life interesting, doesn't it?"

34

Mac drove home in a fog, almost rear-ending a Volvo at a stoplight. There were so many questions he needed to ask, and nobody to supply him with the answers.

Why had his mother lied to him all those years?

When his father was shot, why hadn't she and Luca told him the truth and brought him up as their own son?

He reached his house feeling angry and confused. It was not peaceful. His two sons and several of their friends were gathered in the game room, playing a noisy game of pool. Guns N' Roses blared through the stereo speakers, deafening everyone within earshot.. Sharleen's daughter, Suzy, was sitting in the kitchen with a bunch of girlfriends, watching a tape of *Melrose Place*. They were painting their nails while stuffing their faces with peanut-butter-and-jelly sandwiches, cookies, and Häagen-Dazs ice cream bars. The kitchen was a mess.

"Where's your mother?" he asked abruptly.

Suzy waved at him. "Oh, hi, Mac."

"Oh, hi, Mac," chorused her girlfriends.

They all looked like escapees from a teenage porno movie in their ass-clinging little shorts with cutoff tank tops exposing far too much bare flesh.

"Hello, girls," he said, feeling ancient. "Where did you say your mother was, Suzy?"

"In the gym with her trainer," Suzy said, licking ice cream with a suggestive tongue. "You'd better knock before you go in. Have you *seen* Mom's trainer? He's a hunk. Awesome body! *Big* pecs!"

The girls all thought this was hilarious. They collapsed in fits of giggles.

Mac walked to the back of the house, where they'd converted a spare bedroom into a fully equipped gym. The door was closed. He considered Suzy's warning but entered without knocking because he trusted Sharleen implicitly.

She was lying on the floor in a revealing white leotard, one leg in the air. Her leg was held aloft by Chip or Chuck or whatever her trainer's name was. As far as Mac was concerned, he was nothing more than a twenty-five-year-old muscle-bound jerk. Certainly no threat.

"Hi, honey," she greeted, blowing him a little kiss. "Care to join us?"

"No, thank you, Sharleen. I play squash and I jog. It's enough already."

"Okay, sweetie."

"When will you be finished?"

"I don't know." She gazed up at Chip appealingly. "How much more torture are you planning for me today?"

Chip grinned, displaying a dazzling row of extremely white teeth and a perfectly dimpled chin. "Now, now, Mrs. Brooks," he said with an annoying wink. "No shirking."

"How long?" Mac asked brusquely, hating the

bronzed and muscled trainer, who probably had a two-inch dick.

"About fifteen minutes, Mr. Brooks, sir," Chip said, helping Sharleen stretch her leg high in the air.

What kind of an asshole called him "sir"? "See if you can hurry it up," he snapped. "I need to talk to my wife."

"Everything okay, honey?" Sharleen inquired solicitously.

"Why wouldn't it be?"

"You look kind of pale. What did the studio want?"

"What do you mean?"

"They've called a dozen times."

This woman could drive a man crazy. "Sharleen," he said patiently. "How do I know they've called a dozen times if you don't tell me?"

Chip stretched her leg even higher. "I'm telling you now, sweetheart," she said, dividing her attention between him and Chip.

"Thank you," he said tightly. "I'll find out what they want right now."

He went into his study and slammed the door, trying to drown out the relentless din of Guns N' Roses. Then he fixed himself a large Scotch on the rocks and sat down at his desk. His hand — still wrapped in a towel — was beginning to throb. Nobody seemed to have noticed that he'd been hurt. Nobody gave a shit about anything anymore — including his own family. What did they care, as long as he was around to pay the bills?

He was not inclined to call the production office back, but the phone rang and he snatched it up.

"Mac?"

"Yes."

"It's Bobby. Where have you been?"

"You want I should fill in a report card?"

"I'm not aiming to make this difficult," Bobby said, ignoring his sarcasm. "But I've been trying to reach you for three hours. We've got big problems."

There was always a fucking problem. His life was turning into one major problem after another. "What is it now?" he asked shortly.

"Cedric Farrell died."

"Oh, Jesus!"

"Heart attack."

"I'm sorry to hear that. He was a nice man."

"Look, Mac, our immediate problem is recasting Cedric's role. While you've been away we've been trying to figure out what to do. There's an idea floating around I wanted to run by you. Can you drive in? Or shall I come to you?"

"I've got a bitch of a headache, Bobby. Tell me your idea, and I'll let you know what I think."

"It's not exactly my idea. The studio came up with it, and everybody else seems to like it. I figured it could be a good way for us to dump Barbara. If we can get away with paying her off, it might be the smartest way to go."

"So you're telling me you want to lose our leading lady and that you don't have a replacement for Cedric, is that it?"

"No, that's not it, Mac. We might have a replacement." He took a beat. "They're after me to hire Jerry."

"Jerry?"

"Jerry Rush. They've already got the publicity campaign mapped out."

"How do *you* feel about that?"

"I'm not sure. I figured if you went for it, we'd give it a shot."

"If it doesn't bother you, I'll agree."

"In that case maybe I'll drop by the house and talk to him. If we go through his agent it'll take six months to make a deal."

"Good idea."

"I'll check with you later."

"Do that," Mac said, putting down the phone. He took two hearty gulps of Scotch and slumped over with his head on the desk, which is how Sharleen found him when she entered his study a few minutes later. "What's the matter, sweetheart?" she asked, rushing over. "Something's wrong — what is it?"

He looked up at her with bloodshot eyes. "You ever have something happen to you where your whole world falls apart?"

She was alarmed, her eyes widened. "What?"

"Sharleen . . ." He shook his head. "There's so much to tell you. . . ."

Now she was genuinely concerned. "Baby, you know you can tell me anything."

Before he could answer, his son Kyle burst into the study — all lanky six feet three inches of him. "Dad, can we talk? Like we *really* gotta have a car conversation. Like I'm *really* bummed by that major piece of crap you're forcing me to drive."

Sharleen glared at him. "Can't you see we're in the middle of a conversation? Haven't you heard of knocking?"

"All I wanna do is speak to my dad," Kyle mumbled sulkily. "Big deal."

"We'll talk about your car tomorrow," Mac said, sitting up straight.

"I gotta leave the house early tomorrow," Kyle whined.

"Sorry I can't fit into your busy schedule," Mac said sarcastically.

"Don't get pissed, Dad. When I was in Hawaii, Mom told me she heard that model's not safe to drive. She said I should get a new one like right now."

"I don't give a horse's ass what your mother said!" Mac said, pulling himself together. "Now vanish. And next time you want to talk to me, knock before you barge in."

Kyle backed out. "*You're* in a pissy mood," he muttered, slamming the door behind him.

"I've got to get out of here tonight, Sharleen," Mac said urgently, shaking his head. "Let's book into a hotel."

Her face lit up. There was nothing she'd like better.

Grant took the call from Bosco Nanni and jotted down his requests. A buxom blonde and a short redhead with big tits.

"This is a late order," Grant said, enjoying his new role as superpimp. "I'm afraid it'll cost you."

"What are we talkin' here?" Bosco demanded. "A grand? Two?"

"We only have the best available. Five thousand apiece."

Bosco let out a long, low whistle. "Five fuckin' thou!"

"Believe me," Grant assured him, "they're worth it."

"*Shit!*"

But he didn't cancel the order. They made arrangements, and Grant replaced the receiver, then he quickly checked through Cheryl's files to see who wasn't busy.

Sissy would do for the blonde, he'd taught her well — for an amateur she certainly knew her stuff. Of course, she wasn't exactly buxom, but they'd never had any complaints about her.

The redhead was more difficult to come up with — they had only three on their books, and all three were booked for the night. Goddamn it! He'd just scored them a record price, and now he had no redhead to fill the order.

Cheryl was at the beauty parlor. He called her there, but the receptionist informed him she'd already left.

He waited impatiently, thinking about the consequences if his famous father ever found out what he was doing now — movie stars hated scandal, unless it was good for their careers.

What did their parents care anyway? Sometimes Grant thought he'd been brought into this world to be used as nothing more than a good photo opportunity. Childhood memories. His mother's dulcet tones.

Daddy's being photographed for Life.

Daddy's going to be on the cover of Time.

Daddy's being photographed for Newsweek.

And every so often they'd required little Grant to be in the pictures with Daddy, showing what a wonderful, caring family man Grant Lennon, Sr., was. This was to counteract the gossip magazines who were constantly exposing him as the biggest cocksman in town.

Being a celebrity in Hollywood meant creating an illusion, and the public liked that illusion to remain intact. Grant Lennon, Sr., gave great illusion.

Bullshit. It was all bullshit. That's why Grant hung out with Cheryl, Jordanna, and Shep. Because they all shared the same bullshit. They'd all grown up experiencing identical lifestyles. And it wasn't the most secure lifestyle in the world, although Grant had done a pretty good job of pretending it was.

It wasn't easy having Grant Lennon, Sr., as a father. It wasn't easy carrying the same name. Booze and recreational drugs had soothed the way most of his life, but sometimes it was impossible to avoid reality. And the reality was that he was a mere shadow of his famous father and had achieved exactly nothing on his own.

When Cheryl arrived home, he took one look at her and with a blinding flash of inspiration came up with the answer to his problem.

Her red hair was striking, definitely her most valuable asset. In fact, Cheryl — since her new-found success — was looking decidedly attractive.

"You'll never guess — " he began.

"What?" she interrupted, throwing down her purse.

"Have a drink."

"Will I need one?"

"Maybe," he said, going over to the bar.

She flopped into a chair and kicked off her shoes, wiggling her toes. "It's nice having you around, Grant. I can't imagine how I managed without you."

"How's your sense of adventure?" he asked, pouring her a stiff shot of vodka.

"Fine. How's yours?"

He handed her the glass. "Wanna do a line?"

"Why not," she said, wanting to do whatever he wanted to do.

"How tall are you?" he questioned, tipping a vial of coke onto the glass-topped coffee table.

"Five four. Why?"

"Some people might consider that short, right?"

She took a gulp of vodka and got ready to snort some coke. "Thanks a lot."

"No offense."

"None taken."

Grant arranged the white powder in neat lines, rolled a twenty-dollar bill, and handed it to her.

She bent over the table, put the bill to her left nostril, and inhaled deeply. Almost immediately she felt peaceful and powerful and sensual — all the good things.

"Any action while I was out?" she asked, leaning lazily back in her chair.

Grant's mind circled her like a predatory vulture. She had red hair. She was almost short. Her

443

tits weren't enormous, but in the right outfit they could fake that. He knew it would work. All he had to do was convince her.

"Cheryl," he said, crouching down beside her.

"Yes, Grant?"

"Uh . . . no, it doesn't matter."

"*What* doesn't matter?"

"You wouldn't do it. . . ."

"Wouldn't do *what?*" she asked, exasperated.

"It was just that I had this insane idea — but it's too way out there; I'm not even going to say it."

"Grant," she said patiently, "how long have we known each other?"

"Forever."

"Exactly. So since when can't you tell me your insane ideas?"

He snorted a line and poured more vodka into her glass. "Have I ever mentioned you're very sexy?"

"No, you've never mentioned that," she said slowly.

"I should've."

Was this the moment she'd waited for all these years? Was Grant actually coming on to her?

"You're not so bad yourself," she managed.

He moved closer to her, sliding his arm around her shoulder. "I got a proposition," he said. "And if you're half the girl I know you are, you're really going to go for it."

"Why are we doing this?" Bobby asked, as he drove down Sunset.

" 'Cause you want him for your movie,"

444

Jordanna replied logically.

"Yeah, but why are we doing this together?" he asked, genuinely puzzled. "How come I've got you tagging along?"

"You need moral support," she said crisply. "And that's me. Don't forget I'm your personal assistant. I'm *supposed* to be here."

He narrowed his blue eyes. "You are, huh?"

"I am."

He decided she was a good kid, and in spite of his early misgivings he was really beginning to like her. "There's something I'd better warn you about," he said, thinking of Jerry and his lecherous attitude.

"What's that?"

"Uh . . . Jerry may be an old guy, but he's a horny old guy. He's likely to hit on you."

This amused her. "Oh? He's likely to hit on me, is he?"

"Can you handle it?"

"Bobby, if there's one thing I've been handling all my life, it's old guys hitting on me."

"Your father's friends, huh?"

"Since I was twelve."

"And let's not forget Charlie Dollar."

"*I* can forget him — how about you?"

"That's another conversation."

"It is?" She wondered why he was always bringing up Charlie. Could it be that he was the tiniest bit jealous? "Anyway," she added, "I hope Jerry *does* come on to me."

"Why's that?"

" 'Cause I'll enjoy playing his game."

"Don't piss him off. As you just reminded me,

we're here to get him to do my movie."

"Bobby, listen to me — he'll scale the Empire State Building to get in your movie. Realize your own strength." She paused for a moment before adding, "You're a very special person."

He glanced at her quickly to see if she really meant it. Nobody had ever told him he was special before. Oh, sure — since becoming a movie star he'd received plenty of fan mail from women telling him he was handsome, sexy, gorgeous, fantastic, all of those things. But nobody had ever told him he was *special.*

"Hey — I'm not so special," he said, waiting for her to take it back.

She fixed him with a look. "Yes you are."

"Why's that?"

"Because I say so."

There was a strong moment of silence between them, then he pulled his car up in front of the house on Bedford and the moment passed.

They got out and walked up the driveway. He'd called Darla earlier and told her he was coming over to discuss something with Jerry. Now they were here and there was no backing out.

He rang the bell, and Darla answered the door. She was not looking her usual soignée self. Her face was puffy, her hair not as well coiffed as usual, and her outfit was hardly up to her designer duds standard.

"Bobby!" She seemed almost relieved to see him.

"Hi, Darla." And on automatic pilot: "You look well."

"Thank you, Bobby. So do you."

"Uh . . . this is Jordanna Levitt."

Darla was not slow. "Jordan Levitt's daughter?"

"Actually, Jordan's *my* father," Jordanna said pointedly.

Darla frowned, not quite getting the twist. "Jerry's so looking forward to seeing you," she said, taking Bobby's arm. "He hasn't been feeling well lately."

"He's not sick, is he?"

"No, it's just that things have been a little slow, and you know how your father is — he likes to be surrounded by action." She lowered her voice to a whisper. "The truth is he's been drinking too much."

"So what else is new?" Bobby said with a bitter twist. "Jerry's been drinking too much all his life."

Darla looked distressed. "Don't be like that, Bobby. He needs your support."

"That's why I'm here."

They followed her through the hallway and into the living room, where Jerry was sitting in exactly the same chair that Bobby had last seen him in, nursing what seemed to be exactly the same glass of Scotch — only this time he didn't bother getting up.

"Hi, Dad," Bobby said in an uptight voice.

"My son the movie star," Jerry said, slurring his words.

Why couldn't he be sober for once? Bobby thought. "Meet Jordanna," he said.

"Jordanna *Levitt*," Darla added, making sure Jerry got it. "Jordan's daughter."

Bobby and Jordanna exchanged glances. She shook her head as if to say, *Who gives a shit?*

Jerry perked up at the sight of Jordanna. Anything young, female, and beautiful was cause for a lecherous leer. "Welcome to my house, you pretty little thing," he said, raising his glass in a toast.

"Mr. Rush," she said tartly, "I'm not little, and I'm certainly not a thing."

"I get it," Jerry retorted, with a rude guffaw. "You're one of those feminist broads I'm not supposed to compliment anymore — is that right? Ever since Anita Hill found a pubic hair in her Coke bottle — "

"Mr. Rush," she interrupted, "you really are — "

"Jordanna," Bobby said quickly, catching her eye with a warning glance. "Remember why we're here?"

"Okay, okay," she muttered darkly, shutting up, although she would have liked nothing better than to ream into him.

Darla leaped into the fray. "Would you care for a drink?" she asked, ever the perfect hostess.

"No, thanks," Jordanna said.

"Not for me," Bobby said.

Jerry burped loudly, his favorite habit. "If you've come to borrow money you're outta luck," he said. "According to my lovely wife, we're busted out."

"We are *not* busted out, Jerry," Darla said, flushing with annoyance. "Things are a tad difficult, but nothing we can't manage. And kindly do not discuss our financial affairs in front of Jordan Levitt's daughter."

"Her name's Jordanna," Bobby said.

"So what's going on?" Jerry said, slurping down more Scotch. "You two an item? Jordan's got plenty of bucks — this little girl's a good catch."

"I *work* for Bobby," Jordanna said, trying to control her temper. "I'm his personal assistant."

Jerry laughed in a nasty fashion. "Sure, baby. A little personal assistance under the desk beats punching a time clock any day." He roared with laughter at his own humor.

What a sexist pig! Jordanna thought. *What an asshole! He and Bobby are totally different. Thank God!*

"Mr. Rush," she said, glaring at him, "if *I* had a male assistant I wouldn't expect *him* to crawl under my desk, and nobody expects a female to do so either. It's a sexist old-fashioned concept. Now you wouldn't want to be considered old-fashioned, would you?"

"What's that?" Jerry said, rudely cupping his ear as if he couldn't hear her.

"We'll come back tomorrow," Bobby said, deciding this was a really bad idea. "You're not in the mood to hear what I have to say."

"Yes he is," Darla said anxiously. "He's always like this."

Bobby wondered why he was here. He'd come to offer this man a job, and yet he was staring at a person he could not stand. His strongest desire was to walk out.

Jordanna took one quick look at Bobby and knew he was close to losing it. "How about fixing him coffee?" she suggested.

"Goddamn it!" Jerry shouted, contorting his

449

face. "You're talking about me like I'm not even here. *Jesus!*"

Jordanna shot another quick glance at Bobby. "Tell him the deal and let's split," she suggested.

Bobby realized she was right, he'd come here for a purpose, not to make best friends with his father.

"Okay," he said, speaking fast. "The actor playing my father died this morning. It puts us behind schedule and over budget if we don't replace him immediately."

"Spoken like a true producer," Jerry sneered. "Replace the poor schmuck before he's cold."

"Anyway," Bobby continued, trying not to let Jerry get to him, "I'm offering you the part, on condition you don't come to the set drunk. It's a five-day cameo role. There's no time to jerk around with agents arguing about billing and deals — I'll guarantee you'll get everything you need."

"You want *me* to do a cameo in *your* frigging movie?" Jerry said contemptuously, as if it were *the* most ridiculous suggestion he'd ever heard.

Darla hurried to his side. "Jerry," she said soothingly. "Don't forget we need the money."

"What does he think I am — a frigging charity case?" Jerry thundered.

Bobby took Jordanna's arm, steering her over to the door. "Think about it. I need a fast answer."

"Why should I frigging think about it?" Jerry roared.

Bobby paused at the door. "You know what?" he said. "Jordanna's right. It's a simple deal. Take it or leave it. Your choice."

Darla followed them down the driveway. "Ignore him," she said. "He's been drinking all day. This is exactly what he needs. Send over the script, and I'll talk him into it."

"I don't want him doing me any favors, Darla."

"No, Bobby — you don't understand. You're the one doing *him* the favor."

They reached the car, and he handed her a copy of the script. "Give it to him, Darla. I'll call you later for a decision."

In the car, Jordanna couldn't help laughing.

"Do you want to tell me what you're laughing at?" Bobby demanded, failing to see the humor in the situation.

"You're so funny. You let him get to you, didn't you?"

"No I didn't," he said defensively.

"Yes you did. He pushed your buttons big time."

"Can't you see what a pain in the ass he is?"

"Sure, but you've got to let go, Bobby. Understand what I'm saying. Simply let go."

He contemplated her remark. "It's as easy as that, huh?"

"Think about it. If he wasn't your father he'd be just another old actor with a drinking problem. But he *is* your father, so you've got to view him in a different way. I know I'm not explaining it very well, but believe me — it works."

"How did *you* get so clever?"

"Practice."

"Yeah?"

"Yeah."

There was another long silent moment as their

451

eyes met. Jordanna felt like she'd been jolted with a shot of electricity. Bobby's eyes were so impossibly blue, and she loved the way his hair fell on his forehead, and his body was —

"Dinner?" he said casually.

"Where's Barbara tonight?"

"What's Barbara got to do with anything?"

"I thought you two were an item."

"Who told you that?"

"I've got eyes, haven't I?"

He sighed. "You know, Jordanna, I've had a bitch of a day. Are we having dinner or not?"

She grinned. "It sure beats the hell out of pizza."

"You're so gracious."

Her grin broadened. "So I've been told."

35

Kennedy sat at her computer, checking through her notes. She'd spent most of the day writing the piece on Charlie Dollar, and she was pleased with the way it had turned out, certain she'd captured some of his magic, for that's what Charlie had in abundance — a quirky magical quality, which came across in every role he portrayed.

They'd made a plan to have dinner tonight, and although she was looking forward to spending more time in his company, she'd sooner be seeing Michael Scorsinni. It was unexpected, and she couldn't quite explain it, but talking to Michael last night she'd felt a real connection.

God, wouldn't Rosa gloat if she knew!

The phone rang, and she reached for it.

A woman's voice, "Miss Chase?"

"Yes."

"I'm Gerda Hemsley's mother. I got your message."

"Oh, Mrs. Hemsley, I was hoping you'd call. I'm so sorry about your daughter, it's a terrible tragedy. Please accept my deepest sympathy."

"I know you've been doing everything you can, Miss Chase. I've seen you on television. It's comforting to realize someone cares."

Kennedy reached for a pad and pen. "The reason I needed to speak to you, Mrs. Hemsley, is to find out what Gerda did before working in the bank."

"Before the bank she was with a firm of accountants."

"Was she ever connected to the film industry, by any chance?"

"Why, yes — several years ago she worked on a few films. She was in the production accounts department."

"Really? Would you happen to know which movies they were?"

"I . . . I don't recall. Although of course there was the one . . ."

"The *one?*"

"The one where there was the trouble."

"What trouble would that be?"

"She witnessed a murder."

Kennedy shivered with anticipation. "A murder? What happened?"

"There was an actress in a film called *The Contract*. Gerda was in the production trailer when she saw this crime take place."

"Who was murdered?"

"A young actress, strangled by one of the actors."

"What was his name?"

"I don't remember, but Gerda saw everything. She was a witness for the prosecution."

"Was she the only one?"

"No, there were others."

"Can you remember who?"

"Not offhand. If I went through Gerda's papers

I might be able to tell you more."

"Do you remember anybody called Pamela March or Margarita Lynda?"

"Those names sound familiar, but I can't be sure."

"Mrs. Hemsley, can you tell me exactly when this took place?"

"Let me see . . . sometime early in 1988."

"Thank you. You've been a great help."

Her mind was buzzing. *This was it! This was definitely it!*

She had a number for an uncle of Margarita Lynda's. She tried it immediately. "Kennedy Chase," she said briskly. "We chatted a few weeks ago about Margarita."

"Yes, I remember," the man said.

"Perhaps you can help me with more information. Do you recall if Margarita worked on a film called *The Contract*? Was she a witness for a murder case?"

"Yes. Now that you mention it, I believe she was. Nasty business. It upset her a lot."

Bingo! "Thank you," Kennedy said gratefully. "That's all I needed to know."

Now her mind was really on red alert. She had to find out if Stephanie Wolff and Pamela March had also worked on *The Contract*. Instinct told her there wasn't much doubt about it, she was certain she'd discovered the link.

The phone rang again and she grabbed it impatiently.

"Hi — Kennedy? Michael Scorsinni . . . remember? Your could-have-been date if Rosa had gotten her way?"

He distracted her for only a moment. "Michael, I'm right in the middle of something. Can I call you back?"

"Is that a polite way of brushing me off?" he said wryly.

"Not at all," she reassured him.

"Okay, I believe you. Uh . . . listen, I'm out right now, but let me give you my beeper number." He gave her both his home and beeper numbers.

"Ten minutes — you'll hear from me," she promised, jotting the information down.

"I hope so."

"Honestly."

He felt like he was back in grade school, but he pressed on anyway. "So . . . are you still busy for dinner?"

"I told you — I have a prior engagement."

"How about tomorrow night?"

"I think I'd like that," she said softly.

"Good. That's definite. Call me back anyway, but we're on for tomorrow night."

"Absolutely," she promised, happy to have heard from him. She replaced the receiver and began searching through her notes for contacts on Stephanie Wolff and Pamela March. The doorbell rang, interrupting her thoughts. "Who is it?" she called out impatiently.

"Rosa. Open up. Quick."

"Okay, okay, I'm coming."

Rosa burst in, waving a bottle of champagne. "Guess what?" she announced triumphantly.

"Tell me."

"This is *so* great — you'll *love* it."

She'd never seen Rosa so excited. *"What?"*

"The chief of police and the mayor are holding a press conference tomorrow morning. They made a move, and it's all thanks to our news station and you. We'll attend the press conference together, and right after that my producer would like you to do a live remote. Is that okay with you?"

"Okay with me? It's fantastic!" she exclaimed.

Rosa nodded. "Yes, isn't it great? They're gonna get this sicko, and when they do, it'll be thanks in part to us!"

An hour passed, and Kennedy hadn't bothered calling him back. Michael was disappointed, but he wasn't surprised — he'd known she was different. Kennedy Chase didn't jump, and in a way that was exciting, although the last thing he was into was playing games.

Well, at least they had a definite date tomorrow night; he'd look forward to that.

He drove by the production office and learned that Jordanna had gone somewhere with Bobby Rush. After that he made his way back to his apartment, stripped off his clothes, and stood under the shower for ten minutes.

Bella. Where was Bella? When was he going to find her?

Suddenly he had that feeling again. That dry-mouthed desperate *so what if I had one shot of Scotch* feeling. It frightened him, because he knew that one of these days he might succumb, and if he did it would be all over.

Had to get to an AA meeting. Had to get back

457

into the discipline of knowing that every day was a struggle, but he could beat it if he stayed focused.

When he was finished in the shower he tied a towel around his waist, walked into the living room, and pressed on the answering machine. The first message was from Amber, inviting him for dinner the following night and suggesting he might like her to invite Shelia.

No way, Amber.

The second message was from the woman with the muffled voice who'd called him at the studio. "Got the money?" she said in the same flat voice. "Time's running out."

He played the message back several times, wondering how she'd gotten his home phone number and if she really knew anything at all.

The sound of Bella yelling "Daddy! Daddy!" kept echoing in his head.

Or *was* it Bella?

Who knew?

"Fuck!" Slamming the machine off, he went and got dressed.

Had to find his kid. There was no way he could go on like this.

Out there somewhere was an answer, and it was up to him to discover what it was.

"This is ridiculous," Cheryl said, staring at herself in a full-length mirror, mesmerized by her new glamorous image.

"No it's not, it's a game," Grant observed, standing behind her. He was stoned, and it showed, although he maintained his good looks

458

in spite of his dissolute life. "Remember how we used to play games in school?" he said. "Taking chances, that's what got us through those crummy years."

"How could I ever forget?" she said, wondering why she'd agreed to take part in this particular game. It was crazy, and yet if she backed out now Grant would think she was chicken, and that would never do.

Once, when they were both fifteen, they'd gone on a shoplifting spree at Saks. The winner had to score over five hundred bucks' worth of merchandise. Cheryl had reached four hundred fifty when the store detective pounced.

Her father had been furious. "If you needed more money, all you had to do was ask," he'd yelled, and promptly increased her allowance.

Money meant nothing. Showing Grant that she could do this meant everything. How many other women he knew would be up to the challenge?

Fortunately she was also stoned. She wasn't sure she could go through with it if she weren't.

"Gotta admit you look pretty out there," Grant said, putting his arms around her waist from behind and playfully squeezing.

Then how come you don't take me to bed? Why are you sending me out to sleep with a stranger?

"Do I?" she said coolly, knowing that she'd gotten herself together. For once in her life she looked positively svelte. Everything worked. Sheer black panty hose and very high heels — her legs, along with her hair, were her best assets. A Victoria's Secret bra and a skimpy Azzedine Alaïa dress. Her hair, freshly done and gleaming red. And more makeup than usual.

"*Very* sexy," Grant said, squeezing her even tighter. "I'm beginning to think I should have given you the test run."

She assumed he was joking, wished fervently that he wasn't. *Never let him see you care.*

"Oh, please, Grant," she said dismissively. "Don't talk to me like I'm one of your half-baked all-American cheerleaders."

"Aren't you getting turned on by this?" he asked, hugging her from behind. "I know I am."

"Perhaps you'd like to come and watch," she suggested brusquely, waiting for his reaction.

"Ha! I'm sure the client would get off on *that*."

"Who is the client anyway?" she asked for the third time.

"I told you. Some high roller from out of town. You're perfectly safe."

"Fine for you to say."

"Go to the front desk of the hotel, ask for Mr. Nanni. Use a condom, and don't kiss him on the lips."

"Thanks for the advice," she said, turning away from the mirror and his arms. "Okay, I'm ready. Let's go."

"You're sure?"

No. I am not sure. Why the hell don't you stop me?

"Yes, of course I'm sure."

"Then let's get this party on the road."

"I love hotels," Sharleen said, bouncing up and down on the king-size bed.

"I had to get out of the house," Mac said tensely.

"Those kids are enough to drive a person insane. They're always in my face, asking for something."

Sharleen stretched luxuriously. "You give them too much."

"No more than you give your daughter."

"At least she appreciates it."

"Sharleen — you've got a short memory. Darling innocent little Suzy brought a drug dealer into our house."

"She didn't know."

"Bullshit."

"We're not going to fight, are we?" Sharleen asked, stroking his cheek.

"Not after the day I've had," he said grimly.

"Was it a tough one, sweetheart?" she murmured, her hand moving down, creeping inside his shirt.

"You have no idea."

She tweaked his nipples. "How about telling me? Maybe I can help."

Oh, God, this woman could turn him on whatever his mood. "It's a long story," he managed.

She undid his belt. "And I'm an excellent listener."

"When you want to be."

"Ohh . . ." she said, groping inside his pants and finding gold. "I want to be."

He closed his eyes, shutting out the real world.

Sharleen's talented hands enclosed him, and then her even more talented mouth, and nothing seemed that important anymore.

"You're distracted," Charlie said.

"No I'm not," Kennedy replied defensively.

"Yes you are."

"Okay, so I'm distracted."

"Wanna tell me why?"

They were sitting in Georgia, a restaurant on Melrose. She'd not reached connections for either Stephanie Wolff or Pamela March, and Charlie was right — she *was* distracted, because she needed more information. Rosa was also trying. They'd arranged to speak later.

"I'm thinking about a story I'm working on," she admitted.

"The murders?" Charlie asked.

"You know about them?"

He fixed her with a half-lidded stare. "Hey, green eyes, whaddaya think I do all day when I'm not workin'? I watch TV. I'm a true addict. I saw you last night. You got attitude, strength of character. Seein' that really revs my libido."

"Glad to hear it."

The waiter brought their drinks to the table, two exotic peach daiquiris. Charlie had a shot of rum on the side, which he downed in one quick gulp.

"You like this place?" he asked, looking at her sideways.

"Very much."

"Wait until you suck on a spare rib. Heaven ain't got nothin' like it."

"Can't wait," she said, picking up her drink.

He did the same and clinked glasses with her. "To you, green eyes," he said. "Whatever you want is yours for the taking."

"Really?"

"That's my adage. Lived by it every single day, an' here I am — a big freakin' movie star."

"Is that all you want, Charlie?" she asked gravely. "Fame?"

"It keeps a smile on my face."

And buries the hurt inside, she wanted to say but didn't. Charlie had secrets and demons. He covered his insecurities with a laid-back, stoned demeanor. But Kennedy knew, she could feel his pain.

Did she want to get involved. That was the question.

No.

So why was she here?

Because it had seemed like a good idea at the time, and she hadn't met Michael Scorsinni when she'd agreed to go out with Charlie. And Michael? Well . . . she couldn't help thinking about him. There was something about Michael that went way beyond his good looks. He had a vulnerability she'd immediately hooked into. Never mind the macho Italian thing, underneath the bravado she knew there lurked a sensitive man — and she wanted to get to know him in every way.

She hadn't called him back because by the time Rosa left, Charlie was on her doorstep. It was probably just as well — if she cared to face the truth, she knew she was scared of getting involved. And yet she'd agreed to have dinner with him the following night, and who knew what that might lead to?

"Who're you thinking about?" Charlie asked, zeroing in on her. "What's his name? An' what's he got that I can't give you more of?"

"Why, Charlie, I do believe you're coming on to me," she said, flirting mildly.

"No way, green eyes, not unless you want me to. In fact," he said, sitting back, "not unless *you* ask *me*. I'm available, but I got a feelin' you're not."

"Where are we going?" Jordanna asked, as Bobby's car sped down Melrose.

"I feel an urge for southern fried chicken. Have you been to Georgia?"

"The place — no. The restaurant — yes."

"Okay with you?"

"Perfect," she said contentedly. She was unused to somebody else making decisions for her — it made a nice change, because it was usually she who called the shots — and most of the time picked up the check. This was almost like a real date, although she was sure Bobby didn't consider it a date at all. He probably figured he was buying the kid dinner because she'd gone with him to his father's and he felt he owed her.

"What's your take on Jerry?" he asked, keeping his eyes on the road.

She considered her answer. "An asshole, like you said. Pissed at you 'cause of your success. Sees himself as old and finished, and sees you as what he used to be."

"You're very astute."

"It can't be easy for old movie stars in this town. One minute they're flavor of the year, and the next they're on the slag heap, hosting real-life-drama shows on TV."

He liked Jordanna, she said exactly what she

thought, a refreshing quality in a town full of bull-shit. "Is that what I've got to look forward to?" he asked, amused.

"In about thirty years."

"I'll try to enjoy 'em."

"You should."

Pulling his car up to the restaurant, he handed his keys to the valet.

Brad Johnson, one of the owners, greeted them at the entrance. "Where have you been?" he said to Jordanna. "We've missed you."

"Working," she said, giving him a big hug. "Can you believe it! Me, working?"

"No, I can't," Brad said, leading her into the crowded restaurant. "Welcome back."

Across the room, Charlie had a perfect view of the entrance. "You'll never guess who's coming our way," he drawled. "One of your personal favorites."

"Who?" Kennedy asked.

"Bobby Rush."

"Oh, God!" she groaned.

"You shouldn't've slammed him," Charlie scolded good-humoredly. "Bad karma."

"I told you — I didn't."

"Did you tell *him* that?"

"He wouldn't take my calls, so I wrote and explained."

"You don't wanna apologize?" Charlie teased. "Say you're sorry like a good girl?"

"Are you *serious?*" she snapped, highly embarrassed by the whole thing.

"Just askin'," he said, pushing his chair away

from the table and standing up. "Kiddo!" he exclaimed, grabbing Jordanna in a lecherous hug. "An' Bobby. What a fine young couple!"

"We're not a couple," Jordanna corrected quickly, while observing two ex tight-butt lovers lingering at the bar.

"Don't get excited," Charlie drawled. "I ain't feeding the *Enquirer*. Not this week anyway."

"I owe you a thank you, Charlie," Bobby said. "Jordanna's an excellent PA."

"Anytime . . . An' I guess you know Kennedy Chase."

Bobby did a slow double take. The blonde was sitting there cool as a long drink of water, like she hadn't done a major kill on him. "Yes," he said, distantly. Taking Jordanna's arm, he steered her away from the table. "That's the bitch who wrote about me in *Style Wars*," he muttered.

"Really?" Jordanna said, as they sat down at their own table. "Want me to throw a glass of red wine over her?"

"You'd do that for me?"

"I work for you, Bobby. Just ask, I'll do."

She had him smiling again. "I bet you would."

"Oh, I would," she assured him. "I'm *very* loyal."

"Loyal, huh?"

"When I like someone," she said boldly, staring straight into his amazing blue eyes. If he didn't get it this time, he was either obtuse or totally uninterested.

"Jordanna . . . ," he began.

"Yes?" she asked eagerly.

"I like you a lot, but — "

Before he could continue, Tyrone appeared and hovered by their table — handsome, tall, and totally pissed off. "What the fuck are *you* doing here?" he asked, as if he owned her. It was obvious he'd had too much to drink.

She blinked. "Excuse me?"

"I asked what you're doing here."

"Hey — wait a minute," Bobby began.

Tyrone was not to be stopped. "You break a date with me to have dinner with *him*." He jerked his finger at Bobby. "How about the courtesy of the truth?"

"I'm sorry, Tyrone, this was unexpected. I didn't — "

"Couldn't resist the movie star, huh?" he sneered unpleasantly.

"Hey, buddy, you're out of line," Bobby said, coming to her defense. "This wasn't planned. We — "

"I don't give a fuck whether it was planned or not," Tyrone interrupted, grabbing Jordanna's arm. "Don't play games with me. You — "

She pulled her arm away, throwing him off balance.

Bobby stood up. "I think it's time somebody drove you home."

"Screw you," Tyrone said. "We're not in the office now."

Bobby put his arm around him. "Let me — "

Before he could finish, Tyrone hauled back and hit him, taking him completely by surprise. He almost fell.

Jordanna leaped up, furious. "You jerk!" she yelled. "How could you do that?"

467

Tyrone went to throw another punch. Bobby defended himself. Jordanna hurriedly flung herself between them.

Fists were flying, and somehow or other one lethal punch connected with the side of her jaw.

She fell like an Acapulco diver, and the last thing she remembered was one of her ex tight-butts running across the room — presumably to save her.

Darkness descended.

Her dinner date with Bobby was definitely over.

36

"The show's *finito*," Charlie said.

"It's obvious he never got my letter," Kennedy said.

"What letter?"

"I told you — I wrote to Bobby, explaining it wasn't my piece."

"Too bad."

"What can I do?"

"Forget it. It's old news. How about a drink at my place?"

"Sorry," she replied briskly. "I have an early press conference to attend in the morning. I should go home."

Charlie called for the check. "A press conference, huh?"

"Yes, the chief of police is making an announcement. They're about to form a task force on the murder cases."

"You nudged 'em into it — right?"

"They would have done it eventually, with or without me."

"But you gave 'em a little jog?"

"I hope I had something to do with it."

"So, no nightcap for you and me. An' I was gonna take you to Homebase Central. I own the place."

"Of course you do, Charlie."

He chuckled darkly. "What does that mean?"

"I'm sure you can own anything you want."

He treated her to his insane smile. "You think so?"

"I'm right, aren't I?"

"You're right and you're smart, and when am I gonna see you again?"

"You've got dozens of girlfriends. You live with Dahlia Summers. Why would you want to spend another evening with me?"

"Don't tell me that's a touch of insecurity I hear in your voice?"

"Sorry to disappoint you, but I'm merely curious."

The check arrived. Charlie donned tinted spectacles, scanned it quickly, then signed it with a flourish. "Y'see, the thing is," he said, removing his glasses and pinning her with his roving eyes, "I don't believe in being monogamous."

"You don't?"

"No point to it. We all got one life to live — why not spread a little happiness around?"

"You're incorrigible," she said, shaking her head. "In this day of AIDS you can actually say something like that. I bet you don't even use a condom."

A self-satisfied smile spread across his face. "Not my style."

"Then you're *definitely* off my list."

He cocked an eyebrow. "You've got a list, have you?"

"Y'know, Charlie, I enjoy being in your company, so I really hope you believe in platonic friendships; I've got a feeling we could have a stimulating one."

"Tell you what, green eyes, I'll wait an' see what you write about me first."

"Do that."

Grant dropped Cheryl off at the hotel, instructing her to call him when she was through.

She glared at him. "What do you expect me to do? Sit in the lobby waiting for you? I'll look like the town tramp."

"It'll take me five minutes to drive over. Or better still, call a cab."

"Yes, that's what I'll do — call a cab," she said, her voice heavy with underlying anger.

"Don't get pissed."

"I'm not pissed."

"Yes you are."

She continued to glare at him, willing him to stop her. "I don't even know why I'm doing this."

" 'Cause it's a turn-on," he said encouragingly.

"It might be a turn-on to you — you're not the one doing it."

"Just so long as you tell me every little detail."

She would never admit it to him, but she was nail-biting nervous. This wasn't right, she hadn't gotten into business to become one of the girls. Why *was* she doing it? Simply to impress Grant? What a crock of shit!

She took another look at the name on the piece of paper he'd handed her — Bosco Nanni. What kind of stupid name was that?

She got out of the car, slammed the door behind her, and strode into the hotel, high heels

471

clicking, head held high.

She knew Grant was watching her. Screw him; he didn't give a damn about her feelings.

She marched boldly up to the reception desk. "Mr. Nanni, please," she said with authority. "He's expecting me."

"Mr. Nanni requested you go to the penthouse suite," the desk clerk said. "The elevator's right over there."

"Thank you."

"Oh, God," Jordanna groaned. "Where am I?"

"In the back room of the restaurant," Bobby replied, relieved she was still in the land of the living.

"What happened?" she asked groggily.

"Unfortunately you got in the way of somebody's fist."

"I don't believe this," she said, rubbing her tender jaw.

"Believe it. Tyrone completely lost it. You sent him out of control."

"Yeah," she said, sitting up gingerly. "I have that effect on all the guys."

"Seriously, I've never seen him so out of it. What did you do to him?"

"Exactly nothing."

"Hmm . . ."

"Did *he* hit me, Bobby, or was it you?"

"It happened so fast — I think it was him."

"Sure, you *would* say that."

"Hey — if it was me, I'm not admitting it."

"What a prince!"

"C'mon, I'll drive you home," he said, helping her to her feet.

"I feel lousy," she complained. "What if my jaw's broken?"

"It's not. You'll survive."

"All right for *you* to say," she mumbled crossly. "It wasn't you who got flattened."

"It was an accident."

"Yes?" she said truculently. "I'm gonna sue anyway."

"Who are you planning on suing?"

"*You*, Bobby," she said, with a sly grin. "You're the rich movie star around here, you can afford it."

"At least you're cheerful."

"That's 'cause I'm gonna score megabucks!"

He got her safely outside and into his car.

"What about my southern fried chicken?" she moaned. "Kindly do not forget that I am one starving person. I need nourishment."

"I had the food packed up and put in the car. I didn't think you'd want to go back into the restaurant."

"And he's thoughtful too," she said mockingly.

"We can eat at your place or mine."

"I'm staying at the Sanderson mausoleum. Let's go to yours."

"I'd better call Jerry," he said, reaching for the car phone. "See what he's decided."

He connected with Darla, who sounded pleased to hear from him. "Jerry would love to be in your movie," she said effusively.

It was a shock that Jerry had agreed so fast,

but he remained businesslike. "Good. I'll put everything in motion first thing tomorrow."

"Thank you, Bobby."

"No, thank *you*, Darla. Keep him sober, that's all I ask."

"Well?" Jordanna asked, as soon as he put the phone down.

"I guess he's doing my movie."

"Don't sound so thrilled — you'll enjoy it."

"So she says."

"I'm always right."

"Modest little thing."

"Fuck modesty."

"Did you always have a mouth like a truckdriver?"

"No. I received my education at Daddy's knee." She pressed on the radio, switching stations until she got En Vogue. "Where do you live, Bobby?" she asked.

"I'm renting a house in the Hollywood Hills."

"*I* should rent a house, but I can't afford it on the pittance you pay."

"Your fortunes may improve."

"How's that?"

"Well, you never know. Something might be coming up."

"Like *what?*" she demanded.

"If I tell you, you've got to promise not to say anything."

She held up two fingers. "Girl Scout's honor."

"The truth is I made a big mistake hiring Barbara Barr."

"Oh, you're finally realizing it. She was never right for Sienna, and you know it."

"Don't get into one of those *I told you so* things."

"I'm not."

"You are."

"So go on, tell me what's happening."

"Business Affairs is working out a deal to pay her off. The studio guys promised if I signed Jerry I could cast whoever I wanted."

"Really?"

"Yes, really."

She tried not to let him see how excited she was. "And who's the lucky person?" she asked casually.

"Someone you know very well."

The cool facade was too difficult to keep going. "Don't do this to me, Bobby," she blurted excitedly. "Not unless you mean it."

"I mean it," he said, enjoying her excitement.

"Oh, my God! I'd actually be making more money than the paltry salary you pay me?"

"Exactly. You can rent your own Hollywood Hills house."

"For once in my life I don't know what to say."

"You're very talented, Jordanna," he said, suddenly serious. "Your test was excellent. It impressed me, and I'm not easy."

"Then how come you didn't hire me in the first place?" she asked breathlessly.

"I gave in to pressure. The guys who run the studio chose to go in a different direction." He pulled up in front of his house. "Now don't get *too* carried away," he warned. "There's always a chance it might not happen."

"Yes it will," she said fervently. "I know it will."

"We're here," he said. "Are you sure you're feeling okay?"

"I'm feeling *sensational!* In fact, I've even decided not to sue you."

"You're too kind," he said, getting out of the car.

"Yeah, I'm real thoughtful that way."

He came around to the passenger side and helped her out.

Impulsively she gave him a big hug. "Thanks, Bobby. You won't regret it."

He pushed her gently away. "It hasn't happened yet."

What was with this guy? Had her hug offended him? It wasn't like she was going to jump him or anything. Maybe the old Jordanna would have gone for it. But not now . . . Now she was this new controlled person. Sex was not on her mind.

Or was it?

"I told you," she said confidently. "It will."

"You're into the power of positive thinking, huh?"

"It beats negativity any day."

They walked toward his house.

"Do you always leave your front door open?" she asked.

"No."

"Well, it's wide open. Do you carry a gun?"

"Why would I do that?"

" 'Cause everybody should carry a gun in L.A.," she said wisely. "It's rule one of survival."

"Do you?" he countered.

"Nope, but if I did, I certainly wouldn't be frightened of using it."

"I can believe that."

"What if there's somebody inside?"

He shrugged. "Maybe I forgot to close the door when I left."

"There could be a couple of freaked-out drug addicts, armed with knives and guns." She paused dramatically. "Once we're inside, they'll slice us up and take everything we've got — which in my case is nothing. We should go for help."

He looked at her quizzically. "Just 'cause I left my door open?"

"Yes."

"I've done it before."

"Okay, *you* go in. I'll wait out here."

"Thanks. I appreciate your support."

"Hey, Bobby — tonight I've met your father, missed dinner, been knocked flat on my ass. Altogether I think I've been a pretty good sport. I do not wish to add getting mugged to the list."

He grabbed her hand. "C'mon, Jordanna, live dangerously," he said, pulling her inside the house. "Oh, Jesus!" he exclaimed, surveying total chaos.

His home was completely trashed.

The door of the hotel suite was opened by a fat man with pop eyes and hairy hands. A taller man hovered next to him. Cheryl's stomach dropped. What was she *doing?*

Bosco looked her over and nodded approvingly. "In there," he said, gesturing.

"Not bad," Reno said as she passed him and walked into the living room of the large suite, where she came face-to-face with a short, dark man who looked to be in his late fifties. He had patent-leather hair, a deep suntan, and heavy-lidded eyes. "Hi," she said, in her best very expensive call girl voice. "I'm . . . Bambi." The name came to her in a flash of inspiration.

Luca blinked. She was not what he'd been expecting. She had red hair and decent tits, but she didn't have the usual hooker look. There was a touch of class about her, and he liked that. "Bambi, huh?" he said, clearing his throat. "Well, come on in, baby. Make yourself comfortable."

She stood in the center of the room, not quite sure what to do. What *did* hookers do when they went on house calls? Grab the client's dick and go right at it? Or cool it until he made the first move?

"Is this your first time in L.A.?" she asked. Stupid question.

"Nah, I've been here before," he said. Stupid answer.

"I'm happy to meet you, Mr. Nanni," she said, lowering her voice seductively.

Luca decided Mr. Nanni would do just fine for now, no point in frightening her with his true identity. "You too, Bambi," he said. "Wanna drink?"

Oh yes, I want a drink desperately.

"That would be nice," she said, smoothing down the front of her skimpy dress.

"Scotch?"

"Vodka."

He poured a vodka and handed it to her, standing close. She could smell his strong aftershave; it was overwhelmingly sweet.

"You got pretty hair," he said, reaching out to touch. "You a natural redhead, baby?"

"Just what you ordered," she said, attempting to stick to the low, sexy drawl.

"Where's the nurse's uniform?"

"What nurse's uniform?"

"I told 'em that's what I wanted."

"I never heard about it."

"Shit!"

"Sorry."

"These things happen," he said, thinking she was not a conventional beauty but had plenty of style. And he really got off on her startling red hair. "You wearing a garter belt?"

"Was I supposed to?"

"Jeez! I'm payin' a lot of green stuff for you. Didn't your boss tell you nothin'?"

"I'm afraid not."

At least she was honest. He took the drink out of her hand and put it on a table.

"Turn around, baby," he said. "I'm gonna unzip your dress real slow, then I want you to just stand there an' don't do nothin'. Got it?"

In spite of herself she felt a tingle of excitement. This was so different, so out of her range of experience. She did as he asked and felt his cold hands on her back as he pulled down the zipper of her dress. It fell to the floor, and she kicked it away with the tip of her shoe.

"Hmm . . ." he said appreciatively, regarding her through hooded eyes. "Now I wancha t'take a nice slow stroll around the room just for me."

Once again she did as he asked, parading in her black panty hose with the lace bikini tops and her peekaboo Victoria's Secret bra. This was insane, but she was beginning to get turned on.

"You got hot legs, Bambi," he said, licking his lips.

His admiration was even more of a turn-on. Her nipples hardened as she strutted across the room feeling totally powerful and in control. "All the better to wrap around your neck," she purred sexily.

Grant would *love* that line.

"Lose your bra," he said in a throaty voice. "Only make sure you lose it real slow."

"Excuse me?"

"Do it."

She unhooked her bra, still consumed with excitement. Her breasts were not huge, but she was proud of them — she'd never had any complaints.

He stared hungrily at her bare breasts. "Not bad," he growled, shrugging off his jacket and loosening his tie. "You ain't what I expected," he said gruffly. "But you'll do."

"What did you expect?"

"A real L.A. broad with big tits and a dumb face. You, you're different. You kinda remind me of my mistress."

"It wouldn't please me if I reminded you of your wife."

"I don't have a wife no more."

"I'm sorry to hear that."

"Don't be. I ain't got a mistress either. They both dropped dead on me."

Her adrenaline was pumping. This was excitement with a capital *E:* standing half naked in front of a total stranger, carrying on a bizarre conversation. Jordanna would not believe this scene if she could witness it.

"Come over here," he commanded.

She sashayed slowly toward him, prolonging the moment.

When she reached him he cupped her breasts in his hands as if he was weighing them. "Perfect," he said. "No more than a handful — just the way I like 'em."

Her legs felt weak. This was total submission.

He let go of her breasts. "Lose those stockin' things," he said gruffly.

"My panty hose?"

"Lose 'em."

She peeled off her panty hose — making a show of it, until she stood before him quite naked.

He stared at her, breathing heavily, his eyes taking in every single inch of her.

She'd never felt so exposed and vulnerable in her life. But it was still a turn-on. "Where do you want to do it?" she asked, ever the polite, well-brought-up call girl.

"Don't be in such a hurry. I'm payin' big bucks for you."

"Is there anything in particular you'd like me to do?"

"Walk around again. I get a charge outta eyeballin' you."

She strutted her stuff. This was the most appreciation she'd ever had from any man. Maybe she'd missed her vocation — she could have been a great stripper.

"How long you been doin' this, Bambi?"

"Long enough to know what you want."

"I can see that. How old are you anyway?"

"Twenty-four."

"A good age t'get outta the business. Find yourself a decent guy with plenty of bucks an' settle down."

"How old are *you,* Mr. Nanni?"

"Let's put it this way — twenty-four and countin'." Unzipping his pants, he beckoned her over. "Down on your knees, honey. Gimme some talented tongue."

How simple, Cheryl thought. The customer gets what he wants, and I get a pot of money.

But she didn't plan on making a habit of it.

This one was for Grant, and once was more than enough.

Kennedy paced restlessly around her apartment. She was excited about the next day, and yet at the same time she was confused. What was she supposed to do with the new information she possessed? Should she try to meet with the chief of police after the press conference and tell him what she'd found out? Although he probably wouldn't appreciate hearing it from her. But still, she had to reveal it to someone.

Michael Scorsinni was on her mind. She needed to talk, and maybe he was the person to talk to. After all, he was a former detective, so he'd be able to advise her.

She decided to call him. After a few rings his machine picked up.

"Hi, this is Kennedy," she said, leaving a message. "Sorry I didn't phone you back earlier, but I had to go out. I . . . uh . . . I wanted you to know I didn't forget."

Where was Rosa? She'd said she'd phone, and there was no message.

Her computer beckoned. The names of the four murder victims neatly filed. In the morning she would go through the newspaper files on *The Contract* and try and find out the full story.

Reluctantly she went to bed. Tomorrow she needed to be totally alert, because tomorrow everything was going to fall into place.

The Man sat in his car for a while. He watched Uncle Luca and his companions depart in their long black limousine. Then he waited until it began to get dark. When he felt it was safe enough, he made his way up to the house, parking in his usual discreet spot. No Shelley to plague him now.

The housekeeper was in her room in the back, he could hear the loud noise of her television.

He wondered what the old bitch had told his uncle. Nothing, he hoped, because if she had, he'd be forced to shut her up once and for all.

Fortunately they'd not been able to gain entry to his room. The locks he'd installed were a good investment.

Taking out his keys, he let himself in, moving rapidly. Then he packed up as fast as he could, piled everything in the trunk of his car, and left.

He studied Shelley's new address on his map. The house she was staying in was situated somewhere up Laurel Canyon.

He drove slowly up the winding canyon, turning on a side road and continuing for some way until he came to a wooden mailbox on a post stuck into the ground. The number matched the address he was looking for. He turned off yet another deserted road, way up into the hills.

He'd wanted a remote spot, and now here it was. It was as if the gods had said to him, "Yes, we will deliver you a place where you can wreak the proper vengeance. We will help you."

When he finally reached the house, he was delighted to note it was completely isolated. Shelley's car was nowhere to be seen, and there were no visible lights. It was more than likely she was not home, which suited him fine.

Parking under some trees way over in the shadows, he circled the small house on foot. In the back he discovered French doors leading into a living room. There were no signs for alarms, and no barking dogs.

It took him only moments to force the French doors and break into the house.

Seeing his uncle today had shocked him.

How his mother used to kiss Uncle Luca's ass! She'd fawned all over him. She would've done anything he'd asked . . . anything.

When he was finished with the people in California he planned on taking care of Uncle Luca too. And his mother. And her new husband. They all deserved to die.

The house was laid out on one level. There was a cellar, and he made his way carefully down rickety wooden stairs into the window-less dark storage space. He could hardly believe how perfect it was.

After he'd explored downstairs he checked out the rest of the house. Two bedrooms and one bathroom. A kitchen and a small living room.

He clicked on the television in time to watch that bitch Rosa Alvarez read the news. When she was finished, the newscast repeated the Monday-night appearance of Kennedy Chase.

Another bitch. Another too-clever-for-her-own-good whore.

He should never have left any clues. Let them figure it out for themselves. They were all so stupid, especially the police.

Entering the bedroom, he opened the dresser drawer. Shelley's clothes were stacked neatly — T-shirts, underwear, tights, socks.

He picked up her panties, holding them to his nose, inhaling what he hoped was the aroma of her body. Much to his disappointment they smelled only of laundry detergent.

What would she say when she found him here?

He didn't care.

He knew what he had to do.

37

Bobby could not believe the damage done to his house. The destruction of his possessions was truly vicious. Furniture ripped, every drawer and closet opened and the contents spilled out. Flour, jam, and coffee tipped and smeared over everything. His bedroom was wrecked, and in his dressing room he found his clothes cut to shreds. On the bathroom mirror, someone had scrawled, in bright red lipstick:

WHO DO YOU THINK YOU'RE
MESSING WITH MOTHERFUCKER?

He knew immediately it was Barbara Barr. Obviously Business Affairs had wasted no time in contacting her agent. This was her sweet revenge.

"Nice people you're involved with," Jordanna remarked, picking up half of an Armani jacket and tossing it on the bed.

He made a helpless gesture. The furniture and clothes he could replace — but Barbara had also wreaked her fury in his office, tearing up scripts as well as personal letters and photographs that meant a lot to him.

"Barbara Barr did this, didn't she?" Jordanna questioned, as if reading his mind.

"I didn't encourage her," he said wearily.

"You fucked her," Jordanna said bluntly. "And then dumped her from your movie. If you didn't want to get involved, you shouldn't have let your prick do the walking."

Christ, she could be aggravating! "Do you always say exactly what's on your mind?"

"As a matter of fact, yes."

He phoned the cops, who came by, surveyed the damage, and asked if he knew who'd done it and if he wanted to file a complaint.

He answered no to both questions.

"No?" Jordanna said, pulling him aside. "Why not? You know it's her."

"Do you think I want this all over the front of the *Enquirer* for weeks and months?"

She couldn't believe he was doing nothing. "So you're letting her get away with it?" she asked, outraged.

"What else can I do?"

"Have her arrested and thrown into jail."

"You're too militant for me, Jordanna. You know what the press are like. *I'd* end up looking like the bad guy."

"This is too depressing," she said, surveying the wreckage.

"I'll check into a hotel for the night."

"No way. You'll stay at Marjory's. There's eight thousand guest rooms there."

"I don't know Marjory."

"I'm sure you know her father — Franklyn Sanderson?"

"We're not exactly close."

"He's away. Marjory will love having you stay."

"Do we bring the southern fried chicken?" he asked, trying to make a joke of it.

"Along with your sense of humor," she said. "Which I'm thrilled to see you still have. I'll go phone her — that is if the phone's in one piece!"

He wandered around, inspecting the damage. Great. Get into bed with the wrong girl, and this is what happened. Jordanna was right, he'd let his prick do the walking. When was he going to learn?

"Marjory's psyched," Jordanna said, coming back into the living room.

"I bet."

"Now let's see — I have a T-shirt you can sleep in, and you'll share my toothbrush."

"You never stop joking, do you?"

She tilted her head to one side. "Gotta laugh, Bobby, otherwise you'll cry."

He took one last look around before they left.

"Fortunately," Jordanna said, as they roared down Sunset in his car, "every guest room in the Sanderson mansion is fully stocked for just such an emergency. Hey — you can even borrow a pair of Franklyn's black silk pajamas."

"How do you know he wears black silk pajamas?"

"Didn't you see his interview in *Playboy*?" She imitated a man's voice. " 'I favor black silk pajamas, long thin cigars, and long thin women.' That's a direct quote. At least Jordan would never do the *Playboy* interview. By the way, did I mention Jordan's new wife is pregnant?"

"No, you didn't."

"Yep, I'm going to have a baby brother or sister — ain't *that* a kick?"

"You upset about it?"

"No." She was silent for a moment. "Did I ever tell you about my brother?"

"I didn't know you had a brother."

She took a long beat before replying. "Jamie's not around anymore. He took a jump from a high building. It was the fashionable way to go."

"I'm sorry."

"So am I."

"When was this?"

"Eight years ago," she said matter-of-factly, trying to cover up the hurt and feeling of abandonment that had stayed with her ever since. "I was sixteen."

Bobby glanced across at her. "It must have been very hard for you."

She nodded, choking back a sudden wave of emotion. "Don't know why I'm telling you now," she muttered. "He had a drug habit. Speed. LSD. You name it — Jamie did it."

"How old was he?"

"Twenty. The best-looking guy you've ever seen."

Bobby reached out and squeezed her hand. She held on to him tightly and felt better.

They arrived at the Sanderson mansion at the same time as Michael.

"Hey — Brooklyn!" Jordanna greeted, putting on a cheerful front. "Can't keep away, huh?"

"It's all work."

"That's not what Marjory says."

"I hope you're kidding."

"Jordanna's always kidding," Bobby said, joining in.

"Bobby, this is Marjory's personal detective, Michael Scorsinni — Brooklyn for short. And Michael, meet my boss — Bobby Rush."

"I watched you shooting yesterday," Michael said. "It was pretty good stuff."

"Yeah," Bobby said ruefully. "So good I killed my costar."

"Huh?"

"Cedric Farrell died of a heart attack," Jordanna explained. "Bobby's being facetious."

Marjory met them at the door, hurrying to Michael's side like a dutiful wife. It was obvious she wanted everybody to think they had an intimate relationship going.

Jordanna observed the play between them and felt sorry for both of them — Michael because he was in a difficult position, and Marjory for being so needy.

Bobby yawned and stretched. "I'm beat," he said. "This has been some evening."

"Yeah, sort of like *Adventures in Hollywood*," Jordanna joked. "You should only know what we've been through."

"You could say that," Bobby agreed.

"I *am* saying it. By the way, where's our southern fried chicken? I'm still starving."

"Did I hear southern fried chicken?" Michael said, realizing he hadn't eaten all day. "My favorite."

"You never told me that," Marjory said accusingly, as if she should know everything about him.

"Let's have a picnic," Jordanna suggested. "Everyone to the kitchen."

Michael's beeper sounded. Excusing himself, he hurried into the library and returned the call. It was Quincy, phoning from his car.

"I'm beat," Quincy complained. "I'm sitting outside a hotel, watching the tourists come and go."

"What're you doing at a hotel?"

"Cheryl Landers is here. I checked at the desk, she's visiting some guy. Get this name — Bosco Nanni."

"Who's he?"

"Dunno. All I want is a night's sleep."

"Your arm okay?"

"I'll live. Tomorrow morning the police chief and the mayor are holding a press conference. My connection's got word they're about ready to bust this one wide open."

"That's good news. So we don't have to do anything?"

"Nope. Once they drop this Zane guy's name into the computer, they'll pick him up fast."

"That's a relief."

"You're watching Jordanna Levitt?"

"She's here safely, don't worry about her."

"I'll call you later. We'll meet early in the morning?"

"Sounds good to me."

He checked his answering machine before going back into the kitchen, and was surprised and pleased to hear Kennedy's voice. His first reaction was to call her back, but then he realized it might be too late. Before he could make up his mind if it was worth taking the risk of waking her, his beeper buzzed again. He called back at once.

"Do you have the money yet?" said the woman with the muffled voice.

"Why would I have the money if you can't tell me anything concrete?"

"There's a package outside your apartment. If you want your daughter to stay healthy, get the cash by tomorrow afternoon."

The line went dead.

Cheryl was dressed and ready to leave.

"You're some broad," Luca said admiringly.

She presumed he was paying her a compliment. "Thanks," she replied casually.

"Yeah, baby, you really got what it takes."

Hmm . . . nice to know she was the perfect hooker.

He handed her a fat envelope filled with cash. "Don't believe in checks," he said. "An' there's a tip in there for you. Remember — you don't havta share it with the house. Wanna count it?"

Taking the envelope, she stuffed it into her purse. "I trust you," she said, thinking Grant would be a happy man.

"How about tomorrow?" he suggested. "Nurse's uniform, one of them fancy black garter belts, no panties. Same time, same place."

"I . . . I'm not sure."

"Why? You booked on another job?"

"Maybe . . ."

"You go back an' tell your madam I'll pay double. When it comes to satisfaction, money don't mean nothin' t'me."

"If I'm not available they'll send you another redhead," she said, all business.

"Baby, you simply ain't gettin' it — I want you. No substitutes."

"Me?"

"Yeah, you."

She left the hotel in a daze. The doorman called her a cab, and she returned to her house.

Grant was asleep. She sat down on the end of the couch and shook him awake.

"Hey — how'd it go?" he asked, still half asleep.

She wondered if he'd had a girl over. There was an empty pizza box on the coffee table and two half-filled glasses of wine. Screw him!

"I have a return engagement by popular request," she said, hoping to make him jealous.

"What?" he said groggily.

"My client wants me back tomorrow."

He exploded with laughter. "Are you shitting me?"

"Do you find that funny?" she asked haughtily.

He scratched his stomach. "What did you do that was so out of the ordinary?"

"That's a trade secret."

"Aren't you gonna tell me?"

"Tell you what?"

"Was it a kick? Did it turn you on? Gimme details, Cheryl."

"I'm not in the mood to talk about it."

"You're not, huh?" he said, perplexed.

"No."

He hauled himself off the couch. "Then I guess I'll go home."

494

"Do that," she said, walking into her bedroom and slamming the door.

She was dying to talk to somebody, and it certainly wasn't Grant. How dare he send her out on a trick and then entertain in *her* house. She wished she knew where Jordanna was, then she remembered Shep's mentioning that Jordanna was staying up at Marjory's. Calling there, she waited while one of the security guards put her on hold.

Oh, God, Jordanna would freak when she heard. Eventually Jordanna picked up.

"Jordy? It's me, Cheryl," she said eagerly.

"How did you track me down?"

"It wasn't easy. You're always moving."

"What's up?"

"I can't get into it over the phone. Can you have lunch tomorrow?"

"Hang on a sec, let me find out." Placing her hand over the receiver, Jordanna turned to Bobby, who was munching on a piece of chicken. "Is it okay if I take off for lunch tomorrow — just for an hour?" He nodded. She moved her hand. "Okay, Cheryl, where and when?"

"The Ivy, one o'clock."

"I'll be there."

"I have to go out," Michael said, entering the kitchen.

"Where are you going now?" Marjory asked, as if she had a right to know.

"Business," he said tersely.

"But what if I get another phone call?"

"Look," Michael said, as patiently as he could. "This has to do with my daughter. You're not

495

alone here, Marjory. You've got Bobby and Jordanna, plus the place is surrounded by guards and attack dogs."

"My father is paying you to stay with me," she said stubbornly.

"He's not paying me to watch you twenty-four hours a day. I'll be back later."

He took off fast, driving over the hill to his apartment like a speed demon.

As the woman had said, there was a package outside his door. He tore off the wrapping and opened the box. Inside was Bella's teddy bear — the one he'd bought her when she was two — and a blue sweater, her name tag sewn inside the collar. There was also a plain brown envelope. He ripped it open and read the message inside:

Ten A.M. tomorrow. The pay phone at the gas station on Sunset and San Vicente.

His heart was pounding. If they'd harmed his daughter he would fucking *kill,* no doubt about it.

Now he needed money, and where was he going to come up with ten thousand dollars?

There was an answer. Her name was Marjory Sanderson.

Quincy trailed Cheryl's cab to her house. He watched her go in, then he parked at the bottom of the driveway and settled down for the night.

He had every intention of staying awake, but before he knew it, he closed his eyes and fell into a deep, comfortable sleep.

Michael headed back to the mansion. When he arrived, he picked up the intercom and called Marjory. She answered at once.

"You asleep?" he asked.

"No, Michael. I can't sleep."

"Now that I'm back you can," he said, turning on the bullshit charm.

"Was it so important that you had to leave?" she asked, her voice verging on a whine.

"It was very important, Marjory. I told you — it concerned my daughter. In fact, there's something urgent I'd like to discuss with you. Can you come downstairs?"

"No. You come up here to my bedroom."

He would have preferred to meet on neutral territory, but since he had no choice he ran upstairs and knocked on her door.

"Come in," she called.

Marjory was lying in the middle of an ornate white canopied bed, propped up by several pillows, a thin silk sheet barely covering her breasts. "Sit on the bed," she commanded.

He sat down on the far corner.

"How can I help you, Michael?" she asked sweetly.

"Uh . . . it's about Bella, my little girl."

"What a pretty name."

"She's been missing for quite a while now."

"Yes, you told me."

"I've been getting messages from a woman who claims to know where she is. Tonight there was a package outside my apartment with her stuff. Somebody has her, Marjory."

"That's good news, isn't it?"

"They're demanding money. Big money."

"How much?"

Jesus, this was difficult, but it had to be done. "Ten thousand dollars."

Her expression was blank. "That *is* a lot of money."

"To me it's a fucking fortune. But if we were honest about this . . . to you it's nothing."

She reached up, pushing strands of long fair hair out of her face. "Are you asking *me* for the money, Michael?" she said evenly.

"I'm requesting a loan."

"Ten thousand dollars?"

"I've told you what it's for."

"Shouldn't you go to the police?"

"You don't understand," he said, feeling the frustration building within him. "This is my kid we're talking about. My little girl. I can't risk the cops screwing things up. I've got to take care of this myself."

"My father always warned me that if you lend money, you lose friends."

"Marjory," he said, fixing her with an intense gaze, "am I getting through to you or not? I told you — I'll pay you back every red cent."

"I suppose I could lend it to you if I wanted to," she mused, thinking out loud.

He realized she was holding out for something, and he had a sinking feeling he knew what it was. She was waiting for some kind of commitment from him.

"It would mean a lot to me," he said.

"Do *I* mean anything to you?" she asked plaintively. "Or am I merely a client?"

"Sure you mean something to me."

"Truthfully?"

"Yes," he lied.

"If you weren't being paid to be here, would we still see each other?"

"Is that what you want?"

She stared at him very steadily. "Yes, Michael. I'd like us to spend time together."

He knew he had no choice if he wanted the money. "Okay, Marjory, if it'll make you happy . . ."

"It will."

A deal was about to be made.

"I need it early in the morning," he said.

"What time?"

"Nine-thirty the latest."

"We'll go to the bank together. I'll draw out the cash and give it to you." A pause, then, "Can we have dinner tomorrow night?"

"I don't want to make any promises I can't keep. If I get my kid back — "

"If you get her back, you can bring her here," she said, holding out her arms. The sheet slipped, revealing the tips of her small breasts. "Aren't you going to kiss me good night, Michael?"

He went over and bent down to kiss her on the cheek. She locked her arms around his neck, turning his face until his lips met hers, kissing him with a hungry passion he found quite alarming.

After a few moments he managed to extricate himself. "Gotta get some sleep," he mumbled.

Her eyes were shining. "Don't worry, Michael. We'll take care of everything together."

"Good night, Marjory."

Her cheeks were flushed, her breasts still exposed as she stared up at him. "You can stay if you want," she whispered.

"Not tonight," he said, making it to the door.

"Another time?"

"If that's what you want."

"Yes, Michael, it's exactly what I want."

38

Kennedy awoke early after a restless night. She took a quick shower and dressed hurriedly, then she headed over to the library, where she diligently scanned all the newspaper reports on the murder that had taken place during the making of *The Contract*. Interesting stuff. Everything began to fall into place. She made copies, took some notes, went home, and by the time Rosa arrived to pick her up, she was waiting downstairs in the lobby of her building.

As soon as she got in the car she began filling Rosa in. "I was right," she said curtly. "All four women worked on *The Contract*. And they're being systematically eliminated."

"By whom?" Rosa asked, zooming in and out of traffic.

"A real weirdo, according to everything written about him. Zane Marion Ricca — a New York actor who came out to L.A., got a part in *The Contract*, and apparently had a thing for his co-star, whom he ended up strangling. Six women gave evidence against him. He's killed four of them."

"Who are the other two?"

"Now that's the really interesting part. They're

a couple of Hollywood kids. Rich, privileged, and protected."

"What do you mean by Hollywood kids?" Rosa asked.

"Two little rich girls who were only working on the movie because their daddies wanted them to have summer jobs. Jordanna Levitt, whose father, Jordan, produced *The Contract*. And the other girl is Cheryl Landers — her father owns the studio."

"So Zane — if he *is* the man committing the murders — decided to go for the easy ones."

"Maybe he's going for them all and hasn't gotten around to Jordanna and Cheryl."

"Could be," Rosa agreed.

"We'll have to give all this information to the detectives working the case," Kennedy said. "I've already requested an interview."

She stared intently at the picture of Zane Marion Ricca reproduced in the copies of the newspaper clippings. He had the kind of cold, unemotional eyes that gave a person chills. The eyes of a killer.

Reaching into her purse, she took out her notebook and began making more notes.

"What are you doing?" Rosa asked, narrowly avoiding rear-ending a truck.

"Preparing what I'm going to say."

"Good. The sooner they arrest this guy the better I'll feel."

"Me too," Kennedy murmured.

Luca sat at a table on the terrace of his penthouse suite, eating scrambled eggs and bacon. Not good for his cholesterol level, but who cared.

A magnificent view of L.A. was spread out before him, and he had a smile on his face. It was on account of that Bambi broad last night, she'd really got his juices bubbling. Different. Not the usual hooker type. Young and feisty — just the way he liked a woman to be. He had a strong urge to see her again, especially if she was wearing a nurse's uniform, as he'd requested. Yeah, a nurse's uniform, with no panties and a lacy garter belt. He'd have to get himself prepared for *that* little treat — the heat was certainly rising.

When Reno and Bosco arrived, five minutes later, he was still smiling.

"What's up with you?" Bosco asked, picking up a piece of bacon with his fingers and stuffing it in his mouth.

"Bambi," Luca said. "The broad was a winner."

Helping himself to another slice of bacon, Bosco said, "Yeah? Was she juicy?"

"I'm seein' her again tonight."

Bosco snickered. "What is this — true love?"

"She's a good kid."

"An expensive good kid," Reno pointed out.

Luca abruptly changed the subject. "What did *you* do last night?"

"Had dinner with an old friend," Reno replied.

"Get a blow job?" Bosco asked crudely.

"Whatever I got, I didn't have to pay for it," Reno said sharply.

"Let me tell you something about payin' for it," Luca interjected, dispensing words of wisdom. "You pay, you get the best. An' last night I got the best. A good hooker does anythin' you want.

Every woman should be like that. An' the important thing is she don't open her mouth unless you tell her to."

"You shoulda seen the one *I* had last night," Bosco boasted, rolling his eyes in ecstasy. "A blonde with big tits and an ass to lose your freakin' mind over."

Luca pushed his chair away from the table. "It's time. Let's go take care of that dumb motherfucker while I'm in a good mood."

Bosco and Reno jumped to attention.

An extremely embarrassed Tyrone was waiting in the office when Bobby walked in. "Jesus," he said, rolling his eyes. "I don't know what to say. I had too much booze, and I guess I got outta line."

Bobby shook his head. "You lost it, all right. What was on your mind, for chrissake?"

Tyrone shrugged. "Y'know, I don't usually drink. I feel like a dumb schmuck."

"Good," Bobby said, checking out the mail.

"Can we forget it happened?"

"If you make things better."

"How can I do that?"

"By putting together Jerry Rush's deal. He's agreed to do it, but we have to finalize everything today. Pay him the money he wants, give him whatever billing he asks for — but whatever you do, keep me out of it. If we can change the schedule I'd like to reshoot as soon as possible."

"You got it," Tyrone said, suitably grateful.

Bobby shuffled some papers on his desk. "What is it with you and Jordanna anyway?" he asked.

"I like her. I didn't realize you did too. We had a date — she broke it. I was angry."

"There's nothing between us," Bobby said, still shuffling papers. "She was helping me out. I bought her dinner because it was late and we hadn't eaten. That's it — end of story."

"Hey." Tyrone threw up his arms. "I ain't going near her again."

"Doesn't make any difference to me," Bobby said, too casually.

After Tyrone left, Bobby picked up the phone and spoke to his contact in Business Affairs. "How are we doing with Barbara Barr?" he asked.

"Her agent's throwing a shit fit, but it's all taken care of."

"Okay, thanks." He hung up and called Mac on the set. "Jerry's doing the movie," he said, all business. "Barbara Barr is out, and if you agree, I'd like to go with Jordanna. I think it'll work."

"Fine," Mac said. "I've always thought she could do it."

Next Bobby called Barbara Barr's agent. The guy considered himself a hotshot and was arrogant under the best circumstances. Now he was angry.

"You can't treat actors this way," he said in an uptight voice. "Barbara had the role. What's the matter with you people? How can you fire her before she's done anything?"

Bobby stayed calm. "We're not firing her; she's getting paid off. Call it creative differences."

"Creative differences, my ass."

"You're getting your commission."

"Commission doesn't mean shit when I'm dealing with an unhappy client."

505

"Don't give me that."

The agent switched tracks. "Why are you calling, Bobby?" he asked sarcastically. "You want to sign another one of my clients so you can fire them the next day?"

"Barbara wrecked my house last night."

"She did *what?*"

"Your client broke into my house, cut my clothes to ribbons, and smashed up my house."

"I don't think so."

"Oh, I think so."

"Why are you telling *me?*"

"I want you to have a talk with her. I'm not pressing charges because I don't care to see this on *Hard Copy*. But if she ever comes near me again, she'll be asking for plenty of trouble. Be sure to pass on the message."

Michael reached Quincy and told him he couldn't meet him.

Quincy was annoyed. "Why not?"

"It's to do with Bella," Michael explained. "Something's coming down."

"Can I help?"

"No. I'll be in touch."

A few minutes later Marjory met him in the front hall, dressed smartly in a chic red suit, her hair pulled back in a neat bun. "I called the bank," she said. "They're opening early for me. They'll have the money in cash."

"Great," he said, feeling guilty, but what could he do?

"Which would you prefer?" she asked, clinging onto his arm. "To eat home tonight, or shall I make a reservation at a restaurant?"

He didn't know which was worse, sitting at home with Marjory in the gloom of the mausoleum or going out with her. "Let's go out," he said at last.

"Do you have a preference?"

"Hamburger Hamlet's the only place I know."

"I'll choose somewhere nice," she said, still clutching his arm. "Michael, I'm so happy you came to me for help."

He didn't know what to say. Right now all he was concerned with was finding Bella.

They traveled to the bank in separate cars, met up outside, and entered together.

Once inside, Marjory was treated like visiting royalty. The bank officer counted out the money she'd requested in hundred-dollar bills, then put it into an envelope. She took the envelope and handed it to him. He stuffed it inside his jacket.

"Is everything all right, Miss Sanderson?" the bank officer asked, staring pointedly at Michael.

"Fine, thank you," she replied, an arrogant tilt to her chin. "Your prompt assistance was most helpful."

They left the bank and stood outside for a moment.

"Good luck," she said, leaning in to kiss him on the mouth. "Phone me as soon as you find out anything."

"I'll do that," he said edgily.

He drove directly to the gas station and hung out by the pay phone. Lighting a cigarette, he scanned the area, searching for anything suspicious.

At exactly ten o'clock the phone rang. Grinding his cigarette butt into the ground, he snatched the receiver.

A woman's voice. "Michael Scorsinni?"

"Yes."

"Do you have it?"

"I've got it."

"Get into your car and drive to Century City."

"Where in Century City?"

"Park, go into Brentano's bookstore. Don't forget you're being carefully watched at all times. If you're followed, the deal is off."

"Nobody's following me. Where's Bella?"

"You'll find out in exchange for the money."

"I want my daughter."

"The only way you'll get her is if you cooperate."

"How do I know you have her?"

"That's a risk you must take."

"Where do I go once I'm inside the bookstore?"

"Walk around. We'll find you."

The line went dead. He stood by the phone for a moment, thinking about the ramifications. What if he handed over the money and nothing happened? What if he couldn't find Bella? What if this was some great big scam?

Maybe he should have called in the cops.

No. It was too risky — however sophisticated their surveillance teams were, something could go wrong and blow the whole deal. He had to take care of this himself.

He'd never felt so helpless, and yet there was nothing he could do except follow instructions.

Right now there was no other way.

The press conference at the Parker Center was packed. "Exciting, huh?" Rosa whispered.

"I'll say," Kennedy replied.

"As soon as this is over, we'll do a remote outside."

Kennedy nodded. "I'm all set."

The chief of police and the mayor, surrounded by their minions, made their entrance.

Kennedy settled back, ready to hear what they had to say.

On their second visit to the house, Reno carried a crowbar in a carry all, fully prepared to break into Zane's room.

"There'll be no problem," Luca said confidently. "This time we'll nail the fucker."

"Let's go over this again," Bosco said. "You're tellin' him you want him to come for a ride with us to discuss his future."

"That's it."

"How about the maid and the gardener?"

"You think they're gonna miss him when he's gone? They don't give a shit. Once we got him in the car, we drive out t'the desert an' dump him for good."

The sun was shining and the birds were singing when they arrived at the house. "This place ain't bad," Luca said, his hooded eyes checking out his property. "Fixed up, it could be a fuckin' palace. I could set a girl up here easy."

"What girl?" Bosco asked.

"Bambi."

509

Reno laughed disbelievingly. "You wanna set a hooker up in your house?"

"If I make her my exclusive property, why the fuck not?"

"You mean you'd give her this place?" Bosco said, eyes popping.

"I wouldn't *give* her nothin'. I'd stash her here an', at my convenience, fly in whenever I felt like it. Maybe I should spend more time here."

"You'd better change your way of dressing if you're planning on doin' that," Reno remarked.

"You criticizing the way I dress?"

"No, but a silk suit don't cut it in L.A. You gotta be more casual. We havta take a walk down Rodeo Drive, visit some of them fancy stores where they charge you five hundred bucks for a tie."

"Five hundred for a freakin' tie?" Bosco said, shaking his head in disbelief. "No freakin' way!"

"That's what they pay on Rodeo," Reno said, speaking as if he were the town expert.

"Okay, so we'll do it later — after we've gotten rid of the prick," Luca decided.

They entered the house and headed for Zane's room.

"Knock first. If he don't answer, bust in," Luca commanded, standing back.

"Sure," Reno replied, knocking sharply.

There was no response. He knocked again. Still no response.

"He's out," Bosco said.

"I don't give a fast crap whether he's out or not," Luca said in a hard voice. "This time we're goin' in."

Reno worked on the locks for a few minutes. The door sprang open and they entered the room.

"Fuckin' stench!" Luca complained, wrinkling his nose as he took in the unmade bed, garbage on the floor, and a cockroach scurrying over a Big Mac wrapper. "This place is a fuckin' dump."

"He's gone," Reno said. "Look around — there's nothin' here."

"Someone must've told him we was visitin'," Bosco added. "He took a fast run."

"Fuck!" Luca exploded. "You mean I gotta go searchin' for this *schifoso?* Jesus Christ!"

"We shoulda stayed around yesterday," Reno said. "Waited for him to come back."

"Why didn't you open your big mouth then?" Luca demanded.

Eldessa was in the kitchen when they marched in.

"Where is he?" Luca demanded.

She shrugged noncommittally. "I don' know. He was here yesterday. He musta come back and packed up — I never saw him leave."

"You got no idea where he went?" Bosco asked.

"No. He never told me nothin'."

"What car does he drive?" Reno asked.

"A black Ford," she said.

"You know the license?"

She shook her head.

Luca pulled out his gold money clip, extracted a hundred-dollar bill, and slipped it to her. "If he comes back make sure you find out where he's livin'. You do that and there's more where this came from."

"Yessir!"

"Bosco — give her the number at the hotel."

Bosco scribbled down the number and handed it over.

"C'mon," Luca said. "We've wasted enough time."

Shelley did not come home all night. The Man roamed around the house, becoming more furious as each hour passed.

How dare the bitch stay out.

How dare she do this to him.

She was sleeping with somebody. She was a whore, just like he'd known she was. Every woman he'd ever known let him down. It was a given.

His anger deepened when it began to get light and there was still no sign of Shelley. She was ruining his plans.

He went into the small kitchen, boiled a kettle of water, and made himself a cup of black coffee.

It was impossible to sleep. How could he sleep when he had no idea when Shelley was going to appear and surprise him?

Not that he needed much sleep. He never rested more than three or four hours a night.

Taking a chair, he placed it opposite the front door. Then he sat down to wait.

Eventually she'd come home, and when she did he was ready.

Shelley opened her eyes and immediately realized three things. One, she was not alone. Two, she was not in her own bed. Three, she was naked. It was then that she recalled the previous night. She'd gone to acting class, met a seemingly nice man, who invited her back to his place for pizza with some friends. They sat around talking and drinking wine, his friends left, they talked some more, she drank too much, and that's the last she remembered.

Her head throbbed. Spying her clothes on the floor, she crept quietly out of bed, gathered up her things, and scurried into the bathroom.

She dressed quickly, suffused with guilt. It was so unlike her to sleep around. Before coming to Hollywood she'd only had one boyfriend — a steady from high school. Since arriving in L.A. she'd had no boyfriends at all. The only man she'd even gotten close to liking was John Seagal, but he was a strange one, he'd given no indication of wanting to get involved, even though she'd encouraged him as much as she could.

Once dressed, she felt more secure. Standing in the bathroom, she wondered whether she should slip out of the apartment and go home, or if she should wake her new friend. The embarrassing thing was she couldn't recall anything about their lovemaking; in fact, she didn't even know his name.

She went back into the bedroom and stared at him, willing herself to remember.

He stirred, opened his eyes, and sat up in bed. "You're up," he said, stretching his arms above his head.

She smiled nervously. He had long brown hair,

an extremely hairy chest, and muscled arms. "Shall I make coffee?" she asked tentatively.

"Yeah, I could do with a cup," he said, getting out of bed and padding naked into the bathroom.

She went into the tiny kitchen and boiled some water. "I didn't mean to stay over," she called out.

" 'S'okay," he replied loudly.

"It's just that I . . . I think I had too much to drink."

"The way I feel, we both did."

"I suppose I should have a cup of coffee and go home."

"Yeah," he said, emerging from the bathroom.

Wasn't he going to ask how it was for her?

Wasn't he going to suggest that they see each other again?

"Do you take milk and sugar?" she asked.

"Milk, no sugar," he said, pulling on a pair of Levi's.

She handed him a mug of coffee. "Where are you from?" she asked, groping for conversation.

"Arkansas," he said, taking a gulp of hot coffee.

"How long have you been going to acting class?"

He threw on a plaid shirt. "What is this — question time?"

"It's just that we spent the night together and I don't know anything about you."

He laughed nastily. "Are we supposed to exchange résumés just because we had good sex?"

Was it good sex? she wanted to ask, seeing as she couldn't remember.

"No, but it might be nice, since we spent the night together."

"Listen, honey," he said, putting down his coffee mug. "It's not my intention to upset you, but *you* were the one that begged to stay over, and my girlfriend's coming back this morning, so you gotta leave."

"Your girlfriend?" she said, stunned.

"Yeah, my girlfriend," he answered belligerently. "Wanna make something outta it?"

"Why did I spend the night?" she asked, feeling used and let down.

" 'Cause you wanted it, baby. You wanted it bad."

"You never told me you had a girlfriend," she said accusingly.

"Do us both a favor and split before we get into a fight," he said, walking back into the bathroom and slamming the door.

She ran out of his apartment, sat in her car, and burst into tears.

This was not a good way to start the day.

The Man's eyes must have closed, because he was suddenly awakened by the sound of a car door slamming.

He sat up, springing to attention.

The whore was home, and he had to be ready to greet her.

When Shelley walked through the front door she was still upset about her one-night stand. For a moment she didn't notice Zane sitting there. When she did, she was startled. "Oh, my

God! John!" she exclaimed. "What are *you* doing here?"

He stood up. "I came to see you. You invited me, didn't you?"

She was puzzled. "Of course I did, but . . . how did you get in?"

"I arrived last night. You were out, so I let myself in."

"You mean you spent the night here?" she said, frowning. Although she was pleased to see him, she was not sure he should have taken the liberty of spending the night in her house without her permission. Plus it wasn't even her house — the acting coach she was house-sitting for had impressed upon her that she was allowed no overnight guests.

"Where were you all night?" he asked coldly.

Her frown deepened. "What?"

"I asked where you were all night."

"Really, John — I don't think it's any of your business."

"I'm making it my business."

She was confused. This man whose attention she'd tried to attract for months was acting like a jealous boyfriend. If she hadn't been so upset about last night, she would have known how to deal with him.

"I don't understand your attitude," she said, puzzled and upset. "I think you'd better go."

"No," he said sharply. "You invited me here. You've been chasing me for months."

She flushed angrily. She'd had enough of men for one day. "I have not," she said hotly.

"Yes you have. Inviting me to your room, confiding that you're lonely, telling me all about your-self. Well, now I'm here."

"*I* don't want you here."

"It's inevitable, Shelley."

"What's inevitable?"

"Us. You and me together."

He was beginning to alarm her. "I'm going to call the police if you don't go," she said, moving toward the phone on the hall table.

He reached her swiftly and grabbed her arm.

"You're hurting me," she said, trying to pull away.

"I do not appreciate your behavior," he said sternly. "I do not appreciate you staying out all night. Were you with a man?"

"None of your business," she said, finally losing her temper. "Let go of me!"

"Were you?" he demanded.

She attempted to pull away, but it only seemed to make him more determined to hold on to her. He grabbed both her wrists, pinning them up against the wall.

"If you were with a man I'll know," he said. "When we have sex I'll know."

Shelley realized she was in serious trouble. A feeling of dread overcame her.

The Man stared at her with passionless blank eyes.

"Please," Shelley whispered. "Let me go. I won't complain about this, I won't tell any-body you were here."

"Who would you tell? My uncle? Have you been talking to him?"

518

"No," she said quickly. "I don't know your uncle."

"But you just threatened me. You said you'd tell somebody."

"I didn't mean it."

His head hurt. He hadn't planned on killing her, but now there seemed no other way. She knew something she wasn't telling. She was in cahoots with his uncle, and if he didn't get rid of her she'd give him up.

Besides — and this was the real reason she had to be eliminated — he needed a safe place to bring Cheryl and Jordanna.

It was time.

39

Brentano's wasn't crowded. Michael roamed around, finally settling in front of the magazine stand, where he picked up a copy of *Rolling Stone* and flicked unseeingly through the pages.

He'd had plenty of time to think about what he was going to do. Plenty of time to figure out a plan of action. Whoever approached him would get no money out of him until they produced tangible proof he was getting Bella back.

Putting the magazine down, he walked over to the audio tape section. After a few moments he felt somebody standing behind him.

"Don't turn around," a woman's voice whispered in his ear.

"Where's Bella?" he said, staring straight ahead, although his instinct was to spin around, grab whoever it was, and beat her to a pulp. His anger was ready to explode.

"It's more complicated than you think."

Mustn't blow it, he thought. *Gotta stay calm.*

"Where's my daughter?" he repeated in a low, angry voice.

"We have to trust each other," the woman said. "I'll tell you where she is — but first the money."

"No way."

"Put the money on the shelf in front of you and walk away with me. My partner will pick it up. When he signals it's all there, you and I will talk."

"How do I know you've got something to tell me?"

"Would I be doing this if I didn't? You're a big, strong man. I wouldn't put myself at risk."

His mind was going in all different directions. He couldn't decide what to do. Finally he realized he had no choice. Groping in his pocket, he pulled out the envelope containing the money and placed it on the shelf next to a Tom Clancy audio. Then he immediately turned around, grabbing the woman's arm, moving so fast she had no chance to pull away.

As soon as he had her, he took a look to see who she was. She was in her thirties, with short dyed-blond hair and a suntanned face — most of it hidden behind huge mirrored sunglasses. She had on a blue T-shirt, a short denim skirt, and white ankle boots. From what he could see, her body was good and she was pretty in a cheap way. He noticed she was extremely nervous, her bottom lip quivered, and her manner was jumpy.

"Who are you?" he asked, as they headed for the door.

"It doesn't matter," she said brusquely.

"It matters to me."

"Don't get personal, or I won't tell you any-thing. And believe me, I know exactly where you can find your kid."

"I need to know who you are."

"A friend of Rita's," she said abruptly. "We

521

worked together when she first came out here from New York."

Once they were outside, she pointed to an outdoor restaurant area. "As soon as I get a signal that the money's all there, we'll talk."

He knew his nails were digging into her flesh, but he kept his grip on her arm, for he had no intention of allowing her the slightest opportunity of making a run for it.

"How come you waited this long to approach me?" he asked, his eyes diligently searching the surrounding area to see if he could spot her accomplice.

"Saw you on television," she said. "Felt sorry for you."

"Not sorry enough to give me the information without the money, huh?"

She shrugged. "I've a sister who needs medical attention, the money will see her through an operation."

"You're bringing tears to my eyes."

"I'm here, aren't I?"

"You're here because of the ten thousand bucks. Is Bella okay?"

"She's very healthy," the woman said, reaching into her cheap white imitation-leather purse and extracting a cigarette.

He felt like smoking too, but he didn't dare let go of her.

"We'll sit here," she said, gesturing toward a table out in the open.

"No. The corner one," he said sharply. "And place your back against the wall."

"I'm not going anywhere."

522

"I trust you as much as you trust me."

They sat down. "I trust you," she said. "You weren't followed."

He stared at his reflection in her mirrored glasses. "How do you know I'm not wired? What makes you think I'm not taping our conversation and you'll end up in the slammer for extortion?"

" 'Cause you want to see your daughter," she said, her eyes behind the glasses scanning the passing parade of people.

"What are we waiting for?" he asked impatiently.

Puffing nervously on her cigarette, she said, "I have to know the money is all there." A few more minutes passed before she received the expected signal. "Okay," she said. "Are you ready?"

He nodded slowly. "Yes," he said. "I'm ready."

"It's not what you expect. It'll shock you."

He asked the question he'd been dreading. "Is Bella being used for child pornography?"

"No, nothing like that," she said, taking a long drag on her cigarette. "I'll start from the beginning."

"Do that," he said tightly.

"When Rita first came out here we worked together."

"Where?"

"A topless bar near the airport — a girl can make plenty of money that way." She removed a fleck of tobacco from her teeth. "Our customers liked Rita a lot. She answered them back and they got off on that. I had a small apartment at the time, and I was looking for a roommate. Rita was in a hotel with her kid, so I had the two of them

523

move in with me."

He leaned forward, taking in every word.

"We did okay until the guy running the bar got himself into debt. Then the bar went bust and we were out of a job, so Rita an' me started doing guys on the side — it paid the rent, an' we knew enough men who were happy to pay."

He felt sick to his stomach. "What about Bella?" he asked. "Was she in the apartment when this was going on?"

"She didn't see anything. Rita never brought johns back unless Bella was asleep. She was a good mother that way."

"Is that your idea of a good mother?" he said harshly. "Don't fuck the dicks if your kid's awake?"

"We do what we have to do to survive," she said, shrugging. "It's not easy when you have a child to support, and *you* weren't sending her money."

"The hell I wasn't," he said angrily. "She's had alimony out of me ever since she left."

"Well . . . Rita wasn't always the most honest person in the world."

"Keep talking."

"She walked out on me one day. Didn't tell me she was leaving — simply packed her stuff an' moved out."

"Is that when she went to the Sunset View apartments?"

"Right. Some guy started paying her rent. Then she met Heron Jones, and he set her up with Daly Forrest. Next thing, she's working in the porno business. It would've been nice if she'd gotten me a job too, but Rita wasn't into helping her friends."

"Where is this taking us?" he asked grimly.

"A couple of months after she moved, I went to visit her. She owed me money, and I wanted it. She wasn't exactly thrilled to see me, but there was nothing she could do. I knew she had the money 'cause she was working pretty steady by this time."

"Did she pay you?"

"Yes. And while I was there I noticed the kid wasn't around, so I asked where she was. Rita told me Bella was with her father. I said, 'I thought you hated his guts,' 'cause she didn't exactly talk about you in a flattering way. 'Michael's not her father,' she said. 'Sal's her father.' 'Who's Sal?' I asked. And she told me he's your brother."

He felt a cold, searing hurt deep inside. Jesus Christ! Could this be true? *No fucking way.*

And yet . . . He kept listening.

"So then she starts explaining to me about how she was pregnant when you two got married," the woman continued. "But it was Sal's baby all along, and since he wouldn't marry her, he set it up for you two to meet. Told her you'd do the right thing by her, an' you did. After a while she moved to L.A., got together with Daly, and found Bella too much of a responsibility. She was in constant touch with Sal, and when she heard his wife couldn't get pregnant, she told him he could take Bella. I asked her if you knew about it. 'He'll never find out,' she said. 'He don't give a shit about his kid.' So I said, 'Well, if he's in New York he will.' And she said, 'He don't give a shit about his family either.' "

This was almost too much information for Michael to digest. This woman was telling him that Bella was not his child, that Sal had fathered her, and that all this time, while he'd been driving himself insane with worry, Bella was safely in New York with Sal.

He was filled with a rage so intense he thought he might explode. "How do I know you're telling the truth?" he said at last.

"It would be a helluva story to make up, wouldn't it?" she said, blowing smoke rings. "And if I *was* making it up, how would I know all these details?"

He felt like he'd been rammed in the stomach with a sledgehammer. It was all too much. "Who murdered Rita?" he managed to ask. "Do you know?"

"Daly Forrest had mob involvements. He owed people money, and they threatened him — something to do with distribution of his porno movies. After Rita was murdered, I laid low, 'cause I didn't want anybody suspecting I knew anything."

He pressed on, determined to hear it all. "What about the tape? Bella's voice was on the tape."

"That was my cousin's kid, they all sound alike at that age," she said, picking up her cheap pocketbook and stubbing out her cigarette. "I gotta go now."

"No," he said harshly, grabbing her arm again. "First you're telling me who you are."

"I don't have to tell you nothing. Go to New York — Bella's there. Only what does it matter now? She's not even your kid, is she?"

There was a thunderous roaring in his head. Instinctively he knew she was telling the truth.

It all made sense. Rita and Sal. The perfect couple. How they must have laughed at him behind his back.

It occurred to him that his mother had to have known all along, and yet she'd let him suffer for months. As for Sal — that fat, stinking, piece-of-shit sonofabitch. He'd fucking kill him.

The woman got up from the table and began walking away. He didn't stop her, he didn't care.

He sat there for a long while, his head in his hands, trying to get it straight. Eventually he got up, went to his car, and drove directly to the airport.

Arriving at LAX, he called Quincy from a pay phone.

Amber picked up and informed him Quincy was out. "Listen carefully, Amber," he said, speaking slowly and concisely. "There's been an important development regarding Bella. I have to fly to New York. Tell Quincy it's an emergency."

"Have you found her?" Amber asked anxiously. "Is she all right?"

His answer was guarded. "I think so," he said carefully.

"Michael, I'm so relieved. But I know Quincy will want to speak to you. Will you be with your family?"

"No. Tell him not to call me there, okay? I'll keep in touch with you guys. Don't worry, it'll all work out."

American Airlines had a flight leaving in half an hour.

He booked himself on it.

40

Detective Carlyle glared at Kennedy across the room. The fact that she'd marched into the meeting with her newscaster friend and dumped a load of detailed information on the table had really pissed him off. She was making him look like a fool, and he didn't appreciate it. What right did she have to interfere in his case, pretending she knew what she was doing? As far as he was concerned, the two of them were a couple of ballbreakers with some half-assed theory about who the L.A. Strangler was. They were too late anyway, because, unfortunately for Detective Carlyle, Boyd Keller, the thirty-something hotshot special investigator assigned to head the newly formed task force, had come up with the same information. In fact, he'd already taken it one step further and ordered DNA tests and fingerprint records that might prove Zane Marion Ricca was their man. Everyone seemed pretty certain that within the next twenty-four hours there'd be an APB out on Zane Marion Ricca.

What kind of name was Zane Marion Ricca anyway?

Detective Carlyle burped, not so discreetly.

Kennedy shot him a look. Trust her to catch

it. She definitely needed a man to keep her in line, and so did the other one. He wouldn't mind obliging as far as the Spanish one was concerned, she had the kind of body that really got him going, and he wouldn't say no to her smoldering eyes and full, inviting lips. As for Kennedy, no way — cool as ice, she'd freeze a man's balls off.

He wished Kennedy Chase and her friend would get the hell out. There was nothing he liked less than being made to look a fool, and that's exactly what these two women had done, coming up with facts he should have been aware of — considering that two of the murders had taken place in his division.

Too bad. His workload was a bitch. He could only do so much — he wasn't a fucking machine.

Kennedy stood up, so did the other one. Nice tits. Any other time he might have appreciated them more, but right now he was too pissed off.

The two women were on their way out. And not a moment too soon.

Once Kennedy and Rosa got outside, they turned to each other and started laughing.

"Did you see the faces on those guys?" Rosa said. "What a sorry bunch of schmucks."

"I know," Kennedy agreed.

"And as for your Detective Carlyle — "

"He's not *my* detective," Kennedy interrupted indignantly. "The first time I interviewed him I knew he was an idiot. He had to realize there were connections between the murders, but when I pointed it out he didn't want to know. What kind of detective doesn't investigate?"

"A dumb detective."

"Right."

They began walking toward Rosa's car.

"I can't help thinking that if only somebody had done something about it then, maybe lives could have been saved," Kennedy said.

Rosa nodded. "Well, at least the special investigator seems to know where it's at. He was on top of it before we gave him the facts."

"Thank goodness."

"He's pretty sexy, huh?"

"Who?"

"Boyd Keller."

"C'*mon*, Rosa — you're practically engaged."

"But not dead," Rosa said with a wink. "Did you notice his butt?"

"No, I didn't," Kennedy said firmly.

They reached Rosa's car and got in.

"I must say," Rosa said, "your commentary after the press conference was excellent. You should give serious consideration to appearing on TV full time."

"No, thanks. I already have a job I love. Right now I'm going home to write the story Phil would want me to write."

"Which is?"

"Zane Marion Ricca. I mean, who is this guy? Nobody knows that much about him — except that he came out here from New York and got a part in *The Contract*. Even when he was on trial there was hardly any background information on him. He had high-powered, expensive lawyers. Who paid? And why? I think his story is definitely worth investigating."

"You really get off when you're working on something that excites you," Rosa commented, starting the engine. "It heats you up more than a man, doesn't it?"

"Unlike you."

"You're going to turn into a nun."

"I've got a confession," Kennedy admitted, a touch sheepishly.

"What?"

"Remember how you were always trying to fix me up with Michael Scorsinni?"

"Hmm . . . you really blew that one. He was *great*."

She smiled. "We had a drink together the night before last, and I have to say it was kind of . . . intriguing."

Rosa almost smashed into a Cadillac backing out of a parking spot. "I don't believe what I'm hearing!" she exclaimed.

"It's true," Kennedy assured her, still smiling. "You were right for once, he seems like an interesting man."

"Hey, this is good," Rosa said enthusiastically. "When's the next rendezvous?"

"We're having dinner tonight."

"I feel like a matchmaker!"

"I'm not marrying the guy," Kennedy pointed out calmly. "We're merely having dinner. I'll let you know what happens."

"You know what *should* happen?" Rosa said with a wicked smile.

"What?"

"A crazy night of wild, unadulterated sex!"

"Is that all you think about?"

531

"Only when I'm horny."

Bobby was getting ready to leave his office and head for the location. Even though he wasn't working, he liked to be on top of the action, hovering over Mac — probably driving him nuts, but who cared?

Tyrone caught him on his way out. "It's done," he announced. "I cut a deal with Jerry and his agent. *And* I managed to change the schedule. With any luck, we'll be able to reshoot several of Cedric's scenes tomorrow. Jerry's up for it. Wardrobe's on their way over to his house now."

Bobby nodded. Great. Now he was stuck with Jerry. Deep down he'd hoped Jerry would be too difficult to handle and the deal wouldn't fly.

"That's fast work. I'm impressed," he said.

Tyrone shrugged ruefully. "I figured I had to make amends for last night."

"You certainly did. What's Jerry demanding? An arm and a leg? Or just a kidney?"

"He was pretty reasonable, considering. We pay him mucho bucks, he gets special boxed billing, and he's all set."

"So tomorrow's the big day?"

"Gary and I went over everything. If Jerry knows his lines and doesn't screw around, we may be able to get back on schedule. I've also figured out a way we can cut a day by combining two locations."

"You're pretty good at what you do."

"I try to be."

"So next see if you can take care of Jordanna's deal. We're definitely casting her as Sienna."

532

"Yeah, the rumor's buzzing. Who's her agent?"

"She doesn't have one. I want her to go with Freddie Leon."

"Freddie Leon." Tyrone let out a long, low whistle. "He doesn't handle newcomers."

"I've got a feeling he'll handle Jordanna," Bobby said. "Freddie gets off on challenges."

He stopped by Jordanna's cubbyhole office on his way out. "Good morning," he said. "Feeling better?"

"Like I got hit in the head with a sledgehammer. Apart from that — wonderful! What's up?"

He pushed the door shut behind him and leaned over her desk. "I've talked to Mac and the studio guys, and you'll be glad to hear that everyone approves."

"Of what?" she asked earnestly, nibbling on a pencil.

He took a long, meaningful beat before giving her the good news. "You're doing the movie."

She stared at him for a moment, barely able to speak. Then her face lit up and she gasped. "Oh, Bobby — I . . . I don't know what to say. This is fantastic!"

"Don't say anything."

"Not even thank you?"

"We've got to work out a deal for you first. I'm putting you together with Freddie Leon."

"Freddie won't want me," she said quickly. "I've never done anything."

"Freddie's a good friend. I'm arranging a meeting this afternoon."

"Really?"

"You bet."

She got up from behind her desk, filled with trepidation and delight. "I was just going for lunch. Should I cancel?"

"No. Go enjoy yourself, and don't tell anybody about the movie yet. We'll make an announcement when the time is right. This afternoon you'll visit the costume designer and start picking out clothes. Later we'll read through the script together."

"This is really happening, isn't it?" she said dreamily.

"Yup."

"I can't believe it."

"You will."

She grinned. "I guess I will."

"There's a cleaning crew at my house today, but they should be finished by early evening. How about coming over for dinner?"

She tilted her head to one side. "You and me?"

"No. You, me, and the cleaning lady!" he joked.

"Bobby . . ."

"Yes, you and me, Jordanna. Unless you don't want to."

"Oh, I want to."

"Good."

She smiled softly. "Good."

"Come over to the location when you're through with lunch. I'll be there all afternoon."

She left the office in a daze and drove straight to The Ivy. Now that the dream was actually coming true, she was elated and at the same time scared. Bobby had all this faith in her. Could she really cut it? Would she be good enough? Oh, God, could she live up to the famous Levitt name? It was a scary thought.

Cheryl was already at the restaurant, sitting at an outside table on the flower-filled patio.

Jordanna waved and hurried over. "Hi," she said breathlessly.

"You look terrific," Cheryl said, nodding approvingly. "Very together."

"You look pretty terrific yourself," Jordanna replied, sitting down.

They exchanged smiles, immediately comfortable in each other's presence. "Banana daiquiri?" Cheryl questioned.

"I have to go back to work," Jordanna said. "But why not?"

Cheryl signaled the waiter. "Another banana daiquiri," she said. "And two orders of crab cakes."

"So," Jordanna said, getting right to it. "How's the call girl business?"

"Lucrative," Cheryl drawled. "Grant's working with me now."

"What's he doing?"

"Looking after the girls, overseeing the books, generally organizing things."

"I thought he was an agent."

"He gave it up."

"He gave up his job to work with you?"

"I'm telling you, Jordy, we're making so much money it's a joke. Guys are tripping over each other to pay for it."

"How pathetic."

"You *would* say that."

"It's the way I feel."

Cheryl was not in the mood for a lecture.

"How's Marjory?" she asked, briskly switching subjects.

"She's got a crush on the detective who's looking after her. It's pretty sad, really."

"Maybe not. Patty Hearst married hers."

"You know how needy Marjory is. And this is a great-looking guy who's not into her at all."

Cheryl sipped her drink. "It must be depressing staying up there."

"I'm getting my own apartment."

"How is it, working for Bobby Rush?"

"Sensational!" Jordanna said, dying to reveal her news.

"From what I read about him in *Style Wars*, he sounds like an asshole."

"No way. That writer didn't get him at all."

"And how's Jordan? Did you ever tell him his wife used to be a call girl?"

"Why hurt him? If he finds out, that's his business. Besides, she's pregnant. So let's just forget we know about her past. Okay?"

"Jordy," Cheryl said hesitantly, "there's something I need to talk about."

"Go ahead."

"Well . . . last night I did something crazy."

"So what else is new?"

"No — this was *really* crazy. Grant talked me into it, but . . . the wild thing is I ended up enjoying it."

"Oh, God," Jordanna groaned. "What did you do now?"

"I went out on a job."

"What does *that* mean?"

"We were short a redhead, and Grant thought

it would be a good idea. They were paying so much money that I . . . I did it for a kick. I visited a customer."

"What — you mean you screwed him?"

"Not exactly. I paraded around his hotel suite naked, gave him a blow job, and indulged in a little hooker dialogue. The scary thing is — I actually enjoyed it."

"This is *not* good," Jordanna said sternly. "You'd better get your ass back to your shrink, quick."

"He enjoyed it too."

"Who? Your shrink?"

"No, stupid! The customer."

"Who was he?"

"Some old guy from New York. But he was sort of sweet." She toyed with her drink. "He wants to see me again."

"Back by popular demand, huh?"

"I guess that's where it's at."

"Look, I'd be the last person to tell you what to do, but surely you know you're treading on dangerous territory?"

"I guess so."

"You *guess* so? Get real, Cheryl, and stop this dumb behavior, or you'll *really* be fucked up."

"I'll think about it."

"You'd better do that. And you'd better do it fast."

Quincy was angry that Michael had run out on him. He had enough going on, and he hadn't expected his friend and partner to take off without any warning. On the other hand, if — as Amber

537

said — it was something to do with Bella, he could understand why. Michael had been through a lot, and it was to his credit that he'd managed to stay sober and not fallen totally to pieces.

Quincy drove toward the studio. He had an appointment to see Mac Brooks on the set.

He'd heard that any moment there'd be an APB out on Zane Ricca. If that was so, the cops would take care of putting a watch on Jordanna Levitt and Cheryl Landers, and everyone could relax.

In the meantime, the studio was reaming him out over Barbara Barr. They wanted to know why he'd allowed her to end up on the front page of the *Enquirer*. Because it was inevitable, he'd told them. Because she is an out-of-control white woman.

At the studio, he explained everything to Mac, who seemed relieved. "At least we don't have to worry about the girls anymore," Mac said.

"Right," Quincy agreed. "The cops will be talking to them."

"I'd prefer to keep my name out of this," Mac added.

"*The Contract* was your movie," Quincy pointed out. "It's possible your name will come up."

Goddamn it, Mac thought, why did he have to get dragged into this? "See if you can prevent it," he said, wondering how smart Quincy was and where the other detective was.

"I'll try."

Mac nodded. He was seriously worried that eventually somebody was going to dig deep enough and make the connection. It wasn't an encouraging thought. Although when he'd revealed the truth to Sharleen, she hadn't been horrified. Instead she'd been understanding and wise. "You've got nothing to be ashamed of," she'd said soothingly. "So Luca Carlotti is your father. I know what a shock it must be, but always remember — you're a big success, Mac, and if this comes out in the newspapers it won't reflect on you in any way."

Sometimes Sharleen could be smarter than the image she projected.

He hadn't told her about Zane and their connection. One thing at a time.

Standing outside The Ivy, waiting impatiently for her Porsche, Jordanna wondered why it always took forever for the valet parkers to bring the cars to the front. Cheryl was in the ladies' room, and quite frankly Jordanna was worried about her. It was one thing to supply the talent, but becoming a working girl herself was obviously not a good scene. It was definitely Grant's bad influence. Cheryl had always had a thing about him, not that she'd ever admit it, but Jordanna knew.

An acquaintance strolled out of the restaurant and waved at her. She waved back, then turned around to see if her car was there. As she did so, a Cherokee jeep raced by. Barbara Barr, leaning out of the passenger window, flung the contents of a can of paint at her. It hit Jordanna straight on, almost knocking her to the ground.

The jeep shot away, and she could hear Barbara screaming with laughter. What a screwed-up maniac!

People were staring at her in amazement as she stood there dripping red paint.

Cheryl hurried down the front steps to see what all the fuss was about. "Oh, my God!" she exclaimed. "What in hell happened to *you?*"

She stood in the shower for fifteen minutes before grabbing a towel and calling Bobby on the set. "Your girlfriend threw a can of paint over me," she announced, fairly calm considering what had taken place.

"Excuse me?" Bobby said, thinking he'd misheard.

"Barbara Barr drove past the restaurant while I was waiting for my car and tossed a can of red paint at me. Right now I'm at home trying to scrub it off — it's not easy. And you can pay my dry cleaning bill. Believe me, she'll pay in another way."

"Jesus, Jordanna, I'm sorry."

"It's not your fault. But I wish you'd be more careful who you take to bed."

"I'll come right over."

"No, don't," she said quickly. "I'll be there as soon as I can."

"We have a meeting with Freddie at four o'clock."

"Oh, goody," she said dryly. "I do hope he goes for the Native American look."

Grant was lying on the couch, switching TV channels and nursing a glass of vodka, when Cheryl arrived home. "Your boyfriend called," he said, lowering the volume with the remote.

"Which boyfriend is that?" she asked, kicking off her shoes.

"Mr. Nanni wants you at his hotel at seven."
He jumped off the couch. "Are you going?" he
asked, not looking at her.

"Do *you* think I should?" she said, placing the
decision in his hands.

He slouched over to the bar for a refill, looking
disheveled and not too happy. " 'S'up to you,"
he said casually.

"Maybe I will," she said, waiting for him to
ask her not to.

"Please yourself," he said, pouring more vodka
into his glass.

"That's exactly what I intend to do," she said
crisply.

"How was your lunch with Jordanna?" he said,
returning to the couch with his drink clutched
firmly in his hand.

"Fine. Apart from the fact that she got a bucket-
load of paint thrown over her outside the restaurant."

"No way."

"It was quite a scene."

"Who did it?"

"Barbara Barr. Our local psycho."

"I took her out once. She's a nut."

Cheryl favored him with an amused look. "I
thought you only went for the blond cheerleader
big-tits look."

He did not appreciate her comment. "You
don't know everything about me," he said bad-
temperedly.

"Yes I do," she snapped back.

"No you *don't*."

"I know that you drink too much, use too

541

much coke, and are totally screwed up."

"Like you're so together."

They exchanged a heavy glare. He infuriated her. Why didn't he see that she really cared about him?

"I'm going out again," she said, furious that he didn't seem to give a damn.

"Where now?" he asked, swigging vodka.

Let's see if this would get to him. "I have to buy a nurse's uniform for my appointment," she said, again hoping he'd tell her not to. "And a lacy black garter belt."

"I thought you were going to tell me the details."

The truth was that he simply didn't care. "Too personal," she said, swallowing her disappointment. "See ya."

The five hours spent sitting on the plane were the longest five hours Michael had ever lived through. The whole focus of his life had changed, and he had no idea what was important anymore. One moment he was a father searching for his daughter, and the next . . . he had nothing. He was overwhelmed with sadness, mixed in with the relief that at least little Bella was safe. She might not be his daughter, but he would always love her, whatever happened.

The one thing he was sure of was that he had to have a confrontation with Sal if he was to put it behind him.

Had Sal honestly thought that he'd get away with it forever? What kind of a dumb schmuck was he? Surely his brother knew that one day he'd come back to New York and find out the truth?

And what the hell was his mother thinking? Was she so uncaring about his feelings that she didn't give a damn?

Yes. Fact of life. She didn't care. She never did.

A pretty flight attendant stopped by his seat. She'd been coming on to him ever since they'd left L.A., and now she was making another attempt. "How about a drink?" she suggested brightly.

Yeah, how about a drink? A double Scotch on the rocks would be nice. Two double Scotches. Or maybe three.

The temptation was too much. "I'll have a Scotch," he said, the dangerous words mirroring his thoughts.

"Coming right up," she said, bright smile fixed firmly in place.

He could fucking taste it.

Once, when he was very young, his mother had kissed him in a strange fashion — the way he'd always seen her kiss his father.

The Man had never forgotten it. It represented a closeness between him and his mother he'd not thought possible.

After that he regarded his father as the enemy and treated him as such.

His father was a big, tough-looking man who'd walked with a limp. He overshadowed his son in every way and treated him like an inferior being.

Then there was Uncle Luca — who didn't visit often, but when he did it was always an occasion. His mother would fuss around the house, making sure everything was perfect.

When he was sixteen, he questioned his mother about Uncle Luca. "What does he do?" he asked.

"Your uncle is famous."

"How come we never go to his house?"

"Because he comes to see us once in a while, and that's all right."

He suspected his mother had more than a sisterly interest in Uncle Luca.

"When you're old enough he'll give you a job in one of his businesses."

"What business is that?"

"Commodities," his mother said vaguely.

He stared at her. He wasn't a fool, he knew perfectly well that his uncle was a big-time mobster.

By the time he got out of high school, his father had been sent to jail for armed robbery and racketeering. His father was a low-rent version of Uncle Luca, so it didn't bother him he was no longer around.

With his father absent, his mother labeled him the man of the family, turning to him for support.

Their relationship intensified, and he was relieved when he finally escaped to college — Uncle Luca paid his tuition.

When he graduated his mother insisted he go to work for his uncle.

He refused, informing her he wished to be an actor.

She objected strongly when he told her he intended to go to Hollywood and star in movies.

In spite of her objections, he remained adamant — studying with an acting coach, landing a small role in an off-Broadway play, eventually persuading her that this was what he was born to do. Finally she'd gone to Uncle Luca and requested his assistance.

After a while it came to pass that with his uncle's help he'd flown to Hollywood, gotten a role in The Contract, and met The Girl.

He'd strangled the bitch because she wanted nothing to do with him.

He'd strangled her because she represented all that was bad about women.

Now it all seemed such a long time ago.

In a way Shelley had reminded him of The Girl. He'd felt sorry for her. Even when he tied her up, stripped her clothes off, and had sex with her, he felt a certain amount of regret.

When he put his hands around her skinny white neck and squeezed the life out of her, he made sure it was quick. She'd been too frightened to scream. She stared at him with petrified eyes and remained totally silent.

He didn't like that. It wasn't normal. Killing her was not as satisfactory as he'd expected.

He'd spent the afternoon digging a shallow grave in the backyard, and when he was done he carried her outside and laid her to rest, folding her hands carefully across her chest, so that she appeared quite peaceful when he covered her with earth.

Now he had the house to himself.

He had his privacy.

He had a safe haven where he could bring anyone he wanted.

And he wanted Cheryl and Jordanna.

It was time to punish them both.

41

The meeting with Freddie Leon was going well. At least Jordanna thought it was, although she couldn't really tell because Freddie did not show much emotion, with his poker face, cordial features, and quick, bland smile. His nickname was "The Snake," because it was said he could slither in and out of any deal. However, nobody ever called him Snake to his face.

"You won't regret this, Freddie," Bobby said, acting as her biggest booster. "Jordanna's going to be the next Julia Roberts."

"I don't intend to be the next anybody," she interrupted hotly. "The original Jordanna Levitt will do nicely, thank you."

Freddie liked that. He smiled his quick little smile. "The original, huh?"

"You got it."

"Well, Jordanna . . . how about we take a test run together?"

"Drive with me, Freddie, and we're going all the way," she said boldly. She was not intimidated by men with power, after all, she'd grown up with the best.

"When I consider signing a client, I have them thoroughly checked out," Freddie said, stroking his chin.

"And what did you find out about me?" she asked, prowling around his expensively decorated office.

"That you like to go to clubs, that you haven't really focused on anything in your life, and that you're not exactly close to your father."

"Bullshit," she said, fiercely defensive. "Jordan and I are extremely close."

Freddie laughed. "Bobby, you're right, she's a beautiful challenge, and she'd better be talented too — because I'm taking her on."

Bobby was pleased. "You won't regret it."

"*You* might," Freddie remarked. "Now that I'm representing her, we're going for a killer deal."

"Hey," Bobby objected. "Squeeze our balls the second time around."

Freddie responded with a short, sharp laugh. "The first time suits me nicely." He turned to Jordanna. "Looks like we're in business," he said. "I'll have agency contracts drawn up and over at your house by the end of the day. Where do you live?"

"I'm staying at Marjory Sanderson's," she said, "but I plan on getting my own apartment." She grinned slyly. "If you make me a *really* good deal, I can get a *really* nice apartment."

He stood up, indicating the meeting was over. "You'll get a *really* good deal. That's a promise," he said, walking them to the door.

"He liked you," Bobby said in the car on their way back to the studio.

Impulsively she leaned over and kissed him on

the cheek. "Thanks, Bobby," she said happily.

"For what?"

"Everything."

He concentrated on his driving, staring straight ahead. There was no way he should start anything with this girl. They were just friends, that's all. "I'll drop you off at wardrobe. Make sure Sienna looks sensational."

"I'll do my best."

"And you'll come over tonight — right?"

"Bobby," she said, meaning every word, "I know I keep on saying this, but I'm really grateful."

"Hey," he said casually. "If I wasn't sure you'd cut it, I wouldn't want you in the movie."

"I know." She glanced out the window, then back at him. "Do you ever feel we have so much in common that maybe we've met before? Like in another lifetime?"

"Nope."

He wasn't responding the way she'd hoped. "*I* do," she said surely. "I think we've got a soul-mate thing going big time."

He half smiled, not taking her seriously. "You do, huh?"

"We've both had to go through all that children-of-celebrities crap. You had Jerry for a father. I was stuck with Jordan. I feel such a bond between us. It's hard to explain, but I know it's there."

"I don't get close to people," he said, a touch too quickly.

Why was he making it difficult for her, when she was only trying to be truthful and up-front? "That should be *my* line," she said, pressing on.

"I was close to my mother — she killed herself. I was close to my brother — he checked out. It's only recently that I've begun to realize it wasn't my fault — that I'm not responsible for their deaths."

He regarded her seriously for a moment. "We *should* talk about this, Jordanna, but now's not the time. When you come by later we can get into it all you want."

"I'd like that," she said, staring at him intently. "I'd like that a lot."

Their eyes locked.

They both knew they were on a collision course, and neither wished to stop the inevitable.

"You're really doing it a second time?" Grant asked, when Cheryl returned home.

"You keep on asking me that, and the answer is yes," she said, opening her coat and flashing him. "How about *this* for an outfit?"

He took a long look. She had on a black half bra, sheer black stockings, a risqué garter belt, black panties, and a starched white nurse's apron.

"I didn't think you'd go through with it twice," he muttered sourly, turning his head away.

She continued, desperate to get his full attention. "You like the money, don't you? I'm being paid more than any of our girls, so I must be delivering pretty damn good if he wants me back a second time."

"Christ, don't talk like that. You're starting to sound like a hooker."

"Isn't that what you want me to sound like, Grant? After all, you got me into it."

"I asked you to do it once for kicks. Didn't think you'd make a habit of it."

She allowed herself a moment of vulnerability. "If you tell me not to, I won't go," she said, silently begging him to stop her.

"Not my choice," he muttered.

"Oh — now it's not your choice? Make up your mind."

"Get off my case, Cheryl."

"You'd better drive me to the hotel."

"I'm not driving you to the fucking hotel."

"Fine. I'll take my car."

"Do that."

They glared at each other once more. She hated him — oh, how she hated him! How could he let her do this?

Belting her coat, she hurried from the house.

"You haven't touched your drink," the flight attendant said, hovering next to Michael's seat.

He glanced up at her. "No, I haven't," he agreed.

She licked her lips. Pink frosted lipstick and a pointed tongue. "Too much ice?"

"I wasn't as thirsty as I thought."

"We're landing soon. I have to take your glass."

"Go right ahead," he said calmly, feeling an overwhelming sense of achievement. For the last forty-five minutes he'd sat with the glass of Scotch in front of him and not touched it. Victory was his. It might be temporary, but for now it was enormously satisfying. As soon as he got back to L.A. he'd go to a meeting.

Fastening his seat belt, he stared out the window. According to the pilot it was snowing in New York and freezing cold. Michael began formulating a plan of action. Grab a cab at the airport and head straight for Sal's. Confront the scumbag and see Bella for the last time.

There was a sadness within him that he didn't know how to deal with. It was gradually sinking in that he was not a father and never had been. The loss was devastating, the truth hard to accept.

He remembered the night of Bella's birth — a midnight dash to the hospital, with Rita screaming all the way. He tried to be there for her in the delivery room, but she shoved him away, shouting language that no soon-to-be-mother should ever use.

The first day of Bella's life, he held her in his arms and marveled that he could have created such a delicate perfect little being. It was a memorable experience, one he'd never forgotten.

When Rita came home from the hospital she fell into a deep depression, and after three sleepless nights she refused to continue breast-feeding. He learned how to mix the formula and give the baby a bottle. After that — if he wasn't out on a case — he took over the middle-of-the-night feed while Rita slept. He didn't mind; in fact, he looked forward to it. The moments alone with the child he thought was his daughter were the most special he ever experienced.

Now — because of his lying brother — those moments meant nothing.

Goddamn Sal. He was the lowest of the low. A subhuman with no fucking conscience.

Michael knew that if he was to get through this he had to stay in control. It was going to be difficult with no Quincy beside him to keep a check on his volatile temper, but fuck it — he could do it.

The airport was crowded as usual. Since he had no baggage, he made it out of there fast, hailed a cab, and jumped in.

"Where to, bud?" asked the driver, a gum chewing Arab with an American accent.

He considered his answer. Should he go to his mother's first and drag her along for the ride?

No. He had nothing to gain by involving her.

He gave the driver Sal's address and sat back.

Soon it would all be taken care of.

The Man watched as Cheryl left her house. He could have taken her then and there, but the timing wasn't right. Everything in life was timing. He'd learned that as an actor.

Steven Seagal had good timing. He'd built his career with a steady succession of films, each one more successful than the last. That's what The Man called perfect timing.

Cheryl drove fast down the winding hillside. The Man slipped into traffic behind her. He was in no particular hurry. He had all night. He knew the moment would come when he could pounce and take her, and she would be his. Why rush?

She hit Sunset and made a sharp left, eventually drawing into the forecourt of the St. James's Hotel. Climbing out of her car, she handed the keys to a parking valet.

The Man parked on the street. He could wait. He could wait as long as he had to.

Sitting in his car, he began thinking about his mother and her new husband. She'd remarried when he was in jail. He couldn't believe it. Not that he was any great supporter of his father, but she'd chosen as her new mate a man not worthy to shine her shoes. A man fifteen years younger than her. And, according to friends of the family, a worse villain than her first husband, whom she'd divorced.

All his life she'd caused him nothing but problems and spoiled him for other women. His mother was a true bitch goddess.

He loved her.

He hated her.

Sometimes he couldn't make up his mind which was the truth.

It didn't matter, because soon — when he was finished in California — he would squeeze her white neck between his hands, and when he choked the life out of her he would celebrate.

The Man knew one thing for sure, he was entitled to commit this act, it was justice, really.

She'd given birth to him.

He would give death to her.

A fair exchange.

42

Jordanna spent an exhilarating afternoon picking out clothes for the movie with the costume designer. Then she went back to the Sanderson house, where Marjory was in a deep sulk. "What's the matter?" she asked.

"Michael Scorsinni is the matter," Marjory complained. "I lent him money, and now he's vanished."

"What do you mean, vanished?"

"He was supposed to come back here for dinner. Have *you* seen him?"

"No."

"That's how *I've* seen him."

"He'll be back," Jordanna said. "Why did you lend him money anyway?"

"Because he needed it."

The sooner Jordanna moved out of the Sanderson estate the better, she decided. Marjory's moods were getting boring.

She wondered if Bobby would ask her to stay the night. Just in case, she popped a toothbrush into her bag, then immediately took it out again. Too obvious. Maybe he wouldn't want her to stay. Maybe he wasn't even attracted to her.

Oh shit! How about treating him to a little of

that seductive come-on she was usually so good at.

No, it wouldn't work with Bobby. He was different from her Midnight Cowboys. He was special.

On the way over to his house she thought about Cheryl. Her friend was not in good shape; she was definitely doing coke and God knew what else. It was obvious Grant wasn't the greatest influence in the world.

Bobby greeted her at the door of his house. Clad in jeans and a denim work shirt, he looked great.

She entered the house, checking it out. "Hmm," she said. "It looks like everything cleaned up nicely."

"So did you."

"Huh?"

"The paint job Barbara did on you. Not a trace."

"I was thinking of suing the psycho — but why give her the publicity? Her bad karma will do her in eventually."

"And Miss Levitt is wise, too," he said, taking her hand. "Come with me. I'm fixing us dinner."

"You really think I'm wise?" she asked eagerly, as he led her into the kitchen.

"As a matter of fact, I do."

"You should've seen me in my wild days."

"When was that?" he asked.

"A few weeks ago."

"That's when you were with Charlie — right?"

"I was never really *with* Charlie."

"But you *were* sleeping with him."

"Sleeping with someone sounds so nice and cozy."

Fixing her with his incredible blue eyes, he said, "Were you?"

"Was I what?" she asked, although she knew perfectly well what he meant.

"Sleeping with him?"

"I guess I was — round about the time *you* were in bed with Barbara."

"Twice," he admitted. "Casual sex at its most casual."

She shrugged off her leather jacket. Underneath she wore a white T-shirt and faded jeans. Nicely laid back. Nothing obvious. "Was she any good?" she asked, trying to sound as if she couldn't care less.

He removed tomatoes, lettuce, and a cucumber from the fridge, placing everything on a chopping board. "Was Charlie?" he countered, picking up a sharp knife.

She couldn't help laughing. "What is this — a pissing contest?"

He sliced the lettuce in half. "Is that what you want?"

"*No,* it's not what I want," she said, taking a piece of tomato and popping it into her mouth. "Can I help?"

"Nope. Everything's under control, so why don't you go in my office, grab a script, and start reading through it."

Why don't I grab you, she was tempted to say. *Or better still, why don't you grab me.* She was deeply in lust with this man, and yet for some unknown reason she couldn't bring herself to make a move.

Ha! This was a major first.

"I didn't know you cooked," she said, wishing he'd pay more attention to her.

"Tofu hamburgers and salad," he said wryly. "It ain't Julia Child, but it'll taste good."

She wandered into his office, inspecting everything. It wasn't that she was nosy — she just had a strong desire to know as much as possible about him.

All the torn photographs had been piled neatly in the center of his desk. She picked up a still of Bobby and Jerry when Bobby was just a little boy. A cute little boy at that — long blond hair and big blue eyes. Taking a roll of Scotch tape from the desk, she carefully stuck the photo back together, then, on impulse, stuffed it into her purse. Stolen goods. He'd never know.

"Dinner," Bobby called out. "We'll eat on the patio. Okay with you?"

They sat outside, at a table next to the small, black-bottomed swimming pool. "Umm, delicious," she lied, digging into the strange-tasting hamburger, fervently wishing it were a juicy ground steak.

"Did you look at the script?" he asked, pouring her a glass of white wine.

"I don't need to. I know it by heart."

He was surprised. "You do?"

"When I tested I learned the whole thing."

"So when Barbara got the part you must have been disappointed."

She took a sip of wine. "Try devastated."

"Devastated, huh?"

"Destroyed."

"This part's gonna put you out there. Think you can handle it?"

"Why wouldn't I?"

" 'Cause becoming famous changes a lot of things," he said reflectively.

She tilted her head. "Like what?"

"The way people relate to you, for one. Stardom's a big responsibility. Everyone has their expectations, and you're supposed to live up to them."

"Do you?"

"Do I what?"

"Live up to expectations."

"I try."

I bet you do, she wanted to say, forcing herself to eat. *I bet you live up to expectations in every way.*

"It's given me a sense of my own worth," he continued seriously. "Before I made it, everywhere I went I was known as Jerry Rush's son. Believe me, that is *not* good for the ego."

"Tell me about it," she sighed. "In school we never got into who had the best grades, it was always whose father had the biggest-grossing movie and whose mother was on the cover of *People*."

He nodded. "I know what you mean. I remember one year in high school when Jerry had a dog of a movie. It was his first one that didn't do well at the box office. Boy, was he pissed! I had to beat the crap out of another kid, whose father was a major-league baseball star — 'cause this kid was king of the school, and I was in the shitter due to Jerry's failure."

"But there must have been *some* good times?" she said softly.

"Yeah . . . the parties. Instead of ordinary birthday parties, it was always elephants and tigers — in fact, it was the whole fucking Los Angeles Zoo on our back lawn. That was kind of a kick."

"Must have been the fashionable thing. For my sweet sixteen, Jordan hired the UCLA marching band! And every Friday I was allowed to have all my friends over for a screening of a new movie. Before it even hit the theaters! Beat that!"

"Hey — talk about pissing contests!"

"So now you're happy?" she asked.

He studied her face across the table. "What's happy, Jordanna?"

She shrugged. "Dunno. But I've felt happier these last few weeks than I ever have." Now why had she blurted *that* out. Revealing her feelings was just not cool.

"That's nice to hear," he said evenly.

Their eyes met, and there was no pulling away. It was like an irresistible force drawing them together. She pushed her knife and fork to one side of the plate, finding it impossible to eat.

"Doesn't my cooking cut it?" he wondered.

"I'm not into tofu," she murmured.

He leaned across the table, placing his hand over hers. "I don't want to screw anything up here, Jordanna."

"What are you talking about?" she asked innocently, although she knew perfectly well what he meant.

"You're going to be starring in my movie, we'll be working together every day. I made a bad mistake with Barbara. Let's just be friends, huh?"

The last thing she wanted was to stay just friends, but she nodded as if it were the best idea she'd ever heard. "Sounds good to me."

"Then if Charlie — my favorite icon — visits the set, I won't be a jealous wreck," he joked.

"What *is* this Charlie crap?" she asked. "Why do you keep on bringing him up? Do you want to know what he was like in bed — is that it?"

"No."

"Yes you do," she teased.

"Wrong."

"He was a passable lover, very selfish."

"He's old enough to be your grandfather."

"My father, not my grandfather."

"He looks old enough."

"Hey, one minute he's a fucking icon, the next he's old enough to be my grandfather. Make your choice."

He got up from the table and entered the house. "Ice cream?" he called over his shoulder.

"Is that all you have to offer?" she said, picking up the plates and following him inside.

"Are you coming on to me?" he asked, looking at her quizzically.

Her heart was pounding, he was actually making her nervous. "Yes," she said boldly.

"Didn't we just agree it wouldn't be a good idea?"

She pushed back her long dark hair. "*You* said it wouldn't be a good idea. I didn't agree to anything."

"Hey, Jordanna," he said, opening the freezer. "I was right."

"Hey, Bobby," she responded, finally summoning a vestige of her old self. "You were wrong."

"Good evening, Mr. Nanni."

"How ya doin', Bambi?" he replied, thinking it was about time he revealed his real name.

"Pretty good, Mr. Nanni."

"Whyn't you call me Luca?" he suggested.

"I prefer to keep things on a more formal basis."

"You do, huh?"

"Tonight I'd like the cash up front," Cheryl said, getting straight to the point.

Luca patted his slicked-back patent-leather hair. "You don't trust me?"

"Of course I do. It's just that I like the thought of the cash in my pocket before you see what I'm wearing for you tonight."

"How can I figure what kinda big tip I might wanna hand you?" he asked slyly.

"That's entirely up to you."

He nodded, deciding he'd give her whatever she wanted, plus a generous tip. Vanishing into the bedroom, he returned with an envelope of cash and placed it in her pocket. "You can take your coat off now," he said, licking his lips in anticipation.

"When it gets a little warmer," she said.

He chuckled, enjoying the game. "What're you drinking tonight?"

"Pernod."

"I ain't got no Pernod."

"Order it," she said imperiously. "And while you're ordering, I'll have some caviar."

"You're demanding tonight."

"You don't mind, do you?"

"Nope. In fact, I got a proposition to discuss with you."

"Really?"

"Take that goddamn coat off, an' we'll talk."

"If you want it off," she said audaciously, toying with him, "take it off for me."

He walked over and tugged at her belt, loosening the coat until it fell from her shoulders. He whistled through his teeth when he eyeballed the provocative outfit she had on underneath. "Jeez! You're some hot broad."

"I dressed especially for you," she said, feeling the power again, that surge of incredible power that put her totally in control and made her knees go weak.

"Take a walk around the room for me, baby," he said, settling back on the couch. "Show me what you got."

"Yes, Mr. Nanni," she said coolly. "Anything to oblige."

Glancing at her watch, Kennedy was surprised to see it was past eight. She'd been expecting a call from Michael to confirm dinner arrangements. He hadn't called, and she was disappointed.

For the last few hours she'd been busy at her word processor, putting together her story on the murders for *Style Wars*. She needed more information on Zane Marion Ricca, his past was very sketchy. She already had researchers in New York working on it for her.

She thought she might call Michael, find out

what was happening. As far as she could remember, they'd arranged a definite date.

You're being stood up, a little voice informed her.

I am not.

Oh, yes you are.

She refused to be juvenile about this. She was hardly an insecure teenager waiting anxiously for a date. Picking up the phone, she dialed Michael's number and connected with his answering machine. She hesitated for a moment before leaving a message. "Uh . . . hi. This is Kennedy Chase. It's eight-fifteen and I haven't heard from you, so . . . uh . . . I guess tonight is off."

What else was there to say? Nothing. The next move was his, and if he didn't make it — so what? She was glad she hadn't gone to any trouble, although she *had* washed her hair and taken a long scented bath before sitting down at her computer — but that was merely to relax before working.

Her phone rang, and she pounced.

"This is Kennedy."

"This is Nix."

"Who?"

"Short memory."

"Oh . . . Nix." She remembered him, all right. Tall, talented, and twenty-four. Too young by far, but appealing all the same.

"I'm here for one night, so I thought if you were free — "

"I'm not," she said shortly, cutting him off.

"I would've called you earlier, but L.A. turned out to be an unexpected stop."

"Really," she said. It occurred to her that several months earlier they'd shared a memorable night of passion, and he hadn't called once. It hadn't bothered her, but the fact that now he thought he could walk right back *did* bother her. She got rid of him quickly.

Men.

Who needed them? Most of them couldn't chew gum and talk on the phone at the same time. Her father used to say that to her when she was a teenager and a boy had let her down. Dear old Dad. She missed him.

Suddenly the evening loomed ahead and there was nothing she felt like doing.

Michael Scorsinni.

Damn him, he was evoking feelings she'd thought were long buried.

There was no way she planned on sitting around thinking about him, so on impulse she called Charlie.

He sounded delighted to hear from her.

"Thanks for last night," she said. "I enjoyed it."

"Shoulda come by my club," he drawled. "It was happenin'."

"Can I buy *you* dinner tonight?"

He chuckled, not fooled by her offer. "Okay, green eyes, gimme the happy news — who stood you up?"

"No one."

"My ass."

"Am I buying or not?"

"Yeah. An' since you're buyin', you get to pick me up. How about nine?"

"I'll be there."

"An' don't bring the blues with you."

"I have no clue what you're talking about."

He chuckled knowingly. "Sure, baby. Never bullshit a bullshitter who's been there an' back more times than you'll ever know. See ya."

Maybe Charlie Dollar was just what she needed. Maybe not.

"I've been thinking," Luca said.

So've I, Cheryl wanted to say. *I've been thinking that this is not such a good idea after all.*

The feeling of power, of total control, only lasted until after the sex. And the sex with Luca was not exactly scintillating. His particular kick was watching her parade around the room until he was aroused enough to require a blow job. Twice was definitely enough.

Why had Grant let her go through with this? She was furious with him because he didn't give a damn about her. It was about time she woke up and realized how selfish and self-destructive he was.

"You listening to me?" Luca said gruffly.

"Yes, I'm listening," she answered.

"Okay — this is it, babe. I'm settin' you up."

"Excuse me?"

"I own a big, fancy house here, an' you're gonna live in it. No more hookin' for you, Bambi. You don't havta do it no more, 'cause I'm plannin' on takin' care of you on a permanent basis."

This jolted her back to reality. "Are you serious?"

"Sure am. You'll move into my house; in fact, I'll even let you fix it up, hire an interior designer

567

— that kinda shit. I'll pay you an allowance, an' you'll be mine exclusively. Howdja like that?"

"I'm not for permanent sale," she said sharply.

"Didn't say you were."

"You're talking as if you can buy me."

"That's what I'm doin' now, ain't it?"

"You can buy me for an hour or two, but you can't buy my life."

"You wanna *stay* a hooker? That's not for a girl like you. I can give you plenty more."

"I've never considered the possibility of being somebody's . . . I guess you'd call it mistress."

"You got a boyfriend?"

"No."

"If you was smart you'd be jumpin' up and down creamin' your panties."

His offer was so bizarre that she was tempted to laugh aloud, but she didn't, because she knew it would insult him.

Ha! Wait until she told Grant that this old guy was so crazy about her that he wanted to set her up in a house and pay her money to be his exclusive property. Wow! She'd really scored.

"I'll let you know, Mr. Nanni." She picked up her coat, deciding it was time to get out of the hooker business once and for all.

"Do it fast," he said eagerly.

She left the penthouse promising to call the next morning with her decision. Like she would even consider it!

The moment she was out of there, Luca summoned Bosco and instructed him to trail her.

"I'm in the middle of something. . . ," Bosco

started to complain.

"Forget it," Luca said sharply. "You an' Reno get your asses downstairs an' have the limo follow her."

He'd decided it was time to find out everything about Bambi. After all, whether she knew it or not, she was going to be his, and he didn't appreciate surprises.

When Luca Carlotti wanted something, few people said no.

43

Michael had forgotten what a nightmare New York cabdrivers could be. The ride into the city totally took his mind off everything other than survival.

"Jesus, you wanna slow down," he suggested at one point, tapping the bulletproof partition.

"Yeah, pay my bills, man, an' we'll take it two miles an hour," the driver shot back belligerently.

Dumb jerk, Michael thought.

It was just before six o'clock New York time when the cab screeched to a halt outside Sal's house. Parked outside, like a badge of merit, was the flashy gold Cadillac Michael had heard so much about.

He tensed up, thinking about his no-good brother.

Sal the racketeer.

Sal the scum-faced lowlife who'd stolen Bella.

Sal the lying bastard.

It was time to deal with the slimy sonofabitch. Beat the shit out of him. Do whatever would give Michael peace of mind.

"How about waiting?" he suggested to the cabdriver. "I'll need a ride back to the airport."

"No can do," the driver said, snapping his fingers impatiently.

"I'll take care of you."

"I'm on my way home, man."

"Thought you needed to pay your bills."

"Don't hassle me, man. I toldja — I can't wait."

"Okay, okay," Michael said, paying him off.

The cab zoomed away, and he stood curbside for a moment, staring up at the house. Inside this house was Bella. Would she remember him? Would she remember him as Daddy? Or had they already taught her to forget?

He rang the bell. After a few moments the door was flung open by Pandi, dressed in a lime-green jumpsuit, scuffed white boots, and dangling rhinestone earrings. Her dyed-blond hair was pinned on top of her head, and she was fully made up. She resembled an aging Barbie doll with a nasty attitude.

"Mikey?" she exclaimed, turning pale under her heavy makeup.

"Yeah, it's me."

"Oh, my God, Mikey! Does Sal know you're here?"

"No, but I'm sure he'll be glad to see me. Right, Pandi?"

She immediately panicked. "Uh . . . well, we wasn't expecting you."

"I know that. But we're family. Surprises are nice once in a while, huh?"

Her expression told him that no, surprises were not nice — surprises were a pain in the ass. "Does . . . does your mom know you're in town?" she stammered.

"No. Figured I'd surprise everybody while I was at it. Came by to see your new house and your new car and — hey, what's all this I hear about you got a daughter?"

"Who told you that?" she said uncomfortably, holding firm at the door.

"Yeah, somebody mentioned you've got a kid here now, a little girl. What'd you do — adopt?"

She wasn't a fool. "You'd better talk to Sal," she said, blinking rapidly.

"Where is he?"

"Out," she lied. "Come back another day."

"I'm only in town for a few hours, Pandi. I have to see him now."

She recovered some of her composure. "I told you," she repeated. "Sal's out. We'll havta get together some other time." With that she attempted to slam the door in his face.

He blocked it with his foot. "Cut the crap, Pandi," he said, his voice hardening. "I want to see Sal, and I want to see him now."

"You got no right to force your way in here."

"I've got a right to come in, and you know it."

"Sal!" she yelled, realizing she was in a no-win situation. "We got trouble here."

Michael shoved his way inside the house, kicking the door shut behind him.

Pandi backed away. "This ain't got nothing to do with me," she said defensively. "It all happened long before I came into it, don't go blaming me."

"Blaming you for what?"

"Talk to your brother."

Sal lumbered downstairs, tucking a crumpled blue shirt into a pair of baggy pants. "What the fuck *you* doin' here?" he said, scratching his crotch.

"Paying a brotherly visit," Michael said. "You

have any objections?"

Sal exchanged looks with Pandi. She shook her head as if to say she hadn't told him anything.

"Does Ma know you're here?" Sal asked, peering at him suspiciously.

"Why are you all so concerned about Ma?"

" 'Cause she's the first person you should go see."

"Yeah? Why's that?"

"She's your mother, for chrissake. She cares about you."

"Sure. She cares about me just like you do — you low-life asshole."

"Now wait a minute — "

"How long did you think you'd get away with it before I found out?"

"Get away with what?" Sal bluffed, like he had nothing to hide.

"Don't give me that horseshit."

Sal turned to his wife. "Where's the kid?" he asked abruptly.

"Over at a friend's," she replied, agitatedly biting on her lower lip.

"See she stays there."

"Don't sweat it, Sal," Michael said, hating his dumb brother but managing to stay in control. "I haven't come to take her away."

"What *have* you come for?"

"Maybe to beat the shit out of you."

Sal glared at him. He was fatter than ever, over two hundred pounds, and mean with it. *"You're* gonna beat the shit outta *me,"* he sneered. "I don't freakin' think so."

"I don't want no fighting in this house," Pandi

573

said, asserting herself.

"Why'd you do it, Sal?" Michael asked, shaking his head. "Why'd you have to put me through this?"

"It's all down to you now, huh? You got no thought for Rita. The poor bitch ended up with her brains blown out, an' all you can think about is yourself."

"This has nothing to do with Rita, she's long gone. This is you and me, Sal. You took my child."

"She ain't yours."

"If she wasn't, you should have had the balls to tell me, not sneak her away like some thief in the night. You've got no guts."

"Get outta here, fuckhead."

"Not until I see Bella."

"She's not called Bella no more," Pandi interrupted. "She's got a new name an' a new life. You leave her alone. She's happy with us."

"Shut your mouth," Sal said, shooting her a filthy look.

"Don't tell *me* to shut up," she snapped back, her painted eyebrows rising fiercely.

"I'll tell you what the fuck I like."

"I didn't come here to listen to you two fight," Michael said, still keeping a tight check on his temper. "I want to see Bella one more time, then I'm gone."

"You're pretty freakin' hot with your demands," Sal snorted.

"You're *lucky* I'm not beating the crap out of you."

"Yeah?" Sal sneered. "You ain't got the stones to beat the crap outta nobody. Never did."

"He's not seeing her," Pandi interrupted, her voice turning into a hysterical whine. "She'll get upset. It's not fair on the kid."

Sal threw her another steely glare. "How many times I gotta tell you? *Shut the fuck up.*"

"Who d'you think you're talking to?" she responded hotly. "I ain't some piece of trash you're shacking up with. I'm your wife, so watch your mouth when you're talkin' to me."

Michael was saddened that this was the atmosphere Bella was growing up in, but he realized there was nothing he could do.

Pandi stormed off to the kitchen, muttering under her breath.

"Why'd you do it, Sal?" Michael asked again.

Sal shrugged nonchalantly — he really couldn't see that what he'd done was so bad. "What the fuck. Rita was naggin' me t'get married. I wasn't into that shit — not then. And there you were, always the pretty-boy schmuck when it came to pussy. So I figured *you'd* marry her, that way the kid would stay in the family. After Rita hit L.A. she started getting itchy pants. You know Rita, she had eyes t'be a freakin' movie star — she didn't want to be lookin' after a kid. So we did you a fuckin' favor."

"You're a piece of crap, you know that?"

"No, Mikey, *you're* crap. You're a lousy fuckin' drunk and a lousy fuckin' cop, an' that's all you'll ever be."

"You're wrong, Sal. I'll always be an alcoholic, but at least I admit it. And when I wake up in the morning I have a clean conscience. What've you got?"

"Everythin'," Sal boasted. "You should be so freakin' lucky."

"Everything, huh? Selling drugs to kids and old ladies? Running whores? How do you face yourself in the mirror every morning?"

"Get the fuck outta my house."

"I told you — I'm not moving till I see Bella."

"How about I throw you out?"

"How about you try?"

They squared up, facing each other. They'd had many fights when they were kids, and Sal had usually won because he was bigger. Now Michael was more than ready for him.

Sal went to throw a punch to his chin. Michael blocked the move, grabbed Sal's arm, and twisted it back, at the same time kneeing his brother sharply in the balls.

"Holy *shit!*" Sal grunted, bending double. "What you tryin' to fuckin' do?"

Pandi came running out from the kitchen. "I phoned home, your mother's on her way over with Eddie."

"You stupid cunt," Sal groaned, slumping down on the bottom stair. "Who needs *them* shovin' their noses in."

Michael attempted to control his anger, determined to handle this without totally losing it.

"I could have you killed," Sal muttered grimly. "You know that, Mikey? I could have you fuckin' wiped out."

Jesus, his brother was some piece of work. "You think I'm scared of you and your gun-happy buddies?" Michael said coldly.

"You fuckin' should be."

"I could have *you* arrested."

"For what?" Sal said belligerently. "Takin' back my own kid?"

"Will you two stop!" Pandi screeched.

Michael looked at her with contempt. "And as for you, don't you know how it's been for me these last few months — not knowing whether Bella was dead or alive? What kind of a coldhearted bitch are you?"

"You gonna allow him t'talk to me like that?" she shrieked at Sal. "You gonna let him insult me?"

"Shut the fuck up," Sal mumbled, still clutching his aching balls.

A few minutes later Eddie arrived. Virginia trailed behind him, looking old and worn out. Michael couldn't help feeling sorry for her, but he had to learn self-survival. As far as he and his mother were concerned, it was over.

"What're you doing here, Mikey?" she asked in a tremulous voice. "Whyn't you call? You shoulda told us you was coming."

He took a hard look at his family, his warm, nurturing family. "You all knew about this," he said tightly. "Why didn't anyone tell me?"

Eddie shrugged like it was no big deal. "No need, it would've only caused trouble."

"I'm no longer part of this family," Michael said, feeling unbelievably calm. "Once I've said goodbye to Bella I'm going back to California, and none of you will hear from me again." He turned to his mother. "That goes for you, too."

"Don't be like that, Mikey," she whined. "I was only doing what Sal said was right."

577

"Yeah . . . story of my life. Sal first. Me second. But y'know what, Ma? I'm a big boy now. I don't have to take second place."

"You was never in second place, Mikey," she said unconvincingly.

He seized the opportunity to get a few things off his mind. "Remember how you watched Eddie beat up on me when I was a kid? You never stopped him — you stood back and let it happen. How come, Ma?"

"It wasn't my fault."

"Yes it was. Because you didn't even try."

Virginia clutched his sleeve. "I'm your mother, Mikey. I was always there for you."

Sadly he shook his head. "No. The truth is you never were and you never will be. And I've finally realized it."

The Man watched as Cheryl exited the hotel. He observed her as she stood waiting for her car.

Bitch! Rich spoiled bitch!

She'd helped incarcerate him in a jail full of villains, perverts, and sick people. She deserved everything she was about to get.

He willed himself not to think about the years he'd spent in prison, desperately trying to push those thoughts to the back of his mind. But sometimes incidents filtered to the surface, and he couldn't help remembering the daily humiliations, the tough beatings, and the brutal sex.

One day, he would be able to wash his mind clear of all the hateful memories.

One day, when the women who'd helped put him away were dead and gone. Buried beneath the ground. Strangled by his own hands.

Cheryl tipped the valet, got in her silver BMW, and drove off.

The Man followed, keeping a suitable distance behind her. He knew it wouldn't be long before she ran out of gas. It had been a fairly simple task to empty the tank of her car while *the valets weren't around.*

He wondered if she'd noticed her car was on empty. Probably not. Women didn't bother with such details. And if she did notice, she'd have to stop at a gas station, and then he would put his other plan into action.

Either way he had it covered.

She drove down Sunset, then turned on Alpine, cutting up to Lexington. Two blocks along Lexington, her car ground to a halt.

The Man pulled up behind her just as she was attempting to restart the engine. He had on his dark shades, so she wouldn't recognize him. It was night anyway, and his hair was different.

He strolled over to her car and tapped on her window. "Having trouble, miss?" he asked courteously.

She hardly glanced at him. "Oh, God, I think I'm out of gas," she groaned.

"There's an empty can in my car. I can drive you to the nearest gas station and bring you back, if it'll help you out."

"That's nice of you, but I don't want to put you to any trouble. I can call." She picked up her car phone. It was out of action, he'd made sure of that.

"Would you care to use the phone in my car?" he offered politely.

All Cheryl wanted to do was get home, running out of gas was a real bummer and certainly not on her agenda. "Thanks," she said, getting out of her car, completely forgetting about security and how careful one had to be.

The Man followed, opening his passenger door for her.

"Where's the phone?" she asked as she got into his car.

"It's a portable," he said. "I keep it hidden. Too much crime going on today. Just a minute." He walked around the car and got in, settling himself behind the wheel. Then he immediately activated the special locking system he'd installed.

Now he had her. She was his prisoner, only she didn't know it yet.

He felt a rush of triumph.

"The phone?" she repeated.

The Man was very calm. "There's a gun pointing at you," he said in low, measured tones. "Do not scream. Do not do anything. We're taking a ride. One that I promise you'll never forget."

44

The call from the cops came through long after Cheryl had left the house.

"I'd like to speak to Miss Landers."

"Maybe I can help you," Grant said, thinking it was a would-be client.

"Who are you?"

"Her associate. Who are *you?*"

"Detective Carlyle."

There were a few moments of silence while Grant digested this information. A detective calling Cheryl could only mean trouble. And the last thing Grant needed was to be involved in a Heidi Fleiss type scandal.

"She's not here right now," he said at last. "Can I pass on a message?"

"We need to talk to her regarding a case we're investigating. Are you her husband?"

"No, no, just a friend," Grant said quickly.

"And what's your name?"

"Shep," he lied, deciding it wouldn't be prudent to reveal his proper identity.

"Is there anywhere I can reach her now?"

"No."

"What time did you say she'd be back?"

"Ten, eleven — I'm not sure."

"Well, Shep, have her call me when she gets home. Tell her it's quite urgent." He gave his number.

Grant hung up wondering what the detective wanted. If Cheryl was about to be busted, he had no intention of being dragged along for the ride.

To be on the safe side, he got up from the couch — his favorite resting place — and hurried to his drug stash. Best to get everything out of Cheryl's house and head on back to his own apartment.

He scrawled a message on a piece of paper and left it on the kitchen table.

Call me at home when you get back.

G.

Jesus! He could just see his father's face if he got himself busted. The headlines would really sing:

MOVIE STAR'S SON ARRESTED
DRUG BUST IN BEL AIR

He should've stayed an agent, but pimping was so much more fun.

Taking a final look around the house, he made sure he'd removed all his stuff, then he got in his car and beat a hasty retreat to his apartment.

Charlie Dollar threw open the door of his rambling mansion and ushered Kennedy inside with a theatrical flourish. "How about a drink?" he suggested. "Or a joint?"

"I've made a reservation at Orso's," she said. "I thought we could sit outside on the terrace."

"Does this mean you're picking up the check?" he asked, grinning wickedly.

"It certainly does."

"Dinner two nights in a row," he commented. "Seems to me you're gonna have to put out."

"Not necessarily," she replied good-naturedly. "Don't forget, *I'm* paying."

He chuckled. "Does that mean *I'm* gonna have to put out?"

"Oh, Charlie, Charlie," she said, sighing. "It doesn't always have to be sex. I thought we were going to be platonic friends."

"That's not what you want, Kennedy. Somebody stood you up tonight, and you're running to me to get even. I understand. I've been there."

"Very perceptive."

"Who was he?"

"He was a might-have-been," she said vaguely.

"Might have been what?"

"Might have been involved in my life if he'd come up to expectations, but he didn't."

"You an' me could be very good together, 'cause you're an understanding woman an' that's the kinda woman I'm ready to share with."

"You've already got one understanding woman in your life — the mother of your child. Remember?"

"I get off on those — you know — tribal setups, where a guy has three or four wives an' everybody lives in harmony an' nobody ever gets pissed off. That's the way things should be."

"You're really just a sweet old-fashioned kind of guy, is that it?"

"Well, whaddaya know — she's discovered my secret."

"Can we go, Charlie?"

He took her arm and escorted her outside. "Hey, green eyes," he said, squeezing her elbow, "you written the *Style Wars* piece on me yet?"

"Yes, I have."

"Will I like it?"

"Do you care?"

"Not particularly."

"I've written you as a sexy, unpredictable eccentric. Does that suit you?"

"Didja say I was thin?"

"No."

"Bitch!"

She couldn't help being amused. A man and his ego would be the perfect shout line.

He headed for his Rolls, parked in the driveway. She pulled him over to her car. "This is my date. I'm driving."

He smiled his wild-man smile, slightly ragged around the edges. "Are you sure you don't want to stay here and sample my movie star charms?"

"It wasn't what I had in mind."

"Then I'd better warn you — I am not a cheap date. I do not give head in the car, and I eat everything in sight."

"You certainly know how to turn a girl on," she said dryly.

"Thank you, sweet journalist. Nice words always get me ready for the big seduction."

"Don't hold your breath," she murmured.

The kisses they exchanged were hot and slow, fast and exciting. Kissing hadn't been this much fun in a long time.

Bobby didn't even want to think about what he was getting into. It just seemed right, and that was enough for him.

Jordanna knew immediately that what she felt for Bobby was completely different from anything she'd ever felt before. She really cared about him. There was no logical explanation, it was simply a connection they both seemed incapable of stopping.

They were necking on the couch like a couple of teenagers on a baby-sitting gig, and the kissing was so good she didn't want it to end.

After a while, when things started to progress, she summoned every bit of strength she possessed and pushed him away.

By this time he was ready to rock-and-roll. Her sudden change of direction confused him. "What's the matter?" he asked. "I thought this is what you wanted."

"It is," she said breathlessly, trying to pull herself together. "But first we should have a conversation."

"Jesus, Jordanna. What kind of a conversation?"

"Safe sex," she said, standing up.

He began to laugh. "A safe-sex conversation?"

"Yeah, I know, it's funny, but since we both recently slept with high-risk partners . . ."

"You sound like a doctor," he said, somewhat bemused.

"I'm trying to be responsible."

"Hey," he joked, "it's difficult being responsible with a hard-on."

"Don't tempt me. This is serious," she said, frowning. "What *is* safe sex anyway? Do *you* know?"

"Abstinence."

"Oh, you mean only latex can touch our bodies?"

"Well . . . a condom is safe."

"Do you have any?"

"No. How about you?"

"They're at Marjory's."

"Great. I'll run down to the drugstore."

"Isn't that kind of a mood breaker?"

"Jordanna," he said patiently. "Trust me — you've already broken the mood."

"Do you think I'm being stupid?"

"No, you're being wise," he said, standing up and opening his arms. "Come here."

She fell into his arms as if she belonged there, and felt totally at peace.

He hugged her tightly. "Y'know what? Maybe we've found what we've been looking for."

"Yeah," she said wryly. "A truly great relationship — you, me, and a box of condoms!"

They both burst out laughing, perfectly in tune.

"I'm taking you home," he said.

"No!" she responded, objecting strongly.

"Yes. My call's six A.M. tomorrow. It's my first day working with Jerry, so I need to be prepared."

"But, Bobby — "

"Hey," he said. "Tomorrow night we'll start

early and finish late. I'll have condoms coming out my ears!"

"It's not your ears I'm worried about!"

He took her hand, leading her over to the door. "When we start this, we'll start it right."

"I know," she said softly. "That's exactly how I feel."

"Good."

"Good."

They stood by the door and began kissing again, their bodies pressed close, the heat rising.

"Has anybody ever told you you're extremely sexy?" she gasped, leaning back, wondering why she'd stopped him in the first place.

"Nope," he said, smiling.

"Oh, *sure*. Just about every woman in America. Like you don't get a zillion fan letters a week."

"They see an illusion."

"And what do I see?"

"The real me," he said seriously.

"I'm looking forward to the real you. Every single inch."

"Does that mean you're coming to bed with a tape measure?" he quipped.

"Would I do that?" she asked, widening her eyes.

"Yes."

"Do I need to?"

"No," he said, kissing her one more time. "C'mon, wild child. I'm driving you home."

"You don't have to. My car's outside."

"You're not driving alone."

"Hey — Bobby, it's me you're talking to. I'm quite capable of getting from A to B in one piece.

I've been doing it all my life."

"I'm sure you have."

"I'll call you as soon as I reach the mausoleum."

"Come to the set tomorrow for lunch?"

"Of course."

"I'll be waiting," he said, pulling her so close
she could barely breathe. "Hey — Jordanna . . ."

"Yes?"

"I'm not used to saying anything meaningful — "

"Nor am I," she interrupted, feeling extremely
light-headed.

"But I've got a strong suspicion you're right
— this was meant to be. And I'm looking forward
to tomorrow night."

"Me too."

"Not as much as I am."

"Wanna bet?" she said, grinning.

She began the drive home on a high. Love had
snuck up, taking her completely by surprise. And
the amazing thing was that love had nothing to
do with sex — the sex would be the final prize,
because she knew it was going to be sensational.

Putting in a tape, she sang along to the upbeat
sounds of Salt 'N' Pepa sexily mouthing off on
"Whatta Man." Then she shoved her foot down
hard on the accelerator, zooming her Porsche home
as fast as possible.

Tomorrow couldn't come soon enough for
Jordanna.

The Man had no idea what time Jordanna would arrive back at the Sanderson mansion. He'd already ascertained that she wasn't there, so all he could do was wait.

She might not be as easy to take as the other one. As far as he could recall, Jordanna was tougher, stronger, and more willful. But he was convinced nobody could beat him, because he had the one element that gave him a supreme advantage — surprise.

Cheryl had been easy. Once he got her in his car and she realized she was trapped, she shut up.

At first she thought he was kidnapping her. Going for a big ransom. "Don't hurt me," she said. "My father will pay anything you ask for."

"I don't care about your father," he replied contemptuously. "I don't care about anything except punishing you for what you did to me."

"What did I do to you?" she asked. "I've never seen you before."

"Am I so unmemorable?" he said coldly. "That you could send me away to prison and not even know who I am?"

A few seconds of silence.

"Zane?" she ventured.

"Clever girl," he replied.

"Oh . . . my . . . God!"

Realizing who he was, she desperately tried to get out of the car. But the locking system was in place, and she was caught in the trap, just as he'd planned.

He drove her back to the house in the hills off Laurel Canyon, the isolated, deserted house where nobody could observe what he was doing.

When they'd arrived, he'd bundled her inside, shoved her roughly down on the couch. There was a mug of cold tea spiked with strong sleeping pills on the table, carefully prepared by him before he'd left. "Drink that," he'd commanded.

"I'm not drinking anything."

"Drink it. Or suffer the consequences."

She'd stared at him with frightened eyes and reluctantly choked down the tea.

He'd watched until she slumped into a drugged sleep, then he'd picked her up and carried her down to the cellar, where he'd placed her on a blanket in the corner. Her coat had fallen open on the way, revealing that she was not properly dressed.

He'd stared at her breasts, almost exposed in a black push-up bra. And then he'd touched the insides of her thighs and was tempted. But temptation would only hinder his progress. There would be time later to do anything he desired, so he'd brought the handcuffs he'd pur-

chased at a sex shop into play, handcuffing her wrists to a solid pipe that ran down one side of the wall. Then he'd bound her ankles together with strong rope.

He'd thought about gagging her, but it wasn't necessary. There was nobody to hear her screams. And the strong sleeping pills would keep her unconscious until morning.

He'd pulled her coat closed to cover her strange outfit, and left her alone in the dank, dark cellar.

Now, as he waited for Jordanna, he couldn't help feeling pleased with himself. All those years in jail he'd thought about what he would do when he got out, and in a short period of time he'd successfully disposed of four women.

The betrayers.

The bitches.

And when the other two were gone, he would be able to return to New York and get rid of everyone else who'd tried to ruin him.

The anticipation of strangling his mother filled him with such a burning intensity he could barely stand it. She was a woman. And everyone knew that women were lying, cheating, unfaithful vile scum.

Allowing his mind to wander, he remembered the time shortly after his father had been sent off to prison. A warm New York night. He was sixteen years old and enamored with a girl at school. She was seventeen and didn't want anything to do with him.

He'd arrived home from school and gone straight to his room to study. At eight o'clock his mother had appeared at his bedroom door, dressed in a diaphanous pink negligee, reeling slightly, drunk and flushed. "I need your help, poopsy," she said in the baby-girl voice she sometimes adopted.

"I gotta do my homework, Mom."

"Come with me now, poopsy. Mommy needs you."

Reluctantly he followed her into her bedroom, an oppressive room filled with lace-trimmed cushions, movie magazines, stuffed toys, and shopping bags abrim with the clothes she purchased, wore once, and always returned.

She wandered over to her bed and flopped down in the middle. "Come over here, poopsy," she coaxed. "Sit on the side here and talk to Mommy."

He couldn't stand it when she called him poopsy. He loathed it when she demanded his time.

She held open her skinny arms. "Mommy's having a bad day," she sighed. "Mommy is not happy."

"What is it?" he asked, drawn toward her in spite of himself.

"I received a letter from your father. He writes mean things to me. Cruel things."

"Well . . . ," he started to say, attempting to comfort her.

Before he could get any further, she'd thrown her arms around his neck and pulled him down next to her, kissing him full on the lips.

He smelled booze mixed with cigarette

smoke and a cloying sweet scent. Her tongue flicked into his mouth, exploring, searching. . . . And then her hand crept between his legs, and to his eternal shame he was hard, and when she unzipped his pants —

The Man snapped to attention, breaking out in a sweat, refusing to remember.

It wasn't right, the things she'd done to him that night. It wasn't proper. And yet he hadn't fled. He'd allowed her to do whatever she'd wanted. And she'd wanted it all.

He spotted car headlights coming up the hill. He'd stationed himself not too far from the entrance to the Sanderson mansion, but not close enough so that anyone in the guardhouse could spot him.

Jordanna was approaching. Her white Porsche unmistakable in the moonlight.

Another rich bitch! His for the taking.

It had not been easy finding out where she lived, but he'd done it, and now here she was. His excitement began to build, for he knew that soon he would have her in his power.

He started his engine. As soon as she was near enough he hit the accelerator, swerving his car out of the shadows, smashing into the side of her Porsche, taking her completely by surprise.

Jordanna Levitt would soon be with Cheryl, exactly where she belonged.

And then he would be king. And eternal power would be his.

45

Sitting in his study in front of the television, Mac watched as Rosa Alvarez made a big deal out of the task force formed to track down the L.A. Strangler. Listening to her, you'd think her network was personally responsible for getting it together.

He waited impatiently for her to name Zane Marion Ricca, but she didn't, and he couldn't understand why. He picked up the phone and called Quincy. "What's happening?" he asked tersely. "I thought you said they'd name him today."

"It'll probably hit the news tomorrow," Quincy informed him. "They've put out an APB, but sometimes they ask the press to hold back on naming the suspect."

"Jesus!" Mac complained. "What about the girls? Have the cops warned them?"

"I'm sure they have."

"So they're safe?"

"I spoke to Detective Carlyle this afternoon, he assured me it was taken care of."

"Okay, okay," Mac said, still feeling uneasy. He wanted Zane to be caught, arrested, and thrown back into jail. Only then would he feel secure.

He could barely admit it to himself, but the horrible truth was that Zane was his cousin; they shared a bloodline, and it sickened him.

Feeling edgy, he wondered if he should call Luca. It might be a good idea to get his take on what was happening, for Luca would surely know if Zane had been picked up yet, unless of course he'd handled it in his own way. . . .

Mac had always thought of himself as a righteous man, but now he found himself hoping that Luca *had* handled it. He wanted Luca to have found the prick and buried him six feet under.

Jesus! He truly was Luca Carlotti's son.

It was a frightening thought.

"So like we're followin' Bambi in the limo," Bosco explained. "An' suddenly she pulls her car over to the side of the road and this guy stops behind her — it looks to me like he was followin' her too. So he gets out an' goes over to her car — "

Luca frowned. "What guy?"

"Dunno. They must've been together, 'cause then she gets outta her car, leaves it there, an' gets in *his* car. Then they drive off cozy as two fuckin' peas."

"What was you doin' all this time?"

"We was parked down the street, watchin' the action."

"So then what happens?"

"We trail the car with her an' the guy in. He takes off fast, hits Sunset, turns on Laurel Canyon, an' takes a side road up into the hills. We're behind him as close as we can without them suspectin' they're bein' followed."

"Did you find out where she went?"

"Yeah. Some deserted house way up there."

"Was he her boyfriend?"

Bosco shrugged. "How would *I* know?"

"Did they look *loving* together?"

"You're askin' the wrong person."

"Okay, okay," Luca said impatiently. "You get an address?"

"Not exactly."

"That's okay. You'll go back tomorrow an' check it out."

On the plane to L.A., Michael felt as if he were going home, and it was a good feeling. The relief of getting out of Sal's house was overwhelming.

They'd finally let him see Bella, and the sad thing was she barely recognized him. She wasn't his child anymore, they'd done a good job of brainwashing her.

Pandi had brought her in. "This is your uncle Mikey," she said. "*Uncle* Mikey."

"Hello, Uncle Mikey," Bella said, clutching a stuffed teddy bear, gazing up at him with big blue eyes. Rita's eyes.

"Do you remember me, sweetheart?" he asked, bending down to talk to her.

"Dunno," she said shyly.

"We lived in the same apartment in New York, when you were real little."

"Dunno," she repeated, swinging her teddy bear in circles.

"I'm going to tell you something," he said,

squeezing her hand tightly. "And I want you to listen carefully. If there's anything you ever need, you can always come to me. Can you remember that?"

"Okeydoke," she said, unconcernedly popping bubble gum. "Okeydoke, Uncle Mikey." Then she reached up, put her little arms around his neck, and kissed him.

It killed him. But what could he do? If he wanted to fight this legally, he wouldn't stand a chance.

He spent a few more minutes with Bella, hugged her close, and walked out of the house without looking back. Now he had to go forward, make a new life for himself in California.

He'd taken a cab to the airport and phoned Quincy when he got there. "What's happening?"

"Jesus Christ!" Quincy sounded really annoyed. "You call me and you ask *me* what's happening. What's going on with *you?* Did you find her? Is she safe?"

"You know what, Q? It's a long story, and I'll tell you when I get there."

"Are you bringing her back? Amber will get a bed ready."

"No, she's not coming back. She's with my family."

"You took her there?"

"I'll explain everything when I'm home."

Sitting on the plane, it suddenly occurred to him that he'd blown a date with Kennedy. Marjory had also been expecting him at her house, and knowing Marjory, she'd be furious, considering he'd borrowed ten thousand dollars that very morning.

First priority: find a way to pay it back — and fast.

He called Kennedy, using the phone on the plane. He got her machine and left a message.

Next he phoned Marjory. The butler informed him she'd retired for the evening.

After that he fell asleep, dozing fitfully, dreaming about Bella, Rita, his mother, and Sal.

He was proud of the fact that he hadn't smashed his brother's face in. It was quite gratifying to know he could control his sometimes violent temper, because in his drinking days he would have beaten him to a pulp.

Those days were over now. He was wiser, more responsible.

Finally he was his own person.

"You stupid maniac!" Jordanna shouted, leaping out of her car, practically jumping up and down with fury. "Look what you've done! You've smashed up my car! I can't believe it! What's *wrong* with you?"

Angrily she began inspecting the damage.

Zane acted swiftly. Getting out of his car, he ran over as if he were as concerned as she was.

"What are you — drunk?" she yelled, glaring at him. "I'm calling the police."

"I . . . I'm sorry," he mumbled, playing dumb.

She bent over to pick up a piece of bent chrome.

Swiftly he moved up behind her.

"This is shit — " she began to say, holding a broken mirror aloft.

He took her by surprise, grabbing her in a choke hold from behind, placing the chloroform-soaked pad he'd prepared over her nose and mouth.

She reacted violently, kicking back with an unexpected strength.

*Fast reaction. Not as easy as the other one.
It was all he could do to keep the pad in place.
She was fighting like a wild animal, but he was
strong, stronger, and her struggles were in
vain, because after a few moments she slumped
helplessly to the ground, unconscious.*

*The Man half carried, half dragged her to his
car. Then he opened the trunk and unceremo-
niously bundled her inside, shutting it fast.*

*He looked around. The street was dark and
deserted. Producing a flashlight, he inspected
the front of his rental car — it was only slightly
damaged, while one side of the Porsche was
totally wrecked. Good. He'd enjoyed slamming the bitch. Getting behind the wheel of his
car, he took off fast.*

*Driving along Sunset to Laurel Canyon, he
made sure he kept within the speed limit, looking neither left nor right. At one stoplight a police car pulled up alongside him. He kept his
eyes firmly on the road ahead, his expression
betraying nothing.*

*By the time he reached the house and
opened the trunk, Jordanna was in a semicon-
scious state, mumbling unintelligibly. The
bitch couldn't even stay unconscious for long.*

*He lifted her up, slung her over his shoulder,
and carried her inside.*

*With one hand he unlocked the door to the
cellar and staggered downstairs.*

He shone his flashlight at Cheryl. She lay exactly where he'd left her, shackled to the pipe, still in a heavily drugged sleep.

The cellar was small, approximately eight feet by eight, damp and very dark.

He threw Jordanna down on the ground and handcuffed her to the same pipe as Cheryl. Then he bound her ankles tightly.

When he was satisfied they were both secured, he left them down there and went upstairs.

Jordanna began to groan. "What's . . . what's going on?" she mumbled. "Where's Bobby? Bobby . . ." Opening her eyes, she realized she couldn't see a thing.

For a moment she thought she was in the hospital. Somebody had smashed into her Porsche, and now she was in the goddamn hospital!

She tried to sit up, suddenly realizing her wrists were shackled to the wall.

Oh, God! In a blinding flash it came to her — she'd been kidnapped!

A feeling of dread enveloped her. This was her worst nightmare coming true. Rich Hollywood kid, father would pay a big ransom. Oh, Jesus!

She could smell chloroform all over her face. Sneezing vigorously, she shook her head and tried to make herself alert.

She could hear shallow breathing nearby and realized she was not alone. But it was too dark to make out who was down there with her.

"Who's there?" she called out, controlling any sign of panic. "Who the fuck is there?"

Nobody answered.

Pushing her back up against the wall, she desperately tried to acclimatize her eyes to the dark. Although her ankles were bound together, she was able to move her legs, and she did so, pushing against a body in the corner.

Shoving the person with her feet, she muttered an urgent, "Wake up — wake the hell up!"

Whoever it was didn't move.

She was in the dark. Ever since she was a little girl, being alone in the pitch black had always scared her.

Gotta start thinking straight, she told herself sternly. *Gotta start thinking real straight if I'm to get out of this one.*

She reviewed the situation. She'd been snatched off the street, put in a cellar, handcuffed and tied up. But she was determined not to be frightened. She'd get out of this, and she'd get out of it alive.

With that thought foremost in her mind, she drew her knees up against her chest, rested her head on them, and settled down for a long, cold night.

Halfway through the evening, Kennedy knew she'd made a mistake, a little of Charlie Dollar went a long way. He was his usual stoned, charming self, but she'd had enough. Just because she was angry Michael hadn't called, she should not have headed for the nearest man. It wasn't working out. And the sad thing was that Charlie thought he had a chance.

"You know what, Charlie?" she said. "I've got a really bad headache. Do you mind if I skip coffee and go home?"

"*You're* the designated driver," he reminded, raising an eyebrow. "And *I'm* your date."

"So I'll do the right thing," she said, making light of the situation. "I'll take you home first, then you won't have any complaints."

"I thought we were dropping by Homebase tonight," he said.

"You go. I'm not in the mood. The thing is I'm still working on the L.A. Strangler story, and I have researchers in New York bringing me facts even as we speak. There'll be stuff waiting for me on my computer. You know what it's like when you're on a movie — I bet you get obsessed. Well, that's how I am when I'm working a story."

Charlie pulled a face. "Yeah, yeah, your message is coming across loud and painfully clear. This is called movie star turn-down — something I do not see much of."

"I'm sure you don't," she said, hoping he'd take the hint and get up.

He made no attempt to move. "So you don't want to tell me who the guy is, huh? Maybe I can give you valuable advice, my vast wealth of experience is legendary."

"It's not a guy."

"C'mon, green eyes, put it on the table."

She sighed. "Okay — I met someone. We had a drink together, and tonight we were supposed to have dinner. He didn't call. End of story."

"What's he got that I don't have more of?"

"I don't know. And quite frankly, I don't care. He's out of the loop."

Charlie rolled his eyes. "Women!"

"Excuse me?"

"Sweetheart — surely you know we *never* call when we say we will. It's a male thing."

She was in no mood to listen to Charlie's take on male-female relationships, but he was on a roll. "There were many ladies who, before I was a movie star, would not give me the time of day. I know it's hard for you to imagine, my dear, but it's true."

"Is that why you became an actor?" she asked, signaling a waiter for the check.

"It was unintentional. Rock stars claim they became musicians because of a love for music. This is not true. They became musicians to get laid. The same with actors. Why do you think every horny young guy in high school joins the acting class? To get laid, of course."

"So you're telling me that's why Sir Laurence Olivier decided to be an actor?" she said, with more than a hint of irony.

"Nah . . . the English are different. They're so busy getting whipped by their nannies and boarding school matrons, they don't know their ass from a hole in the ground."

"Very eloquent, Charlie."

"I say it the way I see it."

The waiter brought the check, and she handed him her credit card. Charlie seemed to have no problem with her paying.

"So that's why you became an actor, to get laid?" she asked.

He grinned wolfishly. "I did a lot of other things first."

"And you weren't successful?"

"Being a movie star means scoring with ninety-nine percent of the women out there. Very few say no. You're one of the few."

"Am I supposed to be flattered?"

"Don't be — you're missing out."

"I'd sooner be your friend than your lover," she said, signing the receipt.

"You can be both."

She stood up from the table. "Thanks for the offer, but I don't think so."

She drove them home. He wasn't giving up. He invited her in for a nightcap or a joint. She turned both offers down.

"Okay, green eyes, but I'm gonna get you one of these days," he promised, wagging a warning finger at her.

"Keep waiting, Charlie."

That wolfish grin again. "Oh, I will."

He stood on the steps of his house, watching her drive off.

She wondered if Dahlia was keeping his bed warm.

The first thing Kennedy did when she got home was to contact Rosa.

"They're probably naming Zane Ricca tomorrow," Rosa said. "They've matched a perfect fingerprint, there's no doubt it's him."

"Do they have any idea where to find him?"

"No details. Maybe tomorrow they'll release his picture. If so, it won't be long before somebody turns him in. When they do, our producer wants you to do a story on-air. You know, show his

605

photo, ask people if they've seen him. Do a reenactment of one of the murders, with actors playing the roles. Those kind of shows are real ratings grabbers."

"No, Rosa. I don't want to do tabloid TV."

"Not if it helps track him down?"

"It's not my thing."

"Okay, okay," Rosa said testily. "Maybe *I'll* do it."

Kennedy played her answering machine and was pleased to find a message from Michael, calling from a plane. So *that's* why she hadn't heard from him. Of course, he could have phoned earlier, but still, it was nice to know she hadn't been stood up after all.

Switching on her computer, she checked to see what information her researchers had come up with. Tapping in to review the new facts, she noted they'd done a thorough job.

ZANE MARION RICCA
Born January 10, 1958
New York Hospital

Father — Bruno Ricca (currently serving a twenty-year prison sentence for armed robbery)
Mother — Phyllis Ricca (sister of Luca Carlotti)

Now that was interesting.

She scanned the rest of it quickly — schools, jobs, medical history — nothing of much note.

The name of Luca Carlotti fired her interest. Luca Carlotti was a reputed mob kingpin out of

New York, a man to be reckoned with. And now it turned out that Zane Marion Ricca was his nephew — what a connection!

No wonder Zane had been represented by the highest-paid lawyers in town — Uncle Luca must have paid.

Kennedy sensed her story getting bigger and better. She sat down and started work.

46

Hubert Potter had toiled as a private security guard on the Sanderson estate for almost eight years. It was a cushy job, nothing much happened except a few threatening letters every now and then, tourists driving up to the gate asking dumb questions, big dinner parties twice a year — and that was about it.

Five days a week, Hubert got off duty at seven A.M. Today he drove slowly down the long winding driveway in his old DeSoto, his mind occupied with personal concerns.

A few minutes after leaving the estate, he was startled to come across a wrecked Porsche blocking his way. Pulling his car to an abrupt stop, he got out and went over to inspect the damage.

As he approached, it occurred to him that it looked like Jordanna Levitt's Porsche. Now *she* was trouble. Coming and going at all times, driving too fast, blasting her music. And look what had happened to her now — she'd gotten her car smashed up.

He wondered how he'd missed her when she arrived home last night. He'd been on duty, but sometimes his eyes grew heavy, and maybe he'd closed them for a second or two. Still, he was sure he would have seen Jordanna if she'd come home by foot.

He walked around the white Porsche, noting quite a bit of damage. Yanking open the passenger door, he was surprised to discover a woman's purse on the seat, which he thought was strange, because women always took their purses with them.

He picked up the purse, opened it, and checked out the wallet, searching for a driver's license. Sure enough, the license belonged to Jordanna.

For a brief moment he thought about putting the purse back, getting in his car, and going home. But Hubert was too conscientious for that kind of behavior. Duty was duty, and he was obliged to investigate.

Placing Jordanna's purse under his arm, he got back in his car, made a U-turn, and headed back to the Sanderson estate.

Michael rolled out of bed at seven-thirty, six hours after hitting it the night before. His plane had landed after midnight, so by the time he arrived home it was almost one-thirty.

It gave him a good feeling to be back in L.A. Especially as it was one of those perfect smogless mornings, the kind he'd grown to love.

Seeing his family would soon be a distant memory. The one positive thing was that Bella had seemed quite content where she was now. Maybe Sal and Pandi would turn out to be okay parents after all. He could only hope and pray.

Today is the beginning of my new life, he told himself. *No more hanging on to the past.*

It was too early to call Kennedy.

609

He picked up the phone and called her anyway.

On his way to the studio, Bobby reflected on the night before. He'd had a wonderful time with Jordanna — she was exciting and different — but in the cold light of day he wondered if it was wise to get involved just as she was about to star in his movie. He'd made one mistake with Barbara Barr, he didn't want to repeat it.

Not that Jordanna was anything like Barbara — there was no way he could even think of comparing them.

It niggled him that Jordanna hadn't phoned him last night when she got home. Eventually he'd called the Sanderson place, and the butler informed him that everyone appeared to be asleep, and did he really wish to disturb Ms. Levitt. No, he said, he did not wish to disturb her.

So she'd forgotten to call him. Big deal — he'd see her for lunch.

He was kind of edgy because today was the first time he'd be working with his father as an adult. The last time he'd appeared in one of Jerry's movies he'd been eight, playing Jerry as a boy. That was a thrill a minute — with Jerry's encouragement, the entire crew had nicknamed him "Jerry's kid" and laughed at everything he did. Including Jerry — to whom humiliating his son was sport.

Well, he was no longer "Jerry's kid," and this was going to be an interesting experience, because this time it was *his* set, and *he* made the rules.

If anyone was about to be humiliated, it certainly wasn't going to be him.

First thing every morning George Randall jogged. Even though he knew it was good for him, he loathed every step of the way. He did it for his wife. She was twenty-six. He would soon be fifty-six. Well, in Hollywood what was thirty years between lovers?

Nobody ever mentioned their age difference, but George was extremely aware of it, especially as he was in the youth business. George was an extremely successful plastic surgeon.

Running down the driveway of his three-million-dollar home on Lexington, he activated the remote control to open his automatic gates, and as he hit the street he was annoyed to find a silver BMW half blocking the entrance to his driveway.

What kind of nonsense was this? How was he supposed to get his Rolls out when he left for work an hour later?

George decided that maybe he wouldn't go jogging after all. He'd go straight back inside and summon the police. They were quick enough to give him tickets whenever he left his car in the wrong place. Let's see how quickly they could remove a car from his own personal driveway.

Kennedy wanted more. She always wanted more. As information came through, she checked it out, diligently searching for something to make her story fly.

Zane Marion Ricca being Luca Carlotti's nephew was a big plus. It was possible that only she and her researcher knew.

How close was Luca Carlotti to his nephew? A good question.

Right now she was working on the Hollywood connection. Like how had Zane first gotten to Hollywood and landed a role in *The Contract*? It was hardly likely he'd walked in off the street — a New York actor with little experience. It was more than luck. Was it possible Luca Carlotti had ties to the film industry?

She'd found out that Nanette Lipsky was the casting director on *The Contract*, a movie directed by Mac Brooks. Nanette was currently working on *Thriller Eyes*. Kennedy planned to speak to her.

She wished she could view the scenes between Zane and the murdered actress. They'd both been cut from the finished movie, their roles recast and reshot, but somebody had the original footage.

Hmm . . . she'd really like to talk to Mac Brooks too, although it might not be so easy, as Bobby Rush was producing and starring in *Thriller Eyes*, and she could just imagine his reaction if he heard she was trying to interview Mac.

She'd give Mac Brooks a shot anyway, tell him she was writing a story for *Style Wars* and see what he had to say.

The worst he could do was turn her down.

Luca had forgotten the real purpose of his visit to L.A. He'd been so busy thinking about Bambi that he'd let Zane out of the loop, and he needed to bring him back in and get rid of his dumb nephew before he did any more damage.

Bambi had captivated his heart. She might be

a hooker, but at least she was top of the line, and he was prepared to forget about her past in exchange for her undying fidelity. When Luca gave his heart — not to mention his house — it was a permanent arrangement, until *he* said it was over.

Since Priscilla's death he'd been alone. There'd been a series of women, but none of them had got his juices flowing the way Bambi did. She might be a little young, but he was sure she was the woman for him. And he hadn't even fucked her yet. He had plans to fly his personal physician to L.A., have him check her out, make sure she was disease free, and then he'd go for it. Bambi was in for a big treat.

Right now he had to concentrate on finding Zane and eliminating him, only then could he devote all his attention to Bambi.

He knew she'd accept his offer. The truth was he'd give her no choice.

When Luca wanted something, there was no question that he'd get it.

Detective Carlyle was not having a good day. He had this goddamn murder case to deal with, and Boyd Keller, the hotshot asshole heading up the task force, was no help. Headquarters had been formed in his precinct, and Boyd Keller was all over him. Yesterday Boyd had told him to contact the other two witnesses who'd helped put Zane Marion Ricca away, warn them about what was going on, and offer them police protection.

He'd tried. First he'd left a message for Cheryl Landers at her home, and then one for Jordanna

Levitt at the production office where she worked. Neither had bothered phoning him back.

Now he was personally going to have to shift butt and track down the little darlings.

It pissed him off. You would think if a detective left an urgent message, people would get back to him in a timely fashion. If anything happened to either of them, it was their own goddamn fault.

The only problem was, if anything *did* happen, everybody would blame him.

Since the task force had been formed, his life had turned to shit. Boyd Keller had reamed him out in front of a group of his colleagues. "Two of these murders were in your division," he snapped at him, like a fucking drill sergeant. "How come you didn't figure out they were connected?"

Screw you, he wanted to say. *Who do you think I am — Perry fucking Mason?*

As far as the two girls were concerned, how could he put them in protective custody when he couldn't even get them to return a phone call?

Dammit! There was only one thing to do, and that was visit them both this morning.

He got in his car, put on the radio, and treated himself to a sharp jolt of early-morning reality. Howard Stern at his best.

Maybe there was time to stop off for a Danish and coffee. The diner on Third had a new waitress, and she always winked at him in a most provocative fashion.

What the hell — a man had to have *some* fun.

47

Jordanna slept in fits and starts, waiting for daylight. It wasn't until six in the morning that light began filtering in from a small grill high up on one side of the cellar wall. Only then did she realize that Cheryl was the other person trapped in the cellar with her.

Overcome with relief that she was not alone, she rolled over as close as she could, giving Cheryl an urgent shove with her feet. "Wake up," she said quickly. "It's me — Jordy. C'mon, wake up, get with it. We're in big trouble."

Cheryl stirred slightly.

"C'mon, c'mon, c'*mon,*" Jordanna urged.

"Oh, Jesus!" Cheryl groaned, attempting to move. "I don't feel so good. I think I've been poisoned."

"Don't panic," Jordanna said, keeping her voice low. "We're handcuffed and trapped in a cellar. I think we've been kidnapped."

"It's worse than that," Cheryl said weakly, recalling what had happened to her.

"What do you mean?"

"Remember when we gave evidence against that weirdo actor who murdered Ingrid Floris?"

Jordanna felt her stomach drop. She knew she

wasn't going to like what she was about to hear. "Yes."

"It's him. It's Zane Ricca."

Oh, Christ, they really were in trouble. "How do you know?"

"He told me," Cheryl said, her voice rising. "This isn't just kidnapping. He plans to really harm us."

"No way," Jordanna said, refusing to believe the worst. "There's two of us and one of him. We'll get out of this."

"All right for you to say. But how?"

"Don't lose it, Cheryl. Above all we have to stay strong."

"How can we when we're handcuffed and tied up? He won't give us a chance."

"How did he get you here?"

"I was on my way home . . . my car ran out of gas. I got in his car to use the phone. He had a gun, brought me here and forced me to drink something — I guess it was drugged. That's the last I remember. How about you?"

"He rammed my Porsche, and like an idiot I got out to see the damage. The next thing I knew, he'd chloroformed me."

"Obviously he planned this whole thing," Cheryl said.

"We'll be okay," Jordanna responded, her mind racing. "Eventually he'll have to let us go to the bathroom and give us food. There'll be an opportunity, and when it comes we'll be ready to take advantage of him. Did you ever go to a self-defense class?"

"No."

"I did a couple of times. They taught me that in an attack situation the important thing is to stay calm and wait for the windows of opportunity."

"What's that mean?"

"Search out his weak points. Like in the case of rape, a man has to unbuckle his belt — so that's a weak moment. It's then that you strike."

"Oh, God . . ." Cheryl groaned. "I think I'm going to throw up."

Jordanna kept talking. "Let's talk about his two most vulnerable areas — his eyes and his balls. We go for either."

"I've definitely been poisoned," Cheryl mumbled, trying to sit up, screaming with horror as a cockroach scurried across her leg.

"When you're kidnapped or in a hostage situation," Jordanna said, "the essential thing is to become friendly with your captor. Make human contact. We have to get him talking, pretend we're his friends."

"Friends?" Cheryl exclaimed. "You can't be serious."

"Concentrate," Jordanna said, willing her to do so. "It's more difficult to harm people if you know them."

"*You* do it," Cheryl said, starting to shiver. "All I want is to get out of here." Her coat slipped open, revealing her sexy ensemble.

"What the fuck have you got on?" Jordanna demanded.

"Stop staring," Cheryl said, embarrassed. "It's my sex outfit."

Jordanna shook her head. If the situation weren't so desperate, she'd be laughing. "Oh, that's really good. That's a fine outfit to get kid-napped in."

"Thanks. When I put it on I wasn't planning on being kidnapped," Cheryl retorted, recovering some of her snap.

"Here's what we'll do," Jordanna said, glancing at her watch. "It's early, so he might not come down here until seven or eight. We should get some sleep, 'cause we'll need all our strength. When he comes down and removes our handcuffs, we go for him. Remember — eyes and balls. We've got to do this together, Cheryl. It's imperative we back each other up."

"I feel so bad," Cheryl moaned. "I don't know what he gave me, but I feel like pure shit."

"It's just an allergic reaction."

"I don't know. . . . I never felt this bad. . . ."

"Hey — hang in there, we'll get out of this," Jordanna said encouragingly. "Don't you worry about it."

She sounded strong and cheerful, but deep in her heart she was terrified.

The Man slept for seven straight hours. He knew it was important to get his rest, his mother had taught him that. She'd taught him a lot of other things too, most of which he wished to forget.

Now that he had the two girls safely secured in the cellar, he wasn't quite sure what he would do with them. Eventually he was going to kill them, but he enjoyed the idea of playing with them first. Making them suffer as he had suffered over the last seven years.

Ah, yes — bringing them to their knees watching them shiver with fear, would be a pleasure.

He hadn't quite decided how he was going to do it. Perhaps keeping them trapped and shackled in the cellar was enough. Psychologically they would expect him to do something. And yet what if he did nothing? Merely kept them chained like wild animals until they died a slow and agonizing death.

The idea appealed to him.

Being in control was a heady feeling.

Grant never surfaced before noon, and when he did get up he usually had a major hangover. On Thursday morning he awoke before ten and lay in bed, willing himself to go back to sleep.

It occurred to him that although he'd left a message for Cheryl to call him, she hadn't done so. Abandoning more sleep, he reached for the phone and gave her a buzz.

Her machine picked up. He hated machines; on principle he never left a message.

Sometimes Cheryl could be extremely aggravating. She should have called him back last night, since he'd gone to the trouble of leaving her a note. He wanted to alert her that there was a detective on the prowl, because if there *was* some kind of investigation going on, she might be able to deflect it. Cheryl had power, or at least her father did. More power than his father, who was a mere movie star.

He tried Cheryl again. Surely she wasn't stupid enough to have stayed the night with her client?

No, not even Cheryl would do that. They'd

often played dangerous games, but never that crazy.

It occurred to him that he shouldn't have allowed her to go off on an appointment with some john. Still, she was just as much to blame as he was: she shouldn't have done it.

Now he'd have to start checking up on her.

He climbed out of bed, stared at his reflection in the bathroom mirror, pushed back his long hair, and decided to drop by her house, just to make sure she was okay.

"Can I come over?" Michael asked.

"Excuse me?" Kennedy said.

"This is Michael. Remember me? I'd like to come over and bring you breakfast."

"I don't eat breakfast."

"Make an exception."

"It's awfully early."

"You're up, aren't you? I didn't wake you."

"That's because I'm working on a story."

"What story?"

"Zane Marion Ricca. The L.A. Strangler. They're about to put out an arrest warrant."

"Really?"

"I'm running background on him. There seem to be some interesting tie-ins."

"Why don't you tell me about it when I get there?"

"Aren't you listening, Michael? I don't eat breakfast."

"How about calling it an early lunch?"

"You're persistent."

He hoped he sounded as sincere as he felt. "I

missed seeing you last night, Kennedy. I know I didn't call, but I had to fly to New York — it was about my daughter."

"Have you found her? Is she all right?"

"Yes, she's fine."

"That's great news."

"I need to talk to someone." He paused, then turned on the charm — only this time it wasn't bullshit — he meant it. "And the truth is, you're prettier than Quincy."

She smiled. "Compliments will get you nowhere, but I wouldn't mind discussing Mr. Ricca with you, so you may as well come over."

"An address would be good."

"Boy," she sighed. "You really want it all, don't you?"

"That's about the way it is."

Jerry Rush hit the set like the star he was. Darla followed — the perfect Hollywood wife, coiffed and groomed to within an inch of her life. Behind her came his personal hairdresser — a whiz with discreet hairpieces for aging movie stars — and behind him his personal makeup artist, a pretty girl with amazing tits.

Bobby watched the circus warily, hoping he could get through the experience of working with Jerry unscathed. One thing he knew for sure: it wasn't going to be easy.

Mac liked to rehearse each scene before blocking. When he told Jerry, the old movie star roared with laughter. "Rehearse? Fucking *rehearse?* That's for the theater."

"No, this is the way I work," Mac said quietly.

"You do, huh?"

"Yes, he does," Bobby said, hurriedly joining in.

There was a tense moment while they both waited for Jerry's reaction.

Jerry thought about behaving like a prick, but Darla was there, observing his every move. Had to watch it, she could be very scathing and he wasn't in the mood. Besides, Darla was now in charge of his finances. It gave her too much control, but so what? He was getting too old to screw around anymore. "Okay, I'll rehearse," Jerry said magnanimously. "I know the scenes, my lines, and I haven't had a drink." He clapped Bobby on the shoulder. "Relax. This'll all be fine."

Bobby glanced over at Mac, who nodded reassuringly.

"Good," Bobby said. "Let's rehearse."

He wished Jordanna would arrive early. He was getting used to having her around, and right now he could do with her support, because he had a strong suspicion this was going to be a very difficult day.

Once they started, Bobby got lost in his character. So did Jerry.

After a few awkward moments they were in perfect tune, two actors doing a job — two very good actors.

After they'd gone through the scene three times, Mac said, "I'm satisfied. How about you guys?"

Jerry nodded and turned to Bobby. "You're good — you know that?"

Bobby couldn't believe it. A compliment? From

his father? This was a first.

"Uh . . . thanks," he mumbled, feeling ten feet high. "So are you."

Jerry gave a big shit-eating grin. "Well, *that* goes without saying."

Suddenly Bobby realized it wasn't going to be so difficult after all. One thing about Jerry, he was a true professional, he knew exactly what he was doing, and he did it extremely well.

Bobby began to relax.

Early in the morning, Luca returned to his house, accompanied by Bosco and Reno.

"You seen or heard from Zane?" he asked the housekeeper, who was busy sweeping the front hall.

She stopped what she was doing and slowly shook her head.

"What didja say your name was?" Luca asked, rocking impatiently on the heels of his handmade shoes.

"Eldessa, Mr. Carlotti."

"Okay, Eldessa. I got a big fat reward for anyone who tells me where my nephew is. We're talkin' bucks here. Five thousand of 'em. Anyone comes up with the information is gonna get this reward. Cash. You understand me?"

Eldessa tried to imagine all the things she could do with five thousand dollars. "Yessir, Mr. Carlotti."

"How long you worked for me?"

"Many years, Mr. Carlotti."

"Okay, okay — just makin' sure you know where your loyalties lie."

"I know that, all right," she said, nodding stoically.

Luca turned to Bosco. "Go take another look through his room. An' fuckin' find him, will ya. It's enough already."

"I'll find him," Bosco said confidently, although he had no clue where to start looking.

He and Reno swept the room without discovering much of anything. A few movie magazines — mostly with Steven Seagal on the cover — a flyer from a hardware store on Santa Monica, a dirty old pair of white sneakers, and that was about it.

Luca knew Zane couldn't go too far, because he didn't have enough money. He'd been keeping him on a tight rein, sending him the occasional check. The only way Zane could have any serious money was if he'd taken up a life of crime, like his no-good father. And Zane Marion Ricca didn't have the balls. Killing defenseless women was one thing. Putting himself out there was another.

Back at the hotel, there was a message from Mac. Luca reached him on the set.

"I'm on the portable," was the first thing Mac said.

"So?"

"So I don't know what they do in New York, but in L.A. they listen in."

"I got it."

"Did you take care of our mutual friend yet?"

"Funny you should ask."

"Why?"

"Our mutual friend has done a vanishing act."

"I thought you were in control of the situation."

"I thought so too."

"Can we talk?"

"I'll come by an' visit you. Never watched a movie bein' shot."

"Not a good idea."

"So I won't come by. Big deal. See me at the hotel when you're through."

"I'll be there around seven."

Luca wasn't that interested in seeing Mac. He'd hoped for a more enthusiastic reaction when he'd told him about their relationship. But no. Mac Brooks was a cold sonofabitch when it came to family. Fuck him.

Luca was disappointed, but so what? He had Bambi now. Maybe he'd leave *her* his money.

Now that was a thought. He had to settle matters with her, set her up in his house and arrange to put her on permanent payroll. The dumb broad should be kissing his balls instead of saying she'd let him know. But he got off on her independent attitude, plus she had exactly what he required. Class. And she was going to be his — soon — because he couldn't stick around L.A. forever. He had business to take care of in New York. Big business.

48

They were sitting at the kitchen table when Michael leaned back, stretched, and said, "I've been talking too much."

"No you haven't," Kennedy replied, sipping a tall glass of orange juice while watching him closely. He *had* been talking a lot, but she didn't mind — even though he'd been speaking nonstop for an hour, telling her about the situation with Bella, the problems with his family, and finally his drinking, which he seemed to have under control. It was painfully obvious he'd struggled along without ever finding true happiness, and she didn't know why, but she had a strong desire to reach out and make it all better.

"It's a bad habit of mine," he said, feeling very much at ease in her company.

Regarding him seriously, she said, "You had to tell somebody. I'm glad it was me."

Michael realized that now he'd started spilling everything, he couldn't stop, and she was such an understanding listener he didn't want to. "I loved Bella," he said. "And I still *do,* but you're right — I gotta let her go and stop thinking about it."

"Yes, Michael, and if what you've told me is

true, then in my opinion you've behaved admirably."

"You think so, huh?"

"Absolutely."

"Your opinion means a lot to me, Kennedy," he said, getting up and pouring himself more coffee. "Mind if I smoke?"

"Go ahead."

He came back to the table, lit a cigarette, and continued talking. "My brother was always into giving me shit, but I never thought he'd do anything as bad as this. As for my mother . . ." He paused for a moment, remembering the hurt. "Y'know, there was never one time she stood up for me. She let my stepfather bust my ass whenever he felt like it — and he felt like it plenty. There were times when I was a kid that he'd wake me up just to scream at me about something I'd supposedly done. Couldn't wait until morning — dragged me out of bed in the middle of the night and beat up on me."

"It can't have been easy."

"Soon as I was old enough, drinking became my escape — and believe me, it worked good for a while." He laughed ruefully. "So . . . my childhood was a mess, and I guess that's why I have a difficult time making any kind of commitment."

"You've been emotionally abused, Michael," she said understandingly. "It takes time to get over that type of damaging treatment."

"How *do* I get over it?" he asked, putting his elbows on the table and studying her face, deciding she was more than beautiful: she had compassion and soul and the most seductive lips he'd ever seen.

"By forming meaningful relationships. Knowing you're a good person and that you *can* share things — affection, love, whatever. Not everybody is like your mother and stepfather. One day you'll meet somebody and realize there are such things as good relationships."

He looked straight at her. "Maybe I already have."

She chose to ignore his knowing look, finding his scrutiny unnerving. "Well," she said, slightly flustered. "Breakfast was certainly interesting. Bananas, croissants, and Danish. I'll be suffering from a sugar fit all day!"

He laughed easily. "It's the cop in me coming out. On stakeout that's all we ever ate."

"How unhealthy."

"You should see my partner, Quincy. His wife's always putting him on a diet. Trouble is, he never sticks to it."

Kennedy decided that Michael was illegally handsome and probably had women falling all over him. There was no way she planned on adding herself to the list. "Hmm . . ." she murmured, wondering why she'd suddenly lost all interest in work.

"Hey — I'd like you to meet Amber and Quincy one of these days. They're real people — you'd like 'em."

"I know some real people of my own," she said defensively.

He smiled, stubbing out his cigarette. "I wasn't insulting you."

"I know."

They held another long look. Kennedy broke

it by getting up from the table. She was definitely losing it, had to get back on track. "Uh . . . this story I'm working on, Michael — I've discovered an intriguing connection."

"Tell me about it," he said, following her into the living room.

"I found out that Zane Marion Ricca's uncle is Luca Carlotti. Do you know who he is?"

"Hey — my personal life might be totally fucked, but I *am* aware of what's going on out there," he said, wondering why Mac Brooks had failed to reveal this pertinent piece of information.

"Glad to hear it."

"Do the police know?"

She walked over to her computer. "I have no idea. Should I contact them?"

He was right behind her. "Well . . . if they're looking for him, he might be easier to track through Luca."

She turned around. He had great eyes, she tried to avoid them. "The *L.A. Times* wants to run my piece tomorrow. That means if I *do* inform the police, I'd still have the story out there before anyone else."

He was doing it again, studying her intently. "Is that what does it for you? The thrill of getting the news out there first?"

"You could say that."

He moved a little closer. "It's exciting, huh?"

Her green eyes finally met his and didn't look away. "Yes, Michael, it's very exciting."

He was getting closer every second. "So are you, Kennedy, so are you."

When they kissed, it was the most natural move in the world.

Grant let himself into Cheryl's house and soon realized she had not been home all night. The house was undisturbed, and her bed hadn't been slept in.

He paced around, unsure about what to do. Was his first thought right? Had she lost her mind and stayed the night with her client?

No, even Cheryl wouldn't do such a crazy thing. Although lately she'd been in a strange mood, nothing she did would surprise him.

It was time for somebody to talk some sense into her. Reluctantly he supposed it would have to be him. Of course, she never listened to him, but this time he would make her.

Pouring himself a slug of vodka, he settled on the couch, switched on the TV, and waited for her to arrive home.

"I think I hear him coming," Jordanna whispered. "Stay alert. Try to remember everything I said."

"There's nothing we can do," Cheryl said mournfully. "He's got us, Jordy. We'll never get out of here."

"Don't . . . talk . . . like . . . that," Jordanna replied through clenched teeth. "We're going to survive. I refuse to be a fucking victim."

The door at the top of the steps opened, and they heard footsteps descending.

Jordanna began psyching herself up.

Stay strong.

Make eye contact.

Get him talking.

Treat him like a human being.

Which was more than he'd done to them. They were still handcuffed, their ankles bound tightly together, trapped in a dark cellar.

She had to go to the bathroom and was desperately thirsty. Cheryl must have the same needs, but Jordanna knew it was important they didn't beg. She was determined to get this situation under control.

Zane Ricca. She remembered him well. She'd watched him strangle Ingrid Floris and known he did it without an ounce of regret. And then she and Cheryl had fought their respective fathers to allow them to appear as witnesses for the prosecution, ensuring that Zane Ricca was properly punished for the heinous crime he'd committed. The day he was sentenced, they'd thrown a wild celebration party.

Now — all these years later — he was out of jail and back in Beverly Hills.

What did he want? That was the question.

At first she didn't recognize him. Surely Cheryl was mistaken? Zane Ricca had been a puny-looking specimen. This man descending into the cellar, dressed all in black, was stronger and tougher, with long hair scraped back into a ponytail, a hardened face, and bulging muscles.

Yes, she suddenly realized, it *was* him. The eyes were the same. Flat, dead eyes, completely devoid of emotion. She'd never forget those frightening eyes.

631

Stopping on the bottom step, he surveyed them coldly.

Jordanna stifled an urge to scream obscenities at him. In spite of her fear, she managed to remain cool. Following her own advice, she immediately attempted to create some kind of rapport.

"I . . . I don't know why we're here," she said, her voice sounding surprisingly calm. "But whatever the reason, I know we can work something out."

Silence.

"Look," she said persuasively. "Take the handcuffs off and let's talk."

More silence.

"Okay, so don't let's talk, but we need to go to the bathroom."

His zombie eyes registered nothing.

"I must have something to drink," Cheryl pleaded weakly. "My throat's so dry . . . I'm sick. Please . . ."

Turning his back, he walked slowly up the stairs, slamming the door behind him.

"Jesus!" Jordanna exploded. "He really is a fucking psycho."

"I told you," Cheryl said hopelessly. "There's nothing we can do."

"Oh, yes there is," Jordanna responded fiercely. "We're getting out of this. That's a promise."

Getting the police to have the silver BMW towed was no easy task, but George Randall complained long and hard, until eventually they promised to have the car impounded just to get him off the phone.

He was triumphant.

"I don't know why you're making such a fuss," his exquisite young wife said. "We could always use our other gate."

She was too naive to understand the perverse thrill of forcing the cops to do something they really couldn't be bothered with.

He decided that since he was late for the office anyway, and had blown his appointment with Taureen Worth, the fifty-something sex symbol who wanted him to make her look twenty-two again, he might as well enjoy a leisurely breakfast with his lovely wife.

"I'll take you to The Peninsula for champagne and orange juice," he suggested, imagining a romantic morning that could possibly develop into an even more romantic afternoon.

"Sorry, hon," she replied, trying to think of a suitable excuse — she was having an affair with a nineteen-year-old grocery clerk, who gave the greatest head. "I'm late for my psychic."

"Your psychic!" he exclaimed.

Before he could get into it further, he noticed the tow truck had arrived. Puffed up with his own importance, he hurried off down his driveway to witness the removal of the offending BMW.

It happened so naturally that they were both taken by surprise. Neither Kennedy nor Michael had expected to end up in bed together, but here they were — caught in a mood, enjoying every passionate, sensual moment.

The kissing had gone on for a long time, until he found himself so aroused he couldn't stop. And

633

neither could she. They'd headed for the bedroom without saying a word, divesting themselves of their clothes on the way. Something came over both of them, and there was no stopping the inevitable.

Now she found herself hungry for his touch, yearning for him to be inside her. And he didn't hold back, because this woman was his destiny and somehow he knew it.

When they made love it was so intense it startled both of them. But as they got into it, Michael realized it was more than great sex, it was something so special he never wanted it to end. And he knew that this was how it should be.

Kennedy felt the same way. She hadn't planned on falling into bed with Michael Scorsinni, yet here they were, and for the first time since Phil's death, she wasn't silently making comparisons — she was letting herself go with it, riding an incredible wave of sensuous pleasure with absolutely no inhibitions.

They were naked and wild and tender. He was an exciting lover, with a passion that took her breath away. He was everything she'd ever wanted and more. And as they reached a long drawn-out climax, she moaned her excitement aloud, luxuriating in every inch of him.

"This is probably crazy," she said, sighing languorously, when it was over.

"Yeah, crazy," he agreed, rolling off her.

"And very nice."

"Very *nice*, Kennedy?" He shook his head, grinning. "Very nice, she says. How about sensational? How about amazing? How about — "

"Okay, okay," she agreed, laughing. "I admit — it was better than nice."

"She's so cool," he said, running his fingers up her bare leg. "So ladylike."

"Was I ladylike just now?" she demanded.

"You were somethin' else."

"I'll show you something else," she said, sitting up and reaching for him.

"Hey — wait a minute! Give me time to — "

"You don't need time," she said seductively, bending her head to lick the insides of his thighs.

He immediately started to get hard again as her tongue promised unspeakable ecstasy.

Putting his hands on top of her honey-blond head, he pushed her down and groaned with pleasure.

"I told you," she murmured. "You've really got to learn to listen to me, Michael."

And then she had him in her mouth, and he leaned back, lost in a sea of pure delight.

Being with Kennedy was like coming home.

Having the two girls trapped in the cellar was the most stimulating thing that had ever happened to The Man. He had complete and total control over their lives. He could do anything he wanted to them — anything at all.

He wished it were his mother down there. Yes, his mother, who'd always loved to be surrounded by sweet things, nice things. And the bitch had called him poopsy and ruined every single day of his fucking horrible life.

He'd like to see her *shackled in a basement with rats gnawing at her skinny ankles, crawl-*

ing up her spindly legs, tearing at her flesh.

The thought excited him so much that he considered stripping off his clothes and satisfying himself. But he could always do that later — he had all the time in the world.

He wondered if there were rats down there in the basement. Then it occurred to him that he didn't have to wait and see, he could take care of it himself.

Women were frightened of the furry, long-tailed rodents. If he rigged a tape recorder at the top of the stairs, he would be able to record their screams of terror.

The very thought made him happy and content.

He'd killed four of the women who'd betrayed him. He had the other two trapped.

Soon his mission in California would be over and he could return to New York, ready to deal with the woman who deserved to die more than any of them.

49

Detective Carlyle rang the doorbell of Cheryl's house.

Grant heard the sound of the bell over the television, but he didn't move.

Carlyle kept his finger firmly on the buzzer.

Finally Grant slouched to the door. "Yeah?" he said, still holding his glass of vodka.

"I'm here to see Cheryl Landers."

"She's not home right now."

"I called yesterday. She never returned my call."

"Who are you?"

"Detective Carlyle. Was it you I spoke to?"

"No, not me," Grant said quickly.

"You got any idea where she is or when she'll be back?"

Grant ran a hand through his uncombed hair. "Look, do you want to tell me what this is about?"

"Who are you?"

"Her brother," he lied.

"You'd better have her contact me pronto."

"Why?"

Carlyle shifted position. "Several years ago she testified at a murder trial. It seems that the man she helped put away is out of prison. I'm trying to warn Miss Landers to be on her guard."

"Is this serious?" Grant asked.

"Only if he comes looking for her."

"What makes you think he might?"

"Because he went looking for four of the other women — and he found 'em. They're all dead."

"Jesus!" Grant exclaimed. "Why wasn't she warned before?"

"We've only just found out."

"I don't get it. I — "

"If she feels she needs protection, she can come in and talk to us," Carlyle interrupted.

"I'll have her call you as soon as I find her."

"*Find* her?"

"Oh . . . uh, she's around somewhere."

Carlyle handed Grant his card. "See she does."

Grant couldn't wait to get rid of the detective. At least they weren't getting busted for pimping and pandering.

Once Carlyle was out of there, he searched for his notes, trying to locate the name of the client Cheryl had been visiting at the St. James's. Shuffling through a stack of papers on the desk, he finally came across it, scribbled on a yellow legal pad. Bosco Nanni. Yes, that was the name.

He immediately called the hotel, only to be told there was no answer from Mr. Nanni's room.

Grant was really worried now. It wasn't like Cheryl to stay out all night, and now this detective was telling him there was some maniac out there, tracking down the people who'd testified against him.

What if he'd got Cheryl?

638

Of course it was unthinkable, but what if he had?

Grant decided the best thing to do was to go over to the hotel and see if Cheryl was there.

And if she wasn't?

He'd get into that when it happened.

Eldessa finished her chores, then wearily sat down at the kitchen table, resting her feet. There wasn't much to do in the big old house anymore, especially now that everybody had moved out, but she kept it clean and presentable because Luca Carlotti could turn up at any time — as he'd recently proved.

Mr. Carlotti was a fine man, and even though he'd visited rarely over the years, Eldessa was still in awe of him. He'd probably forgotten, but when she first started working for him she'd been employed by the actress who, at the time, was his mistress.

Eldessa often recalled the night Mr. Carlotti had flown in unexpectedly and caught his girlfriend in bed with her stuntman lover. She remembered the yelling and screaming, and the two of them getting beaten up and thrown out. After that exciting incident, the house had been empty for a while.

She'd worked for him ever since, watching people come and go, observing all sorts of things, but forever being loyal to Mr. Carlotti because he was her boss.

When Zane arrived to stay, she'd known he was the nephew of Mr. Carlotti. Eldessa had a way of finding things out.

Unfortunately she didn't know where he'd gone, although it occurred to her that Shelley might, because she'd seen how Shelley ran after him all the time.

She should have warned the girl that Zane was no good. An evil presence. Eldessa had a nose for bad people.

She decided it was probably just as well she'd never said anything. It wasn't her place. Besides, girls today, you couldn't tell them anything, they all thought they knew it all.

When Shelley left the house, she'd written down her address and made Eldessa promise to visit.

Eldessa had agreed.

Now that Mr. Carlotti had mentioned a big reward, she decided to take the bus down Sunset and pay Shelley a visit. Maybe Shelley would know where Zane had gone. After all, she had nothing to lose and everything to gain.

Later that morning Luca Carlotti got word from his business manager in New York that Zane had tampered with a six-thousand-dollar check, changing the amount to sixty thousand dollars. Luca was one angry man. He immediately summoned Bosco and Reno to his suite. "You've been screwin' around long enough," he snarled, a rigid disciplinarian when he had to be. "Get out there today an' find the cocksucker — you hear me? An' don't come back till you do."

"Where are we supposed to look?" Bosco asked, his pop eyes bugging.

"That's your problem, not mine."

Bosco shuffled his feet. "Whaddaya want me to do first?" he asked. "Track down Bambi? Or find Zane?"

Luca's voice was cold. "Find Zane before the cops, 'cause I personally want the pleasure of splittin' his thieving head open an' scattering it to the coyotes."

The Sandersons' butler and Hubert Potter were having an argument. The butler kept insisting that Jordanna was asleep in her room and couldn't be disturbed, while Hubert was equally insistent that she had to be wakened, because he needed to know why her wrecked car was abandoned in the middle of the street.

The butler had been enjoying a peaceful morning, but it was obviously not to continue. Hubert was getting on his nerves. He did not approve of security guards anyway, it was beneath his dignity to work in a household that had to have these uncouth people around. Once, when he was very young, he'd served at Buckingham Palace. Working for an American billionaire was no match for Her Majesty the Queen.

Reluctantly, he buzzed Jordanna's room.

Just as he'd thought, there was no reply.

"Miss Levitt is still asleep," he said, unable to hide a small note of triumph.

"I never saw her come home," Hubert said stubbornly. "She would've told me about her car. There's something wrong here."

"I can assure you, nothing is wrong," the butler said, looking disdainfully down his long, thin nose.

"Then I'll speak to Miss Sanderson," Hubert

said, refusing to be deterred.

The butler stood firm. "Miss Sanderson cannot be disturbed either."

Hubert scratched his head, unsure what to do next. The doorbell saved him from having to make a decision. The butler opened the front door, and Detective Carlyle entered the fray.

"Can I help you?" the butler asked imperiously.

"I understand Jordanna Levitt's staying here."

"Miss Levitt cannot be disturbed," the butler said. "May I ask who's calling?"

"Detective Carlyle, and yeah — Miss Levitt *can* be disturbed." He'd had enough for one morning. It was not his job to go traipsing around trying to find Beverly Hills brats so he could warn them to be careful. "Tell her I'm here."

Hubert observed the action. The detective couldn't have arrived at a more opportune moment.

The butler hesitated, then stomped off to get Jordanna.

"She smashed up her car," Hubert remarked, folding his arms.

"Excuse me?" Carlyle said.

"It's sitting in the middle of the street. Didn't you see it on your way up here?"

"A white Porsche?"

"That's right."

"How'd she do that?"

"She's a wild one," Hubert said knowingly.

"Really?"

"Too much money. What're you here to see her about?"

"It doesn't concern you."

Hubert puffed up. "I think you'll find it does. I'm security here."

"Security, huh?"

"Been with Mr. Sanderson eight years."

"He that TV mogul?"

"Correct."

"Easy to work for?"

"The best."

"Good pay?"

"Excellent."

Carlyle sighed. "Sometimes I got a hunch I'm busting my ass for nothing. I should get me a cushy private security job like you got."

The butler returned, his face impassive. "Miss Levitt is not here."

"I told you," Hubert crowed.

Carlyle hitched up his pants. "Where is she?" he asked.

"I would imagine she's at the studio."

"Didn't you say her car was out there on the street?"

Hubert couldn't wait to join in. "It's her car, all right, her purse was sitting in it. I don't know any woman who'd leave her purse behind. And what's more, I never saw her pass by my station."

"Was her bed slept in?" Carlyle said patiently, although the last thing he felt like being was polite.

"No," the butler said.

Detective Carlyle had a nasty feeling he was about to find out something he didn't want to know.

"What time is it?" Cheryl mumbled.

Jordanna consulted her watch. "Nearly eleven. How're you feeling?"

"Really bad. It's like my stomach is on fire."

"Try to stay strong."

"How long is it since he was down here?"

"Almost three hours."

"Do you think anybody's missed us yet?"

"They'll find my wrecked car. Where did you leave yours?"

"Lexington — blocking somebody's driveway."

"When they discover our cars they'll realize something's wrong. They're probably already looking for us. This is kidnapping, Cheryl. The FBI will get into it. We'll be out of here soon."

"I wish I felt better," Cheryl complained. "All I want is to close my eyes and pretend this is a bad dream."

"It *is* a bad dream, but we'll be okay."

"He won't even let us go to the bathroom, or give us a drink. My mouth's so dry. I could kill for a sip of water. What are we going to do?"

"I don't know," Jordanna replied honestly. "Something will come up. We'll get our opportunity. First of all we've got to try and get out of these handcuffs."

"There's no way," Cheryl said flatly. "You need a key."

"Wait — I hear something. He's coming down again." Jordanna listened, holding her breath.

The door opened . . . silence for a few seconds . . . then there was a tumbling noise on the stairs.

"Hey, Zane — I need to talk to you," she

shouted. "It's important."

No response.

Keep going.

Attract his attention.

Get the fucker to communicate.

"Did you know that Ingrid spoke about you all the time?" she called out. "Ingrid told me plenty. I want to share some of the things she said with you."

The door slammed shut.

They both heard the squeaking noises at the same time. "What's that?" Cheryl asked, alarmed.

Before Jordanna could answer, two rats descended on them — and, panicked, began racing frantically around the small cellar. One of them nipped at Cheryl's ankle. She let out a blood-curdling scream. "Oh, Jesus! Oh, my God! Jordy, *do* something!"

"Kick 'em, Cheryl," Jordanna yelled as the rodents scurried around the floor, searching for an escape. "You've got to kick 'em hard. We can kill 'em. We can do it." Drawing back her legs, she kicked out with all her might. One of the rats yelped loudly as it was flung up against the wall.

Cheryl was weakening fast. "I can't," she wailed. "I can't, Jordy, I can't. I'm telling you, he's poisoned me!"

"Yes you can," Jordanna said harshly. "You've got to. Just kick the little bastards."

Cheryl shrank into the corner, doubled over with stomach cramps. "Oh, God," she groaned. "I think I'm going to die."

The Man crouched by the door at the top of

the stairs, listening to the shrieks coming from below.

One time, when he was in jail, a couple of the other inmates had forced a live rat down his pants. It had bitten him on his balls and thighs, and the pain had been excruciating. The guards had hauled him off to the prison hospital, where he'd been given a rabies shot. The pain of that shot was worse than the rat bites.

How the other inmates had loved that little trick.

But he'd gotten his revenge. He'd put rat poison in the stew when he was on kitchen duty, and half the cell block were sick for days. A fitting punishment.

He hadn't planned on speaking to either of the girls, they didn't deserve the honor of his conversation. But he'd been intrigued by the mention of Ingrid.

Had Ingrid really talked about him? And if so, what exactly had she said?

He thirsted to know every word, and the only way to find out was to ask.

He'd had enough of the bitches' screams. Besides, he could replay the tape as many times as he cared to.

He opened the cellar door again. One of the rats raced up the stairs, making a frenzied dash into the house.

He shone his flashlight down into the cellar.

Cheryl was huddled in a ball. Jordanna wasn't.

As soon as she saw him she began talking. "Do you want to hear what Ingrid had to say

about you? We should talk about it — it's inter-
esting stuff."

Jordanna was a tough one. He could see that
she'd kicked one of the rats to death with her
bound feet, and she was still ready to talk.

He hesitated for a moment, but the thought
of finding out what Ingrid had said about him
was irresistible.

Slowly he descended the cellar steps.

Bobby had just finished shooting a pivotal scene
with Jerry when Mac called him over to one side.
"This is Detective Carlyle," he said, introducing
him to the stocky detective.

"If it's about Barbara Barr trashing my house,
I'm not pressing charges," Bobby said, wondering
why Mac was getting into it.

"I'm afraid it's more serious than that," Mac
replied, with a worried expression. "Have you seen
Jordanna today?"

"She'll be here soon."

"Were you with her last night?" Carlyle asked,
thinking that his girlfriend would have an orgasm
if she knew he was actually speaking to Bobby
Rush. Her idol. Although as far as he was concerned, Bobby Rush looked like every other over-
thirty movie actor. Kevin Costner, Dennis Quaid,
Michael Douglas — they all looked the same to
him.

"Yeah, I saw her last night. Why?"

"I don't know how to tell you this, but we think
she's . . . missing."

Michael lay in bed, hands crossed behind his

neck, eyes wide open. He was perfectly content. Absolutely at peace.

Kennedy lay half across his stomach, asleep. The scent of her body entranced him. Gently he began stroking her hair.

Was it possible to fall in love with somebody in such a short period of time?

Yes, it was possible. He was living proof.

There'd been a lot of women in his life — one-night stands, short affairs — but in all his experience he'd never come across anyone like Kennedy. She fulfilled him in every way, and as far as he was concerned they were totally compatible, even though they came from such different worlds.

He caressed her hair until she woke up. "Didn't sleep last night, huh?" he asked.

"Not that much," she said, stretching in a very feline way. "I was working on my story."

"You're a hard worker."

"Hmm," she said reluctantly. "I suppose I should get back to it."

"Yeah," he conceded. "And it's about time I checked in with Quincy."

"Well . . . ," she murmured, feeling completely satisfied. "I guess we've both got to work."

"Quincy will be wondering what happened to me."

She touched the back of his neck, sliding her fingers through his thick hair.

"You're turning me on," he said, enjoying every moment.

"It's my intention," she murmured.

"Really?"

"Yes, really."

"I thought we were getting up."

"No, Michael, *you're* getting up," she teased.

He lightly brushed the tips of her nipples. "This is something, huh?" he said.

"I know."

"I didn't come over here with this in mind."

"Oh, yes you did."

He grinned knowingly. "Oh yes, I did."

The phone began to ring. She reached out and clicked the bell off. "No calls," she whispered. "No interruptions."

Then they both forgot about getting up as his lips descended on hers and once again they began the rapturous trip.

He moved on top of her, preparing for the wild ride.

And she knew for sure she was never going to be alone again.

50

"We gotta find the little prick before Luca blows," Reno said. "He's gettin' close."

"I know that," Bosco agreed. "Where we gonna start?"

"We go back to the house," Reno said. "And tear his room to pieces inch by inch."

"We did that."

"This time we'll search my way."

They took the limo to the house, had the driver wait outside, and made their way to Zane's room.

"So now we'll do it good," Reno said, quite pumped at the thought of wrecking a room. "Slit the mattress, peel off the wallpaper, pry up the floorboards. I didn't come to L.A. to spend my time chasin' this cocksucker. I came out here to relax. This time we're gonna nail him."

They went to work.

Bobby and Mac huddled with Detective Carlyle at the edge of the soundstage.

"If this man was let out of jail, shouldn't Jordanna and Cheryl have been notified immediately?" Bobby asked, blue eyes blazing.

"We didn't know it was him," Carlyle explained. "It only came to light in the last twenty-four hours."

"So you're telling me that four women were murdered and you didn't know it was him? Nobody put together the connection before now?" He turned angrily to Mac. "Do you believe this?"

Mac studied his shoes. His worst nightmare was coming true. This should never have happened, and the horrible thing was he blamed himself, he should have gone to the cops immediately instead of hoping Luca would take care of it.

"We've got to find Jordanna," Bobby said grimly. "What's being done?"

"Everything possible," Carlyle replied, wondering why everyone thought they had a right to blame *him*.

"Where's Cheryl?" Mac asked.

"I stopped by her house," Carlyle said. "Only her brother was there."

"She doesn't have a brother," Mac said grimly. "Maybe it was Zane."

"No, I have a photograph of Zane, it wasn't him."

"What happens next?" Bobby asked. "Will there be a ransom demand?"

"If that's what he's after, he'll most likely contact her father."

"Does Jordan know what's going on?"

"I'm on my way to see him now."

"I'll come with you," Bobby decided.

"You can't leave the set," Mac objected.

"Close down for the day," Bobby fired back. "Jordanna's in danger, and I'm going to be out there doing everything I can to help find her."

Grant paced around the lobby of the St. James's. He'd already asked the girl at reception for Mr. Nanni, and she'd said he was out. Next he'd spoken to the parking valets and found that Cheryl's car was not parked there. In fact, one of them remembered her collecting her car and leaving the hotel the night before at around ten.

For the first time in his life, Grant decided he cared about someone more than he cared about himself. Cheryl and he had always been close, the thought that she might be in danger was a frightening one.

He took out Detective Carlyle's card and studied it.

If he called and told him that Cheryl could be missing, he might have to reveal that she'd been visiting a client last night.

So what? He'd face that problem when it arose. If her safety was at stake, it was worth it.

"If we're going to talk, first you've got to let us use the bathroom," Jordanna said insistently. "And can't you see that Cheryl's sick? You poisoned her with that stuff you forced her to drink. She could be having an allergic reaction. Why don't you let her go? All you have to do is drive her to a hospital and drop her off outside. She can't tell anyone where you are, because she doesn't know. You'll still have me."

He ignored her pleas. "What did Ingrid say about me?" he demanded.

"I *want* to tell you, Zane, I really do, but I'm in a difficult position. Give Cheryl a drink, at least, then I'll tell you everything. That's a promise."

He was drawn toward her in spite of himself. "What's there to tell?"

"Ingrid talked about you a lot. She really liked you. It was terrible what happened, but *I* know it was an accident."

"Don't try to fool me. You're the one had me thrown into jail."

"I had no choice. My father forced me to testify."

"Your father didn't force you to do anything. You did it because you're a spoiled rich cunt."

"No, Zane, you've got it wrong. Ingrid confided in me."

"What did she confide?" he asked suspiciously. "If you don't tell me soon, I'll leave you down here in the dark. You think the rats were bad? Wait until you see what else I have for you."

Cheryl groaned. Even though Jordanna was worried about her, she wished she'd shut up, because instinctively she knew Zane would get off on weakness, only strength would intimidate him.

"Ingrid thought you were handsome," she lied, realizing that although she had his interest, she needed more. "Ingrid was always telling me."

The truth was that Ingrid had never mentioned him, except to say that he was the most obnoxious creep she'd ever come across.

A flicker of expression. "She did?"

He actually believed her. "Oh, yes," she said, nodding her head.

Zane sat down on the stairs and regarded her through narrowed eyes. "When did she say this?"

She stayed silent, which infuriated him.

His voice hardened. "I *said* when did she say this?"

More silence. Now she was doing exactly what he had done earlier, and he didn't like it.

"Don't play games with me, bitch," he said stonily. "Because you'll regret it."

"Why do you call me names?" she asked, trying a new tactic. "Ingrid said you were a nice guy, she really liked you — respected you, in fact. If she knew what you were doing to us, she'd be upset."

His voice registered no emotion. "Ingrid played me for a fool."

"You didn't understand her, but she understood you." She paused a moment, gauging his reaction. He was hooked, but she still had to reel him in very carefully, otherwise she'd lose him. "Some of the things she said about you were so interesting. . . ."

He blinked several times. "What?"

"C'mon," she said persuasively. "Be a nice guy and let Cheryl go, then I'll tell you."

"Cheryl stays."

"At least give her some water."

"I don't have to do anything."

"I know that."

"I could kill you both."

There was a long, tense silence while he decided what to do next.

Mentally Jordanna willed him to do the right thing. She'd always believed in the power of positive thinking.

Now if she could only hook him into her mind trip . . .

"Michael?"

"That's my name."

"This all happened so quickly. I'm not used to falling into bed with men early in the morning when I'm supposed to be working."

He raised a quizzical eyebrow. "Men, Kennedy?"

She smiled. "You."

"Thank you."

"You're welcome."

"Are you complaining?"

"Well . . . I don't want this to be a casual breakfast affair."

"Is that what you think it is?"

"No . . . but we did rush into it. Shouldn't we have had some kind of — "

"What?" he interrupted, half smiling. "You want me to take you out on a date and buy you dinner?"

"Why not?"

"Okay, if that's what you want," he said, sitting up and reaching for a cigarette. "We'll go on a double date with Amber and Quincy — how's that?"

She sat up next to him, pulling the crumpled sheet over her breasts. "You mean I get to mix with real people?" she asked, widening her eyes.

"Very funny."

"At least I can make you laugh."

"You can make me do a lot more than that."

"Really?" she teased. "Tell me about it."

He grabbed her playfully. "How about I show you?"

She squirmed out of his grasp. "How about we take a break?"

"You're a difficult woman, Kennedy."

"And you smoke too much."

He took a deep drag and stubbed out his cigarette. "So," he said, "we're going on a proper date, is that it?"

"When will we do this?"

"When do you want to do it?"

"The truth is," she said, stretching like a contented cat, "I never want to leave this bed — not with you in it."

"Me too," he said, staring at her beautiful face. "Y'know, the first time I saw you I knew this was going to happen."

"You did?"

"I sure as hell wanted it to, but first I had to straighten out my life. Now I hope I've done that, and guess what — here we are."

"Hmm . . . here we are." She sighed.

"You're not regretting it, are you?"

"No, Michael," she murmured. "I'm not. How about you?"

"You've *gotta* be kidding. You're the best thing that ever happened to me." He leaned over and kissed her.

She pushed him gently away. "I hate to ask, but what time is it?"

He took a peek at his watch. "Jeez! It's eleven-thirty. Quincy's going to be pissed I ran out on him."

"Let's get up, then."

"Yeah, let's do it."

Neither of them moved.

"We've got this stalker thing going on with Marjory Sanderson," he said. "She claims there's a guy threatening to kill her."

"Is there?"

"I don't know if I believe her." A beat. "There's something I should tell you about Marjory."

"Go ahead. I'm in a listening mood."

"I had to borrow money from her."

"How much?"

"Ten thousand bucks."

"Why?"

"Information in exchange for currency. That was the deal to find Bella. Remember? I told you about the woman who called."

"Ten thousand dollars is an awful lot of money."

"Right — and I've got to pay it back."

"How do you plan on doing that?"

"I dunno . . . I guess I could moonlight as a private security guard, work my balls off, sell my body — "

"Michael!" she admonished.

"Unless *you* feel like paying."

She took a moment. "Will a dollar do it?"

"Lady," he quipped, "we're talking ten bucks or forget it."

"What do I get for ten bucks?"

"Come here and I'll show you."

"Again?"

"If I was seventeen . . ." He put his arm around her and pulled her close.

He made her feel so good. "Y'know," she said softly, "after Phil died I never thought there'd be anybody who could take his place. And yet — here you are."

657

"Yup — here I am."

"You've come into my life like an explosion." Her fingers traced his face. "I hope you're staying around."

"Around?" he said quizzically. "Sweetheart, I'm moving in."

Her voice was low and husky and filled with satisfaction. "Who said you could do that?"

"Kennedy, you may as well face it — we're together, and that's how it's going to be. Unless you don't want it."

She snuggled even closer. "I do."

Was it possible he'd gotten this lucky in such a short period of time? She was so . . . perfect. "You know what?" he said.

"What?"

"You opened up my heart and walked right in."

"Why, Michael, this is a revelation — underneath the tough detective there lurks a true romantic."

"Hey," he said, playfully grabbing her again. "With you I can be anything."

They began to kiss as if they were only just beginning.

Eldessa got off the bus near the bottom of Laurel Canyon. Clutching her black purse tightly to her side, she started the long, steep walk up the hill.

Eldessa was used to walking, it didn't bother her. Her car had broken down a year ago, and she hadn't gotten around to replacing it. It was an old car anyway and had given her more trouble than it was worth.

She thought about her family as she made her

way up the canyon. Five children, all scattered in different places. Not that she saw much of them, but occasionally they came to her for financial help, and she did her best.

Five thousand dollars was a fortune. If she had that money she could retire, go live by the ocean in Santa Monica with her cousin, and finally, after a lifetime of cleaning up after other people, spend her days doing nothing.

Eldessa thought she had a chance of getting it. She was almost sure Shelley would be able to tell her where Zane had gone.

It was worth the long trudge up the steep canyon. Every single weary step.

"Take a look at this," Reno said, cracking his knuckles.

"What?" Bosco asked, sweating profusely in the L.A. heat.

"It's his car rental papers. He hid them under the mattress. I told you — when you toss a room you gotta do it good."

"Okay, so now we've got his car license number. Big deal."

"You don't understand — we got that, we got him. Let's go."

51

Bobby roamed around Jordan Levitt's lavishly appointed study, watching and listening as Detective Carlyle explained the situation.

Jordan Levitt was a tall, handsome man who'd probably intimidated the hell out of Jordanna when she was growing up. Bobby knew the feeling well. In a way Jordan reminded him of Jerry. He had that *I'm a major player — don't mess with me* aura.

When Jordan finally spoke, his deep voice was filled with a barely controlled anger. "Why wasn't my daughter warned?" he thundered, glaring fiercely. "Why wasn't she placed in protective custody?"

"I asked the same questions," Bobby said.

Detective Carlyle shifted uncomfortably. He was finally meeting Hollywood big shots, and what was he getting? A freaking tongue-lashing, as if Jordanna Levitt's disappearance was *his* fault. If she'd returned his original call, this would never have happened.

"We attempted to warn her — " he began.

"Bullshit!" Jordan roared, slamming his fist on his desk. "That's pure bullshit, and you know it. Get on the phone and put me through to whoever's in charge. I want action, and I want it *now*."

"I think I hear your doorbell," Michael said.

"Tell them to go away," Kennedy replied.

"We gotta do something about getting out of this bed. It's past noon. *Definitely* time to get up."

She sighed. "If you say so."

"Do you want me to answer the door?"

"No. You go take a shower. I'll see who it is."

He kissed her and jumped out of bed. "Meet me in the shower in sixty seconds. I'll get very impatient if you're not there."

"If I do, we'll *never* get any work done."

He grinned. "On second thought, who needs work?"

"We both do," she said, reaching for a robe.

Throwing up his hands, he said, "Okay, okay, I'm going to shower."

She padded to the door, calling out, "Who's there?"

"Kennedy?"

Recognizing Rosa's voice, she reluctantly opened the door a crack. "Oh, hi," she said. "What are you doing here?"

"What am *I* doing here?" Rosa said crossly. "I've been trying to call you for the last two hours. Where were you?"

"Working," she said vaguely.

"Are you letting me in or not?"

"Yeah, yeah — I guess."

"You *guess?* What in hell's going on with you? And why aren't you dressed?"

Still reluctantly, she opened the door all the way, allowing Rosa to sail past her and enter the apartment.

"I repeat," Rosa said. "How come you're still wandering around in your robe?"

"I've been working at my computer."

Standing back, Rosa surveyed her with a jaundiced eye. "You've got that recently fucked glow," she said accusingly.

"Excuse me?"

"You heard."

"I'm working on a story. I've been up all night."

"Yeah, baby. It's *me* you're talking to. Who's here?"

"Nobody."

"I can hear the shower running."

"I was just about to take one."

"Uh . . . *excuse* me," Rosa said, bending down to pick up a piece of clothing from the floor. "Whose pants are those?"

Kennedy spun around. "What are you — a spy?"

"Hey — don't get on *my* case. I'm delighted for you, honey. Who is he?"

"Michael," she admitted.

"Oh boy. You work even faster than me! *One* date? Is that all it took?"

"He's an incredible man, Rosa," she said, smiling dreamily.

"Kennedy! This isn't like you. I'm delighted to see that you're a human living female after all."

"Now that I've told you, can you please get out?"

"No, I can't. There's been developments."

It occurred to Kennedy that life went on, and it was time to join the real world again. "Okay, fill me in," she said, attempting to pull it together.

"It hasn't hit the news yet, but it's on the street that Jordanna Levitt is missing."

"Oh, my God! How do you know?"

"Her damaged car was found with her purse still in it. And nobody's seen her since last night."

"What about Cheryl Landers?"

"Haven't heard anything."

"This is unbelievable."

"I know."

"I've been finding out plenty too," Kennedy said, snapping back into the swing of things. "Did you know that 'reputed mob boss' Luca Carlotti is Zane Ricca's uncle?"

"Are you saying there could be a crime connection?"

"Who knows? I'm figuring it this way — his uncle probably got him the role in *The Contract*. Zane came out here, murdered Ingrid, went to prison, and now he's out and wants revenge on all the women who gave evidence against him."

"Have you tried contacting Luca Carlotti?"

"Who, me? No way."

"Somebody should. We must pass this information on to the cops."

"I was going to, but I kind of got sidestepped, or sidetracked, or hit on the head. I don't know, Rosa. Take no notice of me — I'm light-headed."

"So I noticed," Rosa said dryly.

"This is not great timing."

"When it comes to love, kiddo," Rosa said, nodding her head wisely, "*nothing* is great timing."

"Who said anything about love?"

"Take a look in the mirror. There's a smile on

your face could light up Cleveland!"

"Nonsense."

"*Sure.*"

"I should tell Michael what's going on. Fix yourself coffee, I'll be right back."

"Don't you want me to come with you?"

"Rosa, you're not strong enough to see Michael in the shower. I'm telling you, it's quite a sight."

"My God, you're beginning to sound just like me!"

"Never."

"Ha! You should be so lucky."

Zane released Cheryl, took her upstairs, allowed her to use the bathroom, and gave her a glass of water.

When he dragged her back down into the cellar, she could barely walk.

Jordanna felt her heart begin to pound. Her friend was in trouble, but there was nothing she could do to help, she could only watch helplessly as Zane retied Cheryl's ankles. He was about to handcuff her wrists again when Jordanna spoke up. "You don't have to handcuff her," she said, forcing him to listen and take notice. "Look at her — she's out of it. She needs medical care."

"You talk too much," he said coldly.

"I thought you wanted me to tell you all the things Ingrid said about you."

Bingo! She had his attention.

"What things?" he said.

"Special things. Very revealing."

He left Cheryl where she was on the floor, walked over and sat on the bottom step again.

Jordanna noted that he did not put the handcuffs back on Cheryl. At least that was something.

"Ingrid didn't treat me right," he said resentfully. "She didn't treat me with respect. Anybody watching us together could see that."

"I know," Jordanna agreed.

"She led me to believe we were going to be together. Ingrid lied to me."

Oh fuck, how was she going to keep him talking?

"There were pressures on Ingrid you didn't know about," she said, making it up as she went along.

"What?" he demanded, rubbing the vicious scar on his cheek.

Gotta come up with a story here. Gotta really get the hook in solid.

"Mac Brooks, the director," she blurted. "He . . . he was in love with Ingrid. He had her under his power. But somehow he found out she liked you, and he forbade her to be nice to you. So you see, it wasn't Ingrid's fault."

The Man was filled with fury. Was this true? Was Mac Brooks responsible for Ingrid's rejection?

He glared at Jordanna, hating her and hating the other one, who'd gotten sick too quickly. It was going to be no fun watching her die.

Jordanna was the reverse — too strong by far. She needed to be taught a lesson in humility.

The bitch wasn't frightened of him.

Maybe he should strangle her now. Wrap his

665

hands around her neck and gaze deep into her black eyes while he watched the life seep out of her.

No. It wasn't time. He needed to hear more. He needed to hear everything.

The perspiration dripped off Eldessa's forehead as she continued to make her way up Laurel Canyon. When Shelley had written out directions, she failed to mention that the house was so far up the hill.

Eldessa stopped for a moment, took a folded tissue from her purse, and wiped her brow. She was too old to be walking around Los Angeles on a fool's errand. Shelley might not know anything, and then where would she be?

Muttering under her breath, Eldessa plodded on. She had a chance to lay her hands on five thousand dollars. Every step was worth it.

"I'll see you later," Michael said, cupping Kennedy's face in his hands and kissing her on the lips. "I'm meeting Quincy and getting into this. Don't forget to call the cops and tell them what you've found out."

"If they're any good they'll already know," Rosa remarked.

"Rule number one," Michael said. "Assume nobody knows anything."

As soon as he was gone, Rosa let out a long, low whistle. "*That* is one good-looking sonofabitch. And he's not even an actor. How lucky can you get?"

"You had your chance, Rosa."

"Not really," she said truthfully. "He was never into me. I can always tell."

Kennedy sighed happily. "Isn't he great?"

"Listen to her! You sound like a lovestruck adolescent!"

"I think I am."

"Fools rush in . . ."

"I'm not a fool. Michael's different."

Rosa beamed, happy for her friend. "Do I get a finder's fee?"

"You get to be flower girl at our wedding."

Rosa's eyebrows shot up. "Wedding! Has he asked you to marry him?"

"I was joking," Kennedy said, shaking her head and smiling.

"You've turned to mush!" Rosa yelled. "I don't like it."

"Not quite," Kennedy said. "Let me get dressed, and we'll go over to task force headquarters. I want to be in on this one."

"Where in hell you been?" Quincy demanded angrily.

"Somewhere very special," Michael replied, unable to remove the smile from his face.

Quincy was perplexed. "What is this somewhere special shit?" he asked, scratching his head.

"You'll meet her."

"I'll meet her, huh?" Quincy said, glaring at him. "Are you telling me that while I've been carrying the load on my own, you've been out getting laid?"

"Nope," Michael said. "This isn't about getting laid."

"Well, what the fuck is it?"

"Can we talk about it later? There's something Mac Brooks forgot to tell us, and it's important we pay him a visit. Zane Ricca has an uncle. His name is Luca Carlotti."

"Let's go," Quincy said.

"I'm behind you, bro'."

Reno had friends in L.A. He put out a search-and-find order on Zane's car and settled himself on the patio by the pool at the St. James's.

"We'll have him before nightfall," he promised Luca. "It's a done deal."

"Howdja know that?" Luca growled. He wore Versace shorts with matching shirt, Gucci gold-trimmed slippers on his feet. His hair was slicked back.

"Care to take a bet?" Reno said confidently, fiddling with his sunglasses.

Luca trusted Reno. If he said it would be done, Luca knew that it would.

Bosco lumbered outside, sweating liberally as the day progressed.

"There you are," Luca said.

"Yeah, here I am," Bosco replied.

"This is what I want you t'do now," Luca said, issuing instructions. "Take the limo, stop by Cartier's in Beverly Hills, and pick up a diamond bracelet. Have them gift-wrap it, then write a card with my name on it — my first name only, don't wanna scare her off. Deliver it to Bambi personally at that house you followed her to last night, an' tell her I'm expectin' her at eight." He shoved an envelope at him. "Pay cash."

Bosco pocketed the envelope. "Ain't Reno comin' with?"

"Not necessary. He stays here by the phone."

"Should I have lunch first?" Bosco asked, his stomach rumbling at the very thought of food.

"No fuckin' way. You're gettin' soft in your old age, Bosco."

"Who *you* callin' old?"

They might joke together, but everyone knew who the boss was.

Grant felt he had no choice but to go to Detective Carlyle and inform him that Cheryl appeared to be missing.

He hung around the precinct until the detective walked in, then he approached him, keeping it loose. He told him Cheryl had visited a friend at the St. James's, and from the information he'd received, she'd left there around ten last night and nobody had seen her since.

"Why didn't you tell me this earlier?" Carlyle asked.

"I thought she'd stayed the night at the hotel with her . . . uh . . . friend."

Detective Carlyle peered at him suspiciously. "Didn't you say you were her brother?"

"That's right."

"I understand Cheryl Landers don't have a brother."

Grant didn't hesitate. "Technically, no," he said. "What I meant was we're like brother and sister. We grew up together."

Carlyle continued to regard him suspiciously. "Who are you?"

Sometimes it was useful having the name. "Grant Lennon, Junior," he said smoothly.

The detective snapped to attention. "You mean Grant Lennon's your father?"

"That's right." Idiot.

Trying not to look too impressed, Carlyle said, "Give me the make and license of her car, I'll run a check. And I'll need the name of the friend she was visiting."

Grant gave him the information, asked the detective to keep in touch, left his number, and returned to Cheryl's house.

52

Jordanna was running out of things to say, but at least she had his full attention. Zane was fascinated, absorbing every little detail about Ingrid and what she'd supposedly said about him.

Jordanna embellished, making up a life for Ingrid Floris — a young actress whom she'd hardly known. She wove a good story, every so often throwing in more information about Ingrid's feelings for him.

In her story Mac was the villain; Ingrid the princess; and Zane the unfortunate suitor who was never allowed to show his true love how much she meant to him.

"I did love her," he said earnestly, completely drawn into the fairy tale.

"I know," Jordanna replied sympathetically. "And there's more."

"I have to know everything," he said, his dead eyes coming alive for a moment.

"You deserve to," she said soothingly. "But first take me upstairs. It's my turn to go to the bathroom and get a drink."

She could sense his hesitation. "Please," she said calmly, fixing him with an unwavering gaze. "I won't try to escape. I'm enjoying our talk."

The Levitt bitch wasn't such a bitch after all. In fact, she was the first woman who'd been truthful with him.

Everything she said made perfect sense. Ingrid had loved him all along. She hadn't been pretending. She'd genuinely loved him.

So many women over the years had lied to him. They'd broken his heart until he'd learned that to get over the hurt he had to punish them.

Before Ingrid there'd been others — the first one when he was seventeen. A pretty girl named Sally, who'd made him promises she never kept.

Nobody ever found out it was he who'd fixed her car so that the brakes failed.

After Sally there was a young Danish girl, who'd unfortunately drowned on a summer picnic. This young lady had severely disappointed him. It was her fault she'd been punished.

He'd never regretted their deaths, they'd deserved to die.

It had been so easy taking revenge and never getting caught . . . until Ingrid.

All those years in jail, the prospect of getting his hands on the six women who'd put him there had been orgasmic.

He thought about Ingrid, and the fact that Mac Brooks had kept them apart.

And Mac Brooks shall die.

Zane untied Jordanna's ankles and pulled her roughly to her feet. Her legs were numb, and for a moment she could barely stand. She fell against him, straightening up immediately.

A quick glance at Cheryl revealed her to be huddled weakly in the corner.

Zane unlocked the handcuff attached to the pipe, slipped it around his own wrist, and clicked it shut. Now they were shackled together. No chance of escape. At least she was getting out of the cellar. Upstairs there might be something she could do, maybe scream, attract a neighbor's attention. Anything was better than being trapped in this black hole.

He climbed the stairs, dragging her behind him. She hadn't realized how hungry she was — and thirsty. Licking her dry lips, she tried to concentrate on winning him over. Yes. That's what she had to do — continue to gain his trust. It was probably their only shot at survival.

Once upstairs, he slammed the cellar door shut behind them, leading her down a narrow corridor into a small bathroom.

"Go," he said, indicating the toilet.

"Not with you here," she said, appalled. "Take off the handcuffs and wait outside."

The Man had no intention of letting her get away with anything. He had her under his control, and that's where he'd keep her. Under control, like a dog.

Yes, she was being truthful with him — for now — but women couldn't be trusted, any fool knew that.

She glared at him before unzipping her jeans with one hand, pulling down her under-

673

wear, and squatting on the toilet.

He knew he was humiliating her. It gave him great satisfaction.

The end would not be quick for this one. He liked having her around — especially when she told him tales of Ingrid and her love for him.

Yes, Jordanna Levitt would die slowly.

If she'd had a gun she would have blown him away. Shot him right between his already dead eyes.

Screw you! she wanted to scream. *You sick perverted murdering bastard.*

He'd taken away her freedom, and he had no right to do that. He was a killer — he deserved no chance.

She finished peeing and pulled up her jeans as quickly as possible.

Was Bobby missing her yet? Was he out looking for her?

How about Jordan? Did he know? Was he concerned?

They must have found her car by now and realized something was seriously wrong.

"Can I get a drink?" she asked, deliberately sounding subservient, hoping to lull him into a false sense of security.

He grunted and led her into the kitchen.

Where was this place? Glancing over at the window, she observed trees and greenery outside. Big help. They could be anywhere from Malibu to the Valley.

Yanking her across to a water cooler, he filled a paper cup and thrust it at her.

She downed it in one big gulp. "More," she said thirstily.

"No more."

"Why?"

"Because I'm not bringing you up to the bathroom again."

"Why not?"

"You talk too much."

He hadn't heard the half of it. "How about something to eat?"

"No."

"For Cheryl? It'll soothe her stomach."

"No," he repeated harshly, and began pulling her back toward the door.

She glanced over at the window one more time. Freedom. She'd never missed it until she didn't have it.

Oh, God! What could she do to get out of this?

And then she saw a sight that made her spirits rise and filled her with hope. Cheryl, outside the house — stumbling, escaping, running for her life.

There was a chance for survival after all.

53

Mac was driving out of the studio when Quincy spotted him and did a fast U-turn.

Michael jumped out of Quincy's car, flagged Mac down, ran over, and tapped on the window of the Rolls. "How come you never mentioned Luca Carlotti was Zane Ricca's uncle?" he asked sharply. "Didn't you know?"

Mac took a beat. Should he bluff it out — or was it best to go with the truth?

Jordanna was missing. It had to be the truth.

"I knew," he admitted.

"So why didn't you — "

"Hey," Mac interrupted. "What's done is old news. The important thing is to find Jordanna. Luca's in L.A. I'm on my way to see him now."

"Does he know where Zane is?"

"Not the last time we spoke. But he's likely to track him quicker than the cops."

"We'll come with you."

"I don't think Luca would appreciate that."

"Do you give a shit?"

"Well . . ."

"We work for *you*, Mac. It's not like we're in the catching criminals business anymore. Chances are we can help."

"Okay. Follow me."

"Where are we going?"

"The St. James's Hotel on Sunset."

By the time Kennedy and Rosa arrived at headquarters, it was known that Cheryl Landers was missing as well as Jordanna Levitt. Her silver BMW — apparently abandoned on Lexington — had been traced to the car impound.

Detective Carlyle was in deep shit. Thanks to Jordan Levitt, he was getting it from all sides, because now Boyd Keller was being pressured from above, and the hotshot special investigator had to take it out on someone. Detective Carlyle happened to be that lucky someone.

On top of everything else, there were the two ballbreakers to contend with, Rosa Alvarez and Kennedy Chase, who'd descended on them with even more information. Rosa seemed to be getting very palsy with Boyd — she was all over the Boy Wonder, and Boyd didn't seem to object. As for Kennedy, she did nothing but shoot him dirty looks — like it was *his* fault the girls were missing.

Somewhere in the recesses of his mind, Carlyle suspected that maybe it was. If only he'd connected the cases earlier, done a little more detective work . . .

No, he told himself firmly, it wasn't his fault. His workload overwhelmed him. Murders, beatings, stabbings, shootings, pimps, hookers, drugs, pornography, child abuse, runaways, carjackings, robberies, rapes — there was always something to grab his attention.

Boyd Keller stormed out of his newly appointed office and hooked a finger in his direction. "Get in here, Carlyle," he said in an unpleasant tone.

Detective Carlyle sighed. He was just about ready to pack this job in and join a private security force. He, too, was allowed to have a life.

Bosco strolled into Cartier's on Rodeo Drive as if he owned the place. He was trying very hard to emulate Luca, who had a way of making people jump to attention.

Somehow it never worked for Bosco — even though he had the limo parked outside, and plenty of attitude. Unfortunately he did not possess Luca's commanding presence.

A saleswoman approached him.

Swaggering across to a center showcase, he gestured at a diamond bracelet. "Lemme take a look at that one," he said. "Nice, huh?"

"All our diamond bracelets are nice," the saleswoman assured him with a slightly patronizing air.

"Show me a couple of 'em," he said.

Luca had not told him how much he wished to spend, but Bosco knew that when Luca went after a woman, money was no object.

The saleswoman surreptitiously made sure the security guards were watching before she unlocked the showcase and removed two magnificent diamond bracelets. She took them over to a counter and carefully laid them out on a black velvet pad.

Bosco checked them out like he knew what he was doing. Finally he pointed to the one that seemed to have the biggest diamonds. "Gonna take that little mother," he decided, accompanying his decision with a jaunty wink.

"Will that be cash or charge?" the saleswoman asked, totally unimpressed.

"Cash." He guffawed loudly. "Is there any other way?"

The saleswoman didn't crack a smile.

Uptight broad, he thought to himself, she'd smile soon enough if she knew what he had to offer in bed. He might not be Mel Gibson, but he could bring tears to a woman's eyes.

"I'll need that gift-wrapped," he said, pulling out the envelope bulging with hundred-dollar bills.

"Certainly, sir," she replied. "Would you care to wait, or will you send your driver back?"

At least she'd noticed he arrived in a limo. "I'll wait," he said, favoring her with another wink. "Make it fast."

Michael filled Quincy in on his New York trip as they trailed Mac's Rolls down Sunset.

"You did the right thing," Quincy said. "You walked away from it."

Michael nodded. "I know. But it still hurts."

"I bet it does," Quincy said, chasing Mac through a red light. "That sonofabitch brother of yours — he never quits."

Michael reached for a cigarette. "This is bad news about the two girls. If that sick fuck has them . . . Shit! I knew we should have done something about it before. . . ."

"We did," Quincy said grimly. "The cops were supposed to take over."

"They blew this one."

"I know," Quincy said, swerving to avoid a jay-walker. "The St. James's," he said thoughtfully. "That's the hotel I was waiting outside for Cheryl Landers."

"She'd hardly be visiting Luca Carlotti," Michael said, stifling a yawn.

Quincy glanced over at him. "Tough night?"

"No, tough morning. I was flying all night."

"Tough morning, huh? What did you do that was so important you couldn't contact me sooner? We're partners, bro', we got a lot of shit to take care of."

"You want the truth or a lie?"

"Whyn't you try the truth."

"I met someone."

"Where? On the plane? At the airport? She serve you a drink, is that it?"

"What makes you think I had a drink?"

" 'Cause you look too goddamned pleased with yourself."

"Hey — if I'd been drinking, the last thing I'd look is pleased."

"Goddamn it!" Quincy exclaimed, as Mac jumped another red light and he tried to keep up with him. "This guy is nuts."

"What do you expect? He drives a Rolls."

"Yeah, yeah, I know — those kinda cars don't stop for red lights."

"I was thinking we'd all have dinner."

"Who's we?"

"Her name's Kennedy."

"Kennedy's a dead President."

"No, Kennedy is this woman I met. She's a journalist."

"That's dangerous."

"You'll like her, Q. She's wise, intelligent, and beautiful."

"And you're in love — right?"

"You've seen me through plenty of women — you ever heard me talk like this before?"

"Yeah, the day you married Rita."

"The day I married Rita I was drunk and horny. Someone shoulda stopped me."

"You ever tried stoppin' a man with a hard-on?"

"You coulda tried."

"Hey — "

"Okay, okay. I want you and Amber to meet Kennedy. We'll go out to dinner. My check."

"Oh, boy, this *must* be love!"

Eldessa had turned off Laurel Canyon onto a side street a while ago. She was hot and tired, and now her feet hurt. She stopped to consult the crumpled piece of paper Shelley had given her. The problem was she couldn't see a thing, so she took out her old glasses and put them on.

Shelley had drawn her a little map, and as far as she could tell she was heading in the right direction, only she wasn't there yet, and she was getting cranky.

For a moment she thought about abandoning the idea of visiting Shelley and turning back. But that seemed foolish, she was bound to reach the house soon.

Besides, there was five thousand dollars luring her on.

Random thoughts raced through Cheryl's head

as she ran. *Okay, okay, I can do this, I have to do this. It's our only chance. I have to get away.*

Once Zane had removed Jordanna from the cellar, she'd taken action. Without the handcuffs she was able to untie her ankles, stumble up the stairs, reach the front door, and flee.

In spite of being doubled over with stomach cramps, she'd known she had to make the supreme effort — even though she was horribly aware that as soon as Zane discovered her missing he would be after her.

However ill she felt, it didn't matter. Nothing mattered except summoning help.

She reached the end of the small driveway and found herself on a dirt road cut into the hillside — a rough terrain of overgrown shrubbery, trees, and long grass. Desperately she looked around, hoping to see other houses, but there were none up here in this lonely place.

Making a big effort, she began frantically running down the overgrown path — glancing over her shoulder, staying to the side of the road, petrified he would catch up with her. Her heart was in her mouth. Fear pervaded her entire body. Clutching her coat around her, she made it into the bushes.

I must hide, she told herself. *He'll be here in a minute. If he catches me, who knows what he'll do.*

She had no idea where she was or where she was going. She knew only that she had to get away as fast as she could.

Bobby paced restlessly up and down the floor

of Jordan Levitt's study. "Is it all right if I hang out here?" he asked. "If there's a ransom demand, you'll be the first to hear."

"Of course," Jordan said, his forehead creased with worry. "Help yourself to a drink."

Bobby went over to the small bar and poured himself a neat vodka. He needed something to take away the empty feeling of hopelessness in the pit of his stomach. "Can I fix you something?" he offered.

Jordan nodded. "Scotch."

There was silence while Bobby poured Jordan his drink, walked over, and handed it to him.

Jordan cleared his throat. "Are you and Jordanna seeing each other?"

"We're best friends," Bobby replied carefully. "She's about to star in my movie."

Jordan's eyebrows shot up. "Jordanna's not an actress."

"She tested for the role. I have to tell you — she's a wonderful actress."

Jordan frowned. "I'm surprised."

"Surprised that she's wonderful?"

"Surprised and pleased," he said, taking a gulp of Scotch. "Right now I don't know what to say. I . . . I haven't always been the best father in the world. When I get her back, I plan on changing all that."

"She loves you," Bobby said. "Talks about you all the time."

Jordan's craggy face lit up. "She does?"

"I know the two of you have had your problems. But you know your daughter — she's smart, and over the years she's learned to understand you.

I can tell you, she's happy about the baby your wife's expecting."

"That makes me feel good, Bobby."

"I'm glad."

"When Jordanna's mother died, it was a difficult time for me. And then when my son . . ." He trailed off, unable to continue.

"It's gonna be all right," Bobby said, gulping vodka as if it were water. He wished he felt as sure as he sounded. The thought of Jordanna trapped with some maniac . . . "There's gotta be *something* we can do," he said edgily. "Maybe it would be better if we went over to headquarters. What do you think?"

Jordan nodded. "Yes. I'll have all my calls switched through. At least we'll be there if something happens."

"Let's go," Bobby said, already halfway out the door.

Reno was indulging in a mild flirtation with a voluptuous freckled woman in a large white hat and a sundress, who sat under a striped umbrella, delicately picking at a plate of thinly sliced melon.

"Now that's what I call a broad," he said admiringly.

"No," Luca corrected. "That's what you call a lady."

"No," Reno corrected him back. "That's what I call a broad."

"You want her, have her," Luca said magnanimously, as if she were his to give.

"Maybe I will," Reno responded. "I wanna see if she eats all the melon. If she does, she's a pig.

If she leaves some over . . . then we'll see."

Luca chuckled. "Is that how you judge 'em?"

"I have my rules," Reno said, lowering his shades. "Take a look at who's heading our way."

"Who?"

"Mac Brooks. An' he's not alone."

Luca zeroed in on Mac, automatically smoothing down his slick black hair. "See those guys with him — they're cops," he said, frowning deeply.

"How do you know?"

"Cops got a way about 'em," Luca said, continuing to watch Mac as he approached. "Yeah, they're cops, all right," he muttered, sitting up a little straighter on his lounger. "Why is the schmuck bringin' them here?"

"He's your schmuck, not mine," Reno said blandly, and went back to studying the freckled woman with the plate of melon.

Sitting in the back of the limo, Bosco visualized what he would have for lunch when he got back to the hotel. A hamburger, maybe. Or a steak. Not one of those mixed-salad things everybody seemed to eat in L.A. How anybody got any satisfaction out of a pile of grass with some fancy dressing beat the shit out of him.

Yes, he'd have a rare juicy steak, a glass of red wine, and a large slice of chocolate cake with cream on top.

Then, if they were hanging around L.A. for another night, he'd order up a high-class whore. The blonde they'd sent him before had been a disappointment — all Californian teeth and tits. Next time he'd try something more exotic — Chinese or Malaysian, a small woman who'd do anything he required.

He weighed the Cartier's package in his hand. This Bambi broad was one lucky hooker — he hadn't seen Luca so ready to tango in a long time.

The limo turned off Laurel Canyon, heading up a deserted side road into the hills.

"You sure this is the right way?" he asked, leaning forward to speak to the driver.

"This is where we followed the car to last night," the driver replied.

"Okay, okay," he said, imagining Bambi's surprise when he turned up and presented her with Luca's gift.

Luca sure knew how to turn a woman on — but then, Bosco thought with some satisfaction, in his own way, so did he.

54

Zane was pulling her toward the cellar door.

She knew she had to stall, do something to prevent him from finding out that Cheryl had escaped. The longer she kept him from going down into the cellar, the better it would be for Cheryl.

With a sudden lunge, she faked a trip, falling heavily to the ground. "Oh, my ankle!" she cried out, feigning pain. "I think I've twisted it."

He stopped abruptly. "Get up," he commanded harshly.

"I can't."

"Do it."

"I would if I could, but I can't stand."

"You're full of tricks, aren't you?"

"No — no, I'm not," she said, her words coming fast. "I want to be your friend — that's what Ingrid would have liked."

"Ingrid's not here," he said in a strained voice. "Ingrid got what she deserved, and that's exactly what you're going to get."

"The two of you could have been so great together," Jordanna said quickly. "She didn't just want a fling with you . . . she talked about marrying you, having your babies."

"You're lying."

"Why would I lie?" she asked innocently.

"Because all women lie," he answered, roughly yanking at the handcuffs.

"How come you find it so difficult to believe that Ingrid really cared for you? You're an attractive man. You remind me of — "

"Who?" he asked, stopping and staring at her.

She'd hit a nerve. Oh, God, she'd hit a nerve, and now she had to follow through. Flatter him. Go for his ego. Instinct took over. "Oh . . . um . . . a . . . a . . . movie star."

"Which one?"

"Somebody strong," she said, feeling her way. "An action star?"

"That's right. You remind me of . . ."

Steven Seagal. Say Steven Seagal, you bitch!

The Man glared at her, willing her to do so.

Of course, he was better looking than Steven Seagal, but surely she must see the resemblance?

"Jean-Claude Van Damme," she said at last.

She wasn't as smart as he'd thought, but then nobody was as smart as him.

"Steven Seagal," he informed her coldly. Steven Seagal, bitch.

"That's who I meant," she said, clicking her fingers. "That's exactly who I meant."

"I could have been a big star like him," he said. "If circumstances had been different."

"Is that why you came to Hollywood, to be a star?"

"I came because they called me."

"Who called you?"

"Mac Brooks. He wanted me in his film."

"I guess he didn't realize Ingrid would be so attracted to you."

"Women are always attracted to me," he said, closely monitoring her reaction. "Even when I kill them — I can see it in their eyes. Shelley wanted me. She chased me for weeks."

The bitch didn't react the way he'd hoped. Jordanna Levitt was not easy to intimidate.

"Who's Shelley?" she asked.

"Never you mind."

"My father's a producer," she blurted out. "I'm sure he'd love to have an actor like you in one of his movies. They're looking for a new action-adventure hero. Arnold and Sly are getting older, Bruce seems more into caper movies. Would you consider working again?"

He wasn't sure if she meant what she said. Maybe. Maybe not.

He knew who her father was — big-time producer Jordan Levitt. Of course, he would be a sensation as the new action-adventure hero. But the fact that he'd been in prison might go against him.

"I have to stay in the shadows," he said mysteriously.

"There's no reason for you to do that. You can be a big star if you want to."

This woman definitely talked too much, this Jordanna Levitt. And sometimes she even made sense. It puzzled him that she wasn't cowering with fear like the other one. He pulled her to her feet. "We're going back downstairs."

"My ankle," she protested, hobbling.
"Either walk or I'll drag you."
The Man opened the cellar door and they de-
scended into darkness.

She held her breath, waiting for him to realize that Cheryl was gone. It didn't seem to register at first. He looked around, then shone his flashlight, taking a second look around the dark cellar, hardly believing Cheryl was not there.

"Where is she?" he said at last, the hardness in his voice chilling.

"I . . . I don't know," Jordanna said.

"You tricked me!" he screamed, losing control.

Before she could protect herself, he hauled back and slapped her across the face. Blood trickled from a cut on her lip.

She tried to bring her hands up to save herself from a second assault, but as she was still handcuffed to him, it was impossible.

He dragged her hands away from her face and hit her again.

She kicked out, attempting to catch him in the groin, but he moved swiftly, punching her in the face.

For a moment she was stunned. He took the opportunity to unlock the handcuffs joining them together. She rallied and kicked out again, infuriating him.

"You wanna play games!" he yelled. "You wanna play fucking games?" And with that, he withdrew a gun from his belt, pointing it directly at her.

Silently she said her prayers, because she thought this was it. He was about to blow her brains out, and there was nothing she could do to stop him.

But he didn't. He stared at her for a moment, the gun in position, his eyes two flat dead zones.

She licked her lips, tasting her own blood. Oh, God, she might be petrified, but she'd never give him the satisfaction of seeing her beg.

He released the safety catch on the gun and continued to stare at her.

She met his gaze steadfastly, refusing to look away. If this was the way it was supposed to be, she was ready.

After a few seconds he lowered the weapon. "I've got to find her," he muttered, almost to himself.

She didn't say a word, she knew when to stay quiet.

He began stuffing the gun back in his belt.

Window of opportunity.

She took it. Bringing her wrists up, she pounded him under the chin. He fell back, startled, and she followed up with a violent kick to his head and a race for the stairs.

But he was too quick for her. As she passed, he grabbed her by the ankle, twisted hard, and she fell to the floor with a dull thud.

"Cunt!" he screamed. "Dirty stinking cunt!"

She tried to get up, but before she could, he leaped on top of her, straddling her body with his, placing his hands around her neck and beginning to squeeze.

He was very strong. She found herself totally

helpless, trapped beneath him, unable to move.

He was so close she could feel his sickening breath in her face.

This is not good, she thought dizzily. *This . . . is . . . not . . . good. . . .*

He continued to squeeze her throat, shutting out all sound and sensation, until finally everything went black and she lapsed into unconsciousness.

55

"I thought we was meeting at seven," Luca said irritably as Mac approached. "This don't seem like seven t'me."

"I took a chance you'd be here earlier," Mac said. "We had to close down shooting today."

"How come?"

"Jordanna Levitt and Cheryl Landers are missing."

"Who're they?"

"They both testified against Zane at his trial."

"What're you saying?"

"I'm saying he's probably got them."

"Goddamn it!" Luca muttered, slapping his fist into the palm of his hand. Then he looked over at Quincy and Michael. "You wanna introduce me to your friends?"

"They're private detectives working for me."

"Why're you bringin' them here?"

"Because we've got to talk. And they can help."

Michael stepped forward. He was face-to-face with the notorious Luca Carlotti, and the guy looked like just another aging hood with good grooming. "The cops know, or are about to, that you're Zane Ricca's uncle," he said.

693

"Yeah? How d'you figure that?" Luca asked belligerently.

"I have a journalist friend who's been doing some investigating. She came up with these facts, and she's telling the cops."

"Aw, jeez!" Luca complained. "Is this gonna be all over the press?"

"How close are you to finding Zane?" Michael asked urgently.

"I'm not talkin' to no cops," Luca warned.

"You don't have to," Michael said. "This is between us. For now. The cops'll be all over here soon."

"How'd they know I'm here?"

"They'll find out, it's no secret."

Quincy joined the conversation, working on a hunch. "Who's Bosco Nanni?"

"Why?" Luca responded suspiciously.

"Cheryl Landers was visiting him at this hotel the night before last."

"Visiting Bosco?" Reno said.

Quincy nodded. "That's right."

Luca chortled. "The only visitor Bosco had was a hooker."

"So you *do* know him?"

"Wanna make somethin' outta it?" Luca said, impatient at having to answer questions.

"Can we talk to him?" Michael said.

"When he gets back."

"Where is he?"

"He had to go do somethin' for me."

"We'll wait," Mac said.

Bobby and Jordan arrived at the police precinct

694

at the same time as Ethan and Estelle Landers, Cheryl's parents.

Estelle rushed over to Jordan, her lower lip quivering. "My little girl!" she cried dramatically. "They've got my little girl. I always knew this would happen. I warned Ethan we had to be careful of kidnapping."

"Let's hope that's all it is," Jordan said grimly, backing away because Estelle smelled like a bottle of stale wine.

Ethan Landers stepped forward to greet Jordan. The two men hugged — a theatrical gesture they both seemed to take comfort from. Ethan was a heavyset man with thick red hair and matching bushy eyebrows. He and Jordan were old adversaries.

"What do you know about this?" Ethan asked, rubbing his stubby fingers together.

Jordan shook his head. "Not much. They seem to think it could be the actor the girls testified against. He's out of jail, and from what I understand, he's murdered the other four witnesses who testified against him. God knows what he'll do with our daughters if he has them. God only knows."

Bobby extended his hand to Mrs. Landers. He'd known her since he was a child, the Landers were good friends of Jerry's. "Bobby Rush," he reminded her.

She looked at him through a faintly alcoholic haze. "Oh, Bobby dear, why are you here?"

"Jordanna and I are good friends."

"This is so shocking," Estelle said, wringing her perfectly manicured hands.

Try fucking unbelievable, Bobby thought. *Try how can this be happening?*

And once again a dull feeling of helplessness overcame him, because there was absolutely nothing he could do.

The police had set up a room for relatives and friends to sit in. Word from above was to keep these people happy — they were key members of the Hollywood community and therefore had to be treated like royalty.

Ethan Landers took one look at the lackluster refreshments set out — a bowl of Fritos and some warm cans of Coke — and sent out to Nate-n-Al's for a suitable spread.

"Surely we don't have to stay here?" Estelle asked plaintively, yearning for the comforts of Bel Air and a bottle of gin so she could fix herself a decent martini.

"For a while," Ethan replied, wishing he could put her in the limo and send her home.

Estelle was not good in crisis situations. Neither was he.

The butler discovered Marjory Sanderson at noon, lying on her bathroom floor barely conscious. She had slit her wrists with a fortunately rather dull razor blade.

He had the presence of mind to summon Mr. Sanderson's very discreet personal physician, who had her rushed by private ambulance to a low-key exclusive clinic where they were able to take care of her without the ugly intrusion of the press.

It wasn't the first time.

"Take a look over there," Rosa said, as they were on their way out.

"What am I looking at?"

"Bobby Rush, Jordan Levitt, and the Landers."

"Bobby Rush is haunting me," Kennedy groaned. "He's everywhere I go."

"Why's he here? I smell a story."

"Let's go, Rosa. I have a story of my own to finish."

"Wouldn't you like to interview the grieving parents?"

Kennedy jumped on her. "You're sick, you know that? They have nothing to grieve about yet. And I hope they never will."

"Well, I'd sure like to put them on camera and find out how they're feeling now."

"Exactly like any parent would feel in this situation. Leave them alone."

Rosa nodded to herself. "I'm coming back with a crew. This is a big one, and I've got access."

"Why don't you dump your prestigious anchor position and join *Hard Copy*? I'm sure they'd hang out the American flag to have you aboard."

"A story is a story. Don't get holier-than-thou on me."

Kennedy shook her head. "There are some things you do and some you don't. Interviewing the parents of two girls who could be horribly murdered is *definitely* a no."

Rosa sighed. "I really hate it when you're in love."

Three things took place at once.

The limo driver decided he was lost and pulled to a stop in the middle of the rutted road while he tried to figure out where he was going.

Eldessa trudged up behind the big car, maneuvering her footsore way past it.

And Cheryl stared from the bushes, wild-eyed and panicked, clutching her coat around her.

She saw the limo — but couldn't make up her mind whether to ask for help or not. It was possible the car could be Zane's. Best to stay hidden.

Eldessa kept walking, eyes to the front. She passed by the limo, but not before Bosco spotted her. He opened the car door and got out.

"Hey — " he yelled. "Ain't you the maid up at Mr. Carlotti's?"

Eldessa stopped and considered her reply. Had they already found Zane? Was he with Shelley? If this was the case, she'd get no reward, and her long walk would have been in vain.

She glared at the fat man. "I was gonna call Mr. Carlotti," she said resentfully. "When I was sure."

"When you was sure of what?" Bosco asked, puzzled. What was Luca's maid doing in this godforsaken place?

"That he was with Shelley," Eldessa said.

Bosco had no idea what she was talking about. He was just about to ask, when Zane Ricca came into view, proceeding down the road like an armed terrorist, clad all in black, holding onto an Uzi machine gun, which he pointed straight at them.

Bosco felt his stomach turn a loop. "Shit!" he mumbled. "Goddamn fucking *shit!*"

But it was too late for him to do anything.

698

56

Jordanna drifted in and out of consciousness, trying desperately to come back. Rolling over on the cold, hard floor, she opened her eyes and began throwing up, almost choking on her own vomit.

The important thing was she was still alive, she had another chance, and she was taking it. Goddamn it, she was a survivor, she *had* to take it, otherwise she'd never see Bobby again. Or her father. And she wanted to be around for her new stepbrother or sister.

Get up! a voice screamed in her head. *Get up and get out. Move now! Do it!*

She staggered to her feet. No handcuffs, no ties to bind her.

It dawned on her that he'd left her for dead. The cowardly sonofabitch thought he'd finished her off.

She could still feel his hands around her throat, squeezing . . . squeezing . . . squeezing the life out of her.

Zane Ricca, you made a big mistake. I am not dead. I am here. And you will pay for everything you've done to me and all those other women.

Dizzily she started up the cellar stairs, but when she reached the top she was devastated to discover the door was locked.

A moment of desperation.

Only a moment. She would figure something out. After all, Jordanna Levitt was a true survivor.

Steven Seagal, eat shit. I am king. I am the finest. I am the biggest movie star in the world.

The Man thought good thoughts as he trained his Uzi on the three people.

Three rats caught in a trap. Only he was the trap, and he was deadly.

They'd better not mess with him, or he'd blow them away.

He'd never shot anyone before. He'd certainly never killed a man, although there'd been many times in prison when he'd had the desire to do so.

Strangling women seemed like such a gentle way to remove the scum from the earth.

He watched as Bosco reached for what looked like a gun.

The Man let rip, spraying him with bullets.

Bosco didn't fall immediately. He stood for a moment as blood spurted from the newly made holes in his body. His eyes bugged wide open with surprise — then he fell, air whooshing from his open mouth.

The limo driver decided to make a run for it.

The Man liked that. Rat deserting sinking ship. Run, rat. Run, rabbit. Run, fucking run.

The Man aimed and fired, hitting him in the back with a nicely balanced spray of bullets.

Eldessa stood her ground, her gnarled hands

clutching the wooden cross that hung around her withered neck.

He knew who she was, and he hated her. Nosy old bitch. Always watching him, dying to sneak back into his room after he'd installed the heavy-duty locks.

He put down the Uzi, withdrew a pistol from his belt, took a few steps forward, and shot her point-blank in the face.

She dropped like a heavy sack of flour.

Now what? He was confused. He hadn't come looking for these three people — he'd come to find Cheryl, to bring her back where she belonged.

Bitch! Look what she'd made him do.

Jordanna thought she heard gunfire in the distance.

I have to figure this out. Think logically. Get into his mind. Know what he's going to do better than he knows himself.

He probably thought he'd killed her, so maybe he wouldn't come back. On the other hand, he might return to bury her body. She shuddered.

Which would he do?

She hoped he'd come back, because if he didn't she was trapped in the cellar with no way of escape, and unless somebody found her . . .

The thought of being locked down there forever gave her chills.

Although it wouldn't be forever, she reasoned, someone would come looking eventually.

How many days could she last without food or water? Five, six?

Cheryl will fetch help before then, she thought confidently.

Unless . . . Cheryl . . . is . . . dead.

Oh, God. It wasn't possible, or was it? She'd heard gunfire. Maybe he'd caught up with Cheryl and gunned her down like a dog, with no chance.

Mustn't think that way. Stay positive. Stay strong. The power of positive thinking conquers all.

The important thing was to decide what she was going to do if he came back. How could she defend herself?

Desperately she began searching around the small, dark cellar for something she might use as a weapon, finally coming across a long slab of hard wood jammed under a water heater. She struggled to dislodge it.

It wasn't much, but it was certainly better than nothing.

The Man dragged the bodies to the side of the road, piling them together. It was hot, dirty work, and his clothes were soon drenched in blood, but he didn't mind.

Once, when he was twelve, he'd skinned a live cat and hidden his bloodied clothes for days, just so he could take them out and smell them. The clothes worked better than the dirty magazines his father collected — magazines filled with spread-eagled women, featuring shaved twats and vacant smiles.

The physically exhausting work, the relentless afternoon heat, and the smell of blood was getting to him. He felt aroused like a horny bull.

He stopped for a minute and thought of Jordanna, freshly dead . . . her body barely cold.

Cheryl was gone. It was more than likely she would run for help and bring people back here. He had to leave, but first Jordanna. . . .

She set a trap, ready if he did return. Squeamishly she picked up the dead rat, placing it halfway down the stairs, figuring if she was lucky he'd trip and break his neck. Then she gathered dirt from the floor, put it into a rusty tin can, and placed it next to her on the floor where he'd left her.

After that she positioned the block of wood and arranged herself on top of it.

If he came back she was prepared.

57

Cheryl continued on her journey down the hill toward the noise of traffic. Staying close to the bushes, she was too scared to emerge. Her face and neck were scratched and torn, her stockings in shreds, her shoes long gone. The burning sensation in her stomach was getting worse, but she kept going — haunted by the sight of Zane, clad all in black like a ninja assassin, dense shades covering his eyes, shooting those poor people down as if he were enjoying target practice.

It was plain to see he was insane, and she was terrified for Jordanna.

The thought of getting help spurred her on as she stumbled along, moving through the heavy undergrowth as fast as she could go.

For once in his life Grant was stone cold sober. He sat in Cheryl's house, trying to take care of business, but he was unable to concentrate. He had no interest in arranging appointments for their army of expensive call girls. He stonewalled prospective clients — including the regulars — and told all the girls to take a day off. Some of them were severely pissed — they were used to the extra money, which supplemented their incomes as actresses and models. A couple of them threatened to leave and operate elsewhere. "Go ahead," he told them.

Eventually he turned on the answering machine and headed for the police station.

Screw business. All that really mattered was Cheryl's safety.

Luca returned to his suite, trailed by Mac, his two private investigators, and Reno. He shut himself in the bedroom and called Cartier's. A salesperson assured him Bosco had purchased a diamond bracelet and left the store over an hour ago.

Luca was deeply puzzled. Why had Cheryl Landers — a rich Hollywood broad — been visiting someone like Bosco? Did Bosco have secrets Luca didn't know about?

Luca grimaced, he did not appreciate anyone keeping secrets from him, especially Bosco. Something strange was going on, and that he couldn't quite figure it out really infuriated him, because he was sharp — sharper than any of them.

It all had to do with his slimeball nephew. When he found Zane, he would take great pleasure in personally disposing of him.

In the meantime, where the fuck was Bosco?

He went back into the living room just in time to witness the arrival of Detective Carlyle.

Jesus! Timing! If he'd come out to the Coast a day earlier, he'd have nailed his sonofabitch nephew, and he wouldn't be sitting in a hotel room dealing with private detectives, a dumb cop, and his movie director son, who was scared shitless someone was going to find out about their relationship.

When timing was off, nothing went right.

Michael called Kennedy from the hotel.

"Where are you?" she asked.

He told her.

There was a long pause, and then she said, "Uh . . . Michael, did I miss something along the way? I had no idea you were this close to the action."

"We've been working on something for Mac Brooks," he explained, feeling guilty he hadn't told her before. "He brought us to Carlotti."

Warning bells went off in her head. Like Rosa, she could smell a story like a drug-sniffing dog. "Working on what?" she asked curiously.

"Uh . . . it's kinda confidential."

Hmm . . . this from a man she'd just spent the morning in bed with.

"Mac Brooks was the director of the movie Zane was in," she said. "Did he *know* Zane was out of prison, committing more murders? And what's his link to Carlotti?"

"Can we talk later?"

She hated it when someone answered a question with another question. "No, let's talk now. Does Carlotti know where his nephew is?"

"He doesn't seem to."

Her voice rose. "Doesn't *seem* to? There's two girls' lives at stake here, Michael."

"Believe me, I'm aware of that."

"It doesn't sound like you are."

"Kennedy, I know Jordanna, I care very much about finding her — so get off my case."

"Get off *your* case? I didn't know it was *your* case."

He'd called to tell her he missed her, now she was giving him a hard time. He didn't need this. "I gotta go — "

"Keep me up to date on everything," she said, all business. "I'm going back to headquarters."

"Kennedy . . ."

"Yes?"

"Uh . . . nothing."

She hung up feeling let down and angry. Michael knew more than he was telling her, and it disturbed her. What if he'd had information he'd kept back, and because of that two more women were dead?

No. Michael wouldn't do that.

Or would he?

Suddenly she realized she hardly knew Michael at all.

"I want to see photographs of both girls on every TV station, every newspaper — anywhere we can get 'em out there." So spoke Boyd Keller to a roomful of attentive officers. "We've discovered no bodies yet. If these two girls are still alive, the public will help us find them. And believe me, we need all the help we can get. Perry," he added, snapping his fingers at an eager young detective, "take the photos over to Carlyle at the St. James's Hotel. He's expecting them."

Boyd exited his office and surveyed his VIP guests through a one-way window. They were gathered in the conference room. Producers, movie stars, famous people, everywhere he looked.

707

This would not be a good case to blow — he had to rally every resource to locate these two girls.

Frankly, he didn't think there was much hope of finding them alive.

Detective Carlyle sat uncomfortably in Luca Carlotti's suite, fidgeting on the plush couch. Getting information out of the New York mobster was a difficult task. Luca did not seem prepared to give him any of the answers he required.

"I ain't seen the kid since he got out of jail," Luca said, resentful he'd been put in the position of having to answer questions.

"Where was he staying in L.A.?" Carlyle asked in a not too pleasant way.

"What's with this questions shit?" Luca said, suddenly losing it. "I don't havta answer nothin' without my lawyer present."

"Why would you need a lawyer?"

" 'Cause you fuckers ain't interested in the truth. I got my rights, an' I don't havta talk to no one."

Michael stepped into the picture, annoying Carlyle, who liked to think he was in total charge.

"Mr. Carlotti," Michael said, "what we're trying to do here is find these two girls before your nephew does them any harm. Now, if you do know anything, you'd be well advised to give that information to the police. All they're asking for is your help."

"Hey — if I knew anythin', you think I'd allow that dumb cocksucker t'be runnin' around doin' what he's doin'? I ain't proud he's my nephew."

There was a knock on the door. Reno answered it. Perry entered and handed the envelope of photographs to Carlyle.

"What's that — a subpoena?" Luca said roughly. " 'Cause if it ain't, get the fuck outta here. I ain't answerin' no more questions."

Carlyle wished he had the power to run Luca Carlotti in and beat the crap out of him. If there was one thing he hated, it was people who were not intimidated by the fact that he was a police detective and had authority. He ripped open the envelope and handed the pictures of the two girls to Luca. "Jordanna Levitt and Cheryl Landers," he said, fighting to keep an impersonal tone.

Reluctantly Luca glanced at the two photographs. "This ain't Cheryl Landers," he said, frowning. "This one's Bambi."

"Who's Bambi?" Mac asked, wishing he were somewhere else.

"A friend of mine," Luca said cagily.

"I'd like to know more about your friend, because this girl is Cheryl Landers," Carlyle said.

"Hey, Reno," Luca said, beckoning him over. "Take a look at this photo an' tell 'em who it is."

Reno studied the picture. "Bambi," he said. "No doubt about it."

It was frustrating. Now that he was a movie star, Bobby was used to everything going his way. He hated sitting around at the police station, unable to do anything.

Grant Lennon, Jr., turned up. He sat hunched in a corner, looking depressed.

"There's nothing we can do here," Ethan Landers said, walking over to Bobby. "I'm in constant touch with the chief of police. He'll let me know as soon as anything happens. We're going home. You should do the same."

"No," Bobby said. "I'll stay here."

Jordan didn't leave. Whatever Jordanna might say about him, it was quite obvious he really loved his daughter.

Bobby sat down next to him. "Whyn't you go home? I'll keep in touch."

Jordan shook his head. "I'd sooner be here."

"How about your wife? Shouldn't you be with her?"

"No, I should be right here," Jordan said.

They were both surprised when Charlie Dollar arrived, followed by two assistants with trayloads of sandwiches and refreshments.

"Came by to see if I could do anything," Charlie said. "I got this psychic thing — I'm tellin' ya, they'll be fine."

Bobby nodded. He wanted to believe him, but it wasn't easy. The two girls had been snatched the night before, now it was nearly two in the afternoon.

Their chances of survival were getting dimmer and dimmer.

Cheryl sat on the ground and rested for a moment, dizziness and nausea overcoming her. She daren't emerge into the open, better to hide in the thick underbrush.

Jordanna. I've got to get help for Jordanna. The thought kept her going.

The farther down the hill she went, the louder the traffic sounded. Thank God, she was finally nearing civilization.

She tried to compose herself. It was important to stay together long enough to tell the police every little detail.

Kennedy returned to headquarters, unable to stay away. She kept on thinking about Michael and the fact that he might have known something without telling her.

He'd been aware she was working on the story the first time they'd met; surely he should have mentioned it.

The press were everywhere, but Rosa managed to hustle her inside, past the rest of the reporters and TV crews. "Boyd Keller and I are developing a very special friendship," Rosa said, winking conspiratorially.

"What about Ferdy?"

"All good basketball players miss the shot eventually."

"Does that mean it's over?"

"Right now he's on the bench."

It didn't take long for Detective Carlyle to start putting it together. When he had to, he could figure things out pretty well. Luca Carlotti thought Cheryl Landers was Bambi. Bambi was a hooker. Could it be that Cheryl Landers and her boyfriend, Grant Lennon, Jr., were running hookers? And that Cheryl herself wasn't averse to doing a little putting out on the side?

He called Boyd Keller and told him of the new

developments. Boyd summoned Grant into his office and began questioning him. Grant told him everything.

Luca, realizing that Bambi/Cheryl was in trouble, revealed how Bosco and Reno had followed her the night before.

So if Cheryl was really Bambi — and Bosco and Reno had followed Bambi home — it figured that the man they'd assumed was her boyfriend could actually turn out to be Zane.

Luca slumped in a chair. He was in shock. No wonder he'd gotten off on the broad — she was a rich Hollywood kid. And he'd thought she was a simple working girl. What a scam! You had to respect somebody who could pull off something like that. Especially on him, because nobody had ever accused him of being naive.

"Can you find the house?" Detective Carlyle asked Reno.

"It was dark," Reno said. "But I know where it is."

"Let's go," Carlyle said. "I'll call for backup."

Rosa got the news first. She'd attached herself to Boyd Keller, who didn't seem to mind one bit. And because of this, she knew something was going down before the rest of the press knew.

By the time Keller strode from the precinct and jumped into an unmarked squad car, Rosa was in the camera truck with her crew and Kennedy.

"Follow that car," she said dramatically. "We got ourselves a story. Let's hope it has a happy ending."

58

The Man felt powerful and triumphant. He was soaring high — like an eagle.

He was an avenger. A true hero. Even better — an action hero.

He marched back to the house, striding down the middle of the road because he didn't have to hide from anyone. His days of hiding were over. He was the Master of the City.

Steven Seagal . . . Arnold, Sly, all of them . . . they were nothing compared to him. Soon the world would realize.

He reached the house, double-locked the front door behind him, and kicked open the door to the cellar. The bitch was down there waiting for him. Waiting for him to bury her.

He swaggered down the stairs, swinging the Uzi in one hand, his pistol stuffed into the belt of his blood-soaked pants.

What would his mother say if she could see him?

Would she be happy? Would she be proud?

She wouldn't call him poopsy now. She wouldn't dare.

I am the most powerful man in the world.

I am invincible, and nobody will ever touch me again.

Jordanna heard Zane kick open the cellar door. Her heart was beating so loudly she could feel it thudding throughout her body.

Although she was terrified, she was not paralyzed. She lay on the ground where he'd left her, concealing the slab of wood beneath her body. Now that she had a weapon, she could fight back.

Any second, he'd trip over the dead rat she'd placed on the stairs, and when he did, she was prepared.

Her hands clutched the piece of wood, ready for action. She had a plan — go for his eyes first, then smash the weapon across his face, and keep on hitting until she rendered him unconscious.

She was truly petrified, her throat felt dry and parched, and she was sure the imprint of his hands would mark her neck forever. Yet her adrenaline was pumping. She knew she *had* to do it — *had* to be the winner in this deadly game.

She heard Zane stumble and fall, just as she'd hoped. The Uzi flew out of his hands, clattering to the hard cellar floor.

Did she have time to go for it? She wasn't sure. Had to be careful — couldn't take any risks. This was a test of her strength. And she would pass the test, because Bobby was waiting for her, and she didn't intend to disappoint him. Bobby Rush was her future, and no insane psycho was going to rob her of the opportunity to be with him.

She willed herself to stay perfectly still. It was imperative that her timing be just right.

He got up, cursing and muttering. She heard him getting nearer and nearer. Soon she felt his presence hovering over her.

Now was the moment for action. *Now! Now! Now!*

Gripping the piece of wood tightly, she turned her body and struck out with a mighty lunge.

The slab of wood cracked against his skull with a sickening thud, sending him flying back.

She leaped to her feet, grabbed the can of dirt, and ran for the stairs.

He came after her with a furious roar, blood coursing down his forehead, into his eyes. He reached out, his muscled arm once again encircling her leg.

She spun around, flinging the can of dirt into his face and eyes.

He yelled and fell back.

Heart pounding, she scrambled up the stairs, shot into the hallway, and raced to the front door.

He'd locked it. The sonofabitch had locked it!

Stay calm.

Don't panic.

You will survive.

Dashing into the kitchen, she picked up a chair and attempted to smash the window. It didn't break. Desperately she tried a second time. The glass shattered, but it was too jagged for her to climb through.

She turned around. He was at the door of the kitchen, blood pouring down his face now, anger and fury contorting his features.

"Fucking bitch!" he screamed. "Fucking cunt bitch! You're going to die now."

She opened her mouth and let out a primal scream. Then she hurled the chair at him.

It slammed into him, and she ran for the door of the kitchen, trying to dodge past him.

He caught hold of her and dragged her down onto the floor.

They struggled. She clawed at his eyes, bringing her knee up, pounding into his balls.

He wrestled her shoulders to the ground, turned her over and attempted to jam his lips down on hers.

It was too grotesque. His blood was dripping onto her face, and to her horror and disgust she felt him growing hard against her thigh.

"You sonofabitch!" she screamed, striving to shove him off. "You piece of shit *sonofabitch!*"

"There's nowhere you can run to get away from me," he yelled triumphantly. "I had nowhere to run in prison, and you've got nowhere to run here."

"Fuck you!" she screamed. *"Fuck you!"*

He started pulling at her jeans, trying to get them off.

She spat in his face and attempted to knee him again.

He slapped her so hard she was momentarily stunned.

She lay very still for a moment, desperately trying to remember everything she'd learned in self-defense class.

Window of opportunity!
Window of opportunity!

The words screamed inside her head as she saw him going for his pants. But first he had to remove the pistol stuck in his belt.

She watched as he reached for the gun, ready to lay it on the ground while he unzipped his pants.

Window of opportunity!

Fucking go for it!

With all her might, she sat up, surprising him, smashing her head under his chin, causing him to grunt with pain.

Twisting her body, she managed to wrestle the gun from his grasp and point it at him.

"You wouldn't dare use it," he said, taunting her.

"Oh, yes I would," she said, clicking back the safety catch, just as she'd seen him do.

And once more they were in the same position, only this time *she* was in control, ready to blow him away forever.

But she hesitated just that moment too long, and he took advantage of the pause, jerking his hands upward, knocking the gun out of her possession.

They rolled around on the floor, each scrabbling to get the weapon.

Eventually the gun became wedged between them — locked between their bodies as they continued the life-and-death struggle.

And then the gun went off.

One loud blast, and after the explosion there was nothing but a deep and deadly silence.

59

Bobby was swigging Coke from a can when he saw Boyd Keller rush for the door. He knew immediately something was going down. Grabbing the detective, he said, "Wherever you're going, I'm coming too."

"No way. It's against all regulations."

"I don't give a fuck about regulations."

"We'll keep you informed — if anything happens you'll know immediately."

"Screw it," Bobby said fiercely. "If you don't want me to come you'll have to arrest me."

Boyd shrugged. Sometimes rules were made to be broken, and he'd had word from the chief of police to keep all the big shots happy.

"Okay," he said reluctantly. "As long as you stay outta my way and keep a low profile."

"You got it."

Cheryl staggered into the street, desperately attempting to flag a car down. There was a steady stream of traffic traveling up and down Laurel Canyon, but nobody stopped.

She waved her arms frantically in the air. Drivers averted their eyes and kept going.

Oh, God, they think I'm some kind of homeless

718

person or a drunk, she thought, running unsteadily down the hill.

She couldn't believe nobody would stop. For one wild moment she considered throwing herself in front of a car, but they'd probably knock her down and drive off. Didn't people care anymore?

She swayed, almost falling, but then she forced herself to keep going, until eventually she reached a small market.

She ran up to the checkout stand, faltering, hardly able to put two words together. "Call . . . call the police," she said to the woman. "Please . . . hurry."

"What's the matter with you, honey," the woman said, alarmed. "You been raped? What happened?"

Cheryl collapsed onto the floor.

The cars containing Detective Carlyle, Luca, and Reno, Mac, Michael, and Quincy met up with three unmarked police cars at the bottom of Laurel Canyon.

Boyd Keller and Bobby joined Carlyle, Reno, and Luca in the first car, and the convoy roared off up the hill.

The TV van with Rosa and her crew was right behind them, Kennedy a passenger.

Reno sat in the front, giving directions. After a while he spotted the turning. "It's up here," he said. "Keep on going — it's way at the top."

"You got a number for the house?" Keller asked.

"No, but it's the only one up there."

The terrain was getting rougher by the minute.

"You positive there's another house?" Boyd said impatiently.

"Yeah, I'm sure," Reno said. "I got a good sense of direction."

"We passed the last house five minutes ago."

"I told you — we'll get to it."

"Michael's in one of the cars up ahead," Rosa said.

"How do you know?" Kennedy asked.

" 'Cause I was in Boyd's office when it all came down," Rosa said, her pretty face alive with excitement. "There's Mac Brooks, Luca Carlotti — and if I'm not mistaken, Bobby Rush is along for the ride. This is quite a story, and we're on the spot before anyone else."

Kennedy nodded. She couldn't help thinking about what might have happened to the two girls. If the news was bad, it was a story she didn't want to cover. Let the tabloid press take over and go to town.

People's lives were at stake. This was a desperate situation — not entertainment for the masses.

The first vehicle in the convoy slowed down. "There's a car up ahead, blocking the road," Carlyle said.

"Looks like it could be our limo," Reno said, peering from the window.

Carlyle reached for his gun as the car ground to a stop. "How far is the house from here?" he asked.

Reno shrugged. "It's near."

Luca sensed trouble; the hairs on the back of his neck stood up.

"Stay in the car," Carlyle said, his hand on the door.

Fuck that shit. Luca was out of the car before anyone could stop him.

"What's happening?" Michael said, as their car stopped.

"Something's goin' down," Quincy said.

"I'm taking a look." Michael jumped out of the car and came up behind Reno. "Where's the house?" he asked.

"Up the hill."

"Thanks," he said, sprinting up the bumpy road.

They could all deal with the limo; he had a hunch that what was going on at the house was more important.

"Oh, Jesus!" Luca sighed mournfully, as he approached the bodies piled together by the side of the road. "This shouldn't have happened. This ain't right."

Detective Carlyle tried to wave him away, but Luca was having none of it. He bent down to touch Bosco, making sure he was dead.

"Don't do that," Boyd Keller barked. And then to Carlyle, "Get this area roped off. This is a crime scene here, not a fucking picnic."

Rosa, her camera crew, and Kennedy leaped out of the van. Rosa signaled her cameraman to start shooting before anyone could stop them. He began filming the grisly crime scene, while Rosa attempted a quick remote.

"Get that camera out of here," Boyd Keller yelled angrily.

Michael reached the house, pulled his gun, and approached warily. First he tried the front door — it was locked, so he made his way around the side until he came to the back. The kitchen window was shattered, shards of broken glass everywhere.

The air seemed very still. Heat and silence and nothing else. A fly buzzed into his face, startling him.

He was nervous — since he'd got shot, it wasn't the same. He was no longer Superman, running headfirst into any situation. A year ago he would have leaped through the kitchen window. Now he was more cautious, had to work out the safest way in — because he never wanted to experience the searing, flesh-tearing pain of being shot again.

Edging past the kitchen window, he discovered a side door. One heavy kick, and he was inside the house.

More silence.

He was sweating so much he could barely keep a grip on his gun.

Moving slowly, he entered the kitchen. Blood and chaos was everywhere.

Sprawled in the middle of the floor was a body.

He heard a noise and raised his gun, perspiration rolling down the back of his neck.

Jordanna stood in the doorway leading to the

hall. She was battered, bruised, and bloody, but she was alive.

"I killed him," she said quietly. "He's dead."

Epilogue

The story saturated the press and airwaves. Two Hollywood princesses kidnapped and beaten! One of them a madam! Plus a notorious crime boss's psycho murdering nephew.

The movie business, crime, sex, and Hollywood — an irresistible combination.

Kennedy wrote a powerful piece on violence and obsession for *Style Wars*. It created much controversy.

Rosa seized her opportunity and broadcast the tape of the bodies piled by the roadside. She was severely reprimanded by the boss of her TV station, but her ratings soared.

Shortly after that she broke up with Ferdy and began a torrid affair with Boyd Keller.

According to Rosa, he was the best sex ever.

After her suicide attempt, Marjory Sanderson was sent by her father to a private psychiatric clinic in Switzerland, where, with counseling, she was finally able to admit it was she who'd been writing the threatening notes to herself to gain attention.

Her counselor was a forty-eight-year-old German doctor with blond hair and big teeth. Much to her father's fury, Marjory married him in a secret ceremony and brought him back to Hollywood.

At last she was happy. She had a man all to herself, and he truly loved her.

Shep finally came out of the closet with a Eurotrash count who designed women's clothes.

Taureen Worth almost had a heart attack. It was bad enough that she had a twenty-four-year-old son. But a gay one?

This was not good karma for a past-her-prime sex symbol.

She paid for them to vacation in Portofino and hoped they'd love it so much that they'd never come back.

Luca returned to New York with Reno, but not before visiting Bambi/Cheryl in the hospital, where she was recovering from her ordeal.

"My offer still stands," he told her, pacing around the hospital room. "You're some fuckin' ballsy broad!"

"You think so?" she asked wanly.

He winked. "I know so."

She thanked him and declined his offer.

"Any time y'change your mind," he said, "I'll be waitin'." He handed her his card. "This is where y'can find me. Anytime, baby."

Grant was by her side — a somewhat chastened Grant, who informed her he'd decided they made a talented team and should put their energies into something more legitimate than running hookers.

Was this the Grant she knew and loved?

No, this was a different Grant — a more respectable Grant — a man with his eye to the future.

She took a good look at him and decided it was time to move on. Grant had broken the spell between them, she was ready for a more fulfilling relationship. Someone who genuinely cared about her.

Maybe it would be Grant.

Maybe it would not . . .

She would just have to wait and see.

Her illustrious, socially connected parents freaked out at the news she was a madam. Estelle simply refused to believe it. And Ethan gave her the usual *if you needed more money why didn't you come to me* speech.

Fortunately Donna Lacey, the English director's daughter, returned from London, and Cheryl handed back her little black book.

She was out of the hooker business for good.

Mac Brooks managed to keep his secret. No connection. No publicity.

Sharleen suggested it might be an interesting premise for a movie. "Instead of a male protagonist, make it a woman," she said, really getting into the idea. "I can play the lead," she added. "Think of the fun we can have in our trailer at lunch break!"

After some thought, Mac decided she could be right. After all, what better place than Hollywood to turn fact into fiction?

Detective Carlyle finally left his wife. Or rather she threw him out.

He moved in with his girlfriend. After two weeks he realized his wife was a better deal and begged her to take him back.

She refused.

He ended up living with the waitress from the breakfast joint he frequented.

She gave great fried eggs.

Jordan Levitt's fifth wife gave birth to a baby boy. Jordan wanted to name the child Jordan Levitt, Jr. Jordanna and Kim informed him it was the worst idea possible, and he finally acquiesced — calling the boy Sam.

Jordanna was thrilled to have a brother again.

Charlie Dollar met Barbara Barr one fateful night at Homebase Central.

One night of lust, and she was pregnant.

She moved into his house six weeks later.

He was too laid back to stop her.

Their fights were the kind that fueled tabloid dreams.

Three months after the occurrences on Laurel Canyon, Quincy and Amber threw a party.

"Help me, Michael," Amber said, vainly trying to balance a platter of raw hamburgers and a large salad bowl as she exited the house into the backyard.

"You got it, gorgeous," he said, scooping the platter out of her hands.

He'd be forever grateful to Quincy and Amber. They'd dipped into their savings and come up with the ten thousand dollars he'd borrowed from Marjory, enabling him to send her a check.

"Call it an advance," Quincy had said. "I'll take it out of your share of the business."

Luckily business seemed to be busy. It would take only a year or two before he was out of debt!

"Quincy and his bar-b-ques," Amber sighed. "*I* do all the work and *he* gets all the praise."

"It's his birthday," Michael reminded her. "No nagging on his birthday."

"Fat an' fifty," she said with a sly smile. "After tonight that man goes on a strict diet or I am *outta* here!"

"The truth, Amber, you'd never leave him, would you?"

She beamed happily. "Not if he weighed four hundred pounds, but we won't tell him that, will we, Michael?"

"He ain't hearin' it from me."

"Let's get this party going," she said.

They walked into the backyard, where twenty guests were gathered and Quincy was sharing the secrets of his famous bar-b-que sauce with Kennedy.

Michael put down the platter, sliding his arm around Kennedy's slim waist. "You look sensational tonight," he whispered in her ear. "Not that tonight's any different from any other night."

"I made a special effort," she murmured. "After all, it's not every day I get to mix with *real* people."

"Aw, c'mon," he said, grinning sheepishly. "You're never gonna let me forget that, are you?"

Now it was her turn to smile. "Nope."

He pulled her close, kissing her passionately. She melted into his arms. They'd been together twelve weeks and a day, and she loved him more every hour. Six weeks ago they'd moved in together. It was working out just fine.

After the tragedy they'd had a brief falling out, because she felt that once he'd found out she was writing about the murders he should have told her everything. "I didn't even know you, Kennedy," he explained. "My loyalty had to be with the client."

Grudgingly she agreed he was right.

"I want you to promise that you'll never lie to me again," she said.

"It's written in blood," he replied.

What could she do?

She loved him.

Jordanna and Bobby made a late entrance. Jordanna looked glowingly beautiful in a short white dress, with white flowers in her long dark hair.

Bobby was in jeans, T-shirt, and an Armani sports jacket, his dirty-blond hair curling over his collar. They held hands and whispered together as if no one else existed.

All signs of Jordanna's ordeal had vanished — the only scars that remained were within. She would never forget Zane Ricca. His flat dead eyes, the coldness of his attitude, the inherent cruelty of the man.

She would never forget the moment when the bullet entered his body and the blood flowed from his chest, pumping his tainted blood all over her.

Memories.

The bad kind.

Shut 'em out and get on with life.

There were no charges against her. It was a clear case of self-defense.

The tabloids went crazy for a while, trailing her everywhere she went. But eventually a new scandal took place — Barbara Barr got caught cheating on Charlie Dollar with a very married senator — and Jordanna was off the front pages.

She started work on Bobby's movie and soon realized that for the first time she was doing something she truly loved. Acting was in her blood.

She rented an apartment and happily moved in. Bobby didn't make a move — although he was totally there for her. It was as if he sensed she needed time to recover, and he was prepared to give it to her.

When Michael called and invited her to Quincy's birthday party she'd said yes at once. Michael was a comforting presence in her life, almost like an older brother. She'd had dinner a couple of times with Kennedy and him, and liked them both very much.

"Wanna go?" she'd said to Bobby. "I'd better warn you — Kennedy Chase will be there. She's really very nice. And she assured me that story wasn't her fault."

"Sure," he'd said. "I'd like another face-to-face with that — "

"Bobby!"

Now she pulled him over to meet Kennedy again, and before he could say a word, Kennedy spoke, her green eyes achingly sincere. "Bobby, I owe you an apology. What the magazine did was stupid and unprofessional. It wasn't my story. They rewrote everything. So . . . please forgive me."

There was nothing like a genuine apology to throw a man off track.

"Forget it," he said, shaking his head. "I guess if you really didn't know . . ."

"I didn't," she assured him. "And next time — "

"No next time!" He laughed. "You and your pen — stay away from me!"

She smiled. "Absolutely."

The bar-b-que was a success. Quincy's sauce won the night.

There was dancing later in the small back garden.

Michael held Kennedy tight and asked her what she thought their future held. "We'll see, Michael, we'll see . . . ," she murmured.

But they both knew what was in their future, and they were content.

Bobby and Jordanna left soon after. They stood outside, leaning against his car, kissing for a few memorable moments.

"You have magic kisses," she gasped, marveling at how great he made her feel.

"Hey — you should see what else I got," he joked.

"Maybe it's time I did," she murmured.

"In that case . . ."

"What?"

"I have a gift for you. Something I've been saving for just such an occasion."

"Show me!"

He opened the trunk of his car, reached inside, and handed her a large, elaborately wrapped package.

"What *is* it?" she demanded excitedly.

"Open it and see."

Her black eyes gleamed. "Okay — but it better be good."

"Trust me — it is."

She ripped the package open, tore the lid off the box, and was confronted with thirty-five different makes of condoms.

"Oh, no!" she yelled, hysterical with laughter. "Bobby — you are *un*believable!"

He pulled her in close. "How come you feel so good and smell so good? And how come when I'm not with you I think about you all the time?"

"You do?"

"Can't stop."

"Neither can I."

He kissed her gently.

She kissed him back.

"And how come I walk around with a stupid grin on my face I can't seem to wipe off?"

"Bobby . . . I do the same," she said, touching his face with her fingertips.

"Same grin, huh?"

"It looks better on me."

"Spoken like a true actress."

"Well . . . ," she teased. "You got me into the business."

"Let's get out of here."

"Now?"

"Right now."

"Whatever you say, Mr. Rush."

They got in his car and sped off into the night.

Jordanna knew she'd found her soul mate and that she'd never be alone again. It was a wonderful feeling.

We hope you have enjoyed this Large Print book. Other G.K. Hall & Co. or Chivers Press Large Print books are available at your library or directly from the publishers. For more information about current and upcoming titles, please call or write, without obligation, to:

G.K. Hall & Co.
P.O. Box 159
Thorndike, Maine 04986
USA
Tel. (800) 223-6121 (U.S. & Canada)
In Maine call collect: (207) 948-2962

OR

Chivers Press Limited
Windsor Bridge Road
Bath BA2 3AX
England
Tel. (0225) 335336

All our Large Print titles are designed for easy reading, and all our books are made to last.